D1714737

TORN ROBES: CHOICES

BY
K.M. QUINN

Mimosa Lake Press
2023

To find other books (in this series or others) by K. M. Quinn, order additional print or electronic copies of *TORN ROBES: CHOICES* or to contact the author visit:

www.kmquinn.com

Cover Design and Illustrations by Colleen Quinlan and Megan Wallace

First Edition: March 2023

Created and Published in the USA, Mimosa Lake Press

Library of Congress Cataloging-in-Publication Data

Quinlan, Kathleen M.

Torn Robes: Choices/K. M. Quinn – 1st Edition

ISBN: **9798847884488**

DEDICATION

I'd like to dedicate this book to my Heavenly Father and His Son Jesus, my Savior and forever Friend. With whom I can do all things.

My husband and family, for loving and supporting me. Each one a cherished gift from God. I love you all with everything I am.

And to all of you who've decided to join in this journey.

"If you can?" said Jesus. "Everything is possible for one who believes." Mark 9:23

GILFORD TOWNSHIP

THE WHEATONS
PASTOR JOHN
SARAH

PETERS
MARTIN AND DELORES
LEWIS TREMBLAY

GALLOS
ANTHONY AND LINDA
BRITTANY   JOSHUA

RICHARDSON
MARY
SHELBY   LEXY
IAN   STELLA

POOR
TITUS

THE TAYLORS
DWAYNE AND LOUISE
D.J.   SHARISE

RUSSO
PAUL

GRAYS
DONNA
ERICA MADISON

RIVERA
TERESA
LILY

TAGLIO
JOEY (TAGS)

CAMPSITE

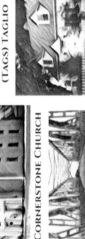

(TAGS) TAGLIO

RIVERA'S

TAYLOR'S

RICHARDSON'S

RUSSO'S

CORNERSTONE CHURCH

GILFORD BRIDGE

THE WHARF

BEACH PARK

HIGH SCHOOL

MAIN STREET

GALLO'S

PETER'S / LEWIS TREMBLAY

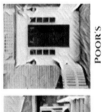

POOR'S

GRAY'S

TORN ROBES: CHOICES
TABLE OF CONTENTS

TORN ROBES: RECKONING

TORN ROBES: CHOICES PREFACE

There are countless descriptions in the New and Old Testaments which refer to the tearing of one's robes or "Rending of Clothes". The tradition of tearing clothes began as an expression of deep grief or mourning. Mental tribulations like the shame David's daughter Tamar felt became part of this custom and were subsequently used in times of anger and stress.

Tearing clothing was also deemed sacrificial. Today clothing is much more affordable and accessible than it was in biblical times. People from the Old Testament did not have our luxuries.

Some illustrations in the Bible depicting this custom are shown below.

"So, his servant put her out and bolted the door after her. She was wearing an ornate robe, for this was the kind of garment the virgin daughters of the king wore. Tamar put ashes on her head and tore the ornate robe she was wearing. She put her hands on her head and went away, weeping aloud as she went." 2 Samuel 13:18-19

"Then Jacob tore his clothes, put on sackcloth, and mourned for his son many days." Genesis 37:34

"Then the high priest tore his clothes and said, "He has spoken blasphemy! Why do we need any more witnesses? Look, now you have heard the blasphemy." Matthew 26:65

"When they saw him from a distance, they could hardly recognize him; they began to weep aloud, and they tore their robes and sprinkled dust on their heads." Job 2:12

"Then David and all the men with him took hold of their clothes and tore them. They mourned and wept and fasted till evening for Saul and his son Jonathan, and for the army of the Lord and for the nation of Israel, because they had fallen by the sword." 2 Samuel 1:11-12

"But when the apostles Barnabas and Paul heard of this, they tore their clothes and rushed out into the crowd, shouting." Acts 14:14

This custom is continued in the Jewish community today it is called Keriah. It is less spontaneous and more ceremonial. Customs may change but the heart's anguish remains. The need to express that pain and sorrow continues.

TORN ROBES: CHOICES
PROLOGUE

The rain fell hard on this May Nebraska morning. Puddles were everywhere. The clouds had erupted throughout the night leaving the mid-morning sky somber and ominous. The majestic cottonwood trees loomed like dark shadows over the grief-stricken mourners. Their silvery bark reflected the delicate light through the gray mist. Less impressive trees stood tall and dark, withering with age. The trees repeatedly witnessed this scene day after day, month after month, year after year.

John stood, as tall and stoic as the trees surrounding them. A funeral worker held an extra-large umbrella over his head in an attempt to catch the raindrops missed by the overhead tarp. John's gaze drifted beyond their family and friends to the cold wet droplets of rain. He wanted to reach out and touch them; it was a desperate attempt to rid himself of the intense agony making its home in his body. John's stomach rumbled, shaking him back to the present. *No not now!* Sweat beaded on his brow despite the brisk temperature.

John licked his lips to keep what little saliva he had from evaporating. *Gulp.* John froze. The rancid taste of bile bubbled up from somewhere in the back of his throat. *Why didn't I eat this morning?*

Inhale, exhale, inhale, exhale, focus…breath. John's breathing and neglected stomach began to settle. He scanned the bereaved group thankful no one had noticed his distress. John's gaze landed on his Pastor, whose lips seemed to be moving but the sound of his voice was coming from somewhere in the distance.

What was he saying? Concentrate! Attentiveness was not John's friend this morning. What solace would he find in the Pastor's words? John watched the blades of green grass welcoming the onslaught of raindrops.

Is this how my parishioners feel when I officiate over their family member's funeral? The realization struck John like the sting of a bee. Jerking, he caught himself before stumbling backward. Those suffering souls were looking to him for hope and answers. John dashed away the tears beginning to form in the corners of his eyes. *Why hadn't I felt the depth of their affliction?*

God answered. *Because you never felt their anguish.*

John provided the 'Good News' and the joy and celebration of the deceased's life. By faith, their loved ones were in the presence of God. Today, his heart needed more. And so, he concluded did the grieving family members he ministered. His stomach tightened like a tangled-up knot. *Help me, Lord!*

John looked down at the young girl standing beside him, Sarah's knuckles were white. She clutched the small bouquet of light and deep purple lilacs, her mother's favorite flower at this time of year. *Where are you looking?*

Was Sarah focused on the brown casket looming at the center of the gathering or toward the enormous array of colored flowers cascading over the sides of the casket like a brilliant waterfall? At thirteen, Sarah looked increasingly like her mother Abby. She had long blond hair, a slender build and Abby's strength in spirit. Sarah looked up. Their eyes locked, mirroring each other's sadness and pain.

Pastor Bennett, a dear family friend, continued to speak of Abby with deep affection. He acknowledged her warmhearted spirit and that she was a loving mother and wife who left this world far too soon.

No! John's hands clenched into tight fists refusing to acknowledge her death. *Why? Why Abby? God, why did you take such a sweet, loving wife and mother? My best friend.* John lifted his square chin high in the air. He was heartbroken. He was angry. John blamed the one who he swore to dedicate his life to, to worship and honor - the one true living God. *How was he going to help Sarah understand why God took her mother when he himself didn't understand?*

John's mind drifted along with the melancholy beat of the rain. *What is the meaning of rain on the day of one's funeral?* He reflected. *Ah yes,* he remembered. *The rain is Heaven's tears. But for who?* John's eyes grew as large as saucers, the answer clear. *Heaven's tears are for those who are left behind!*

TORN ROBES: CHOICES

CHAPTER 1
A STORM IS BREWING

In a small northeastern town along the Atlantic coast, a storm similar to the great Nor'easters of the past was brewing. Issues involving out-of-control high school students needed to be dealt with once and for all.

During the past two years, numerous students had made pregnancy pacts. Girls as young as fourteen were having babies and the residents of the town were becoming loud and irate.

Dr. Spencer Boyle, Superintendent of Schools for Gilford, MA determined that safety protocols should be put in place to help students manage the upcoming school year. He was not going to allow another year of irresponsible behavior to continue. Dr. Boyle, now in his sixties, had little patience for antics of any type. It was time to call an emergency school board meeting. He wanted everyone on the same page to battle the issues they faced in a sensible and professional manner.

The first Thursday of August was hot and humid. The board members found themselves sitting around a long table in the small conference room at Gilford High School. The room lacked the benefit of air conditioning. Even with the windows open, the air was stagnant. The town, which was situated along the coastline, counted on a breeze even during extreme heat waves like the one they were now experiencing. Unfortunately, tonight was the exception.

Spencer sat at the head of the table with Chairman Charlie Martin to his right. Out of shape and balding, Charlie was the perfect complement to Spencer's full head of gray hair and lean 6'1" frame. To Spencer's left sat Assistant Superintendent Robert Johnson with a blank stare on his face that defined his lackluster personality.

Finance Director Bonnie Griffin, sat stick-straight against the back of her chair like a lioness ready to pounce on unsuspecting prey. She held on to the school's purse strings as tight as the stiff bun of gray

1

hair perched tight on the top of her head. Vice Principal Karl Porter, the career opportunist of the group, sat across from Bonnie busy cleaning his fingernails.

"Seriously Karl, must you do that now?"

"What? Excuse me, Bonnie."

"Ugh, you're disgusting."

Shelly Bradshaw, Director of Student Services, had the misfortune of sitting next to Karl. She rolled her eyes. *How did he ever get to be Vice Principal?* Shelly was the student's number one cheerleader. However, tonight she wanted to be anywhere but here. Bob Hanson, the Principal of Gilford Middle School had facial features that matched his pleasant personality.

"The heat has gotten to all of us. With any luck, this meeting won't take too long and we'll be out of here before you know it."

"My thoughts exactly Bob," Spencer agreed. "If you don't mind putting away your paraphernalia Karl. We aren't here for manis and pedis!"

"Sure," Karl replied.

Krystina Davis was anchored on the edge of her seat at the opposite end of the conference room listening to the unpleasant exchange. She was the Principal of Gilford High School and would be the unlucky scapegoat if things didn't turn around.

Settled in between Bob and Krystina was Louise Taylor, School Nurse at Gilford High School, and Spencer's constant irritant.

"Well, I guess that depends. Are we looking for a quick fix or solid proposals?" Louise interjected.

"Here we go," Karl said.

Spencer shot Karl a look to keep him quiet. Then pressed on in a more diplomatic fashion. "We are always looking for solid proposals, Louise."

"Mm hm, I certainly hope so."

Michele Clancy, Spencer's Executive Assistant, was skittish and reclusive with the characteristics of a country mouse. She melted into the background with her recorder pressed to the "on" button.

Spencer was acting more like a teenager than a superintendent, rolling his eyes and shaking his head as he listened to the banter going back and forth like a tennis match. Students weren't the problem this evening; it was trying to get this cast of characters parading as school board to agree on anything.

"Okay. Okay. Okay." Spencer motioned. Standing up, the force of his chair almost toppled over as it went flying toward the wall. Michele jumped from her safe spot with a squeak, scrambling to get out of the way.

Quick as a cat, Spencer's hand reached the chair giving it a furious jerk. The member's attention turned to the continued banging echoing off the conference walls.

Charlie was hunched over the table with the small gavel he used to open and adjourn board meetings grasped in his pudgy hand. Banging ferociously onto the sound block, he was intent on gaining control.

"Bang, Bang, Bang!"

Charlie felt the old, dreaded tingles of past high school memories make their way up his spine. "Bang…Bang…" His head shot up. All the members stared at him. His gavel hung in the air. Poised in mid-flight. Looking around the room into the shocked stares of his fellow board members. A red burn began to creep up from his neck and spread over his face.

"May I continue now?" Spencer smiled at poor Charlie.

Charlie swallowed hard and tried to clear his throat to speak. "Harrumph!" But nothing would come out. With as much dignity as he could muster, he gave Spencer a quick nod. With shaky hands, he placed his gavel back onto the sound block.

Feeling alone, Charlie wiped his sweat-drenched hands on his pant legs. He grabbed a tissue from the box in the middle of the table to wipe the sweat that managed to break free from atop his head and run down his left cheek. Folding his hands, he placed them in his lap and look down at the floor.

"Good," Spencer boomed. "We are ready to continue. Now it seems to me that we are going round and round without getting anywhere." Spencer challenged the group as beads of sweat covered his brow. "We can argue all night long but there's only one solution most of us will agree on. These brochures identifying the hazards and consequences of unprotected sex should be available along with a variety of other options including condoms, lubricants, the morning-after pill, and information about birth control."

Spencer's gaze turned to Louise daring her to argue with him. However, Louise was investigating her lap, pretending to pick an imaginary piece of lint off her sundress.

"These will be available to all high school students with a no-questions-asked policy in the nurse's office during and after school hours."

"Mm, mm, mm," Louise stated with a shake of her head. She was not about to let that statement get by without a comment. "Will we have vending machines? You know, the kind that dispenses condoms with assorted flavors and textures? If we're going to treat the school like a candy store, we should do everything we can to give these kids a healthy variety of choices. Don't you think?"

"What? Are you serious?" Bonnie's questions came with a high-pitched shrill. "Who said anything about vending machines? I mean how much would something like that cost? Is there a supply company that would keep the machines full?" Bonnie demanded directing her questions at poor Charlie.

"Huh?" Charlie managed with an indignant wave of his hand as he tried to gather his wits and refute Bonnie's accusations. "Wh...Why are you asking me? How would I know about something like that?" He pointed a shaking finger at Louise. "She's the one who suggested getting the machines."

Spencer sighed. "Haaaahh! It's obvious Louise was adding a bit of comic relief to the evening. But if there is something a little more realistic you'd like to add Louise, by all means." Spencer motioned his right hand gesturing the floor was all hers.

"Oh, I'd like to add something alright." Louise stood up, all five feet four inches of her. "These are children we're talking about. We need to get to the root of the problem not glaze over it with a Band-Aid or look the other way and hope it gets better. This solution is as bad as their behavior. You're giving them free rein by telling them they're in charge.

These kids show no respect for themselves or the adults in their lives." Louise motioned her hand like she was cutting off a head. "Well, it's not okay with me! There's nothing but trouble ahead." She wanted to laugh at some of the shocked faces staring back at her. *Didn't they know her by now?*

"As the nurse at Gilford High School, I would like it stated for the record that I don't feel it is right to hand out condoms or any other birth control to our babies. Especially without a parent's knowledge or consent!"

"Duly noted," Spencer added, in an exasperated voice. "Did you get all that, Michelle?" It was late. He had a pounding headache and all he wanted to do was go home to his frosty central air. He wiped his brow for the umpteenth time as Michelle, with a nervous smile, held up her recorder in acknowledgment.

"Thank you, Michelle."

The board needed to act; they needed an immediate fix. Parents' concerns were growing and, as principal of Gilford High School, Krystina was responsible. *When did everything get out of control? What happened to these kids?* Even though she agreed with Louise, she'd do everything in her power to make the resolution work. This was her school. Her students. She was in charge. *So why do I feel so powerless?*

Spencer stood looking around the table, he sensed the end of an exceptionally long and strenuous meeting. "Does anyone else have anything else they wish to share?" It was said more as a statement than a question.

"No." Heads bobbed.

With a few. "Uh, Uh's and No's."

Everyone, except Louise, who sat defiant with her lips pursed and chin held high.

"Alright then," Spencer roared. "Charles, we are ready to vote on Resolution 196."

Taking the lead Charles began the vote. From around the table members of the school board expressed a yes vote in voice after voice.

At the end of a very long and heated evening the vote was complete. Nine in favor, one against.

But who knew that in the year to come, that one lone vote would echo louder than the sound of Charlie's gavel hitting the sound block.

They'd made a decision everyone would soon regret.

CHAPTER 2
2 YEARS LATER

"Honey, wake up." With a gentle shake, she urged her daughter into a semi-state of consciousness. "Come on, I have to leave for work, are you listening? I'm serious you need to get up."

"Mom okay, okay! What? Stop shaking me I'm awake!"

"I have to leave early for work today. Natalie called out sick." Short on time she walked over to the window and pulled up the shade bringing the first rays of sunlight into her daughter's darkened room.

"No! No, leave the shade down. Go away!" She cried, pulling the pillow over her head. "Why do I have to get up? She forced open one eye and moaned in despair. "It's summer vacation!"

"Uncle Tomas is sick. He wanted me to bring him over a few things before I go to work. There's a bag on the kitchen counter by the refrigerator. I need you to bring it to him." She sat down on the bed and pulled the light blanket off her unresponsive daughter. "I have no time for this. Come on sweetie, I'm counting on you. Are you listening?"

"I don't want to go to Uncle Tomas' house. He gives me the creeps! All his crazy friends, they're always looking at me weird. Mom, I'll wait until you come home from work, and we can go together." With significant effort, she tossed the pillow off, sat up, and wiped the sleep from her eyes.

Her mother brushed a strand of hair from the front of her daughter's face and asked. "What do you mean he's creepy? He's your father's brother."

"Stepbrother, Mom." She paused. "STEPBROTHER!"

"Be serious honey. I need your help. Uncle Tomas can't wait until I get home from work. With your father gone, the responsibility lies on the two of us. We're all he has left for family, and I can't be in two places at once. So, let's go! The faster you get this done, the sooner you can hang out with your friends. I'll see you for supper." She kissed her daughter's head and walked out of her bedroom.

A couple of minutes later she heard her mom yell up stairs. "I'm leaving, love you!" The front door closed.

She hurled off the remainder of her blanket. Looking at the clock next to her bed, she let out a long loud groan. Her feet searched the wooden floor for her well-worn slippers. They were one of the last reminders of her past life. Mission accomplished!

"Ahhhh-hhaaaaaa." She stretched then shuffled toward the bedroom door. "Yeah. The faster you get this done the sooner you can hang out with your friends, humph!" She mocked her mother.

Downstairs she grabbed a small bowl from the cabinet. Her buzzing cell phone caught her attention. 'Beach', the text read. "Beach!" She said with a smile spreading across her face. She glanced up. The feel of the sun's rays through the windowpanes warmed her body with the promise of a bright and sunny day.

Her cell phone was still buzzing away. The new text message read: 'Beach will be waiting, P.'

The pressure was on now, she'd have to move fast. With a running list in her head, she devised the perfect plan. *Go to Uncle Tomas', get back to the house, change into my bathing suit, and get everything for a perfect beach day.*

She grabbed her favorite cereal, milk, and her bowl and brought them to the kitchen table. Dumping the rainbow-colored morsels into the bowl, she covered them with milk and sat down to eat, rethinking her strategy as milk drizzled down her chin. *I'll put my bathing suit on now under my shorts and tee-shirt and take what I need for the beach with me to Uncle Tomas'. Better than making two trips. Yeah, that should work!*

She checked off each item needing to go into her overused, faded blue-striped backpack, otherwise known as: 'the beach bag'.

With summer in full swing, the beaches filled up by mid-morning. Five minutes could be the difference between getting a good spot to spend a glorious day with her friends or getting left behind. She blushed. There would always be at least one person waiting for her.

Ten minutes later, she was flying back down the stairs. Her hair was pulled into a ponytail and the stuffed beach bag was slung over her shoulder. Grabbing the bag of groceries her mom left for her to take, she locked the door and slipped her keys into the front pocket of her jean shorts.

"Oh crap, the key!" Her bike's lock and chain were wrapped around the bike column. She reached into her pocket and whipped out the keychain with the house keys and the bike key. "Ah, I'm definitely going to need you when I get to Uncle Tomas' apartment." Tossing the keys in the air, she grabbed them in mid-flight and slid them back into her jean pocket.

With care, she placed the bag of groceries into the basked that was bolted to the front of her bike. "Perfect fit. Thanks, Dad," she whispered, looking up into the bright morning sky. Goosebumps appeared on her arms even in the sizzling summer heat. *No sadness today.*

After grabbing her helmet and strapping it onto her head, she flipped up the kickstand. Soon she was peddling off toward Uncle Tomas' apartment. She glanced at her faded leather wristwatch; she was making good time.

Before she knew it, she stood before the large four-story dingy-grey apartment building. After looking it up and down, she moved her helmet and bike to the other side of the black iron fence, out of the sight of prying eyes. Known more for its drugs and robberies, this area was not the better part of Gilford.

"Okay, let's get this over with." She grabbed the grocery bag, keeping her backpack on her back. She ran up to the second floor and knocked on the door marked number nine.

What was that? Her breathing quickened. *Silly girl, stop being so paranoid.* She inched closer to the door. *Nothing! This is crazy! I should leave the groceries at the door. Mom only said to bring them to Uncle Tomas' apartment.* She sighed and then with great reluctance said, "Grr! Well, I don't have to like it!"

Her knuckles were about to connect with the door when a half-hearted moan came drifting out from the apartment and into the hallway. *Could Uncle Tomas be sick after all?* She turned the doorknob.

"Unlocked. Figures." The smell of rotting food was the first thing that greeted her as she walked inside. "Ugh!"

Holding the grocery bag in one hand and pinching her nose with the other, she walked into the dark haze-filled room. She squinted, waiting for her eyes to adjust to the darkness. Remnants of smoke drifted through the slivers of light spilling in from the odd-shaped slashes cut in the worn-out window shades.

"Uncle Tomas? Hello... anyone home?" Her knee hit a piece of furniture stopping her from going any further. "Ouch!"

Taking her hand from her nose she reached through the smoky haze to avoid another run-in and moved in the direction of her uncle's room. She was so distracted by her situation, that she never saw the hand clamp down over her mouth.

The grocery bag went flying, the contents smacked the floor with a thump. The large hand was so tight across her mouth that her screams for help were stifled. Her assailant tore the backpack from her body and threw it across the room. It landed with a muffled thud. Like a wounded animal she fought back, kicking and swinging, giving it everything she had.

Her attacker fended off her defensive attempts without much effort. Then he picked her up like she was nothing more than a rag doll. Body-slamming her to the floor, he pinned both of her arms beneath him.

"Agh!" The breath was knocked out of her. The sweat from his body dripped onto her skin. His appalling odor and heavy breathing bombarded her senses. One of his hands kept her mouth covered, leaving her no choice but to breathe through her nose. His other hand tore at her clothes. *Where? Where was her uncle? Who? Who was this animal? Didn't he know who she was?*

Like a man possessed, he ignored her muffled cries to stop. There was no escape even if an opportunity arose. The hand covering her mouth moved enough for her to bite down as hard as she could into the meaty flesh of one of his fingers.

At the same time, a searing pain tore through the inner parts of her body. Her eyes widened like saucers. "Nooooo!" She screamed.

His bloody hand came off her mouth delivering a heavy-handed slap to her face. Her head bounced off the floor from the impact and she tasted the metallic taste of blood oozing from her lip. Her strength was zapped, her body went completely limp welcoming the darkness.

She didn't remember getting home. Like a kaleidoscope of horror, there were only bits and pieces of memories that collided with each other. Her cell phone lay on the bed where she'd tossed it. The constant buzz coming from a barrage of calls and text messages blew up her phone.

She stepped into the shower, turning the water on to the hottest temperature her body could tolerate. Her skin was covered in bruises and scratches. Her lip had swelled. She scrubbed her body over and over. Finally, the remnants of blood from her attack went down the drain.

Still, she did not feel clean.

The running water, mingled with her tears, couldn't drown out the passionate sobs that racked her. When her tears lessened from frenzied sobs to a faint whimper, she placed one hand on the shower wall to steady herself. The water rained down on her battered body and mind as she flashed back to the nightmare.

She remembered waking up in the front room of her uncle's apartment, nauseous and shaking uncontrollably. She'd crawled around on the floor until she found her torn clothing. She did her best to put her clothes back on. She'd recovered her backpack that was slouched in a corner. Mindlessly, she slung it over her shoulder.

Why didn't her uncle help her? She dared to walk toward her uncle's bedroom and looked inside. When her eyes adjusted to the dim room, the needles and pipe laying on the side table were what she noticed.

Her uncle lay slumped in his bed either passed out or dead. She didn't care or feel the need to move close enough to find out. That's when she heard the noise coming from inside her uncle's bathroom.

"No, no! No!" She banged her hand on the wall of the shower, reliving the terror of knowing her attacker was in her uncle's bathroom. She gagged as bile shot from her mouth. It was the only thing left in her stomach. Watching it disappear into the drain somehow calmed her until her body shook as her stomach lurched again. "Hrrrk!" Her hand shot to her mouth and in a flash, she was reliving it again.

Frozen where she stood, her eyes were glued to the bathroom door. Her hand moved up to cover her mouth, fearing a scream would escape. *Move!* Her mind commanded, but her feet were frozen to the floor and she was filled with dreadful terror.

Everything was confusing after that. She could have sworn someone grabbed her, turned her around, and pushed her toward the living room. She bolted.

It had taken forever for her to reach the door and get out of the apartment. Her hands were so sweaty she couldn't get a good grip on the doorknob. But she wrestled the door free and flew down the stairs tripping over her feet as she ran. She couldn't move as fast as her mind wanted her to go. Outside, she stumbled to her bike.

Her bike and helmet were as she'd left them, still chained to the iron rails. She fumbled through the pocket of her ripped shorts praying the pocket was still in one piece and the key to freedom would still be there.

Then she saw it. With sickening disgust, she looked down at the crude reality of dried blood covering the inside of her legs. She had wretched, emptying the contents of her stomach.

"ARRR!" The water cascaded down her back confirming her ordeal with each new bruise it touched. Her eyes closed tightly to shut out the hideous nightmare. "Go Away!"

"Why? Why did you let this happen? I've tried to be a good daughter. First, you take away my father, and now this. Why? WHY GOD?" Her tears gushed down her face mimicking the shower head.

"I'm sorry, Momma. I am so sorry," her cry stilled to a whisper. She backed against the shower wall and slid down to the bottom. The water rushed onto her like harsh summer rain.

She awoke from her trance, shivering. The cold water pelted her bruised and battered body. With trembling hands, she turned the shower off. She grabbed the towel and dried off her broken and abused body.

Who could help her now? Momma? Her friends? No. Not even…'P'. Not even…'P'. Her heart shattered into a million pieces. Sobs wracked her body as she pulled the towel up to cover her face. "No! No more! It's too much!" The pain was too unbearable.

The shame was unforgivable. She was damaged inside and out.

With the wet towel in the hamper and her terrycloth robe on, she left the bathroom. Just this morning her bedroom had been filled with childhood dreams and bright tomorrows. A few short hours had transformed it into another room, in another house, on another street, in another town.

Her white vanity table and chair with the three-way mirror centered perfectly at the back was a Christmas present from her parents. She'd plead with them day after day making the case that the vanity set was more a need than a want. It sat under her bedroom window.

The firm bright-purple velvet cushion rested on her vanity chair. She sat down and touched the edge of the white table. She felt nothing.

The hairbrush she used this morning lay in the middle of the table just as she'd left it. She looked into the mirror at the face of a stranger. Her jade-green eyes once soft and twinkling, now were cold and vacant. Gone was the positive attitude she worked so hard to maintain after her father's death. If only she could go back in time.

"No use looking for something that isn't there." She rested her hands on the vanity. She was as cold and hardened as the dead wood under her fingertips.

"Hmph." She reached up and touched her swollen lip. A big gift from her attacker for the small dose of pain she'd inflicted on him. *You're going to need ice.*

In the kitchen, she got ice and left her mother a note on the kitchen counter. *Mom, I dropped the bag off to Uncle Tomas… have a headache…went to bed.*

Her shutdown had begun. Her old self was gone, never to return.

He paced back and forth. The beach was getting crowded. Everyone else had gone on ahead. This wasn't like her. She knew he'd be waiting. Looking down at his phone, he wondered why wasn't she answering his calls?

CHAPTER 3
BEGINNINGS

"Hey Dad, I'm home," Sarah yelled as she slipped off her burdensome backpack and jean jacket. She dumped them onto the vintage table in the foyer of the two-story colonial. She walked down the hall to the first door on the left. It was an everyday occurrence that led straight to her father's office.

Sarah found him sitting at his desk like the other permanent fixtures in the room. His fingers moved in a constant rhythm along the keyboard of his laptop. More likely than not, he was working on Sunday's sermon.

Thud! Sarah dropped down into the wide leather chair that sat in front of John's desk. He didn't flinch; it was fruitless to try and interrupt. Instead, she sat in quiet admiration waiting for him to finish the thoughts he'd bring to life from the pulpit. Her deep blue eyes glanced around the room, resting on the picture that sat on the corner of her father's desk. A smile crept across her face recalling the bittersweet memory. One of the last times she would share with her mom and dad as a family.

Sarah and her mom were sitting on the edge of a rock that overlooked the lake they frequented. Her father was about to snap the picture when a considerate older gentleman with a tall wooden walking stick passed by. He volunteered to take a picture of the three of them.

An angel indeed. Sarah sighed. In a snap, she covered her mouth not wanting to explain her sudden gasp to her dad. True to form, he remained completely engrossed in his work. Her mom had been the only one who could drag him away from the computer.

They were a family that loved the outdoors. A family that played and prayed together. The familiar picture brought reflections of the past.

There were no painful "whys" anymore. Now there was the joy of knowing that one day they would all be reunited in Heaven. Her mother's soft blue eyes that mirrored her own, stared back at Sarah filling her with a warmth and closeness that even death couldn't take away.

"Sarah?"

"Oh, sorry Dad. What did you say?"

"How was school today?"

"Bearable. How's the sermon going?" She asked.

"Bearable. I guess we'll find out on Sunday," He replied in a jovial tone.

Sarah laughed. Her father's sermons were anything but bearable. His messages contained humor, thoughtfulness, and insight. They were never condescending or difficult to understand. As pastor of the Angel of Grace Church and her dad, Sarah was glad he was hers.

John sat back in his chair with his fingers intertwined resting under his chin. "I received a letter today. Well, an invitation actually."

"You did? What kind of an invitation?"

"An invitation from a high school principal in the Northeast. Her name is Krystina Dayton. She invited me to speak with the members of their school board."

John studied Sarah's face with care before he continued. "They would like to know about what we've accomplished here at the Angel of Grace Church. More to the point, about the positive affect God's message has had on our youth."

"When and how long will you be gone?" She asked with misty, downcast eyes.

"She would like to schedule a meeting before the beginning of the new school year. Sounds like the end of July, beginning of August."

"Oh."

John knew exactly what was going through her mind. He'd be leaving her for the first time since her mother's death. The past three years had been full of growing pains for them.

"I was wondering." John leaned forward in his chair. "If you would like to join me for moral support. We could make a mini vacation out of it. It's something we haven't done in a very long time."

As soon as the words were out of his mouth Sarah jumped out of her chair bolting straight into her father's outstretched arms. "Would I? This will be the best vacation ever!" Sarah shrieked. She broke away from her father's embrace and started to pace back and forth.

"We have so much to do. But don't worry Dad. I'll take care of everything. We should make a list. Mom always made a list. We don't want to forget anything important."

"Sarah nothing has to be started this minute. We still have a few months."

Amused by his daughter's excitement, John got up from his chair and sat on the corner of the desk. "Aren't you even a bit curious to know where we're going?"

"Oh yeah, where exactly in the Northeast are we going?"

"Glad you asked. Gilford, Massachusetts."

"Dad, Gilford, Massachusetts?" Sarah whispered. "Isn't that the place where those teenage girls made pregnancy pacts?" Her voice got a bit louder. "It was all over the TV and newspapers a couple of years ago. That's all anyone at school talked about for days."

"Yes, that's the place." John answered. "In Ms. Dayton's letter, she referred to a Resolution 196 their board voted on last year. Designed to help the crisis."

"Interesting. Resolution 196. Doesn't sound like it helped."

"Sarah, I don't know. I'm sure the school board did what they thought was best at the time."

"I guess so. It's very sad."

"I know." John agreed. Then he gathered his daughter into his arms. Thanking God for his wisdom and guidance these past three years.

After a moment's thought, curiosity getting the best of her, Sarah asked, "So how did Ms. Dayton know how to get in touch with you?"

"She read, Children of the King, and was intrigued with the concept of the book. After some digging, she found Tracie.

"She must have written her a very convincing letter."

"Maybe. Ms. Dayton thought it wouldn't hurt to seek out other options because what they implemented in Gilford wasn't working."

"Isn't that the truth!" Sarah replied, a bit too sarcastic for John's liking.

"Sarah." John warned.

"I know. I know. No judging. Well, Ms. Dayton must have been very determined if Tracie helped her."

"Determined indeed!"

Tracie Dixon, a petite redhead and an absolute firecracker, was John's publicist. She had an undeniable fondness for stilettos. Being small in stature she believed high heels were invented with her in mind. She had every color imaginable and wore them like an extension of her feet.

"Do you ever get uncomfortable wearing such high heels?" John made the mistake of asking her once.

Tracie reached up and moved her glasses down a bit so as to sit on the bridge of her nose. She peered over the top of the glasses and focused straight on John. This was a common habit of hers when she wanted her response to be precise. "Dear, dear John. These shoes, while as uncomfortable as they may look to you, could carry me up Mt. Everest…and back!"

"I see," John gulped.

With a frosty smile she fixed her glasses and mumbled, "Good."

Even with all her idiosyncrasies, Tracie had passion and tremendous dedication. She loved God with all her heart and had made it her life's mission to market great books that made a difference in people's lives.

She frequently visited the Angel of Grace Church when staying with relatives in Nebraska. She was impressed with the youth group. During the weeknights when the youth group gathered, Tracie would often sit in and witness firsthand the influence of Jesus Christ.

"John, you have a special connection with these kids. They trust you; they honestly like you. You talk with them, John, and listen. No judgments. God has given you a special gift. It's your duty to share it," Tracy observed.

"Thanks, I guess. But Tracie, I'm not sure I understand what it is you want from me. I don't do anything special. To be perfectly honest, I need them as much as they need me."

"Cause and effect John. Journal what it is these kids respond to and what they don't. Mistakes are good; they're learning lessons. See where it goes."

Never one to give up Tracie continued to needle and badger him. She finally wore him down. John's one condition was that the youth group had to approve the idea. To his surprise, they were enthusiastic and hoped their experiences would help others. John started journaling their time together.

There was no official start to the youth group, it sort of happened. After Abby's death, all John's time was spent between Sarah and the church. It became a habit for Sarah and her friends to get together and hang out at the church while John worked in his office.

There was a huge empty room off to the right of the front hall of the cedar wood church. A supply of tables and chairs were stacked in a rear storage room next to the kitchenette. The room could instantly turn into a bean supper, a member's meeting or any special occasion the congregation could muster.

The small group of teenagers gravitated to this room. At first, the group met once a week usually to hang out, listen to music or play games. Later in the evening, John would walk down the hall to check on things or play a game of Scrabble with some of the teens.

It became a habit to gather in a circle towards the end of the night and talk. But then, something amazing happened. One by one the teenagers started opening up and discussing fears they never dared say out loud. Eventually, they felt comfortable enough to start conversations about sex. It was an all-too-real and crucial subject for these young teens. But if they were going to be upfront and talk about it, John was going to listen.

First, he needed to set some ground rules. John's gaze circled the group. "Okay, first things first. When we sit together in this circle

21

of equality, it must also be a circle of trust. If we want truth, we must be able to be forthcoming with each other." To his surprise they were all in agreement and the discussions began.

"There's so much pressure. You really like this guy, and he starts to get super annoying. You know like, come on babe or don't you love me? Ha! If he gets what he wants, he'll dump you and if he doesn't, he'll move on to someone who will. Lose. Lose! What are we supposed to do?"

"Take it from a guy, if you're with someone who isn't listening to you and only cares about one thing. Believe me, he only cares about one thing!"

"Yeah, well it's not just the guys. We get pressure from our friends. They'll give you crap if they know you're a virgin. They call you a baby. You think - I should just do it to make the noise stop."

"I get it. You may not believe me but…guys have the same type of pressure. I mean you're not considered "the man" or you know, "bad enough" if you can't get a girl to sleep with you."

John quickly realized these young teenagers were confusing love with lust and sex. Sarah slouched down in her chair biting her lower lip with downcast eyes.

Without Abby, who could Sarah turn to and ask questions about love, sex, and marriage? As difficult as it was, John realized that if he didn't answer Sarah's questions her friends sitting in this circle would. And they were just as confused as she was.

And so, it began…

"What I'm hearing from most of you, and let me know if I'm getting this right, is that you know what you want to do. But the fear of being alone and the opinions of others make your decisions."

"Yeah."

"I guess so."

"It's not that simple. You should see what some girls do if you try to be different. They're mean. You become a pariah all over social media."

"It's worse than mean; they can be downright brutal!"

John needed guidance so he did what he did best. He prayed.

God, help me convey to these precious children sitting here tonight your love. Inspire me with your words and your wisdom with what you want me to tell them.

"Go with the flow or be penalized. Boy that sounds familiar, I bet that's how Jesus felt over two thousand years ago. But he didn't go with the flow. Jesus came to upset the applecart and upset it he did!

Let's try this, how many of you believe there is a God? Don't look at the person sitting next to you, eyes here." John motioned with his index and middle fingers pointed toward his eyes. Then raised his hand.

"Some of you might not believe God is real. I get that. You've gone through some hard times in your short lives. I'm here to tell you he is real. He wants you to know he loves you all very much."

John shared God's word and they soaked it up. The Word empowered them. It became the light in their darkness. They became the light for others. Their room was named the Lighthouse; it became their sanctuary in the Angel of Grace Church. It was in this room John became a friend and mentor to the group of struggling teenagers.

The Lighthouse held their meetings two to three times a week with new faces sailing through the door all the time.

As much as he loved what was happening. The pressures of being the only pastor of a growing church started to weigh heavily upon John. Sarah saw her dad's passion and energy fading away. Her dad took the responsibility of the teenagers God brought to him very seriously. But he needed help. One night Sarah brought her concerns to the youth group, and everyone agreed they needed a youth pastor.

With growing maturity, the teenagers gathered and did as John had taught them - they prayed. Although the youth pastor did not come right away, the group never gave up. Along the way, they learned a new and valuable lesson. God does things in His own time. *Rest in the Lord and wait patiently for Him.* Psalm 37:7

Tracie eventually got a book. But not just any book. She got *Children of the King.*

This book got to the core of teenager's constant struggles with peer pressure, broken families, sex, and self-esteem. It was a book of struggle and of miracles. Like Paul's transformation on the road to Damascus, the Lighthouse teens met Jesus on their own road and were set on fire with the good news of Jesus Christ!

CHAPTER 4
DECISIONS

Twenty-six-year-old Scott Abbott was a theologian student at the University of Nebraska who needed to land an internship. He had driven northwest toward David City, figuring a lot of the other students would head east toward the bigger cities near Omaha. Unfortunately, he wasn't having very much luck. He headed toward Silver Creek.

Reaching the town of Homestead, he found himself in front of the Angel of Grace Church in his beat-up run-down Ford Escort. Weathered cedar accents adorned the front doorway of the quaint, white church. It was beautiful. This was his last stop before turning around and heading back to the university. Getting out of his car with as much confidence as his bruised ego could muster, Scott walked into the church to the door marked Office.

Knock. Knock.

"Come on in," John yelled as he opened the door to the tall lanky young man who looked awkward. His wavy blond hair was plastered to his face from the heat of the day.

"I was wondering. If ah…The ah church could use an intern?"

John was speechless. Scott took his silence as a form of rejection and rushed on, pleading his case. "I'm in school at the University of Nebraska. I'm a quick learner and willing to help in any area that the church has a need."

"Pastor John Wheaton," John extended his hand to the young man.

Scott smiled and took John's hand in a firm shake. "Scott Abbott. Nice to meet you, sir."

What Scott lacked in experience, he made up for in his willingness to listen and serve. That summer, he followed John around like a puppy dog. Scott was eager to please. After he finished his last semester of school, the Church offered Scott a permanent position as Youth Pastor. He was an answer to prayer and everyone at the Angel of Grace Church became very dependent on him.

"Are you sure about this? I mean I don't have to do this right now?" John asked Scott.

"John, I know how important the congregation is to you, don't worry. The elders will keep an eye on me while you're away. And if that doesn't persuade you," Scott pointed at Sarah. "It would be a hard sell to get Sarah to wait until school vacation. She's ready to go. What's the scripture you're always quoting to me when I'm in doubt?"

"Trust in Him and He will direct your path," They said in unison. John smiled as they walked to Scott's car.

"The congregation is in great hands if we rely on God. Scott, you've come a long way. Remember walking into my office, stumbling over your words.?"

Scott shook his head as his face turned a slight red recalling the embarrassing day. "Please don't remind me!"

"You were the answer to so many prayers." John patted him on the back. "I'm very proud of you."

Sarah put the last of her bags into the trunk. "Let's go Dad! We don't want to be late!"

"You'd better get us to the airport. We'll never hear the end of it if we miss our plane to Boston and Sarah's first glimpse of the deep blue sea."

The men shared an emotional hug before getting in the car.

Scott helped to unload John and Sarah's bags from the trunk of his car at the Central NE Regional Airport in Grand Island. Sarah and John made their way into the airport and boarded their flight in the nick of time.

John gently released the white knuckled grip he had on the arm rests once the plane leveled off in the air. He relaxed a little while still doing his best to remain calm for his daughter's sake.

All he wanted to do was close his eyes and not open them again until his feet were planted on solid ground. Being up so far in the sky didn't feel natural. He couldn't shake the fear. *Lord, when my time is up, I would really appreciate it if it wasn't when I'm so many miles up in the sky!*

John caught a glimpse of Sarah's beaming face in the reflection of the window.

"Dad this is so cool. I might become a pilot, then we could travel all over the world. Wouldn't that be great?"

He gave her an encouraging smile and almost laughed out loud despite himself. "That sounds great Sarah. I'm going to put my seat back and read for a bit." He said, pulling out a copy of Gilford's *Sights and Sounds*.

"Dad, you're going to miss everything, look at how puffy the clouds are. Besides, you always fall asleep before you finish the first page."

"Indeed…" John opened his book and turned to the page where he had left off. "Well, you enjoy the puffy clouds. You can tell me all about it when we land. Someone has to know where to go or what to do on our vacation."

"Suit yourself, but don't get mad at me when you look at my pictures and see what you missed."

"It's a chance I'll have to take." Point made, John pushed the button on his seat and settled in for what he hoped would be a comfortable flight. Soon, he felt his eyes flutter to a close as his mind drifted, his thoughts landed, as always, on Abby. One minute life was wonderful and everything on track then within a matter of six short months it had taken a turn no one expected.

Each time John rewound those bleak days, he noticed something different. Something he'd missed from before.

I guess you had other plans for us. Huh, God? He remembered Sarah wrapped in a tight ball, hugging Abby's pillow and crying with a force that made her small body shake. Through that long and painful night, he'd cradled Sarah like when she'd been a baby. They had cried together. *You're always many moves ahead of us aren't you, Father? Thank you for guiding Sarah and I through the fire.*

Sudden turbulence brought John to the present. His eyes shot open. He looked over at Sarah who was busy looking out the window and taking pictures with her phone.

In a few minutes, John lessened his grip on the arms of his seat when the plane settled into a smoother ride. He left the book sitting in his lap. *Sarah was right, no sense in opening the book.* He got comfortable and closed his eyes.

Where was I? The letters…

Abby had written a letter for each of them with the understanding they were not to open them until they were ready.

The need to feel Abby's presence in their lives gave John and Sarah the strength to open their last earthly communication from her. Abby was certain God had a special plan for the two of them. She asked them to be patient enough to receive it and strong enough to embrace it.

The letters helped. Each day they grieved a little differently realizing Abby's physical presence was no longer with them. Her life and the time she spent with them would remain and be a reflection of who they were and would become. Little by little, the light came back into their lives where darkness once lived.

"Dad? Dad! We're here. We're here!"

John was startled awake when he heard Sarah calling him. The Fasten Your Seatbelt sign was flashing in bright red letters. No problem there. He looked down at his seatbelt which had been fastened the entire flight.

Sarah was busy fastening her seatbelt. The captain announced the descent into Boston's Logan Airport. She strained against her seat belt, with a big smile plastered across her cheerful face. She giggled with pure pleasure. "Dad, look. It's like we're heading straight into the ocean. Look at its beautiful blue color. This is so cool!"

Cool? Did she really say that? John nodded with a grin. The plane began its descent; John held on for dear life. He understood how a person could come off a plane, bend down and kiss the ground. It was something he was seriously considering doing, but not today.

CHAPTER 5
AN ADVENTURE

Krystina Davis waited for her guests from Nebraska to arrive at gate 44. Pacing usually helped Krystina think but her nausea kept getting in the way. Her reputation and future depended on her decision to bring Pastor John Wheaton to Gilford. *Then what?*

He'd still have to face Spencer and the rest of the school board. Well, one person would be on her side. The only person who offered an alternative when Resolution 196 fell apart. Louise had walked up to her in the middle of a crowded corridor of kids placing the book, *Children of the King*, into her hands,

"Read this book, Krystina. It holds the key to Gilford's success."

Louise was passionate when it came to her faith. But a book that could address the teenage crisis in Gilford? Krystina had her doubts. She read the book and was amazed at how she related to the teenagers' questions and fears. Her own teen memories and awkward feelings came flooding back. It was not a Cinderella book; it was hard and it was real. Whether the reader was a believer in God or not, it seemed like miracles were happening in Homestead, Nebraska.

A rush of people came filing out from the plane and into the arrival area. Kristina spotted Pastor Wheaton immediately from the photo on the inside jacket of his book. Accompanying him, on his right, had to be his daughter Sarah, one of the people he dedicated his book to.

"Pastor Wheaton?"

"Yes," John answered. "Ms. Dayton, I presume?" John took her hand.

"Yes. Please call me Krystina," She replied firmly shaking his hand. "It's great to finally meet you, Pastor Wheaton." Krystina let go of his hand and ran her fingers through her wavy brown hair to keep it off her face.

"Please call me John." He smiled showing Krystina two of the biggest dimples she'd ever seen.

"And this young lady is my daughter Sarah," John said pointing to the girl standing beside him.

Krystina extended her hand to Sarah and was rewarded with a smile holding the same deep dimples as her father's. "It is nice to meet you, Sarah. I'm very excited you are here!"

They retrieved their luggage from the bottom floor of the terminal then packed into the cherry red four-door Volvo.

"The drive north from Logan Airport to Gilford is about forty-five minutes. Did you have a comfortable flight?" Krystina asked.

"Yes," Sarah answered.

John smiled and nodded, he had nothing to add.

"What grade are you in Sarah? Do you like your school...teachers?"

Krystina explained the different sites they passed along the way to keep things interesting.

"Over on your right is East Boston. On top of the hill, you'll see a cross that was erected to beckon people to visit the Madonna Shrine."

They drove on toward the town of Salem. "We are passing by Salem, Massachusetts. home of the famous Salem Witch Trials."

John and Sarah learned that the accusations of witchcraft began in Salem Village, a part of Danvers, Massachusetts, Salem's neighboring town. The red Volvo traveled along a stretch of highway that opened to large bodies of water on both sides of the road. Soon they passed the Welcome to Gilford sign.

The Volvo came to a slow stop. "Oh boy!" Krystina sighed.

"Why did the traffic stop?" Sarah asked. "Ahh!"

31

John turned. Sarah was speechless and pointing with one hand toward the bridge ahead. They watched in amazement as the road in front of them moved in a slow, purposeful upward direction. The impressive bridge of gleaming steel and whitewashed concrete split in two.

Krystina put the car in park, shrugged her shoulders and apologized. "This could take a while; I am very sorry about the inconvenience. But as you can see it's unavoidable, there's only one way in and one way out."

"Are you kidding me?" Came the shout of surprise from the back seat.

"No, I'm serious. You know there are some people in Gilford who have never been on this side of the bridge," Krystina informed her astonished passengers.

"This is the only way in or out?" John reiterated.

"That's right. It's exactly what I said."

"This is awesome. We don't have anything like this back home, at least, that I've ever seen!" Sarah affirmed.

"Well then, sit back and enjoy the show." Krystina smiled feeling herself relax for the first time.

John and Sarah watched as boat after boat passed through the middle of the bridge. Their tall masts reaching toward the sky in spectacular splendor.

Finally, the bridge lowered becoming a road once more and the red Volvo crossed over into Gilford. Krystina took a right-hand turn onto a busy, but scenic street. People bustled in and out of shops and restaurants. Some people strolled in a slow casual stride and others stopped to glance inside the decorated store fronts displaying the shop's wares. A few motels and inns were sprinkled about.

Krystina did her best to give her guests a guided tour. They drove along through the different sights and sounds that made up Gilford. Taking it all in John remembered some of the history he and Sarah had read regarding the town. Gilford was a fishing town with a large shipping port.

"The fishing business," Krystina explained, "is a hard and grueling occupation. Families are separated for long intervals of time. The women maintain the home and care for their children."

John and Sarah both shook their heads understanding the harsh reality.

"If you look on the tops of some of the captain's houses to your left, you'll see the old widow walks."

"Widow walks? What's that?"

"Well, Sarah that's where women would pace back and forth searching for the ships that would bring their men home."

"Oh, wow," Sarah answered.

"Of course, it's especially hard on the fishermen, being out at sea for so long. Some endure, and some give it up. Sadly, others never return."

"How awful that must be for families," Sarah interjected knowing full well the enormity of such a loss.

"Yes, it is quite sad. I fear we have let the community down during these tough and struggling years. We've reaped what we've sown, says Louise Taylor."

"Who?' Sarah and John asked.

"You'll find out soon enough."

At the stop sign at the end of the street, the sea laid out before them. Its vast beauty extended beyond the horizon. Krystina turned left. Spotting a parking space beside the sidewalk along the ocean front, she pulled in. Her guests had a glorious view. "Beautiful, isn't it," Krystina asked. "The ocean has many moods and should always be respected. She is glorious and wondrous to behold. As recipients and trustees of this portion of the Atlantic, Gilford has reaped her bountiful rewards and been the student of countless lessons."

Krystina pointed to the right. The harbor was littered with fishing boats coming and going. Fishermen were unloading the day's catch at the warehouses. The trio got out of the car to stretch their legs. Sarah and John watched the vibrant activity play out.

"It looks like the fishing business is still very much alive."

"Not like it once was. Still, it's a major part of Gilford's history and a generational way of life. The lighthouse over there on the jetty," Krystina pointed out, "is a welcome sign for tired fishermen after a long exhausting trip. If you look off to the distance, there's a cruise ship ready to descend upon the harbor." Krystina motioned, holding her hand over her eyes to shield them from the blazing sun.

"Really?" Sarah asked in disbelief.

"Oh yes. Our beaches with their glistening sand and our history attract summer tourists." Krystina answered with pride.

"Look Sarah, there's the Statue of the Fisherman that we read about." John pointed out with enthusiasm.

Sarah smiled and nodded.

Krystina had painted a picture of Gilford's unique and fascinating world for John and Sarah. Back on the road, John and Sarah were silent for the remainder of the ride, taking in the views. Krystina turned left onto Center Street and to their destination, The Seaside Inn. She left John and Sarah to get settled in after inviting them to dinner at Louise Taylor's home.

John and Sarah's room was located on the lower level of the three-story inn. Once in the room, Sarah ran to the sliding glass doors, opening them onto a patio that led to the white sand and the seashore.

"Dad, how can anyone see something this beautiful and expanse and still not believe in God?" She turned to her father before taking off in the direction of the beach with eyes filled with wonder and fascination.

John knew Sarah wasn't asking the question as much as she was pondering it. John answered with a loving smile. "Sarah, don't go too far. We can go for a nice long walk after we settle in."

"No problem, Dad. I just need a closer look. This view is so much better than from an airplane window," She yelled over her shoulder.

John agreed with her on that point.

Sarah marveled at how cool the sand felt as she covered her feet in it, letting the sand sift between her toes. She inhaled a long deep breath. "Aaah!" She breathed in and smelled the salt in the air. She was finally here. Looking out into the blue waves crashing as if on cue, she wasn't disappointed.

Krystina recalled the easy, intimate interaction John and Sarah shared. She remembered her clumsiness with her own father as a teenager. Smiling, Krystina felt a tiny flicker of hope. Maybe a miracle can happen in Gilford. She hoped this tiny flicker would turn into a flame.

It was 6:00 p.m. when Krystina arrived back at the Seaside Inn to pick up her guests. John and Sarah were sitting on the bright multicolored Adirondack chairs. Their gaze directed toward the sun glistening like crystals off the calm blue sea. Krystina beeped and gave them both a quick wave.

The group headed to the Taylors' home for dinner. The trio traveled through the center of the town which was alive with music from restaurants and the solo musicians playing on the street corners. Tip jars, made from old fishing buckets or guitar cases were open beside them, stood ready to accept their audience's gratuities.

The enticing smells of food drifted through the car leaving everyone licking their lips in eager anticipation of their coming meal. The Volvo turned onto Bittersweet Lane and stopped in front of number seventeen. It was a soft yellow cape design with forest green shutters. The white picket gate opened onto a weathered worn brick path leading to the open front door.

"Welcome. Welcome. Welcome," said the very petite woman with a bright smile who stood in the doorway. Louise ushered everyone into her home. "Well now, Pastor John." Louise introduced herself with her low, raspy tone and a large smile. She extended her small, steady hands and gathered John's hands into hers.

"And you must be Sarah. Welcome to our home. We're so happy to finally meet the two of you." Louise turned and scooped Sarah into her smooth almond-colored open arms for a gentle but sincere motherly hug.

Without warning Louise turned quick as a flash motioning everyone to follow. "Dwayne is out on the deck grilling up some steaks for tonight's dinner."

Looking at each other John, Krystina and Sarah smiled. They followed her to the back of the house. Out on the deck, the aroma of steaks cooking on the grill teased and delighted their senses.

As petite as Louise was, her husband Dwayne was an imposing figure at 6'3". Dwayne was as solid as a rock whose skin had a deep mahogany glow that matched his kind eyes.

The graying hair at his temples was the only telltale sign of his age. Sarah was delighted to meet sixteen-year-old Sharise, who was a blend of her parents with a perfect mocha complexion and compelling brown eyes. Sharise was about to begin her junior year of high school. The Taylors' older son Dwayne Jr., DJ, was spending the week at his grandparent's house in the western part of the state. DJ and a friend had gone to help his grandparents with some projects that needed to get done before the boys went to college.

When dinner was ready, everyone moved to the table and gathered hands. Dwayne led the group in prayer. "Father, God, we thank you for the blessings before us that we can share with new and old friends. We ask for Your blessing tonight and for the road ahead. May you guide us and lead us in the direction that is Your will. In Jesus' name we pray. Amen."

"Amen," they all replied.

Dinner was a sequence of laughs and candor; it was like sitting down with old friends. When the meal was finished and the plates cleared, the adults moved their conversation into the house. The mosquitoes were becoming too much.

The teenagers headed upstairs having had enough adult interaction for one night. Soon the adults' conversation turned to what was on everyone's mind. The meeting with the school board the next day.

"Do you think what you and your congregation accomplished in Nebraska could have a chance of working here in Gilford?" Dwayne asked John.

"First, we didn't do anything. God did all the work. He used me. God opened the minds and hearts of our young people. God showed them everything He had to offer. We must never lose sight of that," John answered, choosing his words with care. "The blessings and Glory are the Lord's alone. We are only his humble servants, Dwayne."

"Amen!" Dwayne shouted. "Let's hope the Lord sees fit to open the minds and hearts of our troubled youth, not to mention the almighty School Board of Gilford."

With a slight twinge of jealousy. Krystina sat back in her chair watching the exchange between the pastor and her friends. They shared genuine faith and confidence in God. She felt sadness deep within her, like something was missing from her own life, an empty hole that needed to be filled.

Upstairs Sharise and Sarah were bonding, sitting across from each other on Sharise's bed.

"Do you know any of the girls that got pregnant?" Sarah asked in a quiet voice.

"Most of the girls I've seen around school. I don't know them personally except for Erica Gray. She had a baby girl freshman year. I used to be friends with her in middle school. Then her parents got divorced and we drifted apart. She didn't want to hang out or go to church anymore. I think she blamed God for her parents break up. When we got to high school, she hung around with a wild group of kids who were into drinking and drugs." Sharise looked at Sarah with tears brimmed in her eyes. "It's sad what's happening in Gilford. I really hope your dad can help. There's a lot of people hurting here."

"Me too," Sarah reached over and gave Sharise a heartfelt hug.

And so their conversation marked the beginning of a journey, neither of the girls could ever begin to imagine.

CHAPTER 6
CHILDREN OF THE KING

"You hardly slept last night," Dwayne commented during breakfast.

"I'm anxious to get this meeting underway and to get things moving." Louise answered on her way out the door. She wanted to get to the Seaside Inn early to pick up their guests.

Now, Louise sat tapping her fingers on the steering wheel of her baby-blue Toyota Corolla as she listened to music. As soon as John and Sarah got buckled in, Louise picked up right where she left off at dinner the night before.

"Now John, remember what I said last night. Don't let those wrinkled old suits intimidate you. Some of them only speak to hear themselves talk. Believe me, they seldom have anything worthwhile to say, lately anyway."

John chuckled appreciating Louise's sincere passion and spunk. "Louise, I'm not here to convince anyone, especially the school board, about the awakening our teens have had in Nebraska. I'm here to share God's story and the steadfast commitment we have to our young people. It's up to the school board to decide what they want to do with the information they receive."

"Oh, if it was only that simple." Louise replied.

Krystina's footsteps echoed through the empty halls as she walked toward the school conference room. She wanted this time to prepare for what the Board might throw at her. Vice Principal Karl Porter had been gunning for her job a while. Karl would relish the idea of convincing the board that Krystina had lost her mind.

Had she?

"Stop thinking negatively," Krystina spoke to the empty hall.

She had her allies. Shelly was always in the students' corner; and they had a great working relationship. Krystina always counted on Robert to say black if Spencer said white. Bob voted with conviction and was not one to be swayed.

She reached the conference room and walked to the empty chair at far end of the long table. She liked being able to view everyone's expressions; it gave her a feel for how the meeting was going.

"Ugh," Krystina said aloud in frustration. Then did something she hadn't done in a very long time, she prayed. "God, I know I've ignored you for years. I'm so sorry. I don't know if you're here with me now. If you are and you're listening, please help us like you're helping the people in Homestead. This community is filled with good hard-working folks. We've just lost our way. If you could open the hearts and minds of our board members, starting with me, I'd be so grateful. Help us give the people of Gilford a future to look forward too. Help us Lord to be strong and to believe in you." Trembling, she finished in a faint whisper. "Give us a miracle God. Help Gilford heal."

Krystina heard voices coming from the hallway. Spencer entered the conference room followed by the other board members. John, Sarah and Louise were close on their heels.

Instead of the dread, a peace began to consume her in its place. "Ah!" Krystina smiled. *Let the games begin.*

"Would you mind Pastor John, if we had your daughter wait on the bench outside the conference room? You do understand?" Spencer politely asked John.

John was a bit reluctant, but Sarah assured him she would be fine.

The introductions were made. Krystina stood and walked to the front of the room to address her colleagues. "I'd like to thank you all for coming today. As you know we have a serious problem facing our schools. Not only in the high school but in our middle school as well. We have shown true diligence in trying to combat the problems, but there's been little to no progress. In fact, things are progressing in the opposite direction. With another school year around the corner, it's time to start thinking outside of the box."

Krystina looked over to where John sat, paying little attention to the fake coughs of ignorance. "To that end, I would like to introduce you once again to the Senior Pastor of Angel of Grace Church in Homestead, Nebraska, John Wheaton. Pastor John is the author of the bestselling book, *Children of the King*. John, we are incredibly happy you've come to share your insights about the success you've achieved with the youth group at the Angel of Grace Church."

The clapping was minimal, but John was not one to back down from a challenge. He pushed back his chair and walked to the front of the room. Blank stares greeted him as he took a deep breath.

"Aaah. Good morning. I'd like to begin by expressing my thanks for inviting me to your delightful town of Gilford." John smiled his award-winning smile.

There was a cold chill in the air even though the temperature was sizzling this summer morning.

"It's been exciting for my daughter Sarah. This is her first time coming east and seeing the ocean. Believe me, she was not disappointed!"

Stone cold faces, except for Krystina and Louise, stared back at him without so much as a stir. A little dismayed John cleared his throat.

"Ah hem. Sarah and I come from Homestead, Nebraska. We're from a small town similar to Gilford. To be honest, I don't think Gilford's youth is any different from the youth of other cities or towns in America today. There is not one child born into this world that does not want to feel safe and secure. Children require trust and believe it or not, they want to earn it as much as give it."

"Excuse me. I don't mean to interrupt Pastor John but we aren't talking about children. We have a problem with our teenagers." Karl interjected in a condescending tone.

"Do you have children of your own?"

"Well, no, I don't. But as vice principal, I'm engaged with our students."

"I see. So, you would agree, what I've learned from talking with teenagers is that they are in essence older children."

"Amen to that Pastor John!" Louise chimed in.

"Our children, excuse me for purposes here today, our teenagers, demand unconditional love. Every teenager wants to know they are loved." In a slow and fearless tone, John continued. "No. They don't want, they NEED to know they are special in someone's eyes and that there's a plan and a purpose for their existence."

"If a person, whether a child, teenager or even an adult does not feel loved what is their worth? What is their purpose? Kids today are no different than kids two thousand years ago. They warrant discipline when they do wrong and praise as a reward for hard work and good deeds. Children, teenagers, however, you wish to label them, would rather hear a good word from a parent or have an hour of one-on-one time, than go off to the mall with friends. They would rather hear helpful criticism from a teacher than be degraded in front of a classroom of their peers." It was time John realized for God to speak to these board members.

"If I could speak all the languages of earth and of angels, but didn't love others, I would only be a noisy gong or a clanging cymbal. If I had the gift of prophecy, and if I understood all of God's secret plans and possessed all knowledge, and if I had such faith that I could move mountains, but didn't love others, I would be nothing. If I gave everything I have to the poor and even sacrificed my body, I could boast about it; but if I didn't love others, I would have gained nothing. Love is patient and kind. Love is not jealous or boastful or proud or rude. It does not demand its own way. It is not irritable,

and it keeps no record of being wronged. It does not rejoice about injustice but rejoices whenever the truth wins out. Love never gives up, never loses faith, is always hopeful, and endures through every circumstance." 1st Corinthians 13: 1-7 .

The stunned room was silent.

"The difference between Homestead and Gilford is that we look to God for our answers. In Gilford, you look to the world for yours."

"Excuse me," Spencer piped in. "We are a very proactive town. To combat the problem our town has experienced, we've put a resolution in place. Our students have the best sex education classes possible. We supply different methods of birth control, and we provide childcare for students with babies so they can receive an education. Sorry to disappoint you Pastor John, but not everyone believes that God even exists."

"If you honestly believe this resolution of yours is working so well, why did you invite Sarah and me to come to Gilford?" John countered.

"Good question," Karl remarked, looking at Kristina.

"Really Karl?" Krystina replied.

"I'll tell you why," John aimed at Karl who was sitting with a smug and pompous expression. "Because what you are doing isn't working. You supply excuses, products and a corrupt system to rid yourselves of the guilt you feel so you can sleep at night thinking you're doing all you can to help."

Gasps erupted from around the table.

"Ugh!"

"Agh!"

"What?"

"You are rewarding them for inexcusable behavior and supplying them with contraceptives, then teaching them in Sex Education classes their behavior is justified and supported. Have you ever thought of teaching your students the rewards of abstinence in your Sex Education classes? Of giving them a choice?"

The members chattered under their breath, but John quickly continued.

"When I say abstinence, I'm referring to the way God intended it to be. It's not the belittling and judgmental term it has become. Abstinence is a personal journey, a source of strength and valor. It is humble and steadfast. Abstinence is a gift, and you are its reward."

Some of the members were thinking about what he said.

God urged him on. "I would stop giving out contraceptives to your students; you're only enabling these kids. Lastly, I would not have a childcare facility on the school premise; you are educators not babysitters. I'm not saying the town shouldn't help these young mothers. Childcare should be located away from the school." John ignored the noise. "Children crave attention, and they'll get it by being good or bad." Shocked faces told John all he needed to know. "Look, you didn't bring me all the way out here to sugar-coat your predicament. Did you?"

"No, we did not." Came the lone voice from the other end of the table. John smiled at Louise. Nodding his head toward her in a manner of thanks for the support.

"Someone must tell them NO, but you also have to give them alternatives. Will it be easy? No. But will it be worth it? Yes!" John felt sympathy for their predicament. "Stop talking at them and start listening to them. Show them that their life is worth living. As adults, we need to listen more."

Like a deflated balloon, John felt spent but before he left, he wanted the board members to know it wasn't easy for him either. "Before our youth group was formed, I was oblivious to any problems, questions or feelings teenagers might have. And I'm the father of one of those teenagers. Haven't we all been there? We forget how much they look to us to answer their questions, no matter how silly they may sound or how hard the questions can be. If we aren't there for these kids one way or another those questions will get answered. But they shouldn't get answered from other teenagers guessing at the very same questions." John turned to walk to his seat.

"Pastor John. I agree with a lot of what you said. But, what about the kids living with divorced parents? Those kids are shuffled back and forth. Or the parents who work so much they're never home? How are we supposed to help these kids?"

"Great question. Is there someplace where teenagers can get together? Supervised, of course. I realize there are sports teams and clubs that schools offer. We found in Homestead there are many kids who can't afford the cost of a sports team or the time needed to belong to a school club. A great number of kids are responsible for taking care of their younger siblings after school."

"I agree," Bob interjected. "Our school is involved in so many team sports and clubs. There isn't a place for kids to congregate. Like you said Pastor, who has the time to watch over a bunch of kids? There's no way we can be babysitters too!"

"There are kids who would love to participate in a sport or club, but they can't," Shelley declared. "I've seen it happen so many times. Sometimes, their self-esteem is so low they don't feel like they fit in. Let's face it, kids can be very cruel to each other."

"How well I know that, Ms. Bradshaw. Sarah and I live in a single-parent home. We lost my wife Abigail three years ago to cancer and that's when my eyes were opened for the first time. Have you searched your neighborhoods for places where kids can hang out together? A YMCA? Is there a church in town that can work in conjunction with the school?"

"Oh, easy for you to say." Karl was looking for a way to derail this meeting. Things were fine the way they were; it wasn't his fault parents couldn't control their kids. The YMCA? If they can't afford a club or sports, how will they pay for anything else? A church, that's priceless. "In your infinite wisdom Pastor John, can you please tell us how to get kids already having sex to a church?"

John turned to Karl with a cold stare. "I don't know what kind of places you have in your town to accommodate teenagers since I'm not from this area. Back home we use the church that I pastor. The teenagers play music, they play games and sometimes they sit around in a circle and talk."

"A circle?"

"Yes, a circle. Because a circle defines equality, fairness, no pretense. Everyone is there to help each other. No judgment. Reach out to your community. If the problem in Gilford is as dire as you say, the community should be more than happy to help out. And Karl, everyone is a sinner and praises God for Jesus or none of us would get into Heaven. I'm sure any church in your town is the perfect place for a sinner just like a hospital is for the sick."

John tried to encourage them. "At the very least, reach out to those students you don't think are worth anything because they'll be the ones to surprise you. If you're willing to work hard and look to God for the answers, I promise you he will not let you down. *Don't be afraid, for I am with you. Don't be discouraged, for I am your God. I will strengthen you and help you. I will hold you up with my victorious right hand.*" Isaiah 41:10."

"Well, I believe we have everything we need," Spencer interrupted the deafening silence. He had heard enough and got to his feet. "I know I speak for everyone here today when I say thank you Pastor John for coming all this way and sharing your insight and recommendations. If you would kindly join your daughter, we'd like to discuss the information you've recommended to us a bit further." Spencer reached out his hand to John which he accepted.

"Thank you for having us. We appreciate the opportunity to visit this exceptional area. It was a pleasure to meet with all of you today. May God bless you and your town of Gilford." John walked out the door leaving behind a room full of soul-searching board members.

Father and daughter sat side by side on the worn wooden bench set up outside of the conference room.

"It got heated in there. What do you think will happen now?" Sarah asked.

"Agh." John turned and looked into Sarah's questioning blue eyes. "I don't know what God has in store for the people of this town. What I do know is, through Almighty God, we gave those board members a taste of God's love, mercy, and deliverance."

CHAPTER 7
OUTSIDE THE BOX

The sheer lilac curtains fluttered away from their place on the windowsill announcing the slight breeze that swooped through the living room.

"Ah." Louise sighed before taking a soothing sip of chamomile tea from her favorite mug that displayed the engraved passage. "Every morning when my feet hit the floor, the Devil says, Oh Crap, She's up!"

Louise stretched her legs settling into a comfortable position on the plush chocolate brown sofa and laid her head against the small powder blue striped pillow. Picking up the black leather journal resting by her side and with pen in hand, Louise began writing down the past week's events unleashing the mighty power of God.

Once Pastor John left the conference room. A multitude of conversations exploded. Each board member trying to impose their opinions upon the other.

Taking charge Spencer pleaded with everyone. "Can we please stop talking over each other? We are after all supposed to be the adults in the room." He emphasized. "Now if anyone has any new proposals they would like to offer, Now would be the time."

Scanning the table Spencer continued. "Otherwise, the only logical decision that makes any sense, at this juncture, is to continue with the implementations we already have in place."

Suddenly a hand shot up from within the stillness of the room.

"Ms. Bradshaw is there something new you'd like to share with us?" Spencer asked.

"Yes. I do." Rising from her seat Shelly stated in a strong and concise tone. "We should hire him."

"Hire him. Hire who?" Spencer asked.

"Why Pastor John Wheaton of course."

"What? Do you have any idea what you are suggesting, Ms. Bradshaw?"

"I most certainly do."

"Please," Spencer thundered. "Enlighten us with your grand plan of hiring a pastor for the Gilford Public School System."

Not to be intimated by Spencer's looming figure or boisterous voice Shelly continued.

"We have several students staying after school for detention I would venture to say about every day of the school year. We also have teachers who would rather spend time giving students extra help than serve an hour of detention time. Why not hire Pastor John to sit with the students serving detention? What did he say to us earlier? Reach out to the students you don't think are worth it for they're the ones that will surprise you?"

Despite the incredulous looks from many of the other members Shelly pressed on. "Pastor John will have the student's full attention for one hour each school day. If students want to participate in conversation, they can. If not. They can sit in their chairs and do nothing for the entire hour. The point is we have a chance to turn things around like they did in Homestead. We have nothing to lose and everything to gain and I for one believe these kids are worth saving."

"Well done, Shelly!" Louise encouraged. "I couldn't agree more with you. We owe it to our babies to do all we can. What we've done for them up until now hasn't worked. And the definition of insanity is doing the same thing over and over again. I for one am jumping off the insanity train and giving it all to God."

"Do you hear yourselves? Giving it all to God? We are not talking about a holy crusade, Louise. We are talking about school and students. Has everyone here lost their mind?"

"Separation of church and state. There is no way we can hire a pastor. I can't believe any of you are even considering this option.!" Karl announced in his usually arrogant tone.

"This was a hair-brained idea from the beginning. I knew it would bring nothing but trouble. Now listen to us." Karl turned his annoyance on Krystina. "I'm sorry but at this point, with the high school in such chaos Krystina. You may want to think about resigning!" Like a bully in the playground, he added. "The job seems to be a bit too large for you."

Looking like a frightened little girl Michele Clancy stood up. With her eyes looking down at her feet she declared in pragmatical terms. "Actually. the separation between church and state is to protect the people from the government proclaiming a certain religion for all. Too many times we let a few decide what should be and what should not. Our forefathers never wanted to evict church from society. They recognized that several states did not share uniform values. Much of the Bill of Rights was meant to prevent dictatorships which married church and state in such a manner as to mar many of the freedoms our forefathers sought to enshrine. We could always hire Pastor Wheaton to teach a course. That way anyone who signs up for the class does so of their own free will." Feeling as though she had made her point Michelle quietly sat back down.

Krystina seized the opportunity and jumping into action. "One semester let's hire him for one semester. We can convene after that time and see if any progress has been made. If the situation in Gilford is still the same or worse. I will accept defeat and resign as Principal of Gilford High School." She placed both hands on the table and stared into Karl's ecstatic face wreaking of victory and added. "However, if the situation has improved the School Board will extend the offer to Pastor John to teach his class at the high school for the remainder of the school year."

"Done!" Karl shouted with pure joy jumping to his feet.

"Sit down Karl and get a grip on yourself man. This is not a game show." Spencer directed. All eyes were on Spencer sitting in his chair at the head of the table. His fingers laced together in a thoughtful pose. Turning to Krystina he answered.

"You're putting an awful lot on the line for what could turn out to be a quick hype or the next best thing. This could be nothing more than a publicity stunt to help sell his book. Why you don't know if Pastor John would accept a position at the high school. Even if we were to offer it to him. I mean in all seriousness Krystina he has a life and a church full of parishioners back in Nebraska. You've known him for what two days?

Krystina was gracious in her reply. "I appreciate your concern, Spencer. I do. Honestly, I don't know what to believe. My head is running in a million different directions. But it keeps coming back to the same constant. Our kids are in trouble and as the adults we are to blame.

We've tried many different approaches. The *"don't see don't tell."* The *"slap on the wrist with no consequences."* And the best one of all. *"I'm here for you consider me your friend"* approach. Maybe, it's time to try the *"God"* approach if Pastor John will accept our offer." Krystina shared her own past. "I was not raised a Christian and I do not have Louise's unconditional faith. But for the first time in my adult life. I prayed to a God I wasn't even sure existed. I asked him for strength and courage. To open the minds of our board members and give us a miracle to help heal our town. I believe God answered my prayer today. He opened some of our minds to move in a different direction." Smiling at Michelle and Shelly. "A direction some may consider offensive and controversial. But I can tell you I've never felt more sure about something. God is giving us a chance."

"If God is willing to take a chance on our town, who am I not to put it all on the line for God. Besides, if this is truly from God. Pastor John will accept the position at Gilford High School."

Louise wrote in her journal every word of Krystina's spectacular speech. Well, what she could remember. Krystina took down the school bully and she brilliantly gave it all she had. leaving it all on the conference room table.

CHAPTER 8
A NEW JOURNEY BEGINS

I'm sure putting me in this classroom was no accident. John looked out the window of his third-floor classroom at Gilford High School. *The view isn't much.* He smiled.

Vice Principal Karl Porter had taken extra special delight in walking John up three flights of stairs to the third-floor classroom. Karl had no qualms telling Krystina how much he relished the idea of her resignation.

Poor fool John thought shaking his head. *"Only a simpleton would not know, and only a fool would not understand this."* Psalm 92:6

"What did you say?"

John turned towards Sarah's sweet voice, almost forgetting she was in the room with him.

After agreeing to terms with the school board, Sarah and John packed up their black Subaru for the trek east to Gilford, Massachusetts. Their new residence for the next three months would be the home of Dwayne and Louise Taylor.

There were a few boxes of supplies John brought from Nebraska. They were unpacking some poster art and other paraphernalia.

"Nothing. Just thinking out loud."

"You better watch that Dad, the kids will think you're a little senile in the head." Sarah giggled.

"I don't want the students calling me "Senile Wheaton" behind my back."

Sarah reached into one of the boxes when her newest ringtone of "Trust In You" by Lauren Daigle, suddenly filled the room.

Grabbing her phone from the back pocket of her jean shorts, she read the text message out loud. "Sharise will be here to help in about twenty minutes. She'll be driving the Corolla herself."

"Good! More hands to help empty these boxes," John answered.

"Did you hear me, Dad? Sharise will be driving the Corolla herself!"

"Oh my gosh, did Sharise pass? She got her license." John walked over to Sarah who was nodding her head up and down and gave her a high five.

"I'm going to bring these empty boxes down to the car and wait for Sharise. I'm so excited to see her drive!"

"No problem," John answered throwing her the car keys. "But Sarah remember to make it back up here. No bunny trails. There's only one week before school starts and I really need your help."

"Of course, Dad. We won't let you down. Promise." Sarah gave her dad a kiss on the cheek for reassurance and was out the door.

As Sarah closed the trunk, Sharise pulled the Corolla up next to her.

"Nice job," Sarah said giving her friend the thumps up. Sharise put the car in park and jumped out. Grabbing Sarah by the arms, the two of them jumped up and down laughing. The sight was not lost on the group of football players exiting the back of the gym.

"Hey Sharise, got a new girlfriend?" yelled one of the players. Followed by snickers, laughter and odd remarks from some of the other players.

"Your comments might be funny Steve, if you knew what you were talking about. Oh, I forgot, you don't have a brain because you're nothing but a big dumb jock!" Sharise's quick wit turned the tables on the six-foot one-inch wide receiver along with all the Ooh's and Ah's now directed his way.

Sarah and Sharise sprinted toward the school doors. Sharise held the door open for Sarah who grabbed the door quickly, but not without taking a quick glance behind her. For the briefest of moments, she locked eyes with one of the football players exiting the gym.

"Come on, before they realize we've left the area." Sharise pulled Sarah from her powerful encounter.

"Sorry about that," Sharise declared once they were safely inside.

"Sorry about what?" Sarah asked.

"You know, what I said to Steve. He can be such a jerk. He gets me so mad. They all think they're something because they can run around a field and toss a ball to each other. It's not like any of them are going to the NFL!"

"Oh, Sharise, please. Sometimes people like Steve need to be put in their place. Don't waste your time thinking about it. Besides... you got your license!"

"That's right I did!"

The two ran up the stairs to the third floor to help John finish setting up.

Later, they all stood back taking in their finished product nodding in agreement.

"Great suggestion Sarah, splitting up the passages of 1st Corinthians 13. The lines from the passage align in seamless perfection along the walls of the room," John stated admiring their colorful handiwork. "This way love surrounds the entire classroom."

The two girls burst out laughing.

"What?"

"Dad, love surrounds the room?" Sarah asked trying to contain her amusement.

"Too corny?" John joked.

"Yeah! I warned you...Senile Wheaton!"

"Senile Wheaton?" Sharise asked.

"Never mind, I'll tell you in the car." Turning to her dad, Sarah asked. "That's if it's okay with you, Dad?"

"Sure, but I will be right behind the two of you."

The girls scooted out of the classroom first. Before following them out John reached over to turn off the lights and whispered to himself. *"But blessed are those who trust in the Lord and have made the Lord their hope and confidence."* Jeremiah 17:7

"Perfect," Brittany Gallo announced. Her pleased reflection stared back at her from the long mirror mounted on the bedroom wall. As captain of the football cheerleading squad, she had a certain status and responsibility. "After all," she reminded herself, "Daddy always says." Brittany deepened her tone and pointed her right index finger at her reflection.

"'People look up to leaders, Brittany. You have an obligation to the less fortunate people of the world.' Ah, so much responsibility." With one last look in the mirror, Brittany sashayed out of her bedroom. "Mom, I'm heading over to Julie's house." Her long black hair bounced as she skipped down the stairs.

"Brittany, wait a minute," Linda Gallo called from the top of the polished, wide cherry wood staircase. "What's going on over at Julie's house? Who will be there?"

"Oh, the usual suspects. Andrea, Lisa, you know the girls on the squad." Brittany smiled ever so sweetly. "We thought we'd get together and see if we could come up with some new cheers for the season. Julie's mom invited us to stay for dinner."

"Oh, sweetie that is so smart, getting a jump start on the new year." Linda beamed with pride. "It's what I tell the ladies at the club. My Brittany is always thinking ahead. No wonder you're the captain of the cheerleading squad. Tell Julie's mom I said hello. But remember young lady, you have a curfew. No more excuses."

"I know, Mom." Completely disinterested with the conversation, Brittany headed toward the door. Without warning, the front door opened. Brittany jumped out of the way. A distinct mixture of salt and sweat flowed on a warm breeze into the house and assaulted her nostrils. "You stink!"

"Yeah, that's what happens when you're doing football drills in ninety-degree weather. You sweat. Deal with it." Joshua Gallo expressed bluntly. With his bulky bag of football equipment straddled over one shoulder, he shuffled past his twin sister.

"Josh, wait a minute."

But he kept moving toward the back of the house oblivious to her request. Thoughts of food and lots of it were all that kept him upright and conscious.

Brittany followed him, trying not to breathe in his stench. "Did practice get out?"

"Good guess, Genius. What gave it away?" Joshua dumped his football bag and cleats and headed straight for the refrigerator.

Brittany ignored his wise remark and scooted into one of the high-top chairs at the breakfast bar. "Wow, still funny after six hours of football practice. Could be Coach isn't pushing you hard enough."

"Okay, what do you want?" Joshua's head came out of the refrigerator with hands full of sandwich meats, mayonnaise, and a jar of kosher dill pickles. He laughed at his sister's outright expression of disgust. "It's obvious you can't stand the way I smell, and you don't find my jokes very funny. So, spill it."

Brittany shook her head in complete amazement. *How can we be twins?* At least they weren't identical twins. Sometimes Brittany wondered if Joshua was adopted. "Just curious if Steve said anything to you. Like what he was doing tonight?"

"How would I know what Steve's doing tonight? We had practice not a social gathering! Besides Britt, he's your boyfriend not mine. I'm partial to someone with a higher pitched voice." Then he couldn't resist throwing her one last jab. "Ah, is there trouble in paradise Sis?"

"Hmph! None of your business! But do tell Josh, when was the last time you had a date? I've tried to fix you up with almost every one of my friends. But no! Joshua Gallo is too good to date them." She got off the chair.

"I'm not going to date someone for the sake of dating. That's you Brit. Not me." Joshua drained his Gatorade. Belched, and put the finishing touches on his sandwich.

"Whatever." Disgusted, Brittany waved her hand and headed out of the kitchen toward the front door.

"Joshua Anthony Gallo. I hope you didn't dump your football gear in this house?" Linda called out while making her way down the stairs.

"Yeah, Joshua Anthony Gallo. You didn't dump your football gear. Did you?" Brittany echoed with a giggle.

Linda gave a quick wave to her daughter as she exited the front door, then marched into the kitchen without missing a beat.

"It's out on the back porch, Mom. I needed to get some food into me before I passed out." Joshua pleaded before diving into his masterpiece. The triple-decker sandwich was stacked with baked ham, smoked turkey, Provolone cheese and smothered with real mayonnaise.

Linda stood in the middle of the kitchen with her hands on her hips exposing perfectly manicured nails as she looked her son up and down. Her stylish brown bob with distinct blond highlights shimmered with her every movement while her hazel eyes took in the sight.

"You are a mess. What does that coach put you boys through?"

"It's football, Mom. If I came home looking neat and clean, then chances are I didn't leave the bench."

Ignoring his sarcasm, Linda walked over to the mayhem her son had left on the counter and began putting away what needed to go into the refrigerator. Then she walked to the breakfast bar. "Joshua, you are going to ruin your appetite for dinner tonight. Your father is expecting us at the country club this evening."

Joshua inhaled the kosher dills straight from the jar. A great compliment to his sandwich as he finished the remains of his masterpiece. He got up from the bar stool with care taking note of his tired and aching body. He put the remaining pickles in the refrigerator and placed his plate in the sink. "Sorry Mom, but it looks like it'll just be you and Dad for dinner tonight. I'm going upstairs to take a nice long hot shower, and hopefully I'll have enough strength left in me to do a face plant into bed."

"What?"

"Goodnight Mom, love you." Joshua waved his hand over his head and was about to ascend the long, cruel climb upstairs when he heard a cry coming from the kitchen.

"Your bag Joshua, it needs to be emptied and aired out."

"Leave it, Mom. It's only going to get smelly and sweaty all over again tomorrow." With his strength zapped all he could manage was a chuckle.

In another area of town, life was not so jovial. In fact, for the past couple of months turmoil had taken up residence at the Rivera home.

"Lily, why don't we go out and grab a bite to eat? We can do some school shopping. You'll be starting in a week."

"It's doesn't matter one way or another if I wear new jeans or new shoes to school. It's not like anyone ever notices, or cares." Lily got up from the chair and headed upstairs to her room.

"I'm trying to talk to you; don't walk away from me."

"Mom, think of it as saving money. It's not a big deal what I wear or what pencil I use. Trust me."

"It used to matter. What has happened? You don't care about anything anymore? What you look like? What you eat? You've become distant with all your friends."

Lily stood stick still. Arms crossed, no response.

"I'm thinking maybe the news of…"

"Don't say it!" Lily interrupted.

"I was going to say it happened so close to the anniversary of your father's passing, I am sure it brought back painful memories. I understand. I do, Lily. I lost him too. Don't shut me out. Talk to me."

"Hmph! People die everyday Mom, that's life." Nothing seemed to pierce the cold steel armor that guarded her heart.

"Oh Lily, you sound so resentful. I know you miss him. I do too, every day. But if you continue to bottle up these feelings, it's going to eat you up inside."

Lily's hands balled up into tight fists at her side "Yeah, that's it Mom. I'm angry and bitter because God let Dad die. Leaving you to work, day and night just trying to put food on the table or clothes on our backs for the snobs in this town. Or maybe Mom…I just don't care anymore! I don't know why you do." Lily bolted up the stairs and into her room slamming the door behind her.

Theresa Rivera stood alone in the empty room and pleaded as a tear rolled down her cheek. "Dear God, what has happened to my poor Lily? Please help her."

CHAPTER 9
WELCOME

The auditorium was filled to capacity. The chatter of students was deafening as they caught up with friends they hadn't seen all summer. Sarah sat with Sharise a couple of rows from the front of the stage. Her father was about to be introduced to the students of Gilford High School.

John stood behind the curtain to the left of the stage waiting, thankful for the few moments of isolation. His thoughts returning to earlier in the morning and Dwayne's special prayer.

"Father God, we thank you for giving John the opportunity to connect with the students at Gilford High School. We pray that you will bless him with strength, courage and heavenly wisdom as he begins his ministry. And we would ask for a special blessing of patience and understanding to rain down on the good people of Gilford. In Jesus' name we pray. Amen."

John bowed his head adding, "Lord, fill me with the words you want me to say."

Krystina walked unobserved to the podium in the middle of the stage. Time to begin another school year. Sweeping over the crowd of faces some familiar, some not, Krystina spoke into the microphone.

"Good morning. On behalf of all the faculty members at Gilford High School, I'd like to welcome our incoming freshmen and welcome back our returning students. We hope everyone had a safe and enjoyable summer and that you are ready for a new, exciting year at Gilford High School." Krystina waited for the hoots and hollers from the students to die down.

"There have been a few changes I would like to go over with you before we begin the hectic first day of school. I'd like to take this moment to thank the Gilford YMCA. As some of you have noticed, the childcare center that once occupied the old art room has been relocated to the first floor of the Gilford YMCA on the corner of Fairfield and Main Street."

"Boo! Boo!" The shouts of disapproval silenced Krystina from proceeding any further.

She motioned with hand gestures to quiet them down without success. Krystina glanced at Karl. A spiteful grin was splashed across his face. *You haven't won yet, Karl.* She was still the principal. She would quiet this room.

"Okay, okay. Enough. The change has been made. You've made your displeasure known. If there are any students who would like to speak further regarding this change, my office door is always open. But we need to move on."

"Move on?" Shouted one of the students standing up and pointing at Krystina with one hand and the other on her hip. "I'm going to have a baby in a few months and now because of this change, I'll have to get up even earlier to drop my baby off. Then jump on a stupid shuttle to try and make it to school on time. Now how am I supposed to do that, exactly?"

Shocked by the student's brazenness, Krystina stood at the podium trying to collect her thoughts.

"That's what I thought," the student affirmed. "This is crap. It's not fair." The auditorium erupted with boisterous and negative remarks.

What audacity! They were blaming the school for the consequences of their bad choices. It was about time these students started to take responsibility for their actions. *No sense in trying to silence them now.* Krystina let the emotions of the students take their course. Unfortunately, the chaos seemed to be getting louder.

John decided it was time to meet the students of Gilford High. Sensing the presence of another person, Krystina was relieved to see John's friendly face. She moved aside and let him step up to the microphone.

"Young lady. What is your name?" John bellowed with a firmness and compassion that rose above the disapproving noise in the crowded auditorium.

With a new face taking center stage, the curious crowd's outbursts began to hush. The agitated young girl looked at John with eyes of steel. In a proud and loud voice of her own answered his question. "Kimberly Hanes."

"Well Kimberly it's very nice to meet you. I would like to commend you for choosing life."

Some of the students, thinking John was applauding Kimberly's lifestyle, started to cheer, hoot, and holler.

John motioned with his hands for the students to quiet down. Within a minute the floor was his. "Kimberly, as with all of life's choices, they come with sacrifices. You and your partner chose to have unprotected sex, the result was becoming pregnant. Choices. We make them every day. Some are more significant than others. Having a daughter of my own, I cannot imagine my life without her. Children are a blessing. A gift from God, their love is unconditional. But realize this," John pointed into the audience of students., "not only am I speaking to Kimberly but anyone else making similar choices. A mother or father must be willing to make daily sacrifices for their child. It is demanding and exhausting, especially for one at such a young age." John looked out and scanned his audience. "Do you think you are old enough to raise a child? Not have a child, that's the easy part. But raise a child?"

The entire assembly hall, for the first time that morning, was so quiet you could hear a pin drop.

"Kimberly, I know I speak for all the teachers at Gilford High School when I say we are here to help you. We are rooting for you. But under no circumstances will we be enablers for you or any other student at Gilford High School. Consequential decisions and responsibility go hand in hand. No one is responsible for the choices you make but you." John had made his final remarks for now.

Kimberly stood up from her seat with hands on her hips and her mouth wide open. She was speechless and sat back down.

John moved away from the podium, but Krystina tugged at his jacket sleeve preventing him from walking away.

Krystina smiled tenderly. "Thank you, Kimberly. If you want to discuss the matter further, please come and see me after the assembly. At this time, I would like to introduce our newest faculty member. Please welcome to Gilford High School. Pastor John Wheaton." Krystina continued. "Pastor John will be teaching a new elective course this semester entitled: God and Faith." She motioned John to the microphone and announced, "Pastor John."

John roamed the sea of confused faces settling on the familiar and encouraging face smiling back at him. He returned her tender smile with one of his own, feeling the peace of the Lord sweep over him, reminding him. *I am not alone.*

Joshua sat in the back of the auditorium like always. His attention went to center stage when Pastor John stepped up to the microphone to answer Kimberly's question. Joshua followed the pastor's eyes when he was finished speaking. They rested on the girl he saw walking into the school a few days earlier with Sharise. "Father and daughter, got it." He whispered.

"As Ms. Davis stated, my name is Pastor John Wheaton. My daughter Sarah and I traveled here from the town of Homestead, Nebraska. I was offered a position to teach an elective class this semester entitled God and Faith." Wisecracks and jeers sprung up from the auditorium. John continued without missing a beat. "We don't have the ocean at our back, but we do have the Missouri and the Platte Rivers running through our state. In fact, we have quite a few rivers and lakes. Although according to my daughter, nothing can compare to the great Atlantic Ocean." The students soon realized John was not about to stop talking even with the chatter echoing off the walls. The unruly voices in the auditorium gave up and began listening.

"While Gilford produces fisherman, Homestead produces farmers. I'm sure geographically and economically we have many more differences but even through these differences we hold one common bond between us. We have a generation of confused children growing up in a perplexed world without identity or purpose. A generation of youths that can't say for sure if there is a God."

The auditorium started buzzing again, letting John know he hit a nerve.

"Is this class supposed to force us to believe there is a God? Because I'd take the class just to show you there isn't." A young man with light brown skin and dark, dancing eyes, jumped up from his seat in the third row. The auditorium erupted with loud applause and offensive remarks. Smiling at the young man, John replied in a loud voice to be heard over the lingering banter.

"What's your name young man?"

"Titus Poor," came the proud reply, feeling the crowd behind him.

"Titus, I take challenges very seriously and if you stand behind your words and mean what you say you've just become the first student to sign up for my class. I look forward to our time together. And to be clear Titus. You or any student thinking about taking this class will find out that I won't be convincing anyone there's a God. That's a mountain too high for me to climb. I'll leave that undertaking to God Himself."

Titus adjusted his round-rimmed glasses not sure what just happened. He acknowledged John's proposal with a slight nod and sat down after getting hi-fives and pats on his back.

Not to be outdone by the nerd in the front. Kimberly flew out of her seat as fast as her swollen body would allow. "I suppose that's why there's no more daycare, because the school wants to get all holy on us now. Isn't that against the law to jam God down our throat?"

"Yeah. Separation of church and state." Someone shouted.

Sarah and Sharise looked at each with dread; each said a silent pray for the man standing alone in the middle of the stage.

Even with shouts and wise cracks directed at him, John felt the need to be different. He had to show the students he was not the norm. The fight for the deliverance of Gilford High School had begun.

"This is an elective class. To participate Kimberly, you need to elect it of your own free will. Choices. Like taking Religious Diversity or English Poetry, which are electives. I'm not here to change anyone's mind or heart. I'm excited to hear what you have to say. Those of you who choose to take my class will in turn be open to hear what God has to say to you. I'll leave you all with this scripture verse from the book of Jeremiah; *"For I know the plans I have for you, says the Lord. They are plans for good and not for disaster, to give you a future and a hope."* Jeremiah 29:11 Thank you and have a good rest of your day." John gave the students a sincere double-dimpled smile and disappeared behind the curtain leaving an auditorium full of silent students.

Leaving them speechless is a good start. John smiled.

CHAPTER 10
SCHOOL DAYS

Krystina thanked John and moved on to the day which proceeded without a single outburst from anyone. Joshua stood up searching through a never-ending sea of students. He scanned the faces trying to find the blond girl named Sarah. He had to meet her, even if it meant taking her father's class.

The wave of students pouring in and out of the main office looking to change their schedules hit Krystina when she entered. Three of the four administrative assistants worked frantically behind the counter. Krystina made a beeline toward her own office, tucked in the back corner. She spotted her executive assistant Susan Pinkham scurrying back to the counter waving a piece of paper in her hand.

"I found it. No need to panic" she shouted over the pandemonium.

Krystina watched the four courageous Admins working away. "Oh boy." She turned around, rolled up her sleeves, and dove right in.

Senior Shelby Richardson stood in line. Her torn jeans and oversized green t-shirt unintentionally accented her short curly copper hair.

"Argh!" She had an intense disdain for those around her.

Shelby realized long ago she'd never fit in with any one crowd. She was just fine as a loner, but she was facing a dilemma.

At the counter she spoke with the principal. She needed one elective for her last class on Tuesday and Thursdays and the classes left had much to be desired.

"We have the new elective class, God and Faith. It has openings." Krystina suggested.

"I bet it does," Shelby moaned. "Sure, that's fine. How hard can it be?" She was just thankful to get away from the crazies.

Outside the main office Joshua spotted Sharise with the pastor's daughter. He walked right up to them.

"Hey, Sharise. How's it going?"

'Hi Joshua. Good. I forget how insane the first day of school can be. Ugh!"

"Tell me about it." He looked at Sarah.

"Oh, I'm sorry, you haven't met. Joshua Gallo this is Sarah Wheaton."

'Hi Sarah. Aren't you the pastor's daughter?"

"I am." Sarah smiled. Joshua was the boy she'd noticed coming out of the gym last week.

Joshua was spellbound by the pretty blond. He couldn't put his finger on why he was so drawn to her. Sure, she was pretty. But when she smiled, her face lit up like the sun shining on a bright summer day.

"Are you taking your father's class?"

"Definitely! Sharise and I are in his morning class. He needs all the support he can get." She smiled showing the two biggest dimples Joshua had ever seen. "The students were pretty hard on him this morning."

"I think your father did a great job this morning. He definitely held his own."

Sarah and Sharise shook their heads in agreement.

"Not bad for a rookie I guess." Sarah quipped.

"Ahhh... I was thinking of taking the morning class," Joshua announced. "I have a study hall then, but I could use the extra credits."

"Good luck. You're going to need it in there." Sharise pointed toward the office.

"I better get in there then," Joshua left the girls and headed into the office.

"Look Joshua, I understand you want to take this class, but you'll have to change your whole schedule around to fit it in. There are other electives you can choose that go perfectly with your schedule," Amy Curtis pleaded.

"I understand. Although I would hate to miss the opportunity to learn from someone the School Board thought was so good that they asked him to move all the way from Nebraska to teach at Gilford High."

"Okay. Okay. Far be it from me to hold a student back from greatness."

"Thank you."

Amy started the process, turning his schedule upside down.

"That's the only class available?" She couldn't believe the irony.

"Lily, it'll be fine." A calming voice from behind said. "I'll take the class with you. I can switch out my study hall."

"Stop treating me like a baby, Paul. I'll decide if I want to take the class. It's not like it's going to kill me." She turned back to the woman standing in front of her. "I'll take the class."

"Great, let me put this in the system and printout your new schedule. I'll be right back." Lois Grant smiled.

As soon as Lois handed Lily her schedule, she grabbed it out of her hand without so much as a thank you. Paul stared at her back as she walked away.

"Can I help you?"

Paul snapped his head around collecting himself. "Yeah. I want to change my last period study hall to the God and Faith class, please."

"Wow, two easy changes in a row. Maybe things are looking up." Lois chuckled. She handed Paul his new schedule.

Joshua was at his locker on the second floor when his best friend Steve Marchetti walked toward him.

"Hey man, what's up? What class do you have?"

"That depends what schedule are we using? Monday the first three classes or Monday the last three classes?"

"Steve, do you ever listen to what's going on?"

"Hey, they throw a lot of information at us. How am I supposed to remember everything?" Joshua patted Steve on the back and laughed. Steve's only interest was in a playbook. How he'd made it this far was a question for the ages.

"Fair enough, what class do you have Tuesdays and Thursday mornings at 10:05?" Joshua asked.

"I don't know. I haven't even looked." Steve pulled out a crumbled piece of paper from his pocket. Joshua grabbed the paper out of his hand.

"Let me see?"

"Hey dude, what are you doing?"

"Look. You have study hall. You should take that God and Faith class with me."

Steve laughed. "Are you nuts? Why would I want to do that instead of having a free period?"

"Because you would get two easy credits for doing nothing. Then you could get that free period next year when we're seniors."

Joshua could see the wheels turning in Steve's head knowing he wanted to coast through his senior year.

"You think it's an easy class?"

"Come on, how hard can it be? We went to Sunday school. We already know the answers. Look, I'll even go to the office with you to get it changed."

Without skipping a beat, Joshua put his arm around Steve's shoulders and led him toward the school office.

"This is ridiculous. Because of your error, I have to take a class I don't want."

"I'm sorry Brittany, but if you want to switch your writing class this is the only alternative I can give you."

"But I chose English Classics for my writing class not Poetry with a European Flare. You people screwed up, you need to fix it."

Not one to back down especially from an insolent student like Brittany Gallo, Krystina very calmly explained. "At this point it doesn't matter whose fault it is. What's done is done. If you want to take English Classics and you want elective credits this semester, God and Faith is the only class available."

"Fine, but my parents are definitely going to hear about this."

After handing Brittany the changed schedule, Krystina couldn't resist. "Who knows maybe you'll actually like the class."

71

"Right." Brittany snatched the piece of paper and turned almost knocking over her brother and boyfriend.

"Wow! What's the matter with you?" Joshua asked.

"Nothing," She shouted and stomped off into the crowded corridor.

After waiting for an eternity, Erica Gray finally made it to the counter. "I have study hall last period on Tuesday and Thursdays. I was really looking to fill that time with an elective course for extra credit?"

"Okay, let me see what's still available. Hmm. It looks like the only class left is God and Faith."

"That's it?"

"Sorry, that's it."

"Fine. I want the credits. God and Faith it is."

Daring to peek up at the clock Krystina couldn't believe her eyes. It was 3:05. The last student had just left. The office was empty save for Susan, Elaine, Lois and Amy. Krystina looked at their exhausted faces and disheveled appearances and started laughing. The women looked at Krystina with questioning expressions. One by one they joined in, laughing so hard that tears were rolled down their faces.

Karl emerged from his office and stood at the doorway with his keys in hand, ready to leave for the day.

"What on earth is so funny?" He asked, looking from one woman to another.

No one offered up a logical explanation, which further ignited their laughter.

"Well, Hmph!" He stomped out leaving behind five uncontrollable women.

After much laughter and banter, the women combined their efforts to putting the office back together.

After the last bit of filing was completed, Krystina addressed the women. "I can't thank you all enough. Each one of you went above and beyond the call of duty today. I think the worst is finally behind us."

"It's hard to complain when your boss is not too proud to do what it takes to get the job done. We make a great team," Susan declared as the others spoke up in agreement.

"Indeed, we do." Ushering the ladies out, Krystina turned off the lights.

CHAPTER 11
GOD AND FAITH

Sharise and Sarah rushed up the stairs hoping to arrive a few minutes early for John's first class.

"Good morning, Pastor Wheaton," Sharise announced a bit winded from her climb. Picking a front row seat to drop her backpack beside, she read aloud the sentence on the white board, "Love is Patient."

Absorbed in his bible, John jumped when he heard Sharise's voice. "Oh, wow! Is it time for class already? I didn't even hear you girls come in."

"Careful Dad, kids can smell a rookie a mile away." Sarah sat down in the seat next to Sharise, giggling.

"Funny," John smirked as other students began streaming into the classroom.

"Where do you think you're going, man. I'm not sitting up front. You picked the class. I'll pick the seats," Steve whispered, jerking Joshua by his shirt sleeve. "Back here, dude."

"Fine." Joshua, who had tried to move forward, accepted defeat.

"What's that smile plastered across your face for?" Steve asked.

"Nothing," Joshua replied, "You were right, Bro. It's much better sitting in back." He had a great view of Sarah.

Steve shook his head.

After everyone settled into their seats John looked at the class. While it wasn't full there were more students than he had anticipated. He stood up and walked around to the front of his desk, sitting down on the corner. He hoped he looked more confident than he felt.

"Good morning. I hope everyone is having a much better second day of school than the first?"

Moans and groans were his replies.

"My name is Pastor John Wheaton, you can call me Pastor John. I'll be teaching this semester's class, God and Faith. Now that you know who I am, why don't we go around the room and you can tell me who you are."

Taking note of a few rolled eyes and deep sighs. John could see the students regarded the endeavor a tortuous but unavoidable plight. The students who decided not to talk above a whisper were immediately asked to repeat their names The remaining students caught on fast and spoke clearly.

"I'm sure I'll make a few mistakes here and there, but I look forward to getting to know each one of you. I'll be doing a lot of listening, so class participation will count for a large percentage of your grade." John waved his hand in the air thwarting off all the groans that followed. "Trust me, you're going to love it." He flashed his winning smile.

Steve's eyes opened wide as he shot Joshua a look of panic. Joshua shrugged his shoulders and sent his friend a lopsided grin. He'd have to come up with something good to make Steve stay in the class.

"This semester we're going to take a glimpse into God's world. When I say a glimpse that's exactly what I mean. It would take us an eternity to try and understand every facet of God. He is grace, wisdom, peace, salvation. The list goes on and on so this semester we're going to focus on the greatest of these. God's love."

A hand shot up from the front of the room.

"Mr. Poor?"

"I told you before I don't believe there is a God, so how will I be graded?" Titus adjusted his glasses more out of habit than necessity.

"I understand a few of you may not believe in God. I get that. However, we are here to learn about God and Faith. If you don't believe in God then you can think of him as a fictional character and the Bible a fictional book."

"Okay," Titus acquiesced, "I guess I can do that."

"Good. That goes for anyone else in the class, I can't force any one of you. Not any one of you." He repeated the latter with emphasis. "To believe in God any more than I can teach you to fly. *We know, dear brothers and sisters, that God loves you and has CHOSEN you to be his own people.*" 1 Thessalonian 1:4

Sarah and Sharise nodded. Looking around the class, John felt the issue settled.

"Okay, then let's move on." John walked over to his desk and reached for the sheets of paper sitting in a small stack. He passed out a small amount to the students sitting in the first seat so they could pass them back to the others.

"I would like each of you to write your name and date on one side of the paper, please. Now, I don't want you to think, I want you to jot down on the opposite side of your paper the first word that comes into your mind that describes how you are feeling at this very moment."

Some students were quick to write, some mystified, and some not sure.

"This isn't a test and there's no judgment about what you write," John reassured them. "Write down what word best describes how you feel - whatever pops into your head." When they finished John asked the students to fold their papers up, allowing only their name to show. He walked around the room collecting their papers and dropping them into the jar that was marked with the day's date. Completing his task John closed the lid and placed it back on his desk.

"Okay, let's begin. We can look at love in two ways: how the world defines love and God's love." Opening the book, he held in his hands John read. "The dictionary defines love as a noun. A profoundly tender, passionate affection for one another such as a parent, child or a friend, sexual passion, or desire. The dictionary also defines love as a verb, an action, such as to love music or to need or require.

76

Like plants love sunlight. To embrace and kiss or have sexual intercourse with. "To love up." John stopped and shook his head. "I'm not even sure what that means." His face scrunched up in a ball of confusion incurring much laughter from his students.

"Moving on," John chuckled. "To hug and cuddle. That concludes the dictionary's meaning of love. Does anyone disagree?" John observed his students.

"No."

"Nope." Many smiles. Some faces sported different shades of red, while others shook their heads.

"Okay, let's look at what the Bible has to say about love." John put down the dictionary and picked up his well-worn leather Bible and opened it.

Bible and opened it. "God is love! But there are two types of love expressed in the Bible. One is called Philia. A conditional love, a brotherly kind of love and an emotionally led kind of love. I think we could all describe that as human love. Are we good so far?" Not sure where John was taking them, the students were a little more hesitant to voice their agreement.

"The second type of love described in the Bible is called Agape. Agape love gives and sacrifices. It is unconditional expecting nothing back in return but it can only be achieved with a relationship with God through Jesus Christ." John waved his Bible in the air. "So says the Bible. Our journey begins with learning the difference between worldly secular love and Agape: God's love." John had a remarkable way of breathing life into the words he spoke, and this morning was no different. He held a captive audience.

"The apostle Paul," Not one to take anything for granted, John asked. "Does everyone know who the apostles were?" Satisfied with the agreeable nods he received from his students John proceeded. "Good. Paul wrote of love in a letter to the Corinthians of Greece. In one of the greatest passages in the Bible. He wrote. *If I could speak all the languages of earth and of angels but didn't love others,*

I would only be a noisy gong or a clanging cymbal. If I had the gift of prophecy, and if I understood all of God's secret plans and possessed all knowledge, and if I had such faith that I could move mountains, but didn't love others, I would be nothing."

"If I gave everything I have to the poor and even sacrificed my body, I could boast about it; but if I didn't love others, I would have gained nothing."

"Love… is patient and kind. Love is not jealous or boastful or proud or rude. It does not demand its own way. It is not irritable, and it keeps no record of being wronged. It does not rejoice about injustice but rejoices whenever the truth wins out. Love never gives up, never loses faith, is always hopeful, and endures through every circumstance."

"Prophecy and speaking in unknown languages and special knowledge will become useless. But love will last forever! Now our knowledge is partial and incomplete, and even the gift of prophecy reveals only part of the whole picture! But when the time of perfection comes, these partial things will become useless" John paused a moment before he continued.

*"When I was a child, I spoke and thought and reasoned as a child. But when I grew up, I put away childish things. Now we see things imperfectly, like puzzling reflections in a mirror, but then we will see everything with perfect clarity. All that I know now is partial and incomplete, but then I will know everything completely, just as God now knows **me** completely.*

Three things will last forever—faith, hope, and love—and the greatest of these is love." I Corinthians 13:1-13

Mesmerized by John's poetic and artistic delivery, his students jumped when he voiced his question. "What kind of love is Paul talking about? Secular love or Agape love?"

"Agape," came the few voices brazen enough to answer the question.

"Exactly. Agape love. Now does anyone know the story of Saul's conversion on the road to Damascus?" Avoiding Sarah's and Sharise's raised hands, John looked for someone else to answer his question. John's eyes popped when another hand shot up. "Great, ah," Trying to recall her name.

"Jenny," said the girl sitting in the fourth row with bright pink hair and colorful tattoos trailing up the length of her left arm.

"Thank you, Jenny. The floor is all yours."

"It's a bit fuzzy. I kind of remember it from Sunday School way back when I was forced to go." Giggles escaped from the students who could relate. "This guy Saul was going around arresting and putting the people that followed Jesus Christ in prison. He was a Jew. Right?"

"Yes. He was Jewish," John answered.

"Anyway, this Saul is on his way to get more Jews to bring back to prison and he meets Jesus on the road and Jesus has already been crucified. So, Saul and all the men with him freak out and Jesus makes him blind. Oh, and then his name is changed to Paul."

"Great job, Jenny. Do you mind if I expand on your story a little bit?"

"By all means, Pastor John. The floor is all yours."

John shot Jenny a grin. "Touché."

"The story of Saul's conversion is extremely important. It gives us a better understanding and appreciation of the man. It also helps us experience the transition of who he became."

"Saul was a Jew. He was also a Roman citizen and a Pharisee. A Pharisee can also be called a rabbi or teacher. He was a highly regarded scholar of the Jewish law. Saul the Pharisee had enormous influence and power among the Jewish people and their leaders living in Jerusalem. When Jesus was resurrected on the third day, he appeared to the remaining eleven apostles and lots of other people many times before he ascended into heaven."

"I thought there were twelve apostles that hung around with Jesus," Steve questioned John.

"You're right. However, Judas, the twelfth apostle had killed himself by the time Jesus was resurrected. He couldn't live with the guilt of betraying Jesus."

"Oh yeah. I forgot that," Steve recalled.

Thrilled he had their attention, John continued. "In order for you to realize the enormity of what happened to Saul on the road to Damascus, you must put yourselves in the place of the apostles and recognize the transformation they went through. Remember, Jesus had just been crucified. The apostles were running for their lives, afraid they would also be captured and crucified."

"They must have been terrified," Jenny whispered.

"Exactly. They knew and experienced a wise, loving, peaceful teacher. A man who walked among the poor and the sinners, healing the sick, the lame and the blind, performing miracle after miracle. They believed him to be the one true Messiah who was going to save them from the Romans. The apostles never imagined Jesus would be taken from them and of all things, be crucified. The most painful and disgraceful form of execution."

John stood tall with his arms outstretched to let the word crucified sink in. "So, they ran. And they hid. If this could happen to Jesus, it could happen to them as well.

"Can you imagine the impact Jesus had on the apostles when he appeared to them so many times after his crucifixion? Then on the fortieth day after his resurrection, before Jesus ascended into heaven, the apostles asked him if this was the time Jesus would restore the kingdom to Israel. The Jews were subjected to Roman authority then. Jesus replied to them, *"The Father alone has the authority to set those dates and times, and they are not for you to know. But you will receive power when the Holy Spirit comes upon you. And you will be my witnesses, telling people about me everywhere—in Jerusalem, throughout Judea, in Samaria, and to the ends of the earth."* Acts 1:7-8

"Then Jesus was taken up to heaven and away from the apostles once again." John waited before moving on to give his students a chance to understand the impact of Jesus leaving the apostles.

"Do you think they felt much like preaching the good news, the words of Jesus Christ throughout Jerusalem after their Savior left them for a second time?"

This time many hands went up. John nodded at Joshua.

"No way," Joshua answered. "Rome was still in power, nothing had changed. I think they thought Jesus would stay with them. Get rid of the Romans. They must have been so happy to see him alive. Then he leaves again. I'd be confused. I'm sure they didn't know what to do."

"That's right, Joshua. They still didn't understand that Jesus' sacrifice was a spiritual sacrifice.

The Apostles were looking for a revolution, a way to conquer the Romans. That's precisely why Jesus told them he would send the Holy Spirit who would fill them with knowledge. Jesus knew they would not be strong enough to go out into the world and spread the good news on their own. Jesus told his disciples, *"But when the Father sends the Advocate as my representative—that is, the Holy Spirit—he will teach you everything and will remind you of everything I have told you."* John 14:26 Any questions so far?"

Titus raised his hand.

"Titus, you have a question?"

"Yeah, what exactly is the Holy Spirit? I mean I hear the words, but I have no idea what they mean."

"Great question."

"The Holy Spirit is a person, an equal to God and Jesus. He is the third member of the Godhead: the Father, the Son, and the Holy Spirit."

"Ah, dude. I mean Pastor John," Steve added sheepishly. "Like when you make the sign of the cross." Which he proceeded to demonstrate to the entire class.

"That's right. Thank you, Steve. When you become a believer in the Lord Jesus Christ, God sends himself in the form of the Holy Spirit to dwell in your heart, soul and mind. The Holy Spirit joins us on our journey. He helps us learn the fruits of the Holy Spirit so we can produce God's character in our lives. The fruits of the Spirit are: love, joy, peace, patience, kindness, goodness, faithfulness, gentleness and self-control.

Is everyone good, should I go on?"

"Yes!" "Yeah!"

John reached for his Bible and flipped through the crinkled pages until he rested on the Book of Acts.

"So, the apostles are sitting together in the upper room where Jesus had appeared to them after the resurrection and the Bible says, '*Suddenly, there was a sound from heaven like the roaring of a mighty windstorm, and it filled the house where they were sitting. Then, what looked like flames or tongues of fire appeared and settled on each of them. And everyone present was filled with the Holy Spirit and began speaking in other languages, as the Holy Spirit gave them this ability.*'" Acts 2:2-4

"Tongues of fire? What does that even mean?" Titus spouted.

"The Holy Spirit descended upon the disciples," John answered.

"Come on! Speaking in other languages?" Titus asked, shaking his head.

"I get it, Titus. If you're this worked up, can you imagine how freaked out the apostles felt?"

Titus shrugged his shoulders. He wasn't having any of what John was saying.

"The apostles had no reason to lie about something this extraordinary. Explain to me Titus, how could eleven frightened and

82

confused men leave that upper room after receiving the Holy Spirit? No matter how we envision it happened, they received a passion and urgency to share the good news of Jesus. They were no longer confused or afraid. They had determination and an eagerness, to share their newfound love, knowledge and understanding."

"I don't know. Maybe they thought they would become famous or something, like Jesus," Titus volunteered.

"Famous?" Sharise quipped. "Yeah, famous enough to get killed."

Sarah reached over and touched Sharise's arm in an effort to calm her down.

"Famous? Sorry, Pastor John. Foolish is more like it!"

"It's okay, Sharise. We have to give Titus and any other student in class the right to voice their opinions. No matter how much we agree or disagree. That's how we're going to learn from each other."

Sharise gave John a nod of understanding, but John got the impression she didn't like it.

John nodded back and continued.

"Remember Titus, Jesus was a threat to the Pharisees. The Romans had him crucified. Then they had the eleven apostles out preaching that Jesus is Lord and that he rose from the dead. Think about it. That was blaspheme, punishable by death. I don't think the Pharisees, or the Romans, took too kindly to that type of rhetoric. Especially after they believed they had put an end to it with Jesus' death."

"I don't know. This is hard to believe. Rising from the dead, fire coming down from Heaven and people talking in all different languages?" Titus sighed.

"Do you mean you are starting to believe a little, Titus? I mean if this is a fictional story why not take it at face value?"

"What? Um, no." Recovering a little, he added, "I thought I would play devil's advocate. You know, for class participation and all."

"I see. Well, don't fret. As a matter of fact, one of the apostles, Thomas, had his doubts, too."

"He did?" Titus asked.

"Indeed, he did," John replied. "Thomas was not with the other apostles when Jesus first appeared to them. Thomas told them he couldn't believe Jesus rose from the dead until he saw Jesus for himself with his own eyes and put his finger in the place of the nails and his hand into the side where Jesus had been pierced with the sword. When Jesus did appear to Thomas, Jesus told him, "*You believe because you have seen me. Blessed are those who believe without seeing me.*" John 20:29

John sensed a battle brewing inside Titus's head. "For the sake of time, I'm going to continue with the story of Saul's conversion. But I want you to know I am always available to answer and discuss any questions or thoughts any of you may have. Is everyone okay with me moving on?"

"Yeah."

"Sure."

"Well, yeah. I'm dying to find out how the story ends," Steve added with excitement.

Laughter erupted in the room. As soon as it got quiet, John continued.

"After receiving the Holy Spirit. The apostles went out and began preaching the word of God. They appointed Stephen as the first Deacon of the new church. Stephen was the first to be martyred." John noticed the confusion on some of the student's faces and quickly added. "To die."

"Oh," someone said out loud.

"Saul was witness to Stephen's stoning."

"Stoning? They stoned the dude just for talking?"

"Yes, Steve, they did. That was Jewish law. Stephen was a blasphemer, a liar in their eyes, punishable by death. Unfortunately, stoning was a very popular method at that time. From that point on, Saul made it his mission to get every one of the apostles and have them all receive the same end as Stephen."

Joshua's hand went up.

"Joshua?"

"Yeah, why did Saul want to go after the apostles? Why did he feel like it was his mission? I mean who were they hurting?"

"Saul saw the apostles as a threat to the Jewish way of life. To his way of life. For all of Saul's faults, he was genuinely passionate about the Jewish law, their commandments, and traditions. Remember, he was a scholar, and felt it his duty to persecute and deliver these rebels to justice. Saul truly believed he was doing this for the good of his people and his God. So, we have a vengeful and determined Saul on a mission to arrest the apostles and put an end to every last one of them. When on the road to Damascus the Bible says, *as he was approaching Damascus on this mission, a light from heaven suddenly shone down around him. He fell to the ground and heard a voice saying to him, "Saul! Saul! Why are you persecuting me?"*

"Who are you, Lord?" Saul asked. And the voice replied, "I am Jesus, the one you are persecuting. Now get up and go into the city, and you will be told what you must do. Acts 9:3-6

"Now the men with Saul stood speechless. They saw the blinding light, but they didn't see anyone. When Saul got up, he opened his eyes, but he couldn't see anything."

"Wow," was all Steve said.

"Saul's companions led him to the city where he stayed for three days. Blind, not eating, or drinking anything."

Looking at the clock John decided what to give his class for their very first assignment, "Jesus sends a Christian man by the name of

85

Ananias to Paul. You can read everything that happens from that point on in the Book of Acts, Chapter 9, for your first assignment."

To John's amazement, his students were genuinely disappointed he didn't finish the story. Pointing to the stack of Bibles covering the back table by the door. John informed his students. "Anyone who doesn't have a Bible at home, please pick one up from the back table."

The bell rang. It was time to move on to the next class. "We'll finish up Saul's conversion in our next class. Have a great rest of your day."

"Hey man, that wasn't bad. It was kind of cool. Pastor John's okay!" Steve gave Joshua a punch in the arm when they picked up their Bibles.

Stunned, Joshua recovered quickly. "I know." And they walked out of class together.

Out in the corridor, Steve ran into some of the guys from the team. He motioned for Joshua to come along. Then Sarah came out of the classroom. Not wanting to miss an opportunity to talk with her again, Joshua told Steve to go ahead.

"Where to next?" Joshua asked Sarah.

"Umm…" She unfolded the paper in her hand. "English, with Mrs. Perry. You?"

"Algebra, Mr. Stanford. I'd be happy to walk you downstairs. I mean, I'm going that way. Unless you're waiting for Sharise?"

"No," Sarah giggled. "Titus cornered her in class. The last thing I heard was Sharise blasting him out for being so close-minded. I thought I should go on my way."

"Smart. Poor Titus, he has no idea what he's gotten himself into."

Sarah smiled up into his golden-brown eyes. "Don't I know it." The two walked through the crowded hallway together.

"How do you like it on the east coast?"

"It's different, yet the same. It's hard to explain. The land, the buildings they're different, but people are people no matter where you go. Does that make sense?"

"Yeah, it does." Exchanging smiles, they walked on through the noisy hall. Joshua felt a bit bummed out as they approached Mrs. Perry's classroom.

"I really enjoyed your dad's class this morning. It wasn't what I thought it would be. He's cool."

"Thanks, I think he's pretty cool too. But, he is my dad."

Sharise and Titus came toward them in a whirlwind of commotion.

"You can't admit that I'm right?"

"Are you kidding me?"

"Do I look like I'm kidding you?"

"Impossible. You are impossible!" With that Titus turned and marched off in the opposite direction.

"What was all that about?" Sarah asked.

"Nothing. He thinks he's so smart. He won't even entertain the idea that we were created by God. He'd rather believe we came from a bang. I'm sorry a big bang!" Sharise pulled on Sarah's sleeve. "Let's go, we're going to be late for class. Oh. Hi Joshua. I didn't even see you."

Both Sarah and Joshua looked at each other, dumbfounded.

"I'll catch up with you later." Joshua smiled.

Smiling back, Sarah said her goodbyes.

"Joshua Gallo?" Sharise asked not expecting an answer. "Interesting."

Sarah sat in the seat next to Sharise.

"Oh, please he was only being nice to the new girl in school." She waved her hand.

"Uh, huh."

"Really Sharise?"

Sharise replied with a shrug of her shoulders and a twinkle in her eye.

"Good morning class, let's begin, shall we? My name is Mrs. Perry," said the plump woman sporting a blond bun resting atop her head. Her round black-framed glasses adorned her face. She wrote her name in large letters on the chalk board. Then turning back to the class, she declared in a zealous tone, "I am your English teacher for the school year and this, boys and girls," both of her arms spread out in dramatic fashion to encompass the entire classroom, "is my stage."

"We begin this semester by reading one of the great American classics, *Little Women*, which is written by our very own Concord native, Louisa May Alcott." This disclosure was accompanied with a slight bow of her head and a moment of reflection for the author.

Sharise and Sarah sat with eyes wide open. They were filled with trepidation.

Mrs. Perry paraded back to her desk and resumed her seat, with a gleeful, giddy smile. She folded her hands together and announced to a class full of apprehensive students, "Shall we begin?"

CHAPTER 12
CONFRONTATIONS

Brittany couldn't understand why Steve had elected a religious class as one of his electives. Even more surprising was that he liked it. But what puzzled her most was that it was Joshua's idea to take the class.

Hmm, what was that all about?

Walking into her last period class, God and Faith, Brittany asked herself, *Joshua Gallo, what game are you playing?*

Shelby took a seat in the back row not wanting to be disturbed. She browsed through her army-green backpack for her math book, pencil and notebook. She hoped to get a head start on the night's homework.

Lily glanced around the room at the various quotes displayed on the walls. Noticing the words, "Love is Patient" written in large letters on the chalkboard she groaned. Perfect, just perfect. In a different place and time, I might have enjoyed this class. But, she noted, that was another life.

Erica rushed into the classroom as the bell rang. Flushed from racing up three flights of stairs, she quickly scanned the room in hopes of finding a vacant seat, preferably in the back. As luck would have it, she was forced to take a seat up front.

John introduced himself to his newest class of students and gave the same instructions to these students. Each student filled out a piece of paper which John dropped into another marked jar.

Then he dove right in. "Love is Patient. Can anyone tell me what these three simple words mean to you?" John scanned the room.

Nothing not a word. No one made eye contact and most sat looking at their hands or doodling on some book or paper in front of them. This class was going to be harder than the morning class. Without Sarah or Sharise to bail him out, he'd have to wing it.

"You," John said pointing to a student in the second row. "I'm sorry what's your name again?"

"Paul," came the unwilling reply.

"Paul, a good name. Do you know you share the same name with one of the greatest apostles?"

Paul shrugged his shoulders.

"That should help me remember your name." John smiled looking for a response. Nothing. After an awkward silence John was more determined to get something going with this class and this particular student.

"Okay Paul, let's try again. What does the verse from the apostle Paul's passage in first Corinthians, Love is Patient, mean to you?

"I don't know. I thought I did, but now," he stammered, "I don't know. You tell me, you're the teacher."

John heard the anguish in Paul's voice and saw the torment in him. He let Paul's rudeness pass.

"Fair enough," John conceded. "I believe patience, in the context of Paul's passage regarding love, is being willing to wait. To endure without complaint. Can anyone else add to that?"

"Understanding," Lily disclosed with her attention more on her doodling than her surroundings. Paul's head turned in Lily's direction. He looked like he'd gotten punched in the gut. John witnessed the interaction. So, he'd found the source of Paul's pain.

"Very good, anyone else?"

"Self-control," said a small voice in the front.

A reply laced with contempt sailed from the back to the front of the room. "Too bad you didn't use some of your own advice."

Laughter erupted within the classroom. Erica felt the blood drain from her face. *Why did I open my mouth?* She reached for her things making sure not to make eye contact with anyone. The mocking shrills of Brittany's laughter followed her out the door.

"I have no idea what that was all about, but before I get back into this room everyone had better have an answer to my question. Beginning with you, young lady," John said sternly, singling Brittany out. He exited the classroom as uneasiness spread across Brittany's face.

Erica was walking away as fast as she could.

"Wait. Please wait," John called after her.

She stopped but didn't turn around. Erica waited for John to catch up to her. *I might as well get this over with.* She was still wiping the tears running down her face when John caught up with her.

"I'm sorry about what happened in there. Would you like to talk about it?"

Expecting the judgment she was accustomed to, Erica found John's compassionate and gentle face staring at her. She started to cry all over again.

"Come here," John pointed toward a windowsill wide enough for them to sit on. He waited for Erica to gather her composure and thoughts.

"You might as well know. The whole school does." She blurted out through tears and sniffles. Reaching into his pocket John pulled out a clean folded handkerchief and handed it to Erica, a necessity he always had available thanks to Abby.

"I'm sure whatever you have to tell me isn't as bad as you think."

"Yeah, well it's bad enough," Erica took a deep breath. "Haaaahh. A little over two years ago I had a baby." She said expecting to see disdain, but Erica found soft eyes and a gentle smile urging her on. "Her name is Madison. I'm not sorry I had her. Madison is the best thing that's ever happened to me." Through watery eyes and a red nose, Erica relayed her real dilemma. "It's just no matter how hard I try my reputation follows me, the jokes and nasty remarks."

John shook his head in understanding.

"Madison." As if trying the name out for the first time. John asked, "Is she named after anyone in your family?"

"No."

"How did your parents handle the news?"

With a halfhearted smile, Erica revealed. "My mother and father have been divorced for about four years now. My father works for a big accounting firm in New York and hardly has any time for me, let alone Madison. My mother has become a very angry and sour woman, Pastor John." Erica continued. "I know my dad cheated on her. My poor mother never saw it coming. She was devastated." Erica continued.

"After Madison was born, Mom felt embarrassed between Dad cheating on her and me having a baby. My mom was always head of some committee or taking part in the newest project or cause in town. After the divorce, everything changed. We stopped going to church, Mom was so mad at God and so was I. When I had Madison, it was the final straw. Mom just gave up and wouldn't show her face anywhere."

"I'm sorry she feels that way," John offered. "However, you can't beat yourself up for the way things turned out between you, your mother and father. The past is the past. It's already happened. No one can change it. Holding on to hurt only causes devastating

92

emotions to boil up from deep inside. Trials can do one of two things, Erica. They either hinder a person's growth or, with love and forgiveness, make them stronger. Each of us has a choice to make. We can choose to forgive and move forward or let the hurt and bitterness lead us to live a stagnant life. You owe it to Madison to be the best you can be. Your mother must find her own way through the darkness and back to the light. Just because a person's life path has changed course doesn't mean the happiness they once knew won't follow them down the new path. It will just be... different."

John watched the emotions flicker across Erica's face. He took the opportunity to inquire a bit more. "Does Madison's father play a role in her life?"

"Off and on. I know he loves her more than anything, but he can't seem to stay out of trouble. It's not an environment I want Madison to grow up in."

"I understand that." John silently asked God to give him the right words. "Erica, I am so sorry you've had to go through this alone. It's a tremendous burden for a girl so young. But I see you are a very brave and strong young woman. You have nothing to be ashamed of, certainly not of a beautiful little girl with a lovely name like Madison."

Erica's eyes were downcast toward the floor. John saw a small smile emerge at the mention of her daughter's name.

"More times than not, we stray from the path God has laid out for us. That doesn't mean God leaves us when we stray. He has a plan for each one of us. Look at me, Erica."

Slowly she raised her head.

"God has been with you the entire time, through your pain and anger and through your tears and loneliness. God is waiting for you to get back on the path and fulfill the plan he set for you."

"What kind of destiny can God have planned for me? After what I've done?" Erica blurted out.

"Unfortunately, God has not discussed that with me." John smiled and received a small giggle for his effort. "In truth Erica, I don't know. I'm sure Mary didn't know God's plan for her either when she became pregnant with Jesus. She was alone and unwed. And that was during a time when being unwed and pregnant was punishable by death by stoning!"

"Mary trusted God and knew he would not leave her nor forsake her. Don't sell God short, Erica. His timing is not our timing, and his ways are not our ways but he will always be there. He is consistent and his love for us is forever."

"Thank you, Pastor John you've been very kind. I appreciate your sincerity. But it still doesn't change how I am looked at in school." Erica sighed.

Never one to let an opportunity to share God's love pass. John asked Erica. "I'd like you to come back to class."

"Oh, I don't think so," Erica replied shaking her head no.

"I am asking you to trust me, Erica. No…I'm asking you to trust God. To slay the giant, you first have to face it."

Still hesitant, Erica replied, "I can't promise anything, but I'll try."

John jumped off the windowsill and motioned for Erica to follow. "Good. Shall we?"

The soft buzz of whispering students ended abruptly when they returned to the classroom.

Facing Brittany, John asked, "Do you have an answer for us?"

"Yeah, tolerant," Brittany announced with extreme satisfaction.

"Tolerant. Very good. Isn't it amazing? Excuse me what is your name?"

"Brittany Gallo."

"Brittany Gallo, isn't it amazing how some people insist on others showing tolerance and yet they themselves show very little tolerance in return?"

"Huh?" Brittany's mouth hung open mortified at being called out.

John surmised this was probably the first time anyone dared put Brittany Gallo in her place. Walking over to his desk John grabbed the rock sitting atop a pile of papers. A long-ago gift from a sassy second grader who thought her father needed help keeping his messy papers together.

"Erica," John said looking in her direction. He could see the panic in her eyes. He sent her a smile that said trust me, trust God.

"Erica had a child out of wedlock. She made a mistake, a sin. Out of that sin, God blessed Erica with a beautiful baby girl she named Madison. Erica did not compound her sin, she didn't terminate the pregnancy. No, Erica bore the humiliation and shame she received from others for carrying that baby girl to term. Sadly, to this day a little over three years later, Erica still feels that shame. She's reminded with never-ending looks and remarks. Erica made choices, which determined the lifestyle she lives today. But don't we all?" John tossed the rock from one hand to his other hand.

"Every day we face choices, and those choices have consequences. It's up to every one of us to choose what outcome we want. A mistake is not the end but a chance to change direction. Erica is changing direction. She's choosing to finish her education, no matter the sacrifice or difficulties. She is choosing not to live in a past mistake. *Do not judge others, and you will not be judged. Do not condemn others, or it will all come back against you. Forgive others, and you will be forgiven.*" Luke 6:37

John stretched out his arm and pointed the rock. Scanning the room of students, he said in a loud and clear voice, "Any one of you who is without sin, please take this rock from me and cast the first stone." John finished by pointing the stone at Erica.

Some students looked away or down at their hands. Others smiled at Erica, shaking their heads affirming her.

"We are all guilty of sinning at one time or another, in one way or another. But God still loves us. God's patience is beyond our comprehension. When Paul delivers that beautiful passage in 1st Corinthians he is talking about God's love, not the world's. We can't even comprehend the love God has for each of us."

John looked at the clock and walked to the back of the class where the stack of Bibles lay on the table. "I would like you all to get to know the apostle Paul since he is the author of 1st Corinthians chapter 13 which we will be studying this semester. Your homework for our next class is to read chapter 9 from the book of Acts. There are Bibles on the back table for those who do not have one at home."

"Can't we look it up online?" One of the students asked.

"You can, but while you're sitting in my class, I will require you to open the Bible during our discussions."

The bell rang. A couple of girls headed over to Erica and struck up a conversation. Smiling, he murmured the words from a film he had just seen.

"God is good all of the time. All of the time, God is good."

CHAPTER 13
PUSHING AHEAD

John was preparing his notes for his Thursday morning class. He had to admit the first day of classes were challenging. He didn't expect each class to be so different from the others. There had been troublesome moments accompanied by small victories.

A noise like the sound of a wounded animal jolted him back to the present. Springing out of his chair, he moved with lightning speed to investigate. John stood anchored in the doorway taking in the scene. *A wounded animal indeed.* Karl was slumped over from his waist with one hand clinging to the wall trying to catch his short gasps of breath.

"Oaf. Oaf Ugh!"

"Karl, are you okay? Do you want some water?"

Karl shook his head with all the dignity he could muster. "No, no. I'll be just fine. Whew." He waved his hand at John. "I should have paced myself better instead of running up three flights of stairs."

John chuckled to himself. He doubted Karl ran up three stairs let alone three flights.

"Come on in, Karl. What brings you all the way up to the third floor?"

"We are having trouble filling the after-school detention hour. As you are aware most of our teachers are completely bogged down. It has been decided since you're only teaching four classes a week, you should pitch in and oversee three of the five weekly detentions." Karl added trying to sound reasonable, "That's if you have no objections?"

John looked at Karl's sweaty face and bulging eyes. *How did he even get the brief speech out of his mouth.* "I would love to pitch in and help Karl. When would you like me to begin?"

"Today if you could. I know it's short notice, but these things happen. We must all be willing to step up at a moment's notice for the sake of our students. Don't you agree, Pastor John?"

"Of course, I can start today. What time and where"? John asked.

"Glad to hear it." Karl smirked. "Room 101 at 2:15. There will be a sign-in sheet on the desk for the students, make sure they sign it." Not wanting to get into any further conversation, Karl walked out of the classroom without so much as a goodbye or thank you. Karl's heavy footsteps - clunk, clunk, clunk - echoed his departure down the winding stairwell.

"You're welcome," John muttered under his breath, feeling a bit annoyed, not with the message but the messenger. That was until God laid Mark 2:17 on his heart. *Healthy people don't need a doctor—sick people do. I have come to call not those who think they are righteous, but those who know they are sinners.* "Thank you."

"Does anyone in the class play sports?" John began class with a question.

"Hell yeah, dude. Football," Ending with a great big smile, Steve yelled.

"Steve, right?" John asked.

"Steve Marchetti, wide receiver extraordinaire."

"Steve Marchetti, wide receiver extraordinaire. Your assignment is to practice restraint and respect when answering a question in this classroom." John finished, keeping the atmosphere light, "Dude."

"Oh! Ah, sorry Pastor John. I get so pumped when I talk football."

The students chuckled at Steve's candor.

"Alright Steve. You're in the middle of a game and your quarterback throws you a couple of passes but the cornerback covering you disrupts your route. Do you get upset or down on yourself? Or are you patient?"

Steve shrugged his shoulders in response.

"Do you wait for the chance to slip by the cornerback and fake him out?"

"Yeah, of course!" Steve declared.

"By being patient, you'll eventually catch the football whether it's for a first down or a game winning touchdown."

"Oh yeah. You have to wait it out. When the cornerback thinks he has you all figured out, then BAM! I cut to my left and my man Joshua here," he said pointing to Joshua, "throws the ball right into my hands. Nothing better than that. Nothing! Right Josh?" Reaching over, Steve high-fived Joshua. He loved reliving one of the greatest moments of his life.

Everyone in the class got caught up in Steve's play by play and excitement. Joshua, still smiling, looked out at the rest of the class. His eyes locked on the angelic face with beautiful blue eyes and big dimples smiling back at him.

"That's patience. You wait and you wait and if you have to, you wait some more. You do so because you know the prize is worth waiting for." Students shook their heads in agreement with John's words. "Sometimes we wait and wait, but nothing happens. Rather than waiting a little bit more, we choose to go our own way. Yet, even when we go our own way, God waits for us to come back. God's love never pushes, he loves us that much." He took a moment of silence. "If you knew all you had to do was be patient, willingly patient to receive the prize, would you?"

"Yeah," some answered.

"Sure," said some, while others nodded in agreement.

"Be completely humble and gentle; be patient, bearing with one another in love." Ephesians 4:2

"Is being patient a bad trait or a good trait? Anyone?"

"A good trait," replied Joshua.

"Exactly, Joshua. Love is patient and if God is love, God is patient."

"Do you know what the name Joshua means?" John side-stepped for a moment.

"No," Joshua answered shrugging his shoulders. He shared, "I never thought about it before".

"In the Bible, Joshua is depicted as a great leader, a deliverer of his people. Joshua was appointed by God because he was a strong leader and a patient man. Patience is a great character to have in a leader on and off the field."

"I'll try and remember that."

"Don't just remember it, Joshua. Live it."

The bell rang, it was the end of class. The moment over. The seeds were planted.

"I mean did you hear him talk football. Crazy, right?" John heard Steve broadcast to Joshua on their way out of class.

John found the sign-in sheet where Karl said it would be. It was now 2:25, and there was one more student left to arrive. John waved the sign-in sheet in the air. "I'd like everyone to find your name on this sheet. Put your signature in the space next to it and please pass it to the next person. Thank you." He handed the sheet to the student sitting in the first seat of the first row.

At 2:30, the last straggler came strutting into the classroom. He took a seat in the very back without so much as an excuse or an apology for being late.

Ignoring the straggler, John took the sign-in sheet back from the students and addressed the class. "My name is Pastor John Wheaton. You can call me Pastor John. I'll be with you today until 3:00. If there's anything I can help you with let me know. If you need to use the facilities, please ask so I can give you a hall pass. Just so we are clear, only one pass will be given out at a time." John strode to the back of the room with the sign-in sheet in his hand. "Is there a reason why you're 15 minutes late to detention, Mr.?" John asked the young man slouched in his seat with his long legs sprawled out for anyone to trip over.

"Tags and ah, yeah, no reason, dude," Shrugged the handsome young man with slick, black hair he had pulled back into a ponytail. He looked at John with his hazel eyes and adjusted his leather bomber jacket.

"First, it is Pastor John, not dude. Second, could you sit up so that you are not taking up the entire aisle?"

Tags showed his reluctance but sat up.

"Thank you. Now could I have your full name please?" Wanting to make sure it matched the student's name on the sheet.

"Joey Taglio… dude," Tags replied, icy with insolence, attracting the attention of the other students.

John leaned down inches from Tags' hardened face leaving no doubt about his intent. "We can play this cat and mouse game all day long…Joseph. Or you can show me the respect I deserve by addressing me as Pastor or if you prefer Pastor John. I will in turn give you the same respect and address you as Joey or if you prefer, Tags."

Observing a lack of fear in John's eyes. Tags sat up and replied.

"Joey Taglio… Pastor John," then in a lighter tone added, "but you can call me Tags."

Like air being let out of a balloon, the entire room let their breath out. John presented Tags with the sign-in sheet. "Great. Could you sign the sheet next to your name Tags?"

"I most certainly can." He signed it and returned it to Pastor John with the most striking smile.

"Thank you. I would appreciate it if everyone arrived on time to detention." John announced while walking back to the front of the room. "School is out at 1:55 that gives you twenty minutes to do what you have to do to get here by 2:15. Please make sure you do. Or, you can make up the difference on the other end."

John glanced down at the sign-in sheet and grinned. "That includes you Mr. Mickey Mouse."

CHAPTER 14
BUILDING BLOCKS

"Long day?" Krystina poked her head inside the open door of the classroom.

"To say the least, but not without its rewards. How about you?" John asked.

"Not too bad, but I chose this profession."

"I didn't say no."

"Seriously, I want to apologize for Karl's actions today. I'm sure he played the guilt card to get you to take the detention class. I'm sorry. We didn't agree on this so you don't have to continue."

"Karl didn't guilt me into anything. He connected me to more students and a chance for God to work more miracles." John looked around the room pretending to be secretive and said quietly, "But I think we should keep that between the two of us."

"You definitely have a different way of looking at things. I'll give you that."

"Are there always the same kids in detention class or does it change from day to day?"

"Sad to say it's usually the same old suspects. Why do you ask?"

"No particular reason just curious, that's all."

"I have a few things to finish up in my office. Is there anything I can do for you? Or anything you need?" Krystina asked.

"Yeah, you can show me where to drop off this sign-in sheet," John asked, waving the clipboard in the air.

"Follow me," Krystina said over her shoulder on her way out the door.

John jumped up from his seat, grabbing his briefcase and suitcoat, following Krystina out the door.

"You'll leave it with Elaine. She comes in later in the morning and stays late each day for detention coverage. If you ever need anything she'll be your go-to. I'll introduce you."

"Access in and out of the school at this time of day is only through the front doors," Elaine told John.

John walked out of the office toward the front doors. He was unaware someone was walking beside him.

"Can I talk to you a minute, Pastor John?"

The familiar voice startled John momentarily. He peered into a pair of brown eyes with flecks of gold.

"Paul, of course. How about going outside? It's too beautiful a day to stay cooped up. I, for one, have had enough of school for one day." Paul followed John's lead outside.

"This looks like a good spot," John motioned for Paul to join him on the first bench they came to. John sat patiently and waited for Paul to speak.

"I'm not sure where to begin." Paul looked down at his fidgeting fingers.

"Paul, whatever you have to say will remain between the two of us. What I said earlier in class about judging others, I meant."

"I can see you are carrying a lot of pain. If I can help in any way, I will."

The chains wrapped around Paul's heart, holding him back, were breaking. "Lily. The girl that sits beside me in class."

"Yes. Lily…?"

"Rivera."

"Lily Rivera. Sorry, first week, you'll have to cut me some slack."

Paul tilted his head slightly giving John as much of a smile as his pain allowed.

"Right. Well, Lily and I have been friends forever. I was there for her when her father suddenly passed away. She was amazing through it all. So strong you know not just for herself but for her mom. We've talked about a future together. Then without warning she stops talking. Not just to me, but to everyone! She's become a completely different person. Irritable, moody…just mad at everyone and everything. Ugh!"

John felt Paul's frustration. "Did something happen to Lily that caused such a dramatic change?"

"I don't know. Every time I try to bring it up, she gets mad, furious even. She'll walk away like I'm not even there. You saw her in class. I don't know what to do anymore. I know she's hurting but if she doesn't confide in me, I can't help her. I feel so darn useless," Paul concluded. Exhausted, he hung his head in defeat.

John's gaze fell on the football field in the distance. It gave him a moment with God. "Paul, you're talking as though you have no hope."

"Hope? Didn't you listen to anything I just said. There isn't any hope."

"Not in the manner you're thinking. You're placing all your hope in people. They'll let you down whether they mean to or not. I'm sure you feel as though God has let you down, too. Right?"

"Yeah, I do." Paul never looked up.

"I can tell you from firsthand experience it may feel like He has but believe me, He hasn't. He's been with you every step of the way, through every heartache. When we hurt, God hurts and when we cry, God cries. What I'm going to suggest will be hard for you to do, because we automatically want to hang on to the hurt. If we keep the hurt and sadness buried inside, we're giving ourselves permission to stay a victim, seeking pity from others. That's the wrong kind of attention to be searching for."

Standing up abruptly Paul stared down at John. "I don't want your pity."

"No," John replied quickly. "It's not mine you want, nor would I give it to you. It's easier to submit to the pain than fight it, but that's exactly what God wants you to do. He wants you to fight. *Trust in the Lord with all your heart; do not depend on your own understanding. Seek his will in all you do, and he will show you which path to take."* Proverbs 3:5-6

John continued, "Paul, every time you feel defeated, push it away and repeat Proverbs 3:5-6. I believe with all my heart God will help you through this valley."

"How do you know for sure, Pastor John? How do you know God will help me through this what did you call it? Valley?" Paul stood looking with questioning eyes.

"I know because I have been through the valley of the shadow of death when my wife died." John explained, "It would have been so easy to slip into hopelessness, believing life isn't fair. I can't tell you how many times I repeated Proverbs 3:5-6. Along with many other verses. On my knees in a deep pool of tears. When you have faith in God, even as small as a mustard seed, He can move mountains for you."

Sitting back down Paul admitted quietly, "You sound like my grandmother. I think I understand. I'm no good for anyone in this state, never mind myself. What have I got to lose? I'm going to trust you Pastor John and give it to God." With his decision made, Paul stood up.

"Paul?"

"Yes, Pastor John."

Standing up John reiterated, "Don't trust me, I'll let you down. Trust God."

With a slight smile and shake of his head, Paul reached out to shake John's hand. "Thank you. It's funny how talking about it makes the burden feel lighter."

"Work on giving that burden to God."

"I will," Paul said.

The two walked in silence to the parking lot having left everything that needed to be said on the school bench.

"I knew I'd have to get my feet wet, but geez. I didn't think you'd push me into the deep end right away." In his car, John conversed with God. Chuckling, John sensed God chuckling right along with him.

Indian Summer along the East Coast begins with a chilly start. Eventually, a soft gentle breeze arises triggered by the heat of the sun reflecting off the blue-green sea.

Then the tired leaves from the noble maples, oak and birch trees begin their spectacular process. Changing from tender summer greens to an annual pageant of brilliant colors. Shades of reds, browns, orange, and gold blanket the landscape in a blazing display of burning glory. Such was the day Sarah and Sharise decided to walk home from school instead of taking the bus.

"What good is having your license if you can't use it?" Sharise cried.

"Hey, be happy you have yours. I have to wait until I go home to Nebraska to get mine."

"I guess. Hey, isn't that Shelby Richardson sitting on the porch across the street?" Sharise asked with a single nod of her head toward the red-headed girl sitting on the stairs.

"She certainly has the right hair color. I didn't know she lived this close to the school. Want to go over and say hi?" Without waiting for a reply, Sarah tugged Sharise by the arm and crossed the street.

As they got close enough to the porch Sharise yelled out to Shelby. "Hey Shelby, what's up?"

Surprised to hear her name called, Shelby looked up from her monotonous chore to find Sharise Taylor and that new girl Sarah what's-her-name walking up to her. Bright smiles were painted across their faces as if they were meeting one of their best friends.

"Great," Shelby mumbled under her breath before the girls were on top of her.

"What are you guys doing here?" Shelby inquired suspiciously.

"We decided to walk home instead of taking the bus," Sarah answered.

"It's too nice out to be stuck on that human sweatbox for any amount of time," Sharise joked.

"I guess," Shelby replied.

"What are you doing?" Sharise pressed trying to keep the conversation moving.

Not bothering to look up and turning slightly red from embarrassment Shelby shared, "I'm snapping string beans for dinner."

At that moment a small boy around the age of six came flying out the front screen door of the house screaming.

"Shelby…Shelby? Lexy keeps taking the channel changer from me and won't let me watch my toons!"

Right on his heels was a younger and shorter version of Shelby with longer wavy auburn hair instead of Shelby's short, curly copper toned.

"Ian, stop being such a crybaby. I only wanted to check something; you can watch your stupid toons."

"Really?" Shelby moaned. "Both of you go back inside. Lexy, don't you have homework to do?"

"I finished. Let me help you with the beans?"

"Lexy, I need you in the house to watch the little ones while I finish up," Shelby pleaded. Like an immature child, Lexy stamped her foot and whirled around, running into the house screaming, "I'm sick and tired of watching those two."

"Welcome to my world," Shelby whispered to herself forgetting Sarah and Sharise were standing there.

"Lexy stop," came a shriek from inside.

"Oh great," was all she could manage. Tossing the beans aside, Shelby jumped up as quick as she could to address the commotion inside.

"Maybe we should go," Sharise quietly insisted.

"I don't know, maybe Shelby could use our help." Taking off her backpack, Sarah placed it on the porch. Sitting down on the stair she picked up the bag of beans.

Inside Shelby's voice could be heard shouting at the kids to turn off the TV and go to their rooms. *Bang! Bang!* came the response. Satisfied, Shelby moved on to the front porch and her beans. "Please be gone," she whispered hoping Sarah and Sharise had gone home.

Shelby stopped dead in her tracks. They were sitting on her front porch chatting away snapping her beans like it was an everyday occurrence, appearing to be having fun.

Embarrassed by what they witnessed, Shelby proposed, "You guys don't have to stay."

Sarah smiled. "If you don't mind Shelby I'd like to help. It's been a long time since I've snapped beans." With a tenderness in her eyes, Sarah reflected, "My mom and I used to sit on the backstairs of our house snapping beans just like this. We would talk about everything and nothing. It's probably one of the fondest memories I have of her. So, if it's okay with you, maybe I can add to those memories with my friends?"

Shelby didn't know what to say. What was happening? *I'm a loner! That's the way I like it.*

A stranger from Nebraska moves in, turning the tables on her. Tilting her head to one side and scrunching her forehead Shelby sat down. Together the three of them snapped beans.

A warm breeze drifted off the coast caressing Erica's face. The swing creaked with a strained rhythmic melody. "Up Mommy," Madison squealed.

"Ha, ha," Erica laughed, caught up in the magic of her daughter's delight. "All the way to the moon and beyond. Right Madison?"

Letting go of the swing's handlebar Madison clapped. Cheering. "Moon momma moon." Just as quickly, she grasped the solid bar once again with her chubby little hands.

Tags could see the playground from where he stood in the small knoll above. Watching the carefree scene play out before him, "Aah," his heart swelled with pride and much love.

Gilford was a small town. Ever since he could remember he'd been labeled the small-town hood. The troublemaker. Always being shuffled from one foster home to another.

"Why do you cause so much trouble?" At first, Tags didn't understand. He didn't mean to cause trouble, it sort of happened.

Tags was about five years old when he took the neighbor's dog out on an adventure. How did he know the police had been called to look for him? Soaked and covered in mud after galloping through a small area of marshland, Tags and the dog arrived home hours later. Exhausted. Instead of a strong warm hug of reassurance, he was greeted with a severe tongue lashing. Then he was sent to his cold, dark room without any food or a change of dry clothes. Left alone to cry himself to sleep.

"Don't worry Madison, that will never happen to you, I promise," Tags said as he looked down at the little girl.

Tags moved from home to home where the story kept repeating itself. After a while it was easier to be the bad boy they labeled him. He learned at a young age to harden his heart, until he met Erica. Sweet, innocent Erica Gray. She had an uncanny way of making him feel important and significant. If only he could become the man she believed him to be. "Ugh," He snorted walking down the knoll towards the playground.

"Daddy, Daddy," Madison shouted with glee spying her father first.

Erica whipped around, caught off guard by the ruggedly handsome man walking towards her. She stuttered. "What? What are you doing here?"

"I went by your house. Through the front window, your mom told me in her loud, insulting voice you weren't home and to go away before she called the cops."

"That sounds like Mom."

"I thought you might have taken Madison to the park. So here I am. Do you have a problem with that?"

"You know I don't. It's important for you to be a part of Madison's life."

"And what about her mother, is it important for me to be an important part of her life?" Tags whispered, moving within inches of Erica's face.

Erica backed away feeling uncomfortable with the closeness. When it came to Joey, she needed distance to think clearly. Erica remembered earlier in the day Pastor John's kind words and support.

Gathering her resolve Erica looked Joey square in the face before she spoke. "Joey, you know how I feel about you. But right now, I'm concentrating on finishing school and trying to make a better life for me and Madison." She finished with what she knew would hurt him, but it needed to be said. "To be completely honest, where

111

you are in your life, I can't count on you, and neither can Madison." Erica's whole body tensed waiting for the explosion.

"What?" Not allowing an answer. "What crap is this? Where's this coming from?" Tags demanded.

"It's coming from me."

"That's bull and you know it. Who are you talking to Erica? You might as well tell me, you know I'm gonna find out." He backed her up against the pole of the swing set. Erica heard Madison sniffling, looking around Joey to see her. She looked scared. Still in the swing, her little hands reached out. "Mommy…Mommy?"

Erica went straight to Madison. Getting her out of the swing, she held her tight. Rubbing her back she whispered, "It's okay, baby. Mommy's here."

Tags would never lay a hand on Erica and the last thing he wanted was to scare Madison. But the person feeding Erica this nonsense was another matter.

"Erica, you know I wouldn't hurt you or Madison. I get so frustrated thinking someone is talking to you, telling you to move on from me."

"I don't want to hurt you, Joey. Trust me, I'm not talking to anyone. But something did happen in my last-period class, I ran out. Before I got too far Pastor John caught up with me and we had a long talk. That's it."

"Pastor John. How sweet. Well, Pastor John is going to find out what it means to interfere in Joey Taglio's life."

"Please Joey, don't do anything to hurt Pastor John. He was only looking out for my welfare. Maybe he could help both of us."

"Are you listening to yourself Erica? A pastor? Let's go. I'll take you and Madison home," Joey ordered.

"Thanks, but Madison and I are going to walk home. It's a beautiful day and pretty soon they'll be hard to come by." Erica moved away.

"Erica, stop being so stubborn," he said.

"I'm not being stubborn, and I'm not mad. I'm tired...tired of fighting, of working so hard, and tired of dreaming. You do what you think will make you feel like a man. I'm taking our daughter home to feed her, give her a bath and put her to bed. That's my reality." After she put Madison into the stroller, Erica reflected on the conversation. "You didn't even ask what happened in class that got me so upset. Your priority was your bruised ego and pride." Erica pointed the carriage toward home and walked away.

Tags stood, feeling the effects of Erica's stinging words. Deflecting any blame, he remembered Pastor John from detention. "I think it's about time you and I had a little one-on- one!"

CHAPTER 15
DECEPTION AND HONOR

The Gallo's home overlooked one of the most captivating sections of the Atlantic coastline. The cedar-shingled siding weathered their home from the elements and added to its coastal charm. The sound of breaking waves slamming against jagged rocks made a harsh, but lyrical rhythm.

Standing at the screen door that led to the spacious deep-gray deck, Joshua studied his sister's quiet demeanor. "What are you doing sitting out here all by yourself? It's so unlike you Brittany."

"Thinking. Is that okay?"

Joshua balanced his newest creation, a roast beef, turkey and Swiss cheese sandwich in one hand and a root beer soda in the other as he pushed open the door and plopped down in a navy-blue wicker chair next to his sister. "I've never seen you so deep in thought or looking so serious." Joshua stuffed in a huge bite of sandwich.

"Well, dear brother, I have a lot of thoughts running through my head. But one, in particular."

"Oh, boy, here it comes. What trouble are you trying to cause now?" Joshua asked.

"Why would my twin brother talk his best friend and my boyfriend into taking a class about God? I mean it's not like you needed the credits. You had study hall. You're football players, you can do whatever you want yet you take God and Faith."

She turned to Joshua. "It sounded a little fishy to me, until I saw you talking with Sarah Wheaton." Joshua shrugged his shoulders, looking away.

"Really? I talk to a lot of people. I bumped into Sharise Taylor, and she introduced us. What's the big deal Britt?"

"Don't big deal me, brother. You can't even look at me. Why Joshua Gallo? Because you have a crush on her." Brittany laughed. "Oh my, gosh you do. Look at me?"

Joshua stood up and looked at Brittany to bring home his point. "Don't make this out to be a big deal, it's not. You're letting your imagination get the best of you. As usual."

"Not this time, Josh." she returned.

"What's going on out there?"

Joshua rolled his eyes when he heard his mother's voice. "Nothing!" he answered.

"Josh has a crush on the new girl at school," Brittany blurted out knowing full well her revelation would bring on a full examination into her brother's love life.

Linda stepped out onto the deck and immediately began. "Joshua, you'll have to bring this young lady to the house for dinner. Or even better we could go to the club for dinner. So tell me dear, are her parents members?"

"Yeah, Joshua, are her parent's members?" Brittney sneered.

"I'm not playing your game Brittany. You know sometimes you can be a real jerk. Tell me, is this how you treated Erica today?" Before making his exit, he gave his twin a cold stare.

Brittany's mouth dropped open.

"That's right. Everyone's talking about how horrible you were to her today and how Pastor John had to put you in your place."

"Are you serious? Nobody puts Brittany Gallo in her place. And Erica Gray is nothing but a…"

"Brittany Gallo, don't you dare," Linda shouted.

That was the last thing Joshua heard.

"Mom. You can't imagine how this pastor humiliated me in front of the entire class," Brittany cried.

"What are you talking about? Who humiliated you? Who is this pastor?"

If there was one person Brittany knew she could play, it was her mother. "The school brought in a pastor to teach an elective class called God and Faith. Because they messed up my schedule, I got stuck taking the stupid class."

"Okay. What happened in class?" Linda asked sitting down in the chair Joshua vacated.

"It was awful Mom. The pastor asked us to think of words to describe the word, "patient" and of all people Erica Gray…"

"Erica Gray?" Linda interrupted. "Why does that name sound so familiar to me?"

"You know she was one of the girls that got herself pregnant a couple of years ago."

"Oh, yes. Now I remember, go on." Linda urged with a wave of her meticulously manicured nails.

"The next thing I know Eric Gray blurts out, 'self-control'. I don't know what came over me Mom, but my thoughts came right out of my mouth. I said, 'too bad you didn't use any!' The next thing I know, Erica is running out of the classroom." Brittany whimpered as she managed to cry a couple of tears, before sniffing for good measure. "Then the pastor turned to me and yelled, "By the time I get back to this room you better have an answer ready." Like it was all my fault Erica got upset. Perhaps she should've thought about the consequences of her actions before she got pregnant. Oh, Mommy! It was terrible!" Brittany wailed. Her lower lip trembled while a couple more tears rolled down her cheeks as she reached for her mother.

Linda bought it, hook, line and sinker. "Karl Porter is going to hear from me first thing tomorrow morning." She hugged her daughter, gently patting the back of her head. "What was the school thinking, hiring a pastor to teach at a public school? Oh no. This will not do.

Brush off those tears, Mommy will take care of pastor... Pastor? What's his name?"

"Pastor John Wheaton from Nebraska. His daughter Sarah is the girl Joshua has a crush on."

"This has got to be nipped in the bud." She said as the sun sat on the edge of the ocean's horizon.

"I've got to lie down if you don't mind Mom. I have a terrible headache," Brittany embellished and smiled sweetly. "Thanks, Mom, for being so understanding. You're the best mom in the world. I don't know what we would do without you."

"Oh, Brittany." Linda replied. Standing up and hugging her daughter once more. "You go upstairs and lie down. I'll call you when supper is ready. And Brittany, let's not tell Joshua I know anything about his little crush. I think it would be best if we kept it between the two of us. Don't you?"

Checkmate! "Whatever you think is best, Mom," Brittany answered. With a smug grin on her face, she pulled open the screen door. *Joshua, when will you learn nobody messes with Brittany Gallo!*

"Hey Dad, is everything alright?" Sarah asked. Seeing the puzzled look on her father's face as he hung up the phone.

"Yeah. That was Mr. Porter. He received a call today from a parent that has some complaints about my teaching. He'd like me to meet with him and Miss Davis Monday morning to straighten whatever this is out. No big deal, Sarah. It's nothing to worry about."

Sarah stood up on her tiptoes, kissed her dad's cheek and whispered, "I love you, Dad."

"I love you, too," John replied then added to ease her mind. "*The Lord is my helper, so I will have no fear. What can mere people do to me?*" Hebrews 13:6

"Come on let's eat. I'm starving!" John declared with a gentle squeeze and a crooked smile.

The conversation never lagged at the Taylor house and tonight was no exception. The girls had invited their new friend Shelby for Saturday night dinner.

"Shelby, how is your mother doing these days?" Louise asked.

Caught off guard, Shelby managed to reply. "Oh. Ah... She works a lot. You know the bills have to get paid."

"Yes indeed. How many brothers and sisters do you have?"

"Two brothers and one sister."

"And you're the oldest?"

"Yeah." Shelby said wondering why all the questions.

"That must be an awful lot of responsibility for you being so young," Louise remarked. "I remember when your father passed away and your mom left with little ones to care for. But our God is mighty. A good Father, isn't that true?"

Shelby didn't understand. Did she just hear Mrs. Taylor say God was good for letting her dad die and leaving her mom to take care of four children, a house, and mounting bills? Confused Shelby blurted out, "I don't think I understand what you're implying."

"I remember how hard your father worked and what an upstanding man he was in our community. He taught you children right from wrong, good manners and strong leadership. I bet your mother works very hard to put food on the table. Clothes on your back and to keep you all warm?"

"Yeah?"

"And I bet she depends on you to help with your brothers and sisters when she can't be there. To make sure they complete their homework, have a warm dinner, and get them to bed on time?"

"Yeah?"

"Well, that's leadership Shelby. It started with your father then your mother and now you. You'll pass it on to your siblings." Louise didn't give praise easily. " Your father taught you all the necessary qualities you have needed to depend on when he was gone. I don't know why your father's life was cut short but when bad things happen, God is right there with us. He'll use these times if you let him, Shelby."

Shelby moved the carrots around on her plate. "Are you saying we all have a piece of Dad inside us? I mean the stuff that he taught us and all?"

"Absolutely," Louise replied confidently. "Do you know what God did for your family?"

"No, what?"

"He gave you a woman of character and honor who loves unconditionally and cherishes her children more than her own life. I bet your mother works harder than anyone you know, doesn't complain about her lot in life and knows what she must do then does it. A real superhero in my book. Otherwise, why would she bother to work so hard?" Louise asked posing the question to everyone sitting around the table.

"I couldn't have said it better myself, Louise." John emphasized.

All this time Shelby had only been concerned about herself. She'd never thought about walking a day in her mother's shoes. All Shelby could think of was finishing school and getting as far away as possible from her home and family. How would that affect her mother and siblings? Her mother was working two sometimes three jobs a week. Tonight, she finally got a night off and she said, "Shelby, go out with your friends and have fun." Unconditional love. Mrs. Taylor was right. "You're right Mrs. Taylor. My mother is my hero. I'm not sure if I agree that God did right by my family, but it's something I'm going to think about."

How does she do that? John was dumbfounded.

Dwayne smiled and recited, *"Those who are wise will shine as bright as the sky, and those who lead many to righteousness will shine like the stars forever."* Daniel 12:3

"Hmm, hmm. Louise, you sure know the way to a man's heart. This meatloaf couldn't get any tastier. Isn't that true John?" Dwayne declared.

"I don't think I have ever tasted a meatloaf this good."

Laughter and good cheer were on the menu for the rest of dinner.

When the dishes were cleared, Louise told the girls to get outside for some fresh air before it got too late. They went out on the front porch for a bit. The girls were in full conversation when they heard a beep come from an old silver Monte Carlo pulling up alongside the house. A familiar voice came from the rolled-down window on the passenger's side. "Hey ladies. What's up?"

"Titus, is that you?"

"Don't sound so shocked, Sharise. No need to be intimated by the ride," Titus replied.

"Are you out of your mind, Titus Poor?"

The girls heard him laugh as he parked the car and got out.

"Hey, Titus. I didn't think you lived around here?" Sarah stepped up.

"I don't, I live on the west side of Gilford. I thought I'd take this beauty," he said pointing at the car with a charming smile, "out for a little spin when my eye caught sight of some spectacular colors of red, yellow, and black. And I'm not talking about leaves. I stopped to admire the view." Titus then taunted them with his outstanding smile. "Would you three ladies like to accompany me on a journey into the night?"

All three started to giggle at his ridiculous confidence.

"Do you have a destination in mind? Because I'm not allowed to gallivant around town on joy rides," Shelby asked.

"Neither can I. My parents would have my head."

"Yeah, me too. Where are you headed?" Sarah asked.

Titus had to think fast, time was ticking. "Fisherman's Park, that part of the beach stays open until nine."

"Let me ask. I'll be right back." Sharise ran into the house.

During the ride to the park, Shelby and Sarah noticed what was happening between Sharise and Titus. They flirted with each other with a series of tit-for-tats.

Once they arrived at the beach Sharise and Titus walked off together deep in conversation, unaware of anyone else around them. Shelby and Sarah decided to keep their distance to share their observations and laugh at the realization of what Sharise and Titus were oblivious to.

"Are you serious Titus? You're not pulling my leg?"

"No really. I don't tell too many people. But yes, I'm a descendant of the great Salem Poor, a soldier of the Revolutionary War. He was a hero at the Battle of Bunker Hill. He literally had 14 officers write to the Massachusetts legislature commending him for his bravery and gallantry.

"My family originally comes from Lexington and a lot of them still live there, but my mom and dad wanted to be near the water. So here I am.," Titus exclaimed with an arm-sweeping bow.

Giggling at his display of chivalry, Sharise told him how impressed she was understanding where the strength of his confidence and pride came from. The night ended much too quickly for Titus and Sharise. Shelby was the first to get dropped off.

"The offer still stands. We'd be more than happy to pick you up for church service tomorrow morning." Sarah grabbed Shelby's arm as she got out of the car.

"Yeah. It's the first time I get to drive on my own to church. It would be nice to have the three musketeers together for the ride?" Sharise chimed in.

"Three musketeers?" Shelby and Sarah asked simultaneously.

"That's right, there's three of us. Why not?"

"I like it," Titus stated as if it was a done deal.

"What time tomorrow?" Shelby asked.

"Service starts at ten. We'll get you at 9:45 sharp."

"But I didn't say I was going."

"Don't fight it Shelby, when Sharise makes up her mind there's nothing you can do about it." Sarah laughed.

"Fine, see you at 9:45." Shelby said. Getting out of the car she waved goodbye and scooted up the stairs.

She watched the silver Monte Carlo pull away from the curb and down the street. Before going inside, Shelby glanced through the glass window of the door. Her mother was sitting at the dining room table hunched over a stack of papers, bills probably. Shelby went straight inside to her mother. Bending down she gave her a big hug and a kiss on the cheek, whispering, "I love you, Mom."

"Why Shelby, I love you too. Is everything okay?"

"Everything is fine. I don't get the chance to tell you how much I love you and admire you for being such a great mom."

"You know I couldn't do this without your help, Shelby. You are my right hand and I appreciate you more than you could ever know."

Louise Taylor was so right. Her mother is a hero. Her hero. "I'm going to church with Sharise and Sarah tomorrow morning. If it's okay with you?"

"Really, what church?"

"The one the Taylors go to. The Cornerstone."

Mrs. Richardson recalled. "Funny, your father talked about going to that church before he died. He felt like we were missing something at the church we were going to."

"I remember going to church ages ago. It was boring. I hope it's different tomorrow because I have a feeling Sarah and Sharise are going to bug me to go every Sunday."

"That's not a bad problem to have Shelby. The three Musketeers!" Her mother declared.

"What did you say?" Shelby asked.

"What, oh the three Musketeers?"

"Yeah, Sharise called us that tonight. Weird that you said it too."

"Fitting I suppose since there are three of you. Now scoot, I have to finish these bills before I find an excuse not to."

Shelby hugged her mom one last time. "Alright Mom. I'll check on the kids when I get upstairs. Don't stay up too late."

Mrs. Richardson offered Shelby a warm smile in return then bent her head back to the work at hand, while Shelby bounced up the stairs in search of her younger siblings.

CHAPTER 16
THE TRUTH OF THE MATTER

"Great message this morning, Pastor Peters!"

"Why thank you Pastor Wheaton, that means a lot coming from another pastor."

"It's my pleasure. Your approach to your sermons is enlightening and engaging. It astounds me the way you move from parishioner to parishioner, asking their opinions. The sermon becomes more of a conversation between friends without the angst of being judged. Quite astonishing."

"We have amazing people at Cornerstone who make my job seem effortless. Please, call me Martin. I have a feeling we're going to become very good friends during your stay in Gilford."

Thank you, Martin, that's reassuring. And please, call me John."

"John it is," Martin bellowed with a light slap on John's back.

"I was wondering, John, speaking of sermons. If you wouldn't mind one of these Sundays giving Cornerstone a taste of a good ole' Nebraska sermon?"

"That would be wonderful!" John exclaimed with excitement. A slight blush spread across his face. "I have to admit it's been a little strange being away from the pulpit. I'm sure every pastor feels the same way. Angel of Grace has some of the most selfless, outstanding folks. They were there for Sarah and I when we could barely function. They're our family. I miss that weekly connection."

"Well then, I have the perfect remedy," Martin proclaimed. "I have to go away in a couple of weeks and need someone to fill in."

Stupefied John inquired. "I'm honored but what about Pastor Tremblay?"

"Lewis Tremblay?" Martin chuckled. "Why, he's not a pastor yet, he's still in school."

John's forehead scrunched up and his head titled slightly to the left. Recognizing John's confusion Martin divulged, "Lewis interns as our youth pastor since the church doesn't have one. Once he finishes his studies, he'll be the real deal at Cornerstone." Martin added with a sense of pride. "I'm sure he'll be relieved to know you're more than happy to step in." Martin patted John's back with much enthusiasm. "Think of what a great learning opportunity it will be for Lewis to get a different perspective."

"I'm not sure about that but I'd be honored," John declared accepting Martin's' offer with a firm handshake.

Shelby loved to people-watch. This morning she had a front row seat. This service was far different from the church services she'd attended. There was an unconstrained excitement and a genuine kindness and happiness that emanated from everyone she met. Shelby loved the music, not like the kind of hymns she remembered. No, these songs were captivating and uplifting. They spoke to her soul. Swaying and tapping to each riveting beat. *Make sure to ask Sarah and Sharise about the music,* she noted.

On the ride back to Shelby's house after service Sarah and Sharise were thrilled to learn how much Shelby enjoyed the music. Sarah went straight to her playlists. In a matter of seconds Toby Mac's, "I Just Need You" filled the car. Sharise and Sarah began belting out the words to the song while Shelby moved along with every beat. The occupants of the car were rocking and rolling when they arrived at Shelby's house.

"Do you guys want to come in for a bit?" Shelby blurted, not wanting their good time to end. "I mean you don't have to." Feeling a bit insecure Shelby rushed on, "I thought. You know, maybe you could meet my mom. If you want?"

Sharise popped the car into park. Both girls whipped off their seatbelts.

"Absolutely!" Sarah exclaimed as Sharise bobbed her head up and down in agreement. She wasn't sure what was happening, *To be honest I don't care.* Whatever it was, she was happy.

Inside the house Shelby found her mom in the kitchen and made the introductions. "Mom, this is Sharise Taylor and Sarah Wheaton." Mary wiped her wet hands on her yellow apron that covered a pink blouse. Then she extended a hand to each of the girls.

"It is a pleasure to meet you. Sharise. Sarah."

"It is very nice to meet you, Mrs. Richardson," the girls announced.

"Finally. I get to meet the other two Musketeers!" Mary said. Sharise and Sarah looked at each other with delight.

"Please come in. Sit down." Mary gestured toward the kitchen table. "Would you girls like something to drink? I made some fresh lemonade."

"Yes, please that sounds wonderful. It's quite warm out there today," Sarah declared.

"Sharise, lemonade?"

"Yes. Please."

"Sarah, this warm spell is what we call Indian Summer in Massachusetts."

"So, I've heard. It's different in Nebraska, Indian summer never sets in until after winter has begun."

"Wow, I didn't know that," Sharise announced.

"By the time Halloween arrives in the Northeast, there'll be a cold chill in the air. Summer will be a faded memory. Which reminds me," Mary stated turning to her daughter, "Shelby, October's schedule came out and it looks like I'll be working Halloween night. Do you mind taking the kids out Trick or Treating? I'd hate for them to miss out on the fun because I can't be home."

As if on cue Stella and Ian, Shelby's younger siblings, peered into the kitchen from the living room.

"You know we have a party at the church on Halloween night. A Fall Festival, your brother and sisters might like. There will be all the good stuff. Candy, bobbing for apples, games, stories and lots of music," Sharise shared.

"Can we? Can we Mom?" Stella and Ian shouted repeatedly running into the kitchen.

"Before I agree to anything, you both need to calm down." Mary smiled. Both Ian and Stella clasped their pudgy little hands at once up to their mouths.

"I think it sounds wonderful, everyone in one place having a good time. What's not to like," Mary determined.

Lexy looked on from the bottom of the stairs that led to the second floor. "Sounds kind of stupid if you ask me. I'm not going to some dumb church on Halloween. I want to go out with my friends." Lexy raced up the stairs in a huff.

Bang! came the loud sound of a door slamming shut.

"I'm sorry girls." Mary apologized. "If you'll excuse me. I don't know what's gotten into that girl." She headed toward the stairs to face her latest Lexy challenge.

All three girls were left staring at each other.

"She likes to slam doors," Sharise observed.

"I noticed it a couple of weeks ago, she's been hanging with a rough crowd." Shelby got up from one of the kitchen chairs and started pacing. "I should have said something at the time. I didn't feel like it was my problem but, now everything is different. I don't know what to do."

"Shelby. Whatever happens you don't have to go through it alone. We'll go through it together." Sarah extended her hand. "The Three Musketeers."

"The Three Musketeers." Placing her hand on top of Sarah's.

They both looked at Shelby with an encouraging reflection.

After a few moments of stilled silence, "The Three Musketeers," Shelby whispered, settling her hand on top of the other two.

"Want to hang out on the front porch for a little while? I can braid your hair. Not like mine of course, but we can give it a try," Sharise asked Sarah later that afternoon.

"Hmm, I wonder why you all of a sudden have this fascination with the front porch?" Sarah asked tilting her head.

Sharise tried as hard as she could not to become completely unhinged by the simple question. "Because it's nice outside and pretty soon it won't be. And. And you'll regret not going outside and missing this great day," Sharise stammered and ran up the stairs.

It took Sarah a little bit to comprehend what had just happened. She found Sharise laying on her bed with her knees bent staring at the ceiling.

"Hey Sharise. I was only playing with you. Are you okay?"

"I don't know."

"I have an idea. Do you think you might like Titus?"

Stunned, Sharise abruptly sat up. "What? You think I like Titus?"

"Hmm, hmm, and maybe it's causing you some conflict because you haven't admitted it to yourself."

Sharise shot Sarah a look of indignation. Then the realization hit her hard. "Oh no. I like Titus! What am I supposed to do with that?"

"I guess the first thing you want to find out is if he likes you too. But to be perfectly honest, both Shelby and I have been watching this romance budding for a while now."

"Really? Agh!" She laid back down on her bed. "Sarah, help? What do I do now?"

"I don't know but he's never going to see you if he rides by and you're sitting upstairs in your room. Let's go outside and talk."

No more than twenty minutes went by and as if on cue, Titus pulled up in front of the Taylor's house in his Monte Carlo. "Ladies, may I interest you in a ride this lovely Sunday afternoon?" Titus asked. Peeking out the open passenger window with an easy smile and a head of curly black hair

"Not me, I have some homework I have to get done. Which I should get started on."

Not wanting to give Sharise any time to decline his invitation Titus jumped all over the opportunity. "Sharise, if you want, we can take a walk out to the quarry. The sun will be beautiful this time of day, bouncing off the water like a shimmering sea of crystals."

Sarah got up from the stairs, giving Sharise a smirk before she waved her goodbyes. "See ya, Titus."

Sneaky, real sneaky, Sarah! Sharise smiled through gritted teeth.

"Bye, Sarah. Sharise, wanna go?"

Better to find out now where this was headed. Sharise held up her finger, "Give me one minute I have to ask my parents. I'll be right back," sprinting as fast as she could into the house.

"Mom? Dad?" Sharise called out entering the house.

"Out here," came her dad's deep-throated reply.

Moving quickly through the kitchen. She reached the open sliding glass doors to the deck where she found her parents and John relaxing in conversation. Opening the screen door, Sharise blurted, "Mom. Dad. Is it okay if I go with Titus for a walk around the quarry?"

"Titus?" Louise asked knowing full well who he was.

"Titus Poor, you've heard me talk about him. We all went for a ride to the beach with him last week," Sharise reminded her mother.

"Is Sarah going with you?" Dwayne asked.

"No, Sarah isn't coming. Something about having to get her homework done."

"I guess if you are going out with this young man alone, we'll need to speak with him before you leave. Bring him inside Sharise," came Dwayne's stern response.

Knowing full well she would be fighting a losing battle, Sharise heaved a big sigh. "Aah!" Then turned around sputtering. "I'll go get him." Hoping he wouldn't make a big deal out of coming in to meet her parents, Sharise asked Titus if he'd like to come inside the house.

To Sharise's chagrin, Titus was more than happy to meet her parents.

"Of course." *What parent wouldn't want Titus Poor to escort their daughter on a lovely Sunday afternoon walk?* He thought, until he met Sharise's parents. Titus wasn't convinced who scared him more, Mr. Taylor, who was a giant of a man, or Mrs. Taylor, who was small in stature with penetrating eyes that seemed to go right through him.

"You will be very careful with our daughter. Won't you, Titus?" Dwayne asked.

"With kid gloves, Mr. Taylor."

"Titus when I say careful, I mean in no uncertain terms will there be any theatrics, shenanigans or showing off that might put our little girl in danger."

"Dad, little girl? Danger?"

"Excuse me, Sharise. I didn't think I was speaking to you." Redirecting his steely glare back to Titus. "Now young man, do I make myself clear?"

"Yes, sir."

"Dad?"

"Sharise?"

"Nothing."

Louise could see the terror in Titus' eyes. Good! "Titus?"

"Mrs. Taylor."

"My daughter will return to this house in the same manner in which she leaves it."

Although it was more a statement than a question Titus felt compelled to answer.

"Without question, Mrs. Taylor."

The inquisition over, Sharise and Titus dashed to the front door and on to their adventure. Before they made their escape, Louise stopped Sharise at the front door. "You go on ahead Titus, I want a word with my daughter before she leaves."

"Sure thing, Mrs. Taylor. I'll be down at the car, Sharise. Take your time," Titus responded wisely.

"Sharise, honey." Placing her hands with a firm but tender grip on Sharise's shoulders, she searched her daughter's innocent eyes. "I can see that you like this boy. And even through all that silky smoothness of his, he seems like a real nice boy."

Sharise giggled. "I'm glad you can see that, Mom, Titus comes off a little too assertive sometimes."

Louise reminded Sharise. "Remember who you are Sharise. And make sure Titus knows who you are. It isn't fair for either of you to start something that will only lead to heartache."

"Do not be yoked together with unbelievers. I love you, Sharise."
Louise kissed her daughter's cheek.

"I know Mom. I love you too."

Stepping out the front door Sharise looked down at Titus's smiling
face, waiting for her at the passenger side door. Grasping the handle
as she approached, he gallantly opened the door and with a slight
bow declared, "your chariot awaits."

At some point along the trail leading out to the quarry Sharise
realized she was holding Titus's hand. It felt so natural. It wasn't too
long into their walk before they reached the quarry and decided to
keep walking taking the ocean trail that led out to large boulders and
rock-filled crevices. Sharise hesitantly asked, "Titus? I know you
don't believe in God, but can I ask why?"

He stopped before moving through a doorway of stone that led to a
view of rocky cliffs, a grand display of rushing water and white foam
sprayed up over the jagged edges. Titus bent down and picked
something up.

"Sharise," He opened his hand displaying the grayish blue stone,
dusty and dirty from the trail. "I like to know when I pick up a rock
it's a rock, not because someone tells me it's a rock but because I
can feel it and see it's a rock. Believing in someone or something
because someone tells me it's true doesn't make it true. Especially
up here." He said pointing to the top of his head. "I need evidence.
Proof."

"That's what faith is, Titus. Believing in someone or something you
can't see. Believing without seeing."

"Yeah, I know. I've heard it all before Sharise." He let the rock slip
out of his hands. Titus turned and walked out beyond the trail then
jumped onto an enormous rock. Standing on the edge of the giant
boulder, he tasted the salt on his lips that spewed into the air from

the wave's impact. The sea was real. He felt it, saw it and tasted its reality play out before him.

Sharise took in the stunning scene, admiring the beauty and temperament of the sea. It was an anomaly of rage and peace all at once. The seagulls squawked at each other, diving in and out of the ocean hoping to catch a quick meal. A couple of Ida's swam by, ducking every now and then under the water to find their nourishment.

"I don't always hear God; sometimes I feel him. His presence in my life. I picture it like the wind. When I feel the sudden breeze it's like a kiss from God. You know it's there because you feel it as it passes."

"Yeah well, I've never heard or felt God. Can we get off this subject Sharise and enjoy the day?"

"Deal, but one last thing. Okay?"

"Okay."

"Remember the story Pastor told us the very first day in class about Thomas one of Jesus' disciples."

Titus shrugged his shoulders.

"He wasn't with the other apostles when Jesus first appeared to them and when the other apostles told Thomas what had happened, he replied 'Until I put my hands through the holes of his hands and feet or the hole where he was pierced on his side, I will not believe.'"

"That I can understand."

"Well, the next time Jesus appeared to the apostles, Thomas was there. Jesus went up to Thomas held out his hands showing the holes where the nails went through and he urged Thomas to touch them and to touch where the spear pierced his side. Trembling, Thomas dropped to his knees crying, 'Forgive me Lord I believe. I believe.' Jesus said to Thomas, 'You believe because you see.'" Sharise said opening her hand to reveal the rock she was holding. "Blessed are those who believe and do not see." Sharise dropped the rock. Titus was about to reply when Sharise put her finger to his mouth and said, "Shh. Let it be."

Taking hold of Titus' hand Sharise led him down the rough terrain, over big and small rocks. Some were smooth, others craggy with rough edges. The rocks glistened, wet from the sea's most recent charge. Somehow, they maneuvered their way down to the ocean's edge.

Sharise laughed as Titus played in the puddles of water sitting in the clefts from the incoming tide. They huddled together watching the blue ocean shimmered in the glow of the setting autumn sun. The sea looked like a vision of dancing crystals. Neither said a word, there was no need.

Titus admired Sharise, she was different, not somcone to be taken lightly. She knew who she was. Strong, beautiful, and sure-footed, like she was on the rocks. Like a mountain goat, unshakable. Most times people didn't get him, but Sharise didn't have to say a word. He knew she understood him.

The weather turned and with it came a biting wind and the end of a great day. Titus would later reflect.

Arriving back at the Taylor house, Titus was the consummate gentleman walking Sharise to the front door. He'd built up enough courage to place a sweet but tender kiss on Sharise's cheek when the door flew open and there stood both of her parents. *Ah well, next time*. At least he hoped there would be a next time.

Riding home, Titus thought about the girl with the long black hair, big brown eyes with a will that one minute drove him crazy and in the next made him feel like he was king of the world. "Oh, Titus, my man. What have you gotten yourself into?"

CHAPTER 17
STRAIGHT TALK

John was a little nervous about his Monday morning meeting. Karl didn't bother him as much as the parent of one of his students. He hoped it was an innocent misunderstanding that could be settled quickly. However, that wasn't the impression he got.

"John, what's wrong with you today?" He asked out loud while heading toward the front doors of the high school. *"Trust in the Lord with all your heart; do not depend on your own understanding. Seek his will in all you do, and he will show you which path to take."* Proverbs 3:5-6

Deep in thought, John didn't see the tall lanky figure emerge from the corner at the top of the steps.

"Early this morning, Pastor John?"

"What?"

"Glad I decided to get to the school early today." Tags announced moving closer to the top of the stairs. "I said to myself Tags, you don't want to miss the opportunity to speak with Pastor John this morning. And here you are."

After the initial shock of seeing someone popping out of the shadows, John recovered, surprised to see Joey Taglio staring down at him. "You can make it to school before anyone else gets here, but you can't make it to detention on time? What's that all about?"

"Yeah well, this is important. I didn't want to miss the chance to set you straight on a couple of things."

"Really? I would love to indulge you in whatever it is you think I need to be set straight on, Tags. Unfortunately, I have a meeting in about five minutes, and I cannot be late," John said. Stepping to his right to go around Tags, he continued up the remaining two steps. Relentless, Tags would not be denied.

"I don't think so, Pastor John," Tags said, blocking John's way up the last step. "Not until you hear what I came here to tell you."

"Okay. You have three minutes. What can I do for you?"

"You can stop putting crazy ideas in Erica's head. Everything was fine until you showed up and started giving her advice," Tags started. Pointing his finger at John's chest and continuing through clenched teeth, "I tell her where we're going and what we're doing. You got that Pastor John. Erica is my girlfriend and Madison is my daughter. They belong to me. Understand?"

With as much restraint as he could muster, John got into Tag's face. "First, when you're talking to me don't ever point your finger in my direction again. It's extremely impolite. Second, you need to learn nobody owns anyone. If by the grace of God, we are blessed to share our lives with people we love, we have a duty to cherish their love as we would a precious gift by being respectful and honoring that gift. Nothing I do or say is going to make Erica do anything she doesn't want to do."

John thought this was most likely the first time anyone ever challenged Tags. He looked speechless. "As a child of God, Erica is a very rare and valuable treasure. You dishonor her with the very words coming out of your mouth. Let me share some reality with you, Tags. Your beautiful little girl Madison is watching everything you do. Every move you make and every word you say. Do you open the car door for her mother? How do you treat Erica? Do you respect her? More importantly, how do you honor her?"

Tags looked down at his feet then back up with his eyes narrowing. He was unable to answer John.

"When Madison gets older, she's going to be drawn to the man that most resembles her father. The question you have to ask yourself Tags, is what kind of man do you want Madison to look for? A two-bit punk who likes to bully people and make them feel inferior? Or do you want Madison to look for a man who has integrity? Is trustworthy and reliable? Someone who is loving and kind?"

A hardened expression covered Tags' true thoughts and feelings.

"What I haven't heard you say is that you love Erica and Madison."

"You didn't ask."

"I didn't think I had to. You were sharing everything else, why not the most important aspect of your relationship?"

Not expecting an answer and not wanting one at this point, John climbed the last step and headed into the building. Feeling a nudge from the Holy Spirit he turned back around. Tags hadn't moved. His shoulders were slumped a bit.

"Tags?" John called.

Tags slowly turned, his expression was unreadable.

"Do me a favor and read 1 Corinthians chapter 13. If you need help with it, I am confident Erica would be more than happy to help you. I have a strong feeling she wants to believe in you, as a father, a man and her partner in life. Everyone wants someone to share their thoughts and dreams with. What you have to figure out is how long will she wait for you to become that man."

Tags let out a deep sigh, "Haaaahh."

"Together you can become a mighty force. Apart you'll always be swimming against the current. The choice is yours."

The minutes were ticking away, John shook his head. "Read the passage. If you want to talk about it after, I'd be more than happy to talk with you. Until you understand who I am and where I'm coming from, we are at an impasse. Now I really must go. I'm late for Round Two!" John forged ahead and on to Karl's office.

Completely dumbfounded. Tags watched Pastor John push through the heavy glass door. His thoughts were running a marathon. *Didn't I have everything under control? Wasn't I the one with the upper hand? Didn't I have Pastor John right where I wanted him and then...* "What?" Tags asked the misshapen image mirrored in the glass door. Shaking his head, he tried to make sense of it all. "What the heck just happened?"

Scanning the parking lot, he could see teachers heading his way and students getting dropped off for another miserable day at school. Tags mumbled out loud. "What did Pastor John say 1st Corinthians Chapter 13? What the heck is that and where am I supposed to find it? That's the problem with people these days. If you're going to suggest something at least let them know where to find it."

Tags walked down the remainder of the stairs and over to his car. If Pastor John was right and Madison was going to be drawn to a man just like him, what kind of man would she find? Tags didn't like the answer that flashed through his mind or the sick feeling deep in the pit of his stomach.

Tags knocked a couple of times on the door before Erica answered it. He could tell from her taunt expression and stiff body language the walls had gone up. "Look, Joey, I don't have time to start arguing with you right now." Not bothering to close the door she pressed on to the kitchen.

Tags walked in, closed the door behind him and followed her into the kitchen.

"Erica, I'm not here to fight. I just wanted to see you and Madison."

Madison was sitting in her bright yellow booster seat at the table Tags noticed her face covered in grape jelly and immediately walked over to her. "Madison, what have you gotten yourself into?" The little girl giggled. Erica decided to take advantage of the moment.

"Could you wash her face and hands? There's a face cloth at the sink. I have to run upstairs and get her bag for daycare." Not giving him a chance to say no, Erica ran up the stairs.

Tags wet the face cloth with warm water and squeezed out the excess before he sat down and wiped her hands and chunky little face.

Madison giggled and squealed every time Tags took her hands and covered them with loud kisses or planted gentle tickles at the base of her neck while he wiped her face. Erica came down to the rare display of his affection; she wished time could just stand still.

Sensing Erica behind him Tags asked nonchalantly. "Do you know what Corinthians is or where it's from?"

She looked at him with a creased brow. "Do you mean Corinthians? One of the books from the Bible?"

"It's from the Bible? Well, that figures."

"Yeah, it's one of the books in the New Testament, it's what we are studying in class. Why?" Erica asked.

Tags wasn't ready to reveal the conversation he had earlier with Pastor John. He needed time to sort it all out beginning with Corinthians.

"No reason. Hey how bout I give you and Madison a ride today?"

Erica readily dismissed their conversation for a chance to get a ride instead of taking the bus.

"Really? That would be a huge help. I'm already running late." Before Tags could change his mind, Erica took Madison down from the booster seat. "Come on Madison, let's get your coat on. We're going with Daddy this morning."

Clapping her hands with a big smile Madison shouted, "Yay, Daddy, Yay!"

Joey grabbed the car seat. "I'll put this in the car, while you get Madison ready."

Shocked that he didn't make a big deal about the car seat like he normally did, Erica was not about to spoil the moment. "Sounds good, we'll be right out."

The door to Karl's office was open when John arrived. He was happy to see Krystina's friendly face sitting to the left of Karl. However, Karl's look of doom and gloom and the unfamiliar face watching him was not a comforting sight.

"Sorry I'm late I was sidetracked by a student who had an urgent matter to discuss," John offered.

"Don't worry John, we only arrived a few minutes ago ourselves," Krystina assured him.

"This is Mrs. Linda Gallo." Karl gestured with his hand toward Linda. "You would know her children, the Gallo twins, Brittany and Joshua."

Brittany Gallo. The pieces were starting to come together. He didn't know Joshua was her brother and her twin.

"And Mrs. Gallo this is Pastor John Wheaton one of our teachers at Gilford High School."

"Very nice to meet you," John replied. Standing up, he extended his hand.

Linda Gallo reluctantly took his hand in a brief shake then looked away.

"Yes." In that condescending tone John heard every Tuesday and Thursday afternoon from Brittany. Funny, he thought, Joshua didn't seem to be anything like her. Maybe he took more after his father.

"John. Mrs. Gallo contacted Karl after her daughter Brittany came home from school the other day very upset over something that had happened in your class. Do you recall anything out of the ordinary that would have upset Brittany?"

"Out of the ordinary?" came a sarcastic reply. "He humiliated my daughter in front of the entire class. Unless of course, that's how he conducts his classes. Then I suppose it wouldn't be out of the

140

ordinary. Would it Pastor John?" She finished her sentence with such venom John was taken a back.

"This is unacceptable behavior, especially for a pastor. If news like this were to get out to the media, I don't believe as a public school system we would be able to continue to provide our students with your class. Just because the students don't believe the same way you do Pastor John, doesn't give you the right to use such hate and anger toward our students," Karl concluded with a smug look.

John was not at all sure how to react to the false accusations being slung his way.

What he did know for certain was as long as he was doing the Lord's work, he would always be the target of persecution. So, in some small way he felt a surprised feeling of gratitude, taking it as a sign from God that he was doing something right.

"Karl, as we discussed earlier, we have to listen to the whole story before we rush to any judgments. The media, hate and anger? Really? Let's rewind Karl and hear what Pastor John has to say."

John glanced over at Krystina nodding his thanks then addressed Linda Gallo's accusation.

"Mrs. Gallo, I appreciate that you took the time to come into school today on behalf of your daughter Brittany. There aren't many parents willing to engage in their children's education or for that matter, their life."

The three other attendees in the room did not see John's opening remark coming. Linda sat a little straighter in her chair not knowing whether to thank Pastor John or not. She nodded an affirmation of his intellectual insight.

"The matter you are referring to Mrs. Gallo took place last week during the afternoon class. The semester's focus is on the apostle Paul's passage regarding the gift of Love in his letter to the Corinthians. I asked the students what they thought the meaning of the word patient meant to them, in reference to the beginning of the passage, Love is patient.

141

Brittany thought it would be funny to humiliate a fellow student's answer to the question leading the student to run out of the classroom in tears while listening to Brittany's laughter follow her out of the room."

"How dare you make my daughter out to be the villain in all this when she was the one humiliated!" Linda blasted, starting to rise from her chair.

Krystina immediately took command of the situation. "Please Mrs. Gallo remember you came in here inquiring about what happened. We are obligated to listen to Pastor John's reply. I realize it may not be what you thought you were going to hear, but we are compelled to let him finish. Okay?"

"Fine, let him finish his pack of lies," Linda delivered through clenched teeth.

"Okay?" Krystina asked the group looking at each one individually. When she felt everyone was calm enough to resume. She asked John to continue.

"When I was leaving the class to go after the distressed student, I told Brittany I would like her answer to the question when I returned. After speaking with the embarrassed student and calming her down so she was able to reenter the class, we returned. I asked your daughter for an answer.

She replied with the word. "Tolerance", a funny word for someone who didn't use much tolerance toward her fellow student."

"Why, I never!"

"Mrs. Gallo, please."

"Hmph!"

John looked at Krystina for the okay to finish. He was rewarded with a firm nod.

"I then picked up the rock that was on my desk and addressed the entire class, not individuals. I asked them whether or not anyone had the right to cast stones on a fellow student without walking a mile in that student's shoes. Or if anyone in the classroom could say without a doubt they were without sin? That was it because the bell rang, and class was over. I don't know what you want or what you are looking for, but Brittany was not humiliated. In my opinion, she caused the humiliation."

Jumping to her feet Linda glared at John with contempt. "I don't believe you and I don't care about your opinion. It means nothing to me. You owe me an apology and you owe my daughter Brittany an apology." Unabashed, Linda waited for an apology.

John decided not to stand up knowing he would tower a good foot over Linda. He stayed seated and simply stated the facts.

"I cannot apologize for something I did not do or say. I believe if anyone is owed an apology it is the student Brittany embarrassed."

Linda looked from Karl to Kristina with bulging eyes. Her face tightened and a tinge of red spread across her cheeks. "This is not over Pastor John, you obviously don't know who I am. I will have you thrown out of this school, out of this town and sent back to wherever it is you came from. Karl might be onto something, religion in a public school. I don't think so." With one last glare she left Karl's office with him running after her like a lap dog.

"Mrs. Gallo, please wait one moment, let me walk you out…"

Back in the office Krystina warned. "She's not someone you want as an enemy John."

"I can see that. But the truth is the truth, wherever it leads."

CHAPTER 18
AGENDAS

After a disquieting Monday morning, the remainder of the school week was uneventful. There were a few awkward moments when Brittany entered the classroom Tuesday afternoon but other than that, "No outbursts from any students and no calls to the principal's office," John announced with a slight shake of his head to the empty classroom.

Detention went smooth, although Tags was missing all week. John slid his papers into his briefcase, grabbed his jacket and the sign-in sheet. Walking the short distance to the office, a deafening silence had replaced the explosion of boisterous commotion.

"That's a wrap," John exclaimed, slapping the sign-in sheet on the counter.

"Thank you. Pastor John," Elaine acknowledged. "Can I ask you a question?"

"Of course, Elaine." John smiled running a hand through his mop of disheveled hair. "As long as you call me John."

"Agreed. I thought you were overseeing detention three days a week, not five. Yet I've seen you in this office every day this week dropping off the sign-in sheet. What's going on?"

"You noticed, huh?" John confirmed. "Karl paid me a visit the other day and explained, in the nicest possible way, John, since you are already overseeing three days of detention it would be an enormous help if you could extend yourself the other two days. For the staff and students, of course." John's delivery was an impressive interpretation of Karl's deep monotoned voice, stern expression, and pursed lips.

Elaine laughed. "That was priceless and so on point." In a more sober tone, she added, "In all seriousness, John he shouldn't be able to get away with that, you should speak with Krystina."

"Thanks Elaine, but I believe this is exactly where God wants me to be." John held up his finger and recited, *"You intended to harm me, but God intended it all for good. He brought me to this position so I could save the lives of many people."* Genesis 50:20

"Amen to that."

John put on his jacket and grabbed his briefcase. "Have a good weekend, Elaine."

"Thanks. You too, and I'll see you on Monday."

As soon as John stepped outside, he noticed the sharp change in the weather. He fidgeted with the top button of his coat finally getting it to close. The warmth of the September sea breeze was a faded memory. In its stead were the crisp Autumn winds that suggested it would be a spirited October.

Sharise pulled the car into the empty church parking lot. "No trouble finding a parking space tonight."

"Yeah, I think you have the pick of the lot," Sarah replied, giggling. "I don't see this place getting filled up for a committee meeting just to plan a Fall Festival."

"You'd be surprised who shows up at these meetings, Sarah." Sharise shot back with a twinkle in her eye.

"This ought to be interesting," Sarah mumbled under her breath knowing full well how mischievous Sharise could be.

Joshua grabbed his football jacket off the hook in the mud room. "I'm heading out. I won't be late." With keys in hand, he headed for the door.

Linda jumped up from where she was sitting in the gold, winged-back chair nestled in the corner of the living room and rushed into the front hallway. "Where is it you're going in such a hurry?"

"Out. Why the sudden interest?"

"Since that Pastor and his daughter came to town, that's why. Parents have to be vigilant. Look what he did to your poor sister," Linda retorted, her stance said she had her defenses up arms folded across her chest.

"Really, Mom? I'm going to help plan a Halloween party. That's okay, isn't it?"

"Well, it depends. Where and with whom?"

"Are you serious?"

"Yes Joshua, very serious."

"I'm going to Cornerstone, the church Sharise Taylor and her family go to. I'm meeting Sharise, Sarah, and a few friends from school." Joshua was trying to figure out why she would be so upset.

"I knew it! Sarah, that's the pastor's daughter. I don't want you anywhere near that girl or her preacher father." Linda ordered in a frosty tone laced with ice.

"That's a little difficult to do since Sarah and I are in her father's class together."

"Not for long. That you can count on."

"I'm not dropping the class if that's what you're getting at."

"No Joshua. You won't have to drop a class that isn't being taught at the school."

"Mom, you should take this much interest in your daughter's activities. Any idea where she is tonight?" And with that Joshua opened the front door and walked out.

Aware any further discussion with her son would be frivolous, Linda wasn't in it to win battles. She was in it to win the war. Composing herself, she picked up her phone and found the number she was looking for.

"Hello," came the voice at the other end of the line.

"Hello Karl, this is Linda. It's about time we put a plan into action to run that Pastor John out of our school and out of Gilford."

The small conference room to the right of the church entrance was set up with a large round wooden table surrounded by tired black leather-wrapped chairs. The room had held many visitors over the years, bible studies, small gatherings, and church meetings.

Sharise and Sarah were at the table deep in conversation when Shelby and Titus walked in. "Hey. You guys aren't planning everything without us, are you?" Titus joked, grinning.

"Shelby, Titus, I can't believe you guys are here." Turning her attention to Sharise, Sarah asked, "Why didn't you tell me they were coming?"

"I said you never know who will show up. Now, didn't I?" Sharise answered with a question of her own.

"Why didn't you come with us, Shelby?" Sarah asked.

"I didn't think my mother had off tonight. When I realized she did, you and Sharise had already left so I reached out to Titus."

"How noble of you, Titus," Sarah declared.

"Come on you guys take a seat; we were just getting started," Sharise motioned to the empty chairs.

Titus took his seat next to Sharise when a head popped into the room.

"You think there's room for another person?"

"Lewis Tremblay, there is always room for you at our table." Sharise smiled. "Lewis has an internship with Cornerstone as our youth pastor. Lewis, may I present Titus Poor, Shelby Richardson and you know Sarah."

"Titus, Shelby very nice to meet you." Lewis looked at Shelby. "Did I see you at service a couple of weeks ago?" His deep brown eyes flickered in her direction.

Lewis seemed too young to be a Pastor. Shelby blushed, "Yes. It was a great service, not at all what I expected."

"I'm glad you liked it. Pastor Peters is the best. Maybe you'll come again." Lewis smiled warmly.

"Oh, I will. I had to watch my sisters and brother this past Sunday or I would have attended," Shelby babbled.

"Next time you run into that problem, bring them with you!"

"Yeah Shelby, I'll come pick you all up," Sharise chirped in.

"That would be great, but I have one big problem and it goes by the name of Lexy."

"Oh."

"Hmm."

"Yeah," came the round of acknowledgments from the group, except Lewis.

"Lexy?"

"My fourteen-year-old sister who thinks she's twenty-one and wants nothing to do with church."

"That's too bad. I can see how that would present a problem," Lewis replied with a sympathetic smile.

"Sorry I'm late."

Sarah's heart skipped a beat. Noticing the most beautiful big brown eyes looking in her direction.

"Joshua, we're so glad you came." Sharise walked over to help him with the bags he was carrying. "What do you have here?" Sharise took one of the bags from him.

"I met your mom in the parking lot and she asked me to deliver these to you."

Looking inside the first bag, Sharise pulled out two bottles of Root Beer soda and plastic cups. Placing them on the table she dove into the other bag. To everyone's delight, Sharise displayed a clear container full of homemade chocolate chip cookies.

"Your mother is something else, Sharise. I can smell those decadent cookies even with the cover on," Titus said.

"That she is," Lewis agreed, smiling at Sharise as if they were sharing a secret.

That didn't sit very well with Titus, but for now he would sit back and observe.

The night flew by. The ideas were plentiful, the laughter infectious and the cookies delicious.

"I had a great time tonight. I'm glad I came." Joshua finally got to speak with Sarah alone.

"It was a lot of fun, I'm glad you came, too," Sarah said returning his smile. Thinking it was a long shot Sarah asked anyway. "Would you like to come to service Sunday? There's great music. Everyone is so nice, and my dad will be preaching."

"I don't know Sarah, church has never been my thing." Adding quickly not wanting to miss his chance, "But maybe we could go out for a movie sometime?"

Sarah's heart did a deep dive into the pit of her stomach. Her face glowed a slight tinge of red, she should've known better. Sarah swallowed hard. "Joshua, I like you. I do. But church is my thing, you can't have one without the other. So, friends?" Sarah extended her hand in friendship, but that was as far as the relationship could go.

Joshua's eyes traveled from Sarah's extended hand into her beguiling blue eyes. Ignoring her hand, he asked, "What time on Sunday?"

"Service is at 10:00 am. But Joshua, it won't mean anything to you or me if you attend service for any other reason than you want to. Does that make sense?"

"Yeah, I get it. I do. What did your dad say… of your own free will."

"Exactly." Sarah rewarded him with a radiant smile that lit up the room.

Joshua was curious to hear Pastor John deliver a sermon. *Would he be like he was in class?* Joshua's only obstacle on Sunday would be his mother. *Why was she reacting to Pastor John in such a vicious manner?* For now, he decided the best thing for all parties concerned was to keep his whereabouts to himself.

"It was very nice to meet you tonight Shelby, and if you ever want to bring those siblings of yours to church, I'm only a phone call away." Lewis caught up with Shelby, taking her thin, porcelain hand in his honey-colored hands.

"Thank you, Pastor, I appreciate the offer." She smiled.

"Not a pastor yet," Lewis chuckled. "Call me Lewis, it's what my friends call me."

"Lewis. Thank you, Lewis." Shelby settled.

The night came to a close. Everyone pitched in to clean up and put the room back in order before locking the church up behind them.

Shelby happily took a ride home with Sarah and Sharise. Once they were on their way Shelby inquired, "How old is Pastor Lewis?"

Sharise was quick to answer. "He'll be twenty in November, and he isn't a pastor. He's still in school. One day he'll be our youth pastor. Why do you ask?"

"That's right, he told me to call him Lewis and not pastor. No reason, I thought he looked young, that's all."

Sarah and Sharise shared a quizzical look while Shelby whimsically looked out the window as Crowder filled the air waves.

The first year of high school was surpassing all of Lexy's expectations. There was no way she'd walk in the shadow of her drab, unpopular sister Shelby. She was determined to become one of the popular girls at high school and it was starting to come to fruition. Tonight, she was going with her new friends to the quarry to see for herself what went on after dark instead of the hearsay whispers. Lexy couldn't believe how easy it was to get out of the house. Her mother was clueless thanks to plain, non-sociable Shelly.

Lexy's mother was practically pushing her out the door to go study at her friend Jamie's house. She didn't even notice who was driving the car that picked her up.

"Lexy, this is Pete, he's going to be our ride tonight." Jamie explained from the front seat.

"Hi Pete."

"Aren't you a cute one. Hey, Lexy. Are you ready to party tonight?"

"I sure am." She replied trying to sound more confident than she felt.

"Jamie, be a babe and pop her one."

"Bottoms up." Jamie handed Lexy a beer.

"Bottoms up," Lexy echoed and took a sip.

Both Jamie and Pete laughed out loud at Lexy's attempt to drink the beer.

"First rule, Lexy, act like you've been here before. We don't sip beer, we drink it." Jamie downed a good portion of her beer.

Lexy raised the beer can to her lips and took a huge gulp and then released a very unladylike belch. "Oh, sorry. I didn't mean to, um…"

"Take it easy little one, it's only the three of us. I won't judge, if you won't."

Lexy didn't realize she was holding her breath, she let it out and smiled. Sitting back, she relaxed. *Jamie and Pete were so cool. Finally, I found some real friends,* oblivious to the smirk Jamie and Pete were sharing. The night was spent driving around town parking a few times at different hangout spots.

"Jamie, I thought we were going to the quarry tonight?" Lexy asked.

"Not tonight, Lexy. You aren't ready. You don't want to go there and make a fool of yourself, do you?" Not waiting for an answer, Jamie continued, "We're only looking out for you. I promise as soon as we think you're ready we'll take you to the quarry." Changing the subject she asked, "I've never asked Lexy. Do you smoke?"

"Cigarettes ah, no. How can you stand the smell?" Lexy contorted her face in a grimace of utter distaste.

"Not cigarettes silly. This." And passed her what looked like a cigarette. Lexy knew it was pot, she took it from Jamie and looked at it for a moment not knowing exactly what to do.

Jamie saw Lexy's confusion and instructed her. "Deep inhale, hold it in. Then let it out."

"Where the heck are you, Lexy?" It was well past midnight. Pacing back and forth in the kitchen, Shelby watched the minutes tick by. Thankful she'd sent her mother to bed volunteering to wait up for Lexy.

A little while later, tired of pacing Shelby warily sat on the couch fighting to keep her eyes open. She was roused from her slumber to witness a disarrayed, obviously drunk and reeking of pot semblance of her younger sister tumbling through the front door. "Whoa!"

Like greased lightening, Shelby reached Lexy in the nick of time before she fell to the floor in a loud heaping mess. "Where have you been? And what have you been doing?" Shelby shouted in a loud whisper.

"Why do you want to know? You're not my mother," She slurred her answer. "Jealous much Shelby? That I have coooool friends and you're a big fat nobody. A zero."

Lexy unsuccessfully tried putting her right thumb and forefinger together to make a zero. Giving up, she looked up at Shelby from the floor laughing.

"Quiet Lexy. Yeah, you're cool alright, you can't even stand up and you smell horrendous. If you're smart, you'll keep it down." Bending over, Shelby reached under the back of Lexy's arms urging her up. "Stand up. Ugh! It's going to be a long night."

Trying to stand with Shelby's help Lexy groaned. "I don't feel so well. Uh! I'm gonna be sick."

"Oh no, you don't. You hold it in until we get into the bathroom," Shelby commanded, dragging and carrying Lexy into the bathroom. Thankful there was a small bathroom downstairs. This is not what her mother needed to deal with now.

Yes, it's going to be a long night!

The next morning Shelby had a plan to stick it to Lexy for what she put her through last night. At the door to Lexy's room, she heard her mother talking in a soothing gentle tone. "Lexy honey, stay in bed today you'll need to sleep as much as you can." Mary touched her daughter's forehead. "You're a little warm but no real fever. Whatever you ate that made you so sick last night must be almost out of your system."

Shelby marched into the room ready to do battle, her mother turned to her. "Shelby thank you so much for taking care of Lexy last night. She told me how you were up with her most of the night making sure she was okay, because you didn't want to disturb me."

Shelby stopped short in her tracks, taken completely by surprise. Very confused she burst out with. "I'm sorry, what?"

Mary got up from the bed. Standing in front of Shelby she conveyed the details of the night from Lexy's point of view. "Lexy said she came home early because she wasn't feeling good and went straight to bed. About an hour later she got up feeling sick as a dog." Mary looked warmly upon Lexy. Sighing. "Poor baby."

"Interesting account of the night, Lexy."

"Shelby, I don't know what I would have done without you." Lexy countered, then said to Mary, "She's the best sister. I am so lucky."

It was Shelby's turn to be sick. She underestimated her younger sister. "I was hoping you might be better this morning Lexy so we could all go to church together. Since it is such a rare occasion when Mom is home."

"I would love to go Shelby, but I am too weak. You guys should go though, don't stay home on my account." Lexy finished with a little moan for good measure.

"Shelby, you go. I'll take care of Lexy. Stella and Ian can help me."

"If you don't mind Mom, I'd like to take Stella and Ian with me this morning. That is if Sharise can pick us up."

"Are you sure Shelby? I mean this way you get to spend time with your friends?"

"I know Mom, but I think it's really important they go." No way was Shelby going to let Lexy's bad choices influence Stella and Ian.

"Okay. I'm sorry I can't go with you. Next time for sure." Mary added. Her attention swinging back to Lexy she suggested, "Let me get you a cool cloth for your head, Lexy."

"Maybe I should try to take some aspirin now since the throwing up has stopped. What do you think Mom?" Lexy sighed.

"Sure, honey," Mary breezed by Shelby and out the door.

"You think you won this Lexy?" Shelby whispered.

"In case you haven't noticed Shelby. I think I did."

"Now that I know the extent that you'll go to, you better watch out. I'll be watching your every step. Wherever you go, whoever you meet up with I'll know it. I promise you Lexy, I'm going to be your worst nightmare." Not waiting for a response, Shelby did an about-face straight out of the bedroom.

CHAPTER 19
SUNDAY

People were pouring into the sanctuary. Even though she didn't want to admit it, Sarah hoped Joshua would come to service. If he didn't, *better to be disappointed now than deal with the heartache later.*

The morning service began with joyful song and spirited praise. At the time of the much-anticipated sermon, John patted Sarah's hand and walked up to the pulpit. He opened the small clip from behind the mini-microphone Lewis had put in place for him. John attached it to his shirt.

As was his custom back home in Nebraska, John got down from the pulpit and proceeded halfway up the middle aisle to get closer to the people.

"I am humbled to be here with you today. Pastor Peters is an extraordinary man, and I will do my utmost to deliver a sermon worthy of him." John received smiles. Heads nodded up and down in agreement. A few "Amens" were called out here and there.

"Before I begin, I'd like to share with you a little background as to how Sarah and I," he smiled in Sarah's direction, "ended up in this little Northeast fishing town all the way from Homestead, Nebraska. A while back I was invited by the principal of Gilford High School to come and speak to the school board, regarding the approach we adopted in Homestead. I shared some of the successes we were experiencing in our schools and the noticeable surge of positivity amongst the attitudes of our younger population. One of your parishioners," John pointed out sneaking a quick peek at Louise, "read the book I wrote called, *Children of the King*."

As soon as he mentioned the book loud applause along with numerous shouts of "Amen" broke out from amongst the parishioners.

John could feel the heat creep up his neck, with a humble smile he tried to silence the appreciation. "Thank you. Thank you so much." The shouts and clapping subsided leaving John honored and brimming with emotional.

"I only mentioned the book because it documents our discoveries and success stories and it is the reason Sarah and I came to Gilford. I am deeply moved by all of you. Our God is a great God. He takes the bad and turns it into good. He takes the lowly and brings them high. He is all knowing and all loving." Choking on the rest of his words John cleared his throat. "Ahem." And whispered, "He is my Lord."

Once again shouts of agreement exploded throughout the sanctuary. "Amen!"

"Amen!"

"Amen!"

"Amen, indeed! Jesus Christ came to earth to befriend the sinner, the outcast, the sick and the poor." John's voice intensified. "He did not come to mingle with the proud, the wealthy or men of power. Jesus came in peace and in love. To serve. Not to be served." John magnified the latter. "As Christians, our role in life is not to judge our fellow man but to serve and love him. Judgment belongs to God. Love thy neighbor as thy self. Who is my neighbor?" John paused momentarily. "Everyone we meet."

"Praise the Lord."

"Amen!"

John continued through the soft murmurs and praise. "The apostle Paul thought he knew everything. Didn't he?"

"Mm-hmm!"

"He sure did," others replied.

"After all he was a scholar of the Jewish law. A Pharisee from the tribe of Benjamin. He hated the followers of Jesus even consenting

157

to the stoning of the beloved deacon, Stephen." John finished in a crescendo.

"How merciful is our God that he chose Paul to preach the good news to the gentiles in order that they...we can have everlasting life? What better way to show his people that he is the great: I Am, than to take a hater of the way and turn him into one of the most zealot apostles for our Lord Jesus Christ."

"Paul, who once caused pain and suffering to the followers of Jesus, was transformed and suffered himself. Paul was put in prison many times." John held up his right hand to impress upon the congregation. "FIVE times! He was whipped with thirty-nine lashes by the Jews, not once, not twice, but THREE times. The Romans whipped Paul as well. He endured being stoned to the brink of death." John paused. "How ironic?"

Many shook their heads in acknowledgment.

"Paul was shipwrecked three times, once spending twenty-four hours in the water. He went without sleep and many times was thirsty and hungry, longing for shelter. Yet he still praised Jesus. In prison, he sang songs of praise. Each time the Lord heard him and delivered him. Shall he not hear us and deliver us as well?"

"Amen!"

"Yes sir!"

"Praise be to God!"

"Thank you, Jesus!"

John sensed the emotion and conviction expressed by the congregation this morning.

"If you could bear with me a little bit longer." John chuckled as did some of the parishioners. "I'd like to share with you about the class I'm teaching at the high school."

"After much prayer, the Lord decided," John smiled, receiving many knowing smiles in return, "that I accept the offer from the Gilford School Board to teach an elective class entitled God and Faith for

158

the semester. I prayed long and hard, where in the Bible should I start? And God pointed me to 1st Corinthians 13:4-7."

John threw his hands up in the air. "Of course, he did. Where else would I find a better declaration of God's love?"

Chuckles erupted throughout.

"Easy right?" John shook his head. "Not so much."

"I needed help. I asked, 'Lord, how can I teach the students at Gilford High School about love? About you?' I received silence. I thought I would try a different approach maybe I wasn't explaining myself well enough. I guess we expect an answer to all the questions we ask God. How many of you can relate to my dilemma?"

Hands shot up in the air. Heads shaking affirming John's impasse.

"I asked again, 'God, what is my purpose of going to Gilford? I mean how can I impact any of these students' lives?' After more silence and much prayer on my part, God gave me my answer." John bowed his head briefly. Raising his eyes to the congregation, he sighed.

"I couldn't. I can't teach them anything. I can only share what I know. Only God and God alone can change a person's heart. He will show the students in Gilford just like He did in Homestead who He is and how much He loves them. God will talk to them as we read His word. All children deserve to know that they are sons and daughters of the most High King. Each is born with a special gift from God. Each is loved beyond measure born from royalty."

Amen! after Amen!" was heard throughout the sanctuary.

"The high school students may not know it right now. But, if God can transform Saul into Paul, who am I or anyone else to stand in His way of victory? It is our duty to share this good news with everyone. Because God does not belong to only you and me, He belongs to the world."

The congregation stood up clapping, cheering and praising God. It took about five minutes for the excitement to subside.

John was finally able to say, "Let us pray…"

After prayer was over Sarah had a habit of looking back over the congregation to see the expressions her father's homily left in their hearts. Today was no exception. Turning around Sarah was drawn to the gleaming brown eyes resting upon her. Her head snapped back as the butterflies tickled the inside of her stomach. *He came! He came just like he said he would.*

John stood at the back of the church thanking each person for coming as two familiar faces approached. Unable to contain his excitement, John reached out and grasped Paul's hands. "Paul, I am so happy to see you here today." Looking to Paul's left, John recognized another familiar face. "Lily, what a pleasure." He let go of Paul's hands and reached out to catch Lily's hands within his own.

"Hi, Pastor John," Lily replied. Tilting her head towards Paul she confessed, "Paul can be very persistent when he wants to be. He's been bugging me for weeks to come and check out this church. I finally said yes when I heard you were going to be preaching."

Sensing the tension between the two of them. John asked, "Well, I'm very happy to see you both. What did you think of the message?"

"I thought it was great, Pastor John. I never realized how close God really is to us," Paul replied.

John smiled seeing the peace that filled him.

"What about you Lily? What did you think?"

"Honestly?" she asked.

"Always," came John's reply.

"I don't see God as such a loving Father to his children when he lets bad things happen to people who try very hard to be good and then

160

he deserts them." Lily defied John, as if she wanted him to prove her wrong.

John could sense it went beyond what she thought about today's sermon. Something bad happened to Lily and whatever it was she blamed God for not helping her. "God doesn't desert us, Lily. I know sometimes his silence feels like he does. Scripture says, *When you go through deep waters, I will be with you. When you go through rivers of difficulty, you will not drown. When you walk through the fire of oppression, you will not be burned up; the flames will not consume you.*" Isaiah 43:2

Lily said in a steady tone void of emotion, "Hmm. Go figure, another scripture. Like that's supposed to fix everything." Without another word, she turned and walked away.

Paul shook his head. "Lily won't tell me anything. I know she's hurting but…"

"Paul, don't give up. Lily needs your strength and your hope now more than ever."

"I know. I know. *Trust in the Lord with all your heart; do not depend on your own understanding. Seek his will in all you do, and he will show you which path to take.*" Proverbs 3:5-6

"You remembered?"

Paul shook his head and ran down the stairs after Lily.

John spoke with the parishioners as they left church. Erica stepped up with little Madison holding the edge of Erica's coat for dear life. "Great sermon, Pastor John, full of hope and love. Something we all need to hear more often." Focusing on her little girl. "I want to feel like you said, special, like royalty, and I want the same for Madison, Daughters of the most High King. Thank you for that."

"I only preach what God wants me to say, Erica. Thank Him." John bent down to eye level with Madison. Holding out his hand, he introduced himself. "Hi Madison. I'm Pastor John. It's a pleasure to meet you."

Madison shoved her entire right fist as far as she could into her mouth. Letting out a squeal, she backed behind Erica's legs, peeking her head out.

"Well, if you don't want to shake hands how about a high-five?"

Thinking very hard, she giggled then Madison took her wet fist out of her mouth and presented it to John.

Not wanting to miss the opportunity John tapped her wet little hand. "Very nice to meet you, Madison."

Squealing again, she scooted back behind Erica's legs. "Madison is quite shy, Pastor John. No offense, she's like this with everyone."

"Are you kidding me? She's perfect."

Erica laughed. Picking Madison up, they said their goodbyes.

Titus, Sharise, Sarah and Joshua were talking together. John knew it was only a matter of time before Sarah would be interested in someone. He hoped it wouldn't happen until they returned home. Long distance relationships didn't have very good track records. He'd be there to help her pick up the pieces if, or when, they fell apart.

Louise stood behind John. "Do not be yoked with unbelievers…" Louise let drift from her lips.

"Who knows what the Lord has planned, Louise? Who are we to say?"

"Hmm, we shall see John. We shall see."

"Stella, Ian, it's time to go, Sharise is waiting to take us home," Shelby demanded.

"Ah Shel, do we have to go? We had so much fun today," Stella cried.

"Yeah, pleasssse Shel?" Ian begged.

"Guys I'm very happy you had so much fun, but church is over. We'll come back next Sunday, okay?"

"If you don't mind helping me clean up, I'd be happy to give you a ride home. That's if you don't mind, Shelby?" Lewis asked from the doorway of the children's room.

"Lewis, I didn't see you come in. I guess that's okay. Stella, Ian would you like to help Pastor Lewis, I mean Lewis clean up?"

"Yes," Stella and Ian shouted in unison.

"I guess you have a couple of helpers for clean-up duty. Are you sure it's not inconvenient to give us a ride home?"

"Shelby, I'd be happy to give you a ride home anytime. I mean it."

Shelby's face glowed like a blazing torch. "Thank you. Both of you stay here and help Lewis clean up while I let Sharise know we have another ride."

"Yay!" Shelby heard as she rushed out of the room in search of Sharise.

CHAPTER 20
BONE OF CONTENTION

Lewis pulled up to Shelby's house. "Would you like to come in and meet my mom? And Lexy?" The last part of the question dripping with venom.

"As long as you think it's safe."

"Oh, my gosh, I didn't mean for it to come out that way. Lexy has become quite the handful lately."

"Yeah," chirped Stella. "Lexy is sick today so Mommy couldn't come to church. She said next time she has off she will," Stella finished innocently.

Intrigued, Lewis parked the car, got out and opened the doors for Shelby and her siblings. Shelby led the way inside. Where they found her mother at the stove stirring a big pot.

"Something smells really good," Lewis observed.

"Mom, I would like you to meet Lewis Tremblay, he interns as the youth pastor for Cornerstone Church. Lewis, my mother, Mary Richardson."

"Mrs. Richardson, it's a pleasure to meet you."

"Lewis, please join us for dinner. I'm in the middle of making chicken soup with some homemade bread," Mary announced.

"I would love to. Is there anything I can help you with Mrs. Richardson?"

"I believe you have helped plenty today. Go on in and relax in the living room. Shelby will get you something to drink."

"This way," Shelby directed. "What would you like to drink, we have bottled water, ginger ale or milk?"

"Bottled water sounds good. Thank you."

In the living room, Ian was building something very tall with his Legos. Stella, with crayons in hand, was laser focused on her coloring book. Shelby placed Lewis' water on the table next to his chair.

"That was my dad's favorite chair." Shelby said heavy-hearted.

"Shelby?" Lewis asked.

"Sorry, Dad passed away almost five years ago from a heart attack, you caught me a little off guard."

"I can sit on the couch. I didn't know." Lewis jumped up.

Shelby smiled at Lewis and patted his shoulder. "Don't be silly Lewis, besides, you look good in the chair."

"I do? Well then," Lewis managed. "Stella what's that you're coloring?"

Along with the internship at the church Lewis was offered a place to stay at the Peters' home. On his drive home after Sunday dinner, Lewis went over everything he'd learned about Shelby. She was a senior this year unlike Sarah and Sharise. She was seventeen years old with a January birthday fast approaching and a lot of responsibility placed upon her. Shelby didn't have much time for fun and games. Lewis wanted to help her with the many burdens she carried, but he wasn't sure how, or why. What was he thinking? Didn't her mom say Shelby was looking at schools far away? Who could blame her? He felt sadness at the thought of her leaving Gilford and Massachusetts.

A chuckle escaped him, thinking about the infamous Lexy Richardson. She was quite something alright, as sweet as a wolf in sheep's clothing. Just as quickly as the chuckle came so did the groan. "Argh!" If Shelby was gone, Lexy would be on her own.

That night Sarah and Sharise recalled the wonderful day. Louise and Dwayne had invited the boys, Joshua and Titus, to join them for a good hearty Sunday dinner; meatballs and sausage, pasta, and warm bread along with a hot apple pie for dessert.

As Dwayne liked to say, "If anyone leaves hungry from the Taylor's table it was their own fault."

After a hearty meal the teenagers went out for a walk down to the neighborhood playground. They frolicked and played on the swings, slide and merry-go-round like kids. Sarah sat on the merry-go-round and Joshua sat beside her; they held onto the bars and dangled their feet. Sarah was happy Joshua had come to church.

"I'm glad I came. Not just to see you, even though that was my initial reason, but because I really liked the message. Your father has a way of keeping things upbeat, he doesn't just say stuff to get his point across. Am I making any sense?"

"More sense than you know. Dad definitely has a special gift."

After a few quiet moments Joshua added, "I'd really like to read his book. *Children of the King*. It sounds very interesting. Besides I'd love to know about where you came from and what it's like."

"When we get back to the house, I'll give you my copy."

Joshua shared about his home life, about his sister and father who he hardly sees, about his mother threatening to make him drop Pastor John's class. "I'm not sure what she is planning. She's good at causing trouble for people she doesn't like."

"Joshua, as someone who lost her mom and would do anything to have her back - your mother is your mother. No matter what, she's doing the right thing to protect you because she loves you. When you get angry with her, remember where she's coming from. Maybe in time, she'll redirect that energy toward good."

"Amazing! You really are amazing!" Without a thought he brought her in close and kissed the top of her head.

Paul parked his black Nissan Sentra in front of Lily's house saying a quick prayer. "Lily, I don't know what happened this past summer, but I wish you wouldn't shut me out. I thought we shared everything. We were planning our future then, without any warning, you started looking at me like I'm a pariah or something. What did I do to make you so mad at me?"

Lily felt bad for the way she was treating Paul. He was the kindest and gentlest of all people. But the future they talked about was not the future she saw. She tried many times to tell him it wasn't him it was her. Life changes. "Paul, can't we be friends right now? I have a lot to sort out and you badgering me doesn't help."

"Badgering? Lily? Lily, look at me?" Instead, she kept her eyes fixed on her hands clasped in her lap. Seizing her heart-shaped chin in his hands, Paul gently guided it upward and slightly turned Lily's face so it was inches from his own. "I have never told you this and maybe I should have - I love you, Lily. I always have and always will. But if you see me as badgering you, I'm going to do the one thing my heart really doesn't want me to do. I'll leave you alone." The seconds ticked by in awkward silence. Recognizing Lily wasn't going to put up a fight or protest his decision, Paul let out a painful sigh.

Starting the car back up Paul said, "I hope you find peace with whatever it is that's tearing you apart. I'll be praying for you, for me, for us." Leaning over Paul grabbed the handle of the car door, pushing it open he said. "Bye, Lily."

For the first time in months Lily felt something other than pain stir inside. Reaching for his face she peered into his tender autumn eyes and gently grazed his cheek. Without saying a word, she got out of the car. She watched Paul drive away until he vanished out of sight. A single teardrop fell on her cheek.

Erica was walking up the street to her house with Madison in the carriage chattering away. Tags was sitting on the front porch steps of her house. Getting closer, she noticed he had a book in his hand, turning the pages as though he was looking for something specific.

As Erica and Madison reached the house, Tags said, "Thank goodness you're home. I could really use your help."

"Okay, with what?"

Tags headed over to the carriage and planted a great big kiss on Madison's cheek.

"How's my big girl today? I've missed you, Madison."

"Daddy. Yay!" Madison screeched. hands clapping enthusiastically in her mittens. Unstrapping her, Tags picked her up and whirled her around amidst squeals of delight.

"What is it you need help with?"

"Is it okay if I come inside and show you?"

"Sure, Mom shouldn't be home for a while. I want to give Madison some lunch and put her down for her nap."

"Great. I can feed her if that's okay?" Tags asked shyly.

Who is this and what have you done to Joseph Taglio? "Okay," was all she could manage, trying to figure out what was going on.

After putting Madison down for her nap, Erica found Tags sitting on the couch with what looked like a small pocket Bible. No, she had to be mistaken.

Tags announced while holding up the small book in the air for Erica to see, "I finally found the passage Pastor John was talking about, Cor ith ans?"

"Corinthians," Erica offered.

"Yeah, isn't that what I just said?" Not waiting for a response Tags moved on. "Anyway, this dude talks all about what love is and stuff. What I really want to know is who is this dude, Paul? What gives him the right to tell me how to love someone?"

Erica moved over to the couch by Tags. She took the small Bible from his rough, calloused hands and turned to Corinthians 13:4.

"I'm going to start from the beginning of the passage, so you hear everything Paul has to say." Erica recited the passage.

"That was beautiful Erica, so much better than when I read it."

"Thanks." Erica blushed. "When Paul talks about love he is explaining how it's the "be all end all." It should be kept pure like a child's love. He doesn't say it's easy, but he does maintain this is how love should be. We should keep trying to get as close as we possibly can."

Erica watched Tags process what she said and added quickly, "At least this is how I interpret the passage."

"What about this Paul dude? What's his deal?"

"Paul is a really interesting "dude". His real name was Saul."

Tags sat on the couch captivated by the story Erica shared with him. When she finished, he was speechless. "Pretty amazing stuff, huh?"

"It's incredible. I need time to process this whole thing. I want to know more about him and why would he go through so much for this other guy, Jesus. Someone he didn't even know."

"Great questions, but I think you should be asking Pastor John, not me. I'm just learning all of this myself."

"I have a great idea, how about we learn together? I'll talk with Pastor John and tell you what he says, and you can teach me what you learn in class," Tags offered.

"I think it's a great idea."

Without warning the door swung open and in like a tornado came Erica's mom. Bags of groceries in hands, her hair in complete disarray and a disdained look on her face. Tags immediately offered to help Mrs. Gray with her bundles. Backing away she snarled at his offer.

Proceeding to the kitchen with bags in tow, Donna Gray sarcastically uttered over her shoulder without so much as a glance back, "Looking to make baby number two I see. That will be quite the accomplishment Erica and with such an upstanding hoodlum. I'm so proud. So proud."

Tags first reaction was to run into that kitchen and tell Mrs. Gray a thing or two. However, Erica put her hand on his chest and begged him, "Please don't let her ruin what we just shared. She's a very angry woman who is mad at the whole world, we just happen to be in her path today. Joey, you've placed a hope in my heart I didn't think could happen. We need to keep moving forward not backward. Okay?"

Drained of the emotional fury he felt only moments earlier, Tags reached down and touched Erica's cheek ever so gently and murmured, "Okay, I'll see you tomorrow." Grabbing the door, Tags turned to Erica and said, "Give Madison a kiss for me and tell her Daddy loves her."

"Always," Erica replied.

CHAPTER 21
A DIAMOND IN THE ROUGH

Fall festival was fast approaching. Lewis and the gang were busy preparing for the event. They decided to take a break from putting together prizes for the Fall Festival events.

"Lewis, why don't you give us a tour of the church? I've only seen the sanctuary and this conference room," Sarah suggested.

"Sure, follow me," Lewis replied directing the group on a tour. At the last stop, the kitchen, everyone mulled around.

"Where does that door go to?" Titus asked.

"I almost forgot about this room," Lewis said turning the doorknob.

"Is there a light?" Titus asked.

Reaching blindly to the right wall, Lewis flipped a switch. The overhead light displayed an old, dusty room full of cobwebs. One by one they entered the rickety room. The distressed wooden floorboards creaked with every footstep. Their eyes and mouths were wide open at what they found.

"Look another door. You think it leads to another room?" Titus asked.

"We are at the end of the road." Lewis unlocked the door and opened it. Their reward was a rushing, frigid breeze.

"Look there's another switch. I wonder what it goes to?" Titus flipped it.

"Oh, look it's for outside. There's a stone path that goes out toward the front of the church," Sarah said.

"Does anyone use this room anymore, Lewis?" Joshua asked.

"Not that I'm aware of. I believe the room was used as a small function room for meetings when the church was first formed. But the church eventually outgrew this small space."

Everyone was astounded by the character and old charm of the room.

"Do you think if we clean the room up, and it's okay with Pastor Peters, we could use it as a gathering room?" Joshua asked as he turned to Sarah. "You know, like you guys did in Nebraska. What did you call it? The Lighthouse?"

Sarah beamed. *He'd read the book.*

Lewis placed his hand thoughtfully under his chin. With a twinkle in his eyes and a big smile, he looked over at Joshua. "Joshua, that is a great idea." Adding in a more serious tone, "I'll have to run it by Pastor Peters, but I don't see a downside. Now, don't get too excited," Lewis cautioned. "Remember, it has to be approved by Pastor Peters first."

A little after 2:00 p.m. on Monday afternoon, John sat at the teacher's desk waiting for the customary regulars to show up for detention.

He had to admit, he got the biggest kick out of interacting with this particular group of students. Once they let their guard down, they weren't so tough at all. They showed a real curiosity about who he was and what he had to say. He had begun ending each detention session with a passage from scripture.

Looking over the list, John noticed something peculiar, Tags wasn't one of the students listed for the day's detention class. "Hmm," John puzzled.

As he was wondering why Tags wasn't on the list, he came strolling into the classroom. "How's it going Pastor John?"

"Tags what are you doing here? You're not on my list for today's detention."

"Ah, yeah I was on time for class today." Tags nonchalantly replied.

"Well then, what can I do for you?" Intrigued, John relaxed in his chair and gestured for Tags to sit down.

"I read that passage you told me to, Corriths…"

"Corinthians?" John assisted.

"Yeah, whatever…Corinthians. I talked to Erica about it yesterday and she helped me out with some of my questions. But she thought it was a good idea if I talked with you, cuz she's in the learning stages and all, too."

Taken completely by surprise John sat up straight. *Are you kidding me? Of course, God can do anything. Okay, slow down John, don't mess this up. God show me what you want me to say to this young man. I can't do this on my own. Help me.*

Tags watched John making weird expressions. Asking out of concern, "Pastor John, man, are you okay? Do you want me to come back later?"

John collected himself realizing his conversation with God was written all over his face. "Yeah, I'm great. What is it I can help you with?"

"Okay, Erica explained to me how Paul, who used to be Saul, changed when he saw some blinding light. It all sounds a little messy to me."

"Did Erica turn to Acts and read about Saul's conversion to Paul?"

"Turn to what?" Tags asked. "Maybe this is a stupid idea." Finishing with a shake of his head he started to rise from his seat.

"No, this is my fault." He eased Tags back down into the chair. "Let's start over. Acts is another book in the Bible. It describes Paul's journeys."

Tags pulled out the little pocket Bible from his inside coat pocket and handed it to John. "Can you show me where?"

He took the Bible from Tag's hand and turned to the Book of Acts Chapter 9, then gave it back.

Students were coming into the classroom so John suggested Tags read chapter 9 and then they could discuss it after detention was over.

"Sure," Tags agreed. "But do you mind if I stay in here and read, Pastor John? I mean it's kind of cold outside."

"That's fine with me if that's what you want to do."

Tags got up and went to the back of the room taking his usual seat.

John and Tags were both hunched over the small Bible conversing, when Elaine walked in. "John, I hate to bother you. It's 3:30 and I have to close the office up. Can I get today's sign-in sheet?"

John snagged the sign-in sheet and handed it to her. "I can't believe it's this late Elaine. I am so sorry. I guess I lost track of time. I should have brought this to you right away."

"No problem. I was finishing up some things myself." Elaine said taking the sheet from John.

"Is it okay if we use the classroom for a few more minutes?"

"Of course," Elaine replied. "Have a good night, John."

"You as well Elaine, again, thank you."

"Wow!" Tags said shaking his head in disbelief. "This is very important stuff Pastor John. I mean Saul did a complete 360. He was a mean dude."

"Saul didn't think he was doing anything wrong, he thought he was on the side of right. He thought he was helping God. Saul didn't believe in Jesus."

"Guess he had to rethink that one huh? I mean he was lucky that Jesus is one cool dude. Forgiving him and all."

"Yes, he is one cool dude, Tags. Jesus forgives everyone who confesses their sins to him."

"Everything?"

"Yes, if they are truly sorry…everything."

"Pastor John," Tags began. "Do you think we could get together a couple of times a week so you can teach me some of the stuff you're teaching your classes? I mean I get to homeroom late, so I do get detention."

"I think being in homeroom on time would be best. Still, we can meet here on Tuesdays and Thursdays. I'll give you what we discuss in class, and you can go over it during detention. Then we can discuss it after. How would that be?"

"That would be awesome! Then I can get with Erica, and we can talk about it. I think she'd like that." Tags finished with a lopsided smile.

"I think she would too. It sounds like you two are both trying to work things out?"

"We are, but her mother isn't making it easy. She accused Erica and me of plotting to have baby number two." Shaking his head, he admitted, "Believe me even if I wanted to, Erica won't come near me right now."

"Tags, you aren't doing all this just to get Erica back, are you?"

"I know you don't have any reason to believe me, but Erica and Madison mean so much to me. What you said about Madison looking for a man like her father made me sick to my stomach." Trying hard not to let John see his vulnerability, Tags cleared his throat, "Ahem. I want Madison to be proud of me and I want Erica to see me as a good man."

"I believe you Tags, and I believe you can become that man. I'm here to help get you there."

"Thanks Pastor John. You are the only person besides Erica, of course, to say that to me." He raised his Bible shaking it in the air. Tags said, "See you tomorrow".

John smiled praising God for His blessings.

CHAPTER 22
MISCALCULATION

Whether it was the Fall Festival or Steve's incessant football talk, her mother's nonstop chatter about her brilliant plot to bring down Pastor John or her lovesick brother making a complete fool of himself over Sarah Wheaton, *how pathetic,* even her friends were starting to get on Brittany's nerves.

It was time for a day trip into the city. Let them all wonder where she was. The train pulled up, Brittany stepped up from the wooden platform onto the train. She was excited about surprising the one person who understood her the best.

She remembered the last time she surprised her father at his Boston office. He wasn't the least bit upset that she'd skipped school to come in and see him. No, he'd thought she showed gumption. Smiling, Brittany couldn't help but picture her arrival. He'd be glowing with pride, overjoyed to see her. No doubt they would eat at one of the many upscale restaurants. They'd sit amongst the elites talking about anything and everything. "Aah! My knight in shining armor." Rousing from her daydream, Brittany heard the conductor announce, "North Station."

She passed Hay Market Square and Faneuil Hall, observing the many street vendors out and about selling their wares. Food vendors offered everything from hotdogs to fruits and vegetables to exotic assortments of fish and carts overflowing with lobster, shrimp, and crab.

And the variety of Irish, Italian, French and Indian restaurants unleashed their savory aromas preparing for the midday rush.

Moving swiftly along Boylston Street, Brittany watched the bustling sounds of people, cars, buses and trolleys. The duck boats were catching the season's last bit of activity. Falling leaves blanketed the sidewalk in brazen golds, greens, and reds, and made displays of spicey, colorful accents against tall brick buildings. Yes, indeed the city was alive, she felt it's energy and excitement exuberating from every corner.

Getting close to her destination, she noticed a man walking toward her that looked a lot like her dad.

No! Her eyes were playing tricks on her. This man's arm was interlocked with an unfamiliar woman. Hoping she was mistaken, Brittany noted the man's attire. Black wool coat falling just above his knees. Faux buttons of large silver anchors resting at the tips of the man's collar. She'd know that coat anywhere. After all, she was the one who bought it for him last Christmas. Unable to turn away, her eyes confirmed what her mind refused to believe.

The man and woman stopped steps away from the revolving glass doors at the front of her father's office building. Facing one another, the man reached up with his right hand and intimately caressed the woman's cheek. He bent down and placed a long lingering kiss on the woman's mouth which she happily accepted.

Shocked, Brittany stopped a couple of feet from the engaged couple, staring in disbelief as the dreadful scene played out on the sidewalk in front of her. The absorbed couple broke apart. The woman was the first to notice Brittany staring at them.

Following the woman's eyes, Anthony Gallo called out, "Brittany?" Immediately shifting the woman away from him. "What are you doing here? Why aren't you in school?"

"I'm watching my father make out in the middle of the sidewalk with a woman who is not my mother."

Before he could reply, the woman in question turned hastily and disappeared through the revolving glass doors.

"Look Brittany, this isn't what you think."

"No Dad, it's exactly what I think. I'm old enough to recognize when someone is being friendly and when someone is being overly intimate," She answered in an even tone.

Anthony put his arm around Brittany's shoulder. He didn't notice her flinch. "Let's keep this between the two of us Brit. We really don't want to upset your mother. You know her, she's capable of doing anything. She can be rather crazy at times."

Thinking he was the crazy one, she couldn't find the words to answer him.

"Brittany, we need to be on the same page right now." Taking her silence as approval of his deception. "I mean after all Brit, you and me we're cut from the same cloth. We have to look out for each other. Your mother and Joshua, they just don't understand us."

Why was she staring at him like some simpleton? What was wrong with her?

"I don't have time for this right now. I have to get back to work. How about you and I talk about this later tonight?"

"I am not a liar or a cheat. I am NOT like you!" Pulling away and fighting back the tears, Brittany turned and ran as fast as she could down the street and away from the man she considered her hero.

The train ride home seemed to take forever. Thank goodness the compartment she was in was practically empty. It was too early for anyone she knew to be riding home. Between her tears and the few people on the train offering sympathetic glances, Brittany's head was about to explode.

It seemed like hours she had been sitting on the big rock overlooking the park. She didn't have a clue what she was going to do. Nothing would ever be the same. Everything was different.

"A lie. It's all been a lie." She tried to sort out the biggest crisis of her life.

Brittany desperately needed someone to talk to, someone who would understand. Steve had football practice, he wouldn't even answer a text from her at this time of day.

Maybe Joshua? No, I need to sort this out first. Would he believe me? Why would anyone believe me? My friends? They didn't have a clue, someday they'll realize. "We're not as important as we think we are." The tears spilled.

Brittany heard noises from the playground below. The little girl being pushed on the swing was laughing and screaming with delight. "Careful little girl. It can come crashing down on you someday too."

Brittany's attention turned to the ocean in the distance, oblivious to the mother taking the child out of the swing and putting her into the carriage.

Pushing the carriage toward home Erica saw the girl sitting on the rock. "She looks cold, Madison." Immediately Erica recognized her and wasn't sure what she should do. After all, Brittany made it very clear that Erica was dirt in her eyes. But the thought of passing her by without finding out if she was okay seemed wrong.

"Brittany? Are you okay?" Erica asked timidly. Erica waited for Brittany to reply but she just kept staring straight ahead. Moving closer, hoping not to startle her, Erica asked again a little louder, "Brittany, are you okay?"

Turning, Brittany faintly heard someone speak to her. She wiped her eyes and focused on the face beside her.

"Oh, how perfect. You, of all people? The perfect ending to the perfect day."

"Is there anything I can do to help you?" After what seemed like the longest minute of Erica's life, she noticed Madison's little eyes fluttering to stay open and decided to continue her walk.

"Tell me something Erica why would you want to help me after all the things I've done to you?" Brittany sniffed and asked in a hoarse voice.

Erica stopped. "Brittany, we're not in school right now. You have nothing to prove. Besides you can always deny you ever saw me. But if you need someone to talk to. I'm here. Or... I'll just listen. Whatever."

"Have you ever felt like the whole world is crashing down on you and everything you believed in is not true?"

Erica had to see if she was genuine. "Seriously?" The two of them looked at Madison sound asleep in the carriage.

Brittany and Erica cracked up laughing.

After catching her breath Brittany managed, "Of course, you have. What was I thinking?" Suddenly, Brittany stopped laughing. She suddenly realized exactly who and what she was. "When all you do every day is think only of yourself, it becomes easy to believe all the lies people tell you are true. It's hard to look at someone else and see exactly what they're going through. I've been such an egotistical, self-indulgent, spoiled brat."

Erica kept quiet; she couldn't argue. Brittany was all those things and more. She was mean and insulting, too.

"Erica, I'm sorry for what I did to you in class and all the nasty things I've said over the past couple of years. I don't blame you if you don't believe me. I don't know if I could believe me, but... I really am sorry."

Erica looked for the smirk that usually followed when Brittany was playing someone, but she only saw sadness and dismay. Erica felt sorry for Brittany. "Thanks Brittany, that means a lot to me." Erica smiled then asked, "Do you feel like taking a walk? I don't want Madison to wake up."

"Haaaahh. Sounds like the best plan I've heard all day." Untangling her stiff legs, she jumped down with care from the rock. Feeling like the weight of the world was getting a tiny bit lighter she began shaking. "Wow it's cold out here!"

The sun was beginning to set. The day was starting to come to an end and unfortunately so was their walk. Before reaching the point of separation, Brittany recalled, "I remember when you lived just a couple of streets over from me."

"That seems like so long ago, a completely different life. A different world."

Brittany wasn't sure she wanted to know the answer, but she asked anyway, "How did you get over… you know what your Dad did? I mean have you forgiven him?"

"Hmm." Erica was taken aback from the question. "He's never asked for my forgiveness. To be honest, I don't think he believes he did anything wrong. But if he did ask me, I think I would say yes, I forgive you."

"Really? How could you?" Brittany asked, amazed.

"Because I don't want to live with the anger and bitterness that is destroying my mother. People make mistakes, but it's the road they choose to travel that will either strengthen or consume them. Every choice has a chain reaction and affects everyone around them."

"But he left you and your mother with nothing. You lost your house, your way of life because he was selfish and chose another woman. How can you be so accepting?"

"Oh, believe me, I was furious in the beginning. I hated my father. I hated my mother. I blamed her for not keeping him at home. But in the end, I got so tired of trying to keep up with all the negative emotions. The only person I was hurting was myself. I wasn't hurting my father, he left. He's never looked back and started his new life."

Erica put two and two together and shared as much as she could with Brittany. "Everything changed when I had Madison. The rejection I felt from my father and my mother's disappointment in me didn't matter anymore. Madison showed me what love is, or what it should be. It's unconditional and given gladly. I owe it to her to give her the best life I can. I want to give her the best life no matter what I have to sacrifice," Erica confessed. "It was the choice I made… chain reaction." Trying to lighten the mood before they both headed home Erica said, "Do not judge or you will be judged."

Both girls giggled saying in unison, "Pastor John."

"Mommy, eat?" The sleepy voice from inside the carriage asked.

"I better get going, we don't want Madison to cause a scene. It's time for supper."

"Yeah. I've taken enough of your time, I'll see you tomorrow, Erica."

"I'll see you tomorrow. Come on Madison, let's get home."

Each girl went home to a different section of town, but tonight the distance between them didn't seem so far apart.

Brittany opened the front door and headed straight for the stairs ignoring her mother's calls from the kitchen. She slipped into her bedroom.

Linda took to the stairs like a soldier on a mission. She was in no mood to be trifled with. First, her husband called to say he had a late meeting again and wouldn't be home in time for dinner. Then, the school had called to verify Brittany's absence.

"Absence?" Linda was sure the secretary was mistaken. She suggested the secretary do her job and check the school attendance record again, then promptly hung up the phone. The office secretary called again confirming Brittany was not in attendance.

Linda burst through Brittany's bedroom door. Her left hand positioned on her hip while her right hand was busy pointing in Brittany's direction. "What do you think you are doing skipping school today? Do you want to get kicked off the cheerleading squad?"

"To be perfectly honest, I don't know what I want right now Mom." It was useless to quelch the tears welling up in her eyes.

"Brittany what's wrong? What happened? If it's that Pastor again, I swear I will run him out of town this very day."

"No, it isn't Pastor John."

"Then what? Where have you been?"

Wiping her eyes with the back of her hand Brittany didn't know what to tell her mother.

It had to be something she'd believe but bad enough to get Brittany this upset. "Steve and I had a terrible fight, and I couldn't go to school looking like a total mess. So, I went to Fisherman's Park." Brittany shared how she bumped into Erica Gray at the park.

Linda swiped a couple of tissues from the brightly flowered tissue box on the white polished desk and handed them to Brittany. "Here, clean yourself up, your face is a mess." Adding in a cold tone, "I'm a little disappointed to hear that you spent time with Erica Gray. I mean she really isn't the type of girl you should be associating with. Did anybody see you with her?"

"Mom, that is so mean. Erica used to be okay to hang around with."

"Things change. Now she's a whore with a bastard child and her mother is as nutty as a fruit cake. Now, did anyone see you?"

"I was at Fisherman's Park alone and Erica happened to be there with Madison, her daughter." Brittany tried a different approach. "You know Mom, Erica and her mother didn't ask for what happened to them. Her father left them for another woman. He sat by and watched them lose everything and didn't lift a finger to help them out."

"Hmm. Who can say what really happened? Maybe her mother could have tried a little harder or maybe she was cheating on her husband. We only have their word about what actually happened."

Brittany wanted to blurt out everything she saw earlier but kept silent. Not because she didn't think she could tell her mother. No, on the contrary she didn't think her mother would believe her. Instead, she warned her, "You never know Mom it could happen to anyone."

"Oh, don't be silly Brittany," Linda replied. "Don't go near Erica Gray again. I can't imagine what your real friends would think. Besides, I don't need the people of this town gossiping about me and my family. Do I make myself clear?"

"Crystal clear, Mom."

"One more thing, "I'll be driving you to school tomorrow."

Brittany nodded her head in agreement. Barely above a whisper Brittany said to her empty room, "Try and stop me from being friends with Erica."

The next morning Brittany woke up feeling stiff and sore. She stretched one leg then the other, wincing a little from the discomfort the stretch was causing. Still in her clothes from the day before, Brittany had laid awake in her bed as the hours passed slowly by.

She heard Joshua come in but not her father. She wasn't sure if he'd stayed in Boston like he sometimes did – it made perfect sense now.

Sacrifices are a part of life, Brittany, if you want to succeed and give the people you love everything possible, her dad had said.

"Liar!" Brittany cried. "You're nothing but a self-righteous, pompous, cheat!"

The minutes ticked by. She needed to take a shower. The last thing she wanted to hear was her mother complaining about being late. When she was done getting dressed and disguising her puffy eyes, she headed downstairs. Joshua was sitting at the breakfast bar inhaling his cereal. Her mother stood in front of the glass doors that led to the deck sipping her coffee.

"Morning," Brittany managed.

Taking a break from his cereal Joshua observed in between chews, "Boy Brit, you look rough. I was wondering why I didn't see you at the bowling alley last night. You sick or something?"

Before Brittany could reply her mother turned around and answered for her, "Josh you must have heard that Brittany and Steve got into a huge fight yesterday. Your poor sister developed a migraine and decided to come home and head straight to bed. Isn't that right,

Brittany?" Linda gave her no time to respond. "I didn't want to disturb her, so I just let her sleep."

Wow, she didn't realize how good her mother was at lying. Maybe her parents were more alike than even they knew. "Sure Mom."

Joshua stopped eating and looked at Brittany now sitting next to him. It wasn't so much her answer that set off alarms. It was the tone.

"I'm sure you and Steve will have whatever you argued over all worked out by the time you walk through the school doors this morning. Right?"

"I don't think so Mom, since I'll be walking into school with you. I'm not hungry right now, probably the lingering effects of that darn headache. I'm going to get my things and meet you in the front hall."

"Why are you driving Brit to school? I can drive her, we're both going to the same high school."

"Joshua, that is so sweet of you but I have a meeting with Vice Principal Porter and I want to let the office know why Brittany was out of school yesterday. But thank you for offering."

Okay, something was off. Really off. Were the two of them plotting with Porter to get rid of Pastor John? Joshua was resolved to find out.

Brittany sat on the stairs in the front hall, her elbows on her knees with her chin resting in her hands.

"Brittany, what's really going on? I talked to Steve yesterday. He never mentioned you got into a fight. He was wondering where you were and why he hadn't seen you all day?"

"If he really wanted to know where I was or if I was okay, he could have called or texted me, but he didn't."

"Look you better not be in cahoots with Mom and Porter to get rid of Pastor John. I'm warning you, Brit."

Hearing keys jingling and her mother's footsteps Brittany stood up.

"I wouldn't do that and if I hear that Mom is, I'll let you know. I promise."

"Promise what?" Linda asked.

Brittany answered. "I promised to let Joshua know the next time I don't feel good and decide to leave school."

"Oh." Relieved Linda put on her red leather driving gloves and motioned to Brittany. "Okay, let's go Brittany. Joshua don't dawdle."

"Right." He said staring as the front door closed behind them.

CHAPTER 23
CONFRONTATIONS

Mandisa's music filled the room.

Sarah shot up from a deep sleep, rubbing her eyes to clear the fog, what the…Sharise?

Singing along, Sharise was up and out of bed dancing around the room as she made her way toward the bathroom. "Come on Sarah get up and get moving. It's a great day."

"Yeah, I've heard," Sarah groaned pulling the pillow to cover her ears.

"Come on Sarah time to get up. It's Fall Festival Day! *It's a good morning.*"

Sarah laid back down, staring up at the wall. "It may be a good morning, but it's going to be a long day!"

Dressed in their costumes from the moment they woke up, Ian Richardson, alias Spiderman, and Stella Richardson, the blond, sweet, faced Alice in Wonderland, were excited. It was Halloween and Fall Festival Day.

Mary sat at the kitchen table soaking it all up. She thoroughly enjoyed watching her two youngest children pretend remembering how she and her husband, Joseph, had watched Shelby and Lexy romp around the same way. "Oh, how I miss you, Joseph."

Working so much didn't bother Mary except when it interfered with family life. Thankfully she had Shelby. Selfless Shelby. Mary didn't know what she would do without her.

Mary had hoped Lexy would change her mind about going to the Fall Festival with Shelby. But in the end, she decided to go out with her friends from school. Mary recalled when she was Lexy's age how much fun it was going out with friends in the neighborhood. What harm could there be? Shelby had insisted they all go to the Fall Festival together. In some ways, Mary thought Shelby was more protective of the kids than she was. More like Joseph, she smiled feeling the deep ache just mentioning his name. "Will it always be like this?"

She picked Madison up from the floor. "Time for a nap." Heading for the stairs, Erica heard 'Knock. Knock.' Going over to the door with Madison in tow, she lifted the curtain window to see who it was.

Spying her father standing on the outside porch Madison screamed for joy, "Daddy!"

Tags waved happily at the joyous reception he was receiving and waited patiently for Erica to open the door.

"What brings you by this early?"

"I knew your mom wouldn't be here. I figured I'd come by and see you. I won't stay, I only wanted to say hi." He was feeling rather silly.

"Since you're here would you like to bring Madison up for her nap?"

"Really? I'm not sure what I should do," He replied fidgeting.

"I'll come with you, and we can put her down together."

"Sweet."

Erica remarked when they got back downstairs, "You did a good job up there with Madison. She loves having her daddy around."

"Thanks. I really enjoyed it. I can't tell you how much it means to me."

"Mom isn't due to come home for another couple of hours. Do you want a cup of tea or coffee? Some water?"

"How about a bottle of water."

"Here you go."

Tags sat down at the kitchen table watching Erica clean up Madison's lunch.

Ever since the blow up with Donna Gray a week earlier, Erica thought it would be best if they met at the library to have their bible studies, which was working out great. Erica recalled the first time the three of them walked into the library. Carriage and Bibles in hand. The librarian seemed a bit hesitant, but within a week it seemed like she actually looked forward to their visits. Madison won her over.

Spinning the water bottle in his hand Tags looked at Erica. "Erica, can I ask you something?"

"Sure," She answered still standing at the sink.

"Erica, can you turn around?"

Sensing the seriousness in his voice, Erica slowly turned around. "Do you want me to sit down?"

"Yeah, sure."

Erica pulled out the chair across the table from him.

"I'm just gonna cut to the chase. Okay?"

"Okay."

"Do you think we'll ever be together again?"

A lot of thoughts raced through Erica's mind. She loved Tags, but she wasn't going back to the way things were. This change in him was nice but she needed to see more, lots more.

"Joey, I love you and probably always will. This past week has been amazing, but…"

Tags interjected, "But?"

"But." Erica repeated. "It's only been a week. I would love nothing more than for you, me, and Madison to be a family. A real family. But if we are going to succeed as a family, we have to give up our old lives. You can't be selling drugs because that's not a life Madison or I can be a part of. God has to be the center of our life if we have any chance of making it. I can't explain it." Erica looked down at her hands and took a deep breath before continuing. "God gives me strength. He gives me courage and hope. He loves me unconditionally. Besides, Madison is the only constant in my life. If you agree then yes, I think we can be a great family."

"You ask a lot. How would I provide for you and Madison? I don't know any other way, Erica. I want to be the center of your lives, and you want God to be." Tags stood up and shook his head in disbelief. "Erica, I don't know what to say."

Erica didn't want to lose him; they'd come so far. She walked over to where Tags was standing and touched his arm. "Joey with God at my center I can love you and Madison, *completely*, so much more than I can without him. I know it's hard but we… you, me and Madison have to trust God."

"I don't know Erica, it's a lot to think about." Tags walked to the door with his hand on the knob not bothering to look at her he said, "I'll pick you and Madison up about 5:30," and walked out the door.

The Gallo house was tense this morning. Joshua couldn't explain it. His mother was already up and out, his father was locked away in his study. Maybe his parents had a fight. Something was up and he bet his sister was in the middle of it. She was not acting like herself, no jibes, no sarcasm.

Walking into the kitchen draped in the morning's bright sunlight, Joshua found his sister sitting alone at the kitchen table staring deeply into her teacup. "I don't think you'll find any answers in that cup of tea. It's probably not the right brand," Joshua joked.

"If only the tea could talk," Brittany responded.

Joshua grabbed a glass, and some freshly squeezed orange juice out of the refrigerator. He sat across from Brittany and poured. "So, what's up for tonight, Brit?"

"House party at Julie's."

"Not what you wanted to do tonight?" Joshua asked.

"It doesn't matter to me one way or the other."

That was it, he'd had enough, something was wrong, and he wasn't going to play this cat and mouse game any longer. "What's going on Brit? I know you and you're acting way out of character."

What did he want from her? Was she supposed to tell him she went to surprise their father the other day in Boston and instead she was the one that got surprised? After everything she'd done and said over the years there was no way Joshua would believe her. He'd ask, *'What's your angle Brit?'* Getting up from the table she thanked her brother for his thoughtfulness. "It's probably growing pains. I'm bored, that's all." That was more like the arrogant Brittany everyone knew.

It was almost 4:00 in the afternoon when Linda poked her head into Joshua's room. "Are you going to Julie's Halloween party tonight?"

"No, why?"

"Okay, you can help me give out candy tonight to the trick or treaters."

"Sorry Mom, I have other plans," Joshua quickly added.

"What other plans?"

"I'm going to The Cornerstone tonight, it's the Fall Festival." Seeing the stunned look on his mother's face Joshua rushed on. "I've been part of the planning committee for a few weeks now."

Regaining her composure Linda asked, "The Cornerstone, the Christian church downtown?"

"Yeah, why?"

"Does Pastor John and his daughter have anything to do with this Fall Festival?"

"Well, Sarah is on the planning committee, along with other kids like Sharise, Titus, Lewis, Shelby. It's not Pastor John's festival, Mom, it's Pastor Peter's. He's been doing it in Gilford for years. What's the big deal?"

"I'll tell you what the big deal is. Ever since that pastor and his daughter showed up in town there has been nothing but chaos. Holy rollers, that's what they are. Did you know he wrote a book? A bunch of phonies. This town and its unsuspecting people are probably the newest chapters in his second book. I don't like them and I don't trust them. Shoving their ways on everyone, converting our students without a parents' permission." Linda's voice was getting higher and higher with each sentence.

Joshua had heard enough. He was sick of the double standard. "Funny Mom, you don't ask permission from the teachers shoving their liberal ideas on us. If we disagree with their ideas, those open-minded liberal teachers flunk us. I thought learning was about open discussion not "my way or the highway." You're offended because someone has a different point of view. At least he's open to hear what the students have to say. We get to discuss everyone's opinion, that's what has you so pissed off?"

"Joshua Anthony Gallo, don't you dare talk to me like that." Hearing the loud exchange, Anthony came running from the master bedroom to the hallway where Linda and Joshua stood toe to toe.

"Alright. Alright." Anthony said stepping in between the two. "What's all this yelling about?"

"I don't want Joshua going to the festival at that church tonight. He should stay home and help me give out candy. Brittany is going out and you have to work again. I refuse to be the only person in this house that does everything," Linda ended with the pout she used to get her own way.

"Dad, I've been working on this festival for weeks and because Mom has something against the church and the people that go to it, I have to be punished?"

"Is this a cult or something?" Anthony asked Joshua.

"No," "Yes," Both Linda and Joshua said simultaneously.

"Dad, it's The Cornerstone Church downtown, it's been there for decades."

"Oh yes, the big one downtown. As a matter of fact, I know a couple of lawyers who go to that church. A little too strait-laced for me, but normal people none the less."

Turning to his wife Anthony agreed with Joshua. "Linda, if he's been planning this for weeks, you can't tell him the night of the festival he can't go. Be reasonable," Anthony pleaded. He wanted this to go away, he had his own plans for the night.

Out of the shadow came a small voice. "I'll stay home with you Mom, I don't mind missing the party. Really, I don't."

"There it's all settled. Brittany will help you tonight and Joshua can go to his fall whatever it is." Anthony stated with a wave.

"Festival, Dad."

"Festival," he repeated directly to Joshua. Turning to his wife he asked a little too condescendingly, "Is that okay with you, Linda?"

"You're missing the point as usual Tony. No, it's not okay. I don't care what any of you do tonight. Go. Stay. It really doesn't matter to me," Linda said storming off.

Joshua walked into his room, then he thought about thanking Brittany for offering to stay home. Instead, Joshua settled on cutting through the bathroom he and Brittany once shared before she took it completely over. He came to an abrupt halt before entering her bedroom.

"It looks like we're on the same page after all. I was beginning to worry about you, Brittany."

"What? That I'd let your little secret out?"

"Oh Brittany, so young, so naïve. You'll understand more when you're older. There are some men that like to live on the edge, live in the moment, the excitement, push the limits. It's not like this little fling is going anywhere. It's nothing. Means nothing. Think about it… deep down I think your mother knows, but she chooses to ignore it. For the family, you know how she hates messes Brittany. So, if she can, you should too."

"Do you really believe what you're saying?" Brittany asked.

"Of course, I do. So did my father and his father before him. It's the way of the world. The sooner you learn these things the better off you'll be." Hesitating Anthony asked once more, "We are on the same page right, Brittany?"

"And if I wasn't?"

Leaning in a bit closer to her to make his point he said, "Let me put it another way, in a way you'll better understand. Let's say you go to your mother and tell her your little tale. Who would she believe? You? You've done an incredible job of putting Brittany first. Always making up stories to the detriment of others only to benefit Brittany Gallo. Maybe Daddy would say he wasn't going to buy you a new car or where is it that your friends want to go during spring break?"

"Aruba," She whispered looking down at the floor.

"Aruba. I'm having second thoughts about that trip. I don't think it's safe for my little girl. Look at me, Brittany." Looking at the floor Anthony took his daughter's chin and pushed it upward to look at his face." So you understand. Don't think you can play games with me, my name, or my livelihood. I've been at this a long time, long before you were a twinkle in your mother's eye. I always win."

If Brittany was being truthful with herself about changing her ways, there was no better time to declare it than now. "From a very young age, I idolized you. You were my knight in shining armor. My hero."

The tears flowed, but she stayed firm. "But when I saw you in the arms of another woman kissing her and laughing without a care in the world everything that you were came crashing down. I saw you for the liar and cheat you are. When you said we were cut from the same cloth you were saying I was a liar and a cheat too. The whole train ride home I had to confront who I am. A selfish, spoiled brat who always got what she wanted no matter who she hurt along the way. I didn't like what I saw. You keep your secret life but know this, I will never be a part of it, and I will never be anything like you."

"You're right. You are nothing like me. I'm a winner, Brittany. A winner, and don't you forget that."

Joshua was ready to pounce on his father.

Just then, Linda yelled from the bottom of the stairs. "In case anyone is interested I made burgers and fries. Even though you're all deserting me, at least I'll know you'll have a full stomach while you do it. Now let's go."

Anthony walked downstairs.

Brittany stood at the entrance of her room watching him go. Joshua got to his sister's side and gave her a big hug.

"It's okay, Brittany. You're right, you're not like him and never will be."

CHAPTER 24
FALL FESTIVAL

Children of all ages were dressed up like their favorite story book characters. Little Red Riding Hood, Snow White and Mickey Mouse followed closely by Minnie were waiting to dunk for apples. Donuts hanging from strings held the attention of Spiderman and a cowboy. Still others stood in line waiting to get their face painted dancing to Toby Mac's "Funky Jesus Music."

Lily stood in the doorway not sure which way to turn when she heard a familiar voice calling her name.

"Lily Rivera, what a lovely surprise!"

"Hi, Mrs. Taylor," Lily answered. Louise Taylor walked toward her.

"If you're looking for your friends, they're all about." Louise informed her with a swoosh of her arm. "You'll have to scoot yourself down the hall towards the Sanctuary." Sensing Lily's uneasiness Louise asked gently, "Is there someone you're looking for?"

"Um, Paul. Paul Russo?"

"Well, you'll find him down the hall, that's where the face painting is." Louise smiled. "Go on now, he could probably use some help." Louise steered her in the right direction.

Lily found Paul sitting calmly on a stool talking to a little boy dressed up like Batman. Paul was painting away like he was Picasso on the little boy's cheek.

"Well, I think that will do it," Paul announced putting his paint brush down on the paper plate.

"Let me see? Let me see?" Batman insisted.

"Okay, hang on there. Are you ready?" Paul asked holding the mirror.

"Yes!" Batman cried.

"Tada!"

"Wow, they look so cool!" Exclaimed the little boy looking at the black and blue Batman symbols on both cheeks. Batman ran past Lily yelling, "Mommy, Mommy look at my cheeks."

"Lily, you came." Paul smiled.

"I did." Lily replied adding. "I heard you could use some help."

"Yes, I can." Paul pointed to the never-ending line of characters. "Grab a seat and some paint and let the creativity begin,"

Turning back to the crowd of kids Paul announced, "Look you guys, Miss Lily is here to help with the face painting."

Cheers and claps erupted. Lily found some paint and brushes and sat down on the stool next to Paul. "You know I can't draw worth a lick."

"It's okay, neither can I and they haven't yelled at me yet," Paul joked.

Sarah and Joshua were at the popcorn machine making sure no one went without.

"You've been quiet tonight, is everything okay?" A stoppage in the flurry of activity prompted Sarah to ask Joshua.

"I just have a lot on my mind, that's all."

"I didn't mean to meddle. It's just I can tell something's off."

"Family issues and to be perfectly honest, I haven't really wrapped my head around it yet."

"If or when you're ready to talk, I'll be here. But for tonight, quiet can be good."

Erica was having Madison's face painted with colorful balloons, so Tags decided to go search out Pastor John; he had a few questions.

Finding John by the sound system, Tags shouted over the music. "Hey, Pastor John, can we talk for a minute?" Instead of replying John shook his head to let him know he could and led the way out to an office at the front of the church.

"Looks like Madison and Erica are having a good time tonight," John observed.

"Yeah, I guess."

"What can I help you with?"

"Pastor John I've been hoping that one day me, Erica, and Madison would be a family. You know a real family. But she doesn't see it that way. Well, that's unless I give up certain things. The problem is if I give up these certain things how am I supposed to provide for the two of them?"

"Looks like you're at a crossroad, Tags."

"It's not that easy, Pastor John. I have no education, they pass me from grade to grade because they don't want to deal with me. How am I supposed to make a living? Washing dishes?"

"I think you're missing the big picture, Tags. Erica doesn't care how you make your living as long as it's honest. I don't get it you go to school every day, why don't you do the work?"

"Funny Pastor John. Sometimes you're a real funny man. I'm so far behind I could never catch up. I go so I can see Erica and besides I don't have anywhere else to go."

"Tags, what do you feel when you read from the Bible? When you and I go over different passages do you feel anything?"

"Honestly?"

"Yes, honestly."

"You won't laugh at me, right?"

"I would never laugh at you, Tags."

"I feel great like I can do anything, that maybe God thinks I'm worth something."

"You are worth something Tags, and you can do anything you put your mind to. Joseph Taglio, you are a child of the most high God, an heir to His kingdom. When you give yourself to God you are giving Him reign over your life in all ways, food, clothing, provisions. *Don't worry about anything; instead, pray about everything. Tell God what you need and thank him for all he has done. Then you will experience God's peace, which exceeds anything we can understand. His peace will guard your hearts and minds as you live in Christ Jesus."* Philippians 4:6-7

"Easy for you to say you have everything. I've got nothing. Nothing! Never have. I tried trusting people and look where it's got me."

Looking off into the emptiness of the room John stared into the pain still lurking within the walls of his heart. "No Tags, I don't have everything. Believe it or not, I'm really just like you. Behind this infectious smile you see," John joked, "I have questions and doubts, too."

Turning more serious, John shared, "A big part of my everything, my Abby..." Collecting himself, he reminisced. "Abby told Sarah and me that God had something special planned for us. She could feel it in her heart. I thought it was the work in Nebraska, but now I know that was just the beginning. Abby said to never give up or back away from your path. Embrace it and God will direct you."

"Pastor John? You, okay?" Tags asked.

"I believe I am. Tags, whether you know it or not, you have everything, a woman and a daughter who love you and a God who wants to shower you with his love. Don't give up on yourself Tags, because it can be taken away in an instant. God isn't going to give up on you and neither will I."

200

"Okay."

"You need to know what kind of man God wants you to become. Are you up for a challenge?"

"I guess."

"I'd like to introduce you to another Joseph. He went through some pretty difficult times. But, he never gave up on God even when he thought God had given up on him. I'd like you to read in the Book of Genesis, Chapters 37 through 50."

"The Book of Genesis?"

"Yes, it's the very first book of the Bible in the Old Testament. There are 50 chapters in this book, but I only want you to read about the life of Joseph, Jacob's son".

"Joseph, huh, like me. Is he important?"

"Very important. Promise me if you have questions, you'll write them down and we'll go over them together?"

"Yeah. Sure."

"And Tags, please don't make any life decisions until you have finished the chapters. Agreed?"

"Agreed." Heading out of the office Tags felt compelled to add, "Um, Pastor John, I'm really sorry about Abby. I mean it sounds like she was really something."

"She was and still is. God does provide Tags. He left a very distinct part of her in Sarah. Every time I look at my daughter, I am reminded of Abby and of God's promise that one day we'll all be together again."

Tags was about to ask what he meant that they would all be together again, when a familiar voice rang out.

"There you are, we've been looking all over for you. Right Madison?"

Agreeing with her mother Madison reached out her chubby little arms to Tags saying, "Dada."

"Come here you, look at all those red and yellow balloons on your cheeks." He snuggled her neck releasing shrieks of joy from his princess.

Cleaning up after the festival, Pastor Peters stuck his head into the kitchen and asked the group of teenagers if he could have a few words with them before they left. Sharise, Titus, Paul, Lily, Sarah, and Joshua found Pastor Peters inside the sanctuary. The tired group sat down on the first pew while Pastor Peters finished what he was doing.

"I've spoken to Lewis and Pastor John about the spare room, and I've been watching all of you the past couple of weeks." He paused for a moment and could tell they were on the edge of their seats. "I think you are well behaved and responsible young adults. It might be a good idea if someone were to use that back room for something positive. So… if you want to use it for your weekly bible studies and small group gatherings, I'm all for it." Jumping out of the pews, clapping, and smiling at one another, the teenagers were ecstatic.

"But remember," Pastor Peters cautioned, "this is the house of God, treat it as such."

"Yes, sir!"

"Yes, Pastor Peters!"

"Thank you!"

"Thank you!"

"I've given Lewis the key and I believe he said something about getting together to clean up that old room." Pastor Peters turned, chuckling all the way down the hallway.

Although they were totally exhausted from the activities of such a long but rewarding night the small group of teenagers were intoxicated with the idea of having their own sanctuary.

On the drive to Shelby's house Lewis told her the news of Pastor Peters allowing the group to use the back room. "Of course, we will have to clean it up with all that dust and those cobwebs lurking around."

"That is one dirty room, but we can definitely fix it up and make it sort of homey."

"Homey? What kind of word is that? I wonder what the other kids will think of the room being…homey." Lewis teased.

"Ah, that's not what I meant." Shelby blushed. "It will be cool but still have that sense of warmth."

"I knew what you meant. I just couldn't resist teasing you." Lewis smiled.

Ian and Stella were sound asleep in the back seat of Lewis' Jeep Wrangler and missed their playful banter. Arriving at the Richardson's home, Shelby reached in back to wake the little ones when she noticed Lewis's quizzical expression and followed the direction of his eyes.

Something or someone was slumped over on the lawn in front of her house. Lewis and Shelby jumped out of the car and ran over to the figure. Dropping to her knees Shelby knew immediately it was Lexy. Turning her face toward the streetlight in an effort to see her better, Shelby gasped at the sight.

"We need to get her to the hospital. I'm calling 911," Lewis spoke in a serious tone.

"Lexy, wake up. Come on Lexy!" Shelby cried shaking her sister's limp body. Lexy felt cold and clammy. Her lips had a bluish tint and her breathing was shallow.

Shelby could hear sirens in the distance. Lewis knelt next to her and looked down at Lexy. "Shelby, I think you should call your mother and let her know what's happened. She needs to meet us at the hospital."

Shelby didn't respond instead she tried shaking Lexy again. "Wake up Lexy? Please?"

"Shelby, go into the house and get a blanket for Lexy." Lewis took over.

Shelby didn't move.

"Shelby," Lewis demanded grabbing her shoulders, "go into the house and get Lexy a blanket now."

Shelby looked at Lewis, jumped to her feet and ran into the house. Lewis laid Lexy on her side with her arms over head. Bending down he listed to her breathing, it was shallow but she was breathing. Then he called Mrs. Richardson.

Shelby came running back out of the house with a blanket in hand and draped it over Lexy's shivering body. "She looks so small."

The sirens were just turning up her street when Lexy's body start to convulse. "No! No Lexy! Lewis, do something!' Shelby shouted.

"We have to make sure she doesn't hurt herself.

"Lewis the ambulance…it's here!"

The paramedics rushed over to Lexy. The seizure stopped as they checked her vitals and asked what happened. Getting the information they needed, the paramedics lifted Lexy onto the gurney and into the ambulance with Shelby on their heels.

A silver dodge van came screeching to the curb in back of the ambulance. Mary Richardson came flying out of the driver's seat. Shelby turned to see her mother running to catch up to her as the gurney was being placed in the ambulance. "Mom?"

"It's okay Shelby. Where are Stella and Ian?"

"In the car, asleep." Shelby said turning to Lewis's car, realizing she'd forgotten all about them.

204

"I need you to take Stella and Ian in the house and put them to bed. I'll call you as soon as I know anything."

"What? No, I'm going with you."

"We need to get her to the hospital now." One of the paramedics explained. 'Who's coming?"

"I am", Jumping into the ambulance with a pleading look, Mary begged Shelby, "Please Shelby, I need you now more than ever. Please help me with Stella and Ian. I promise, as soon as I hear anything I will call you." Leaving her with no choice, Mary looked at the paramedic and said, "Let's go." The doors shut tight and the ambulance went tearing down the street, sirens blaring.

Standing on the side of the street Shelby stared after the ambulance.

Lewis took Shelby by the shoulders. "Let's get the little ones into bed. I'll call Pastor John so he can meet your mother at the hospital. Maybe Sharise and Sarah can come and stay with Stella and Ian, so I can take you to the hospital. Okay?"

Tears streaming down her face Shelby, nodded in agreement.

CHAPTER 25
FREE WILL

At the hospital's emergency room Shelby and Lewis asked where they could find Lexy Richardson.

"Are you family?" Asked the woman sitting behind the desk.

"Yes, I'm her sister."

"And you?"

"I'm…" Lewis stuttered.

"He's, my brother. Please can we see her.?

Accepting Shelby's answer. The woman directed the two of them to follow her.

"Brother?" Lewis whispered to Shelby.

"Yeah, you are my brother in Christ, right?"

Lewis answered Shelby with a huge smile.

Escorting them down the hospital corridor, the woman stopped outside one of the rooms. "This is Lexy's room. You can have a seat for now, I believe the doctor is with her."

Pastor John was sitting in one of the chairs sipping a cup of coffee. Shelby rushed over to him

"How is she, Pastor John?" Shelby blurted.

John stood up and smiled slightly. "Good, now. She had her stomach pumped out and is hooked up to an IV to replenish her fluids. She is very fortunate you and Lewis came home when you did."

"Can we see her?"

"The doctor is in there talking with your mom and Lexy, but as soon as he's finished I think it should be okay to go in. Your mom could use the break. While we wait, why don't you both sit down and tell me what happened?"

Shelby filled Pastor John in on everything from the friends Lexy was hanging out with, to the guilt she feels for not putting a stop to Lexy's bad behavior.

"Whoa, Shelby you are not Lexy's mother and from the sounds of things I don't think Lexy would have listened to you anyway. She was lying to both you and your mother. Hopefully this scares her enough to make better choices."

"I hope so," Shelby replied with a hint of doubt. "Pastor John, can you talk to her, make her stop hanging around with those good for nothing…"

"Shelby, don't go there, these kids Lexy is hanging around with seem just as troubled as Lexy." Lewis placed his hand on Shelby's arm.

"He's right Shelby. There's a spiritual war going on, that's why choices matter." As John finished, the door to Lexy's hospital room opened and the doctor came out.

"Is it okay for us to go in?" Shelby ran to the doctor.

"I don't see why not but remember, Lexy has been through a lot tonight," The doctor advised.

"Lewis, why don't the two of you go on in? I'll wait with Mrs. Richardson," John suggested.

"I'll let her know you're out here," Lewis replied.

Mary came out of the room, her eyes were glistening and her nose red. Mary's hands were wringing the tissues she held. John stood up and guided her to an empty seat.

"Pastor John, what am I going to do?"

"Mrs. Richardson," John answered.

"Mary, please. Mrs. Richardson is much too formal from where I'm sitting right now."

"Mary. The first thing a person is tempted to do is blame themselves, but the truth is we can't control the choices others make. Maybe, if we had done this or that, it would have turned out differently."

"But Pastor John, if I had been home," Mary cried.

"Mary, you work because you have to, not because you want to. Even if you were home Lexy would have found a way. We can change the scenarios a thousand times in our minds, but the outcome will always be the same. The choices must be different."

"Then what can I do?" Mary asked.

"Give Lexy more choices. If you agree, I can talk to a couple of people. A lot is happening at the Cornerstone church Shelby's been attending."

"Pastor, at this point we need all the help we can get. I have noticed a change in Shelby."

"Good. At times like this I like to pray. If you would like to join me that would be wonderful. However, the choice is yours."

"I'd like that very much."

"Mary, the Lord said, *'I tell you the truth, if you had faith even as small as a mustard seed, you could say to this mountain, 'Move from here to there,' and it would move. Nothing would be impossible.'"* Matthew 17:20

"Thank you, Pastor John, for coming tonight and staying with us. I can't tell you what it means to us."

John gathered Mary's hands in his own, bowing their heads, John began, "Dear Heavenly Father…".

It was the start of a new week. The beginning of November and the middle month of the autumn season for the East Coast. Joshua noticed Brittany walking down the stairs and yelled to his mother,

"Mom, I'll drive Brittany to school today. And don't worry, I'll make sure she gets to class."

"Joshua, that would be great. I do have a few things to do this morning." Turning to Brittany standing on the last step of the stairs, she said, "Brittany, don't let me get another call from the school today. Understood?"

"Don't worry Mom. I've learned my lesson. I will not skip school again."

"I hope so, that was extremely embarrassing, thank goodness no one saw you."

In the car, Brittany thanked Joshua for the ride.

"No problem. I think you've been through enough this week. What do you think we should do?"

"About Mom and Dad?"

"Yeah, about Mom and Dad."

"I don't know. If we tell Mom, she'll only be mad at us for ruining her perfect world."

"And if we don't tell her?"

"I don't know Joshua, maybe we let them work this out on their own. They are the adults, aren't they?"

"Sometimes I wonder."

The remainder of the ride to school was in silence, each twin deep in their own thoughts.

Pulling up to Shelby's house, Sarah and Sharise decided to go to the front door and knock instead of beeping the horn. Mrs. Richardson answered the door, her hair hanging loose on her shoulders instead of in her usual ponytail. Dark circles underlined her eyes further revealing her exhausted state.

"Come on in girls, it's chilly out there," She said ushering the girls into the kitchen.

"Shelby should be right down. I'm staying home with Lexy today, she's still weak from her ordeal."

Sarah and Sharise nodded murmuring words of understanding.

Suddenly, Stella and Ian emerged filling the room with shouts of excitement.

"Mommy is taking us to school today! We don't have to take the bus," exclaimed Stella.

"Yeah, we don't have to take the bus!" Ian repeated.

"Wow, you guys are so lucky," Sarah replied.

"Okay. Okay. That's enough you two. Let's go upstairs and brush your teeth." Mary corralled them toward the stairs. Heading up the stairs Mrs. Richardson remarked, "Ian, where is your other sock?"

"What's so funny?" Shelby asked walking into the kitchen.

"Oh, just your cute-as-a-button little brother that's all." Sharise declared through her giggles.

"Yeah, cute-as-a-button until you live with him. Let's go. Sorry I'm late. I wanted to check in on Lexy before I left."

"Shelby, really? We're here for you, remember the Three Musketeers."

On their way to school, singing along to the Newsboys, Shelby blurted out, "I don't get it. Lexy doesn't want to tell the principal or the police what Jamie and Pete did to her."

"What do you mean?" Sharise asked turning the music down. "What did Lexy say?"

"She says they could have left her at the quarry but instead they helped her get home."

"Hmm."

"Hmm, is that all you can say? Lexy could have died. Sure, they brought her to the house, but they didn't alert anyone. They just dumped her."

"Shelby, we know you feel responsible for what happened to Lexy, but you can't. Just like you can't make Lexy do something she doesn't want to do. She'll have to figure this out on her own. Don't judge her, support her," Sarah suggested.

"I'm with Sarah on this one Shelby," Sharise echoed.

"Easy for you guys to say, she isn't your sister."

"No, she's not. But she's yours and what you go through we go through, together."

"Again, I'm with Sarah on this one too, Shelby."

"Argh!" Shelby groaned knowing she couldn't argue their point, even if it didn't change how she felt.

Walking toward her locker, Brittany stopped to watch the exhibition her best friend and boyfriend were putting on.

"Ahem," Brittany cleared her throat loudly. The two jumped apart stammering for words.

"Did you two had a good time at the party last night?"

"I've got to get to class. I'll catch up with you later Brittany." Steve announced, not one for confrontations.

Brittany opened her locker, reaching inside she got the books she needed for her morning classes. Julie was still standing beside her. Brittany tilted her head with a questioning glare. "Look Brittany."

Brittany held up her hand in front of Julie's face. "Save it for someone who cares."

Julie was left standing at her locker, her mouth hanging open and green eyes blazing.

Thinking she should be devastated by what just happened, Brittany was surprised that she really didn't care. Steve was never going to change; he was always about Steve and no one else. Sooner or later, it was going to happen, whether it was Julie or someone else. Her so-called friend would have to find that lesson out on her own.

Spying a friendly face, Brittany called out, "Hey Erica. Wait up?"

Erica saw Brittany heading towards her with a big smile on her face. Old feelings of panic and dread stirred deep inside her.

"Where are you headed?"

"Homeroom," Erica answered hesitantly.

"I know silly, what room?"

"104, why?"

"I'll walk with you I'm going to 105. Crazy that we have been next door from each other, and we didn't even know it." Brittany giggled.

"I guess." Not wanting to play this game any longer. Erica dared to ask. "What's up?" Puzzled by her question Brittany replied. "What do you mean?"

"I don't know. I just thought you'd keep your distance from me in school."

"Yeah, that would be something old Brittany would do, but not anymore. The other day at the park I was being truthful. I really am sorry for all the mean things I've done and said to you. You did not and do not deserve any of it. I want to be friends, truce?"

Erica looked down at Brittany's extended hand then looked up at her contagious smile and smiled in return. The two mismatched girls from opposite sides of the tracks stood in the middle of the crowded hallway and shook on a truce.

"Brittany, what's going on?" Andrea and Lisa confronted the two girls. Knowing this was her first test at being a true friend, Brittany turned looking at Lisa and Andrea she said, "Shaking on a truce with my friend Erica."

"Really?" They walked past Brittany and bumped Erica in the process. Holding their noses up high as if they couldn't stand the stench.

"Okay what's the game plan? You're pretending to be friends, why? What nasty little surprise do you have in store for Erica this time?" Once in homeroom Andrea walked over to Brittany and asked quietly.

"I hate to disappoint you Andrea, but I'm not playing any game. I'm serious. I have done some pretty mean stuff to Erica. We all have. I wanted her to know I was sorry and would like to be friends."

"You want to be friends with that little tramp? What about us, Brit?"

"Erica isn't a tramp; you don't know her. Besides it could have been anyone of us who was put in her predicament. We play Russian roulette every time we have unprotected sex," adding, "Andrea, why can't we all be friends?"

"Because she's not one of us, Brittany. Erica Gray made her choice. She let this town know exactly who and what she is. What's gotten into you?"

"Erica is a lot braver than we are."

Andrea looked at Brittany like she had lost her mind. "You're joking, right?"

Knowing it was a lost cause to even attempt to try and explain how she felt, she moved on to see how brave and trusting a friend Andrea really was. Brittany stood up from her seat towering a good couple of inches over Andrea. She wanted to see her friend's reaction. "Andrea did you go to Julie's Halloween party?"

"Of course, I did," She answered reaching up to her short blond hair and twirling a piece between her fingers. A true tell when Andrea was nervous. "So did the rest of the squad and most of the football players. Why?" She finished a little too defensively.

"Is there anything you want to tell me?" Brittany asked watching Andrea's face progress through a plethora of emotions. The right thing would be for Andrea to tell Brittany what happened between Julie and Steve. "You missed a good party, nothing much to tell."

"That's the difference between a true friend Andrea and a phony one. You're only interested in yourself and what's good for Andrea. It's nice to know you don't have my back, that way I don't spend a lot of time and energy on a friendship that really doesn't exist." Brittany sat back down and opened her book letting Andrea know she was dismissed.

Huffing loudly for the entire class to hear. Andrea quickly turned on her heels and walked purposefully to her seat slamming her book bag on the floor.

CHAPTER 26
AN IDEA EMERGES

When cleaning was complete the group stood back observing their handiwork.

"What are we going to sit on?" Titus mentioned the elephant in the room.

"Maybe we can use the folding chairs in the kitchen?"

"Problem with that is we'd have to put them away every time we use them."

"Plus, you never know when the church will need them."

"Um, I have an idea." Lewis jumped into action. He sent an emergency email out to the parishioners at Cornerstone. The response was immediate. By Saturday afternoon, the group received so many donations they ended up donating whatever they couldn't use to the women's shelter in town.

Surrounded by a sense of comfort and relaxation, the gathering room was perfectly 'homey'. Two overstuffed chairs that were patched in spots to hide old tears were tucked cozily into the corners. An old beat-up brown leather couch made its home alongside the longest wall with a handmade crotched blanket designed with colorful autumn squares of Alpaca yarn draped on its back like fallen leaves. It was perfect for those long cold Northeastern nights. Tucked away under the window stood a small rectangular card table surrounded by four, shaky fold-up chairs. More folded chairs were stored in the small alcove under the pitch of the roof at the back of the room. They decided to call this The Gathering Room.

After service on Sunday, Louise and Dwayne invited Pastor Martin Peters and his charming and delightful wife, Delores to dinner.

Louise made her famous mouthwatering, finger-licking fried chicken along with mashed potatoes, yellow corn, green beans, and rolls dripping with butter.

When dinner was finished Sarah and Sharise offered to clean up while the adults made their way into the living room coffee in one hand and plates of Delores's freshly made blueberry cobbler topped with vanilla ice cream in the other.

Everyone was relaxed and filling their mouths with blueberries when Martin asked John how things were going at the high school.

"It seems to be going well. Some of the students attending detention are becoming more responsive."

"Really, how so?" Martin asked.

"Well, the students won't leave until I give them a passage from the Bible to go home with."

"That sounds encouraging, do I hear some hesitation in your voice?"

"I don't know, I feel like we're missing something," John answered with some frustration in his voice.

"Missing, like what?" Louise asked jumping into the conversation.

"In Nebraska, we would do things together whether it was hiking, fishing, camping. But I guess everything in good time."

"It's too bad it's November and not the end of the school year. The church owns a retreat right on the beach, and we just completed some much-needed renovations on the buildings. We added insulation and updated the plumbing. Why we even put in a couple of wood burning stoves. It's all set to use come the spring. Unfortunately, you and Sarah will be back in Nebraska by then."

A sense of sadness fell over the room. Not wanting the evening to end on a somber note Dwayne's jovial spirit kicked in as he began to go down memory lane.

"I remember camping out there quite a few times. Remember Louise, there were some fun times spent there swimming, playing

216

volleyball in the sand and those bonfires at night toasting marshmallows. Hmm, hmm! Those were some good times."

"Oh yes. And smores, Dwayne. Don't forget the smores," Louise exclaimed excitedly. "Sharise and D.J. loved it there."

"That sounds like a lot of fun Louise. Please promise me you'll make sure the youth group takes advantage of the facility. It will definitely strengthen them as a group," John said.

Everyone was deep in conversation reminiscing about their time at the beach when John intervened. "Why can't we use the beach facility now? You said there was insulation, plumbing and electricity, a couple of wood stoves and a fire pit. It's exactly what we need."

John stood in the middle of the living room looking for a response. The adults were silent, then everyone began talking at once. There was such a commotion that Sarah and Sharise came running downstairs to see what was going on.

"Okay, hold up here. Hold up for a minute. John, don't you think it's a little late in the year? I mean that wind can come right off the ocean and whip through the buildings at this time of year."

"Martin with all due respect, we are talking about kids: young, energetic, adventurous kids. They can pack flannels and bring sleeping bags."

"There are wood burning stoves," Dwayne interjected.

"Yes, there are." Turning to John, Martin asked, "John, are you sure about this?"

"I am. There are some things I need to share with these kids. They have to be able to see and feel. I really believe with all my being Martin that God has placed this on my heart."

"Well, if you are serious about doing this and you really believe it's what God wants you to do, who am I to argue with God. However, I do think the sooner the better. The weather is only going to get worse as the year goes on. After all, we are in New England." He smiled as everyone shook their heads in agreement.

"If I may Martin, I'd like to extend the invitation to my classes at the high school. As a field trip?"

"If you're going to go forward with this camp out you might as well go all the way, but you'll have to get permission from the principal."

Louise jumped up getting caught up in all the excitement. "Dwayne and I will be chaperones. You'll need chaperones John, maybe we can even get the principal to volunteer?"

"We still have to pick a date. What weekend do you think would work best?" John asked.

"What about the weekend after Thanksgiving, it's a long weekend," Sharise suggested.

Everyone turned toward the kitchen doorway realizing Sarah and Sharise were standing there listening to their lively conversation. Rushing over to Sharise, John planted a big kiss on her cheek. "Perfect! Thanksgiving weekend is the perfect time for the campout. We don't have much time, so I'll speak with Krystina tomorrow morning and get the permission slips ready."

"Awful sure of yourself John. Are you always this confident?" Martin asked.

"If God is for us, who can ever be against us?" Romans 8:31

"I'm afraid once he feels the hand of God, it's hard to stop that running train," Sarah shared.

The next morning couldn't come soon enough. John found himself in Krystina Davis's office with Louise with him for support. "Before I commit to this field trip, John and Louise, I would like to go and see the campsite myself.

You understand first and foremost, I am the principal at Gilford High

School, and I cannot take chances with any of the students who attend here. Safety is my priority," Krystina expressed.

"We totally understand your position Krystina and agree, but time is of the essence. If we want this to happen Thanksgiving weekend, we should do it as soon as possible. How about after school today?" John threw out.

"How about we meet at the campsite at 3:30 today?" Louise suggested. With everyone in agreement, John and Louise left Krystina's office as Linda Gallo walked into Karl's office.

"I wonder what that's all about?" Linda asked.

"I don't know but I will find out," Karl snarled

"Make sure you do Karl. I want that Pastor and his daughter out of this town as soon as possible. They've wreaked enough havoc on my family." Stepping a bit closer Linda finished. "Karl, if you want to be principal of Gilford High School, you'll get those wheels in motion." Smiling sweetly, Linda turned and walked out of the school office.

Sweat beaded on his brow. Linda was a vicious woman. Thank goodness he was on her side, for the moment anyway. He had to find a way to get rid of Pastor John and his daughter. Nothing was going to stop him from crushing Krystina and becoming principal. The Pastor was bound to slip up sooner or later and Karl would be there to take him down.

Since Halloween, Shelby was in the habit of walking Lexy to her classes when she could. It was during one of these times that Shelby spied Jamie walking towards them. Eyes locked on her target Shelby went straight for Jamie and lifted her up by the collar against the school lockers. The girls came running over with Lexy in the lead.

"Shelby, what are you doing? Take your hands off her."

"After what she did?" Shelby shouted in Jamie's face pulling her fist back. The hall was beginning to fill with students murmuring and fingers pointing.

Sarah, the voice of reason, laid it out. "The way I see it you have two choices; you can let go of Jamie right now and walk away. Or you can punch her in the face which in the end, will make you twice as angry with yourself, and Lexy very upset with you." Not wanting to excite Shelby anymore or have this scene go on any longer Sarah persisted, "What's it gonna be, Shelby?"

Shelby felt such rage but one look at Lexy's pleading face told her Sarah was right. Shelby's fist hit the locker beside Jamie's head with a loud bang. Shelby put Jamie down and let go of her, but not before she said, "Don't ever go near my sister again. Do you understand?"

Jamie shook her head and took off as fast as she could. Shelby rubbed her right hand and walked away from the crowd of onlookers, Lexy, and her friends.

John realized he had detention class after school, turning to Louise he explained his dilemma.

"John, if it's alright, I'll show Kristina the campsite?" Louise asked.

"You of all people would know the site inside and out. But I don't want to inconvenience you, Louise."

"Inconvenience me!" Exclaimed Louise. "John, I'm the one who brought you to Gilford, you just get working on those permission slips. Let me handle Krystina. Not only is she going to love the campsite, but she'll be one of the chaperones." With that upturned smile of hers, Louise stopped in front of the nurse's office. "I'll meet you back at the house later today and we can plan our next step."

"You are a mighty warrior, Louise Taylor."

CHAPTER 27
INTENTIONS

The bell rang announcing the end of detention. John looked up and noticed no one was moving.

"Oh right." Grabbing his Bible, he flipped through the pages until he found what he was looking for. *"Trust in the Lord with all your heart; do not depend on your own understanding. Seek his will in all you do, and he will show you which path to take."* Proverbs 3:5-6

John placed his Bible back in his briefcase. He looked up, everyone was still in their seats. "You do know detention is over?"

"What does it mean?" one voice asked.

"Yeah, can you explain it to us?" someone in the back asked.

John looked out over the sea of bobbing heads, then to the far-right corner at Tags.

John sat back down. A moment of teaching was at hand and patience was its subject.

Leaving for the day, Karl swore he heard voices as he walked through the empty hallway. Puzzled he walked toward them and came to the detention room. "It's almost 3:30." He moved close to the open door, making sure he was concealed. What he heard made him smile from ear to ear. "Got you!" Taking out his phone, he pressed record.

The last of the detention kids had left and only Tags remained. John looked up at the clock and couldn't believe his eyes. "Wow 3:45!" Glad he ran the sign-in sheet to Elaine before he got too involved with the students.

"That was incredible. How do you feel about the power of God now?" John asked.

"I think he works in mysterious ways," Tags replied.

"How are you doing with your assignment? You should be halfway through by now."

"A bit more than that. This Joseph dude has the worst luck. I mean first, his brothers want to kill him, but decide to sell him off instead. Although to be fair, he bragged a lot and was a snitch. Not good in my world."

"Obviously not good in his world, either."

John turned off the lights, thankful for the time God gave him with the students. Walking down the hall, Tag's cell phone went off. Looking at the text message he blurted out, "Oh crap! Sorry about that Pastor John. It's Erica, we have to pick up Madison." Running down the hall he shrieked, "I'm late!"

Louise was pacing, stopping every few minutes to peek out the front window. "Pastor John Wheaton, every day you walk through that front door between 3:15 and 3:20. Today of all days, you decide to change it up."

Abandoning her post for some chamomile tea, the doorknob turned and in walked Pastor John.

"Well, it's about time, where have you been?"

"Louise, I am so sorry. I had every intention of sprinting out that door at 3:00 but God had other plans."

"Other plans?"

"Remember I told you the kids wait for me to read them a passage before they head out?"

"Yes."

"I thought they were playing me, being wise guys. I didn't mind. I figured the joke was on them knowing God has a way of turning things around. And don't you know that's just what he did. Those kids wouldn't leave today until I explained what the passage meant." John plopped down on the couch. "It was one of the most memorable times of my life, Louise."

"That's wonderful, John. Maybe you should consider starting the class with a passage."

"That's a very good idea."

"Well, I have some news of my own if you would like to hear it?" Louise teased, walking into the kitchen.

"Right." John followed her.

"It was my only thought all day. I was literally counting down the minutes. Then detention happened. I am so sorry, Louise. How did it go? Did Krystina like the campsite?"

"Very good, yes and yes."

"Hallelujah, praise God!" John picked Louise up spinning her around.

Dwayne walked through the door and saw his wife in the Pastor's arms. "Pastor John there better be a good reason why you have my wife in your arms?"

Turning to see Dwayne, John put Louise down and rushed over to Dwayne to give him a hug.

"God is good, Dwayne."

Lips pursed and one eye raised, Dwayne looked over at Louise.

"Krystina approved the field trip. Minimum of 10 up to a maximum of 25 students."

"All right," Dwayne hooted.

In a quiet café off Main Street, Karl and Linda were making their own plans.

"This is perfect Karl, we can use this," Linda confirmed holding up his phone. "How dare he keep our children captive while he brainwashes them."

"Well, I don't think he held those kids captive. I'd say it was the other way around," Karl chuckled.

"Karl, don't you want to become the principal of Gilford High School?"

"Of course."

"Good, let's start again. Pastor John held these poor students captive. Detention is over at 3:00 and it was after 3:30 when you realized they were being held against their will. That's when you started recording."

"That's exactly what happened."

"The most sensible and mature approach is to bring a snippet of the recording to the school board. No use burdening them with the entire recording. Pastor John has overstepped his boundaries. Don't you agree Karl?"

"I do, I do. It's our duty to protect our students."

Jumping out of his car and sprinting down the cobbled lane, Lewis checked his watch and didn't notice the girl walking up the path until it was too late…the two collided.

"Are you okay?" Lewis asked.

Lexy looked up into Lewis's wide and worried eyes.

"I am so sorry. I wasn't paying attention.

A deep blush crept up Lexy's face. "I'm fine, really. Maybe a little startled and a bit embarrassed is all."

Straightening themselves out the two looked at each other and chuckled.

"Lexy what are you doing out here when everyone else is inside? Is everything okay?

"Oh, I invited someone to come to youth group tonight and I didn't want her to walk in alone."

"That's really nice of you Lexy. I'd better get inside. I'll see you and your friend in a little bit."

Lewis continued down the path to the youth group's new home. He stopped just outside the door and listened to the wonderful sounds emerging out from inside. "Thank you, God."

Lexy was about to give up and go back inside when a car pulled into the church parking lot at the edge of the pathway. A girl with long blonde hair tied up in a ponytail stepped out of the car.

"Bye, Mom."

"I am so happy you came. I was beginning to think you weren't coming," Lexy exclaimed.

"Believe me, I thought about it at least a hundred times tonight. I have no idea how your sister is going to react. To be honest, I'm really nervous." Jamie admitted.

"I know. I'll be right by your side. Shelby always tells me to put God to the test, so... God, we are asking for your help tonight. Please let Shelby stop being mad and see Jamie for the kind and caring person she is. Amen." Lexy grabbed Jamie's hand. "Okay let's go, no turning back now."

The group had decided to begin each gathering in prayer. Lewis was about to begin when the door swung open. sweeping the cold November chill into the room. Two familiar faces stood at the door.

"Lexy, you found your friend. Why don't you introduce her to the group?" Lewis recommended.

Shelby shot up from her chair and screeched accusingly at Lexy. "How could you bring her here?" Shelby's disdain was evident.

Jamie panicked and went for the door.

"Please, wait." Lexy grabbed her arm.

Jamie stopped and turned with her eyes looking down at the floor. Lexy could feel her shaking. Lewis stood up ready to spring into action.

"Shelby, you're the one telling me how God forgives us when we do wrong. This whole time I've been struggling with my bad attitude, what I put everyone through. I've been humiliated and embarrassed."

"Lexy," Shelby tried to interject.

"No Shelby, let me finish. Am I supposed to believe that God can forgive me, but he can't forgive Jamie?"

"That's not what I'm saying, and you know it, she's trouble." Shelby pointed at Jamie.

"Yeah, well then, I'm trouble. No one made me do anything I didn't want to do. I could have said no."

"Right. So what." Shelby snorted. "Then her and her minion Pete would have pressured you."

"Would they have pressured you, Shelby?"

"Heck no".

"What makes you so much better than me?"

"What?"

"Maybe this isn't the place for me. I thought God said, 'Do not judge others, and you will not be judged. For you will be treated as you treat others.' Matthew 7:1-2 Isn't that what you said to me. Were you lying to me, Shelby?"

Shelby didn't know what to say.

"Shelby?"

When did my younger sister become wiser than me? Tears streamed down her face. Shelby went over to Lexy and hugged her tightly. "You are so right. I've been filled with so much anger. I felt like it was my fault. I should have protected you. I let you down."

"Oh Shelby." Lexy sobbed. "You're the best big sister in the whole world. You work so hard at home with us kids. At school, always sacrificing. You weren't supposed to be the one in charge Shelby. I think the two of us have been so mad that Dad died. He used to take care of everything and then…he didn't."

Erica jumped up and grabbed the box of tissues from the card table and handed them out to anyone needing one, including herself.

Shelby turned to Jamie. "It took a lot of guts for you to come here tonight, especially after what happened at school."

"At school? What happened in school?" Lewis asked.

"Shhh!" Titus and Sharise demanded, both riveted by what was happening.

Lewis looked around and saw everyone sitting on the edge of their seats captivated.

"Hi, I'm Shelby, Lexy's older sister. Welcome to youth group." Shelby extended her hand.

Hesitantly, Jamie reached out to shake Shelby's hand and said softly, "Very nice to meet you, my name is Jamie Welch."

One by one they gathered around Jamie to introduce themselves and welcome her.

"Phew." Crisis averted and a lesson taught. Lewis smiled. *'Lord this is a great beginning.'* Glancing to his right, he saw Lily sitting in her chair, her hands tightly gripped the edges. Staring at the wall directly in front of her, she seemed mesmerized by something, her forehead and nose were scrunched up.

227

Lewis looked but didn't see anything.

Then Paul tapped Lily's shoulder, and she was back in the room with everyone.

"Come on, let's meet Jamie." He motioned for her to join the others; she stood up to follow.

Even her smile is controlled, something is going on inside that girl's head. Lewis prayed that when the dam broke, she would be surrounded by love.

CHAPTER 28
ORDER OF THE DAY

John spotted Krystina walking into the school, he hoped she didn't have an early morning meeting. Louise mentioned that Krystina had drafted a permission slip to be signed by the students' parents before they could spend the night at the campsite.

"Good morning, Susan, Amy, ready to start a new week?"

"We certainly are Pastor John. It doesn't get any better than this." Amy smiled.

"Yeah, living the dream, right Amy?" Susan asked.

"Isn't that the truth."

"Is it okay if I speak with Krystina for a few minutes?" John asked.

"That's about all you'll get. She has a meeting with a parent in about 15 minutes. Now's your chance, go on in."

"Terrific. I promise I won't be that long." John knocked on the door.

"Come on in."

"Good morning, Krystina," John announced walking into her office. "I was hoping to speak with you about the field trip. The ladies out front informed me you have a parent coming in, so I'll make it quick."

"No worries. I wanted to connect with you today, please sit down. Louise showed me all around the campgrounds, it's an incredible site. There are three buildings, more like cabins that sit up on a hill overlooking the water. There's a short path running through a couple of sand dunes that takes you directly to the beach. And there's a good size fire pit for roasting marshmallows or making smores." Krystina was obviously smitten with the place.

Smiling, John listened to Krystina's animated description.

"How are the cabins arranged?" He asked already knowing the

229

answer after speaking with Louise. But, he enjoyed Krystina's attention to detail.

"There are two medium-sized cabins for sleeping. Of course, the girls will stay in one cabin and the boys in another. The larger cabin is in between them and houses the kitchen. It has two stoves and a dining room. Each building has bathrooms and the two sleeping quarters have showers. Oh, there's a generator just in case we lose power." Krystina concluded.

"It sounds impressive. I'm excited to see it." Realizing his reason for stopping in, he surged ahead. "Oh, Louise said something about a permission slip?"

"Oh yes, I almost forgot," Krystina replied reaching into the middle drawer and pulling out a sheet of paper. "My concern is that we don't get enough students to attend the campout. We need a minimum of ten students, and with the holiday weekend families tend to go away. It's just a little late to be announcing a campout on Thanksgiving weekend."

"Agreed. I better get some copies made and start handing them out if we want to reach at least the minimum." John took a copy of the sign-up sheet.

A knock sounded on the door. "That's my appointment."

"I'll let them in, and keep you updated."

"Thanks John."

Opening the door John almost got hit in the face with Linda Gallo's fist getting ready to bang louder on the door. Startled, Linda regained her composure. "My, my, if it isn't Pastor John Wheaton." And with a tilt of her head, "Still here?"

"Yes, for the semester." John was confused.

Bustling past John as if he didn't exist, Linda focused on Krystina. John sent Krystina a smile of encouragement and quietly closed the door.

"Good morning, Mrs. Gallo. You were a bit vague on the phone as to why you wanted to meet."

"Well, I hardly know where to begin."

Linda Gallo made no secret that she would rather have Karl Porter as principal of Gilford High School. Karl would make the perfect puppet for her.

"I always tell my students the best place to start is at the beginning."

"How original. It has come to my attention that Pastor Wheaton is now forcing his beliefs on students outside of his classroom This crosses the line. Who knows where all this insanity will go? I want to know exactly what you intend to do about it."

So much for not knowing where to begin. Krystina tried diplomacy. "I appreciate your concern, but this is the first I've heard these accusations. Is there a specific instance you're talking about?"

"Specific? I guess if you count holding an entire detention class hostage, teaching his ideology well past 3:30. Yes, I'd call that pretty specific."

"The detention class?"

"Did I mumble? I thought I was very clear."

"No. No. I heard you, I'm just a little surprised. I've had to oversee the detention class myself on more than one occasion. Most days the students that have detention don't show up or if they do, they're standing at the door waiting for the bell to ring. It's hard to imagine Pastor John holding any of those kids hostage thirty seconds past the bell."

Noticing Linda Gallo was not amused, Krystina decided to find a middle ground. "I will be happy to address your concerns. If I may. You said he was preaching outside of his classroom?"

"That's correct, I did.'"

Krystina shook her head. "I must tell you. The detention students are essentially Pastor John's other class now." Noticing the confusion spread across Linda Gallo's face, she added quickly, "I'm surprised you didn't know. Ever since Karl specifically requested Pastor John, he has been overseeing the detention class five days a week."

Linda Gallo's face contorted with unmitigated fury. Krystina could almost see the steam coming out of her ears. Jumping out of her chair, Linda gathered her coat then, pausing at the door Linda warned. "This isn't over. Pastor John and his repulsive daughter are poison. If you won't do anything about it, be assured I will."

Krystina stood up. "Mrs. Gallo, please sit down. I am not dismissing your concerns." Linda Gallo was out the door before Krystina finished her sentence. Linda swung open Karl's door and poked her head inside, "You weasel." She slammed the door with force and stormed out of the office.

Krystina did not like where things were headed. Why so much animosity toward Sarah? What could a sixteen-year-old do to her?

Sitting at his desk in the detention room, John sensed he was being watched. Looking up from the notes, he was compiling for the campout, he saw the students looking at him.

"Ahem," John asked, "What, did I forget something?"

Tags, the official spokesman for the straggly group, answered. "Pastor John, we were all wondering," pausing he scanned the room. "Right, you guys?"

"Yeah." "Sure." The group of misfits answered. Some gave quick nods and head pumps.

"If you wouldn't mind sharing with this group of uninformed students," Tags emphasized., "the great story of Joseph, how important he turned out to be."

"I see. Tags, does this mean you've finished the assignment?"

"To be perfectly honest Pastor, I finished a few days ago. I couldn't stop reading. I wanted to know how it was going to end."

"Okay." He shrugged. "The story of Joseph…"

John was still answering questions when the bell rang.

"Why was Joseph acting like such a punk?"

"Why did Joseph get the new coat?"

"Didn't his father realize his older brothers would be jealous?"

John was thrilled with the interaction. The students were placing themselves in the story. They realized not much has changed after thousands of years, a punk is still a punk and jealousy is still jealousy. What they were about to learn is what can happen when we act upon those feelings. Some actions have consequences, and they have rewards.

The next morning the last student barely made it in the door when John jumped up from his chair and walked to the front of the class.

"I am very excited to announce that Principal Davis has approved a fieldtrip for the am and pm God and Faith classes," John explained, waving a handful of papers in the air.

Sarah and Sharise were the only ones smiling. "The field trip is for an overnight campout at the campsite of Cornerstone Church on Harbor Side Beach." Within seconds, John was bombarded with questions.

"Overnight?"

"When?"

"Are there individual cabins?"

"Hold up. Come on, settle down. I'll go over everything and if you have questions after that, raise your hand in an orderly fashion, please."

The students quieted.

"Okay, good. Now, these are permission slips. For anyone who would like to go, they will have to get their parent's permission. Return the signed form to me as soon as possible," John emphasized, passing the slips out to the class. "We'll meet in the school parking lot at noontime on November 26th, the first Saturday following Thanksgiving, and return to the school parking lot on Sunday at 5:00 pm. There are two buildings or cabins for sleeping, one for the girls and one for the boys."

"No co-ed Pastor John?" Steve called out.

"Really Steve? No, absolutely no co-ed."

"Food will be taken care of, if anyone has a food allergy or if you take medication there is a spot on the slip. Your parent will need to fill it in. There's a list of what you will need to bring stapled to the permission slip. You'll notice your class Bibles are on the list, don't forget them. Alright, any questions?"

Immediately hands shot up.

Observing the time, John had a question of his own.

"Okay, my turn. Does anyone play guitar?"

"Paul does," Lily offered.

"I can play a bit," Paul returned.

"Not true. He's really good," Lily countered.

"Great, if you go on the field trip, could you bring your guitar?"

"Sure," Paul answered bothered by Lily volunteering him.

"My buddy Josh here, dabbles with the old guitar chords every now and then. Right, Josh?" Steve blurted out giving him an elbow.

Joshua's eyes widened. *Why did Steve announce that to the class?*

"Oh my gosh, Sarah plays the guitar too," Sharise said.

"If you don't mind Joshua, if you decide to go on the campout, could you bring your guitar?"

"No problem," Joshua answered.

"Actually, bro, there is a problem." Turning from his buddy Joshua to Pastor John, Steve informed them both, "That Saturday is the end of the season bash. This year Julie Stewart's parents are hosting, not a party we can miss. Right, bro?" Steve finished with a quick wink to Joshua.

"If you change your mind Joshua, we could always use another guitar player."

"Remember get those permission slips signed and back to me ASAP!" John shouted as the bell rang.

Out in the hallway, Paul stopped Lily. "Really? Paul plays the guitar," He said in a high voice, imitating her.

"You do and you're very good. What's the big deal?"

"The big deal is I don't play in front of people. I've only played for you," Paul whispered. "Hey, does this mean you'll go on the campout?"

"Wait. What?" Shaking her head, her fists pumped at her side. "Paul, I can't." Lily ran off through the crowded hall.

Watching her, Paul mouthed. "Why not?"

"Isn't that a coincidence?" Sharise asked Sarah walking to their next class.

"Isn't what a coincidence?"

"Both you and Joshua play the guitar. I mean I never knew he played, did he ever tell you?"

"No, why would he? I'm sure it's something only his closest friends know."

Sharise gave Sarah a sideways look.

"Sharise, we just met," Sarah replied shaking her head.

"Hey Josh." Steve called, catching up to him. "Too bad about that campout, it might have been pretty cool camping out on the beach and all."

"Did you have to go and tell the entire class that I play the guitar? You know I like to keep that to myself. Really Steve, sometimes you have such a big mouth."

"What's the big deal? It's not like you're going to the campout anyway. No harm, no foul."

"I haven't decided what I'm going to do," Joshua admitted.

"Come on bro, you're playing with me now. We're having our best season and we have scouts looking at us. Scouts! It'll be the biggest season-ending bash of all time. Of course, you're going," Steve stated factually.

"No Steve, I don't have to go to some dumb party. It's always the same thing, everyone gets loaded and high, sex is rampant and there's nothing but drama. Maybe it's time we grew up."

"Is it the pastor's daughter? Or are you mad at me because of Brittany and me?"

Josh didn't answer he just looked at Steve.

"You know your sister isn't as innocent as that pastor's daughter. Remember bro she's going back to Nebraska and you're not." Softening a bit Steve said, "Josh, we're in our junior year. We have plenty of time to grow up, bro. Until then, it is what it is." Shrugging his shoulders, he walked off, catching up with some of the other football players. Joshua watched Steve jump onto one of the guy's backs horsing around, bumping into anyone who got in their way.

Steve was right. Sarah will go back to Nebraska. What kind of a relationship could they have? In the midst of darkness, being with

Sarah made everything bright. He wasn't going to waste another minute, he had to let her know how he felt.

Hoping to talk to Erica about the field trip, Brittany waited for her in the hallway after class. "The field trip sounds like fun. Don't you think?"

"Yeah, it really does," Erica sighed. "But I won't be able to go."

"What do you mean? Why not?"

"Who'll watch Madison? I can't take her with me."

"What about your mom, can't she watch her"?

"My mom doesn't have much to do with Madison. It's alright, maybe the next one."

"Absolutely not. We'll figure it out. I'm not going without you."

"You want to go?"

"I think I do." Brittany smiled.

CHAPTER 29
SECRETS

Entering the house, Joshua and Brittany heard their mother barking out commands. They walked quietly toward the dining room. Linda Gallo was talking on her cell phone with her back to them.

"Karl, I don't care how you do it. I don't care who you have to convince. You get a town meeting scheduled, preferably after the Thanksgiving break. I'll make sure the right people are there, including the School Board. If Principal Davis won't do anything about that pious Pastor, I will. I want them out of this town and things back to normal. Do you understand me, Karl?"

Listening to Karl's reply, their mother's onslaught was momentarily paused. "Very good Karl. Oh yes, I almost completely forgot. I want the press notified. Best-selling author, Pastor John Wheaton leading children astray. What a headline!"

Having heard enough Joshua moved toward his mother, but Brittany pulled him back. She put her finger to her lips and pulled him out of the room toward the front foyer.

"What do you think you're doing?" Brittany asked.

"Someone has to stop this. She's going too far Brit," Joshua whispered as loud as he could.

"Joshua, think! If we go in there all gangbusters, she'll know we heard what she's up to. Right now, she doesn't know we heard anything. It's the only way to fight her, we need the upper hand."

"I don't know Brit, maybe we tell Principal Davis what we know."

"Trust me Joshua, if there's one thing I know, it's how to handle our mother. We need to find out more. In the meantime, give me your permission slip."

"What? Why?"

"Because from the sound of that conversation, Mom is not going to

238

sign it. There is no way she'll let us go on this field trip. I've signed Mom's signature on many forms, she wouldn't be able to tell the difference."

"Even if you sign the forms, she's bound to catch wind of the campout and won't let us out of her sight."

"Josh, we're going to the end-of-the-season bash and staying overnight at Julie's with everyone else."

"That's right it's the same night," Joshua realized. "I don't know Brit it doesn't seem right, lying like this."

"Do you want to go or not?"

"Yeah, of course I do. More than anything."

"Okay, then follow my lead," Brittany said.

Opening the door quietly Brittany slammed it shut and announced. "Hey, Mom we're home. Mom?"

"Gosh look at the time I've been so busy I completely lost track of time." Linda said as she met them in the kitchen, acting as if nothing unusual was happening.

"Doing anything interesting?" Josh asked innocently.

"Nothing you'd be interested in. Boring, boring, boring." Linda answered. Then she asked, "Would you like me to make you and afterschool snack?"

"I'm not hungry," Joshua mumbled and excused himself.

"What's up with Joshua? He's always hungry after school." Linda noted. "Is he feeling okay? Maybe I should check on him?"

"You know how boys can be and they say girls are moody, ha!" Brittany brushed it off.

After a quick snack and frivolous chit-chat, Brittany went upstairs to talk with her brother. Knocking once, Brittany opened the door and walked in finding her brother laid out on his bed tossing a football in the air.

"Way to follow my lead," Brittany whispered shutting the door behind her.

"Sorry Brit, I'm just not that good at hiding my feelings. I thought it best to go upstairs and let you work your magic." Josh replied with a sheepish grin.

"I'm not sure if I should take that as a compliment or an insult."

"Huh, the old Brittany would definitely have taken it as a compliment. There's hope for you yet."

"You really like her, don't you?"

"Who?"

"Seriously? Sarah Wheaton, that's who."

Not sure how to respond Joshua tossed the football in the air ignoring her question hoping Brittany would let it go. He knew better.

"I like her. Not only is she very pretty but she's smart and seems genuinely sweet."

Taken aback by Brittany's observation, Joshua was beginning to like this side of his sister. "Yeah, she is, and more. But she's going back to Nebraska, and I'll be here in Gilford. How's that supposed to work?"

"Where's your faith, Josh? We're definitely going to need it to get through the next couple of weeks." Brittany headed to the door.

"We're gonna need more than just my faith, Brit."

"I know," Brittany said.

The silence was heavy between them during the car ride home. After their confrontation, Lily and Paul's interactions were short and curt. Paul pulled up in front of Lily's house and watched her unbuckle her seat belt.

"You know Lily, this field trip could be good for you. Just hear me out." Paul couldn't help himself. "You love the beach and campfires. And I know you love smores."

To his surprise, Lily giggled at the mention of smores.

"All I'm asking is that you think about it. Okay? No pressure."

Lily didn't respond.

So he gave it one more shot. "To see you relaxed and enjoying yourself is all I care about." Then he added for good measure, "I'll even bring my guitar."

Lily's mind scrambled. Her face mimicked the raw emotions she still had left unaddressed. Paul was so patient, so loving and kind. But her fear held a mighty grip. Lily decided it was time to meet him halfway. "Maybe. It's not a yes," She hastened.

"But it's not a no either," Paul bartered.

Reaching for the door handle, Lily hesitated. Before she got out of the car, she turned and gave Paul a smile that finally reached her eyes.

"Do you want me to pick you up tonight to go to Cornerstone? Say 6:30?" Hoping he wasn't pushing his luck.

"Give 'em an inch and they take a mile." She grasped the door handle.

"What? No, I didn't mean. I mean…" Paul stammered.

"Paul, 6:30 is fine."

"Ah," Paul exhaled and drove off.

Driving to the daycare center to pick up Madison, Tags told Erica the exciting news. "Pastor John passed out permission slips during detention today for the fieldtrip to Cornerstone's campground."

241

"The detention class?" Erica was a little surprised.

"Yeah, we're like his students. He has more or less the same criminals each day." Tags snickered, adding, "Besides he's been teaching us about Joseph and everyone is really connecting with it."

"Wow, I didn't realize that. I thought it was just you and him. That's awesome!"

"You don't seem too thrilled with the idea. I thought you of all people would be thrilled to get a night away," Tags said. "Hey Erica, if you don't want me to go just say so. I'm a big boy. I can handle it."

"Joey, no. I can't think of anything better than going on a field trip with you… to be a teenager and not have to worry about anyone else." Twisting the gloves in her hands she revealed, "I won't be able to go."

"Why not?"

"I'm… because I have a little girl to look after."

"What about your mom, can't she watch Madison for one night?"

"Really? You know my mom. She'd never believe I was going on a field trip with the school. Besides she doesn't want anything to do with Madison." Her tears spilled over like a running faucet.

Panicking, Tags looked for a spot to pull over. Putting the car in park he reached for Erica, gathering her in his arms he whispered, "Shh, it's alright. It's gonna be alright."

Collecting herself, Erica left Tag's warm embrace in search of a tissue.

"Erica, I'll watch Madison. You deserve this and you're going."

Erica smiled at Tag's gallant attempt at taking charge, "I appreciate the offer, Joey. Really, I do. But Madison can't stay in an apartment with drugs and dealers living there. We both know my mother will not let you stay at my house. So that's that." Taking a deep sigh, Erica looked down at her watch and said, "We have to get going or we're going to be late getting Madison."

Tags touched Erica's shoulder and assured her, "This is not over."

Later that evening in the Gathering Room at Cornerstone Church plopping down on the leather couch, Lexy cried. "That's not fair."

"Oh please. It's a field trip for Pastor John's classes and you aren't in any of his classes." Shelby pointed out finding a seat on one of the overstuffed chairs.

"We'll never get the opportunity to have a campout. Pastor John will be going back to Nebraska after the semester," Jamie chimed in.

Listening from the doorway, Lewis inserted himself into the conversation. "It is Cornerstone's campground. I think starting an annual retreat for the youth group would be a great idea."

"That's genius, Lewis. You can lead it since you'll be Cornerstone's youth pastor." Lexy smiled.

"Sharise, Sarah," came the call from downstairs, "your ride is here."

Sharise jumped up from her bed. "Titus is here. Hurry up, you know how my mom loves to give him the third degree."

"Go ahead, I'll be right down," Sarah said.

"Okay, but not too long. Please?" Sharise begged.

"I'm right behind you," Sarah assured her. Alone in the room Sarah, walked over to the box sitting on top of the bureau Sarah was using during her stay at the Taylor's. Opening the box, she picked up the picture lying inside. "Oh, Mom. I wish you were here. There are so many things I want to ask you, I want to know." Placing the picture back in its place she swiped the tear rolling down her cheek.

"Oomph." She breathed and walked out of the room.

"Where are you heading off to?" Joshua heard as he was zipping up his coat. Turning around, he saw his mother standing in the middle of the hallway with that questioning glare.

"Out, why?"

"I can see you're going out. You have your coat and keys in your hand. The question was and let me rephrase it so there is no mistake as to what I mean. Where are you going out to?"

"I finally got him to go over to Andrea's with me." Brittany replied from the top of the stairs. Running down the stairs lest Joshua open his mouth Brittany continued, "Can you believe it? I've been telling him for how long now, Mom?" Without taking a breath she finished, "I've always said Andrea and Joshua would make an awesome couple."

"Wonderful," Linda responded with glee clapping her hands together.

"Grab me my coat Josh, would you please?"

"Sure." Joshua mumbled trying to figure out what was going on. "Here you go."

"Thanks." Turning to her mom she said. "We won't be out that late mom, after all it is a school night." Moving close enough to Linda's ear she whispered, "A couple of hours. Enough time for Joshua and Andrea to get to know each other a little better."

"Have fun you two." Linda called after them.

Walking to the car Joshua asked, "What was that all about?"

"You want to go to your youth group, don't you?" Brittany questioned.

"Yeah, I do. But Brit all this lying… it's going to catch up to us and then what?"

"To be perfectly honest Josh I don't know."

"Why Andrea?"

"Because Mom doesn't know her parents well enough to call and check on us. But," she added cautiously sliding into the passenger seat, "you're right, it's only a matter of time. Hopefully, we don't get found out until after the campout."

After they picked up Madison, Erica invited Tags in for a while. Tags was hesitant after his last encounter with her mother.

"Mom's working late that's why I can't go to youth group tonight. I guess I should be very thankful she watches her so I can go to youth group every now and then."

"Don't you have to put Madison in bed before you go? I mean it's not like she has to do anything," Tags snorted.

"Joey." Erica reminded him, "She could always say no even to that. I have to be thankful for the small things. I've accepted the fact that she's never going to be a loving grandmother."

Madison was eating her supper while being entertained by her father when the door opened. Donna Gray came storming into the house after seeing Tags' car outside.

"Get out of my house. How dare you!"

"Wait a minute Mrs. Gray," Tags tried.

"Mom please, your scaring Madison."

Everyone turned to see Madison was close to tears with her little index finger in her mouth, lips trembling.

"This is the repayment I get for letting you and her," pointing at Madison, "stay at my house?"

"Mom please, I only invited Joey in to help feed Madison, that's all. He's leaving right after," Erica pleaded.

"No. He's leaving right now. One more thing, just because I'm home doesn't mean I'm watching her so you can go to that youth group tonight." Her voice was rising into an unintelligible pitch as she pointed to Madison. "Especially after this." With her hands flaying in the air, she stormed out of the kitchen yelling, "As a matter of fact I'm not sure if I ever will again after this stunt." She stomped up the stairs.

Erica and Tags stood paralyzed as Mrs. Gray's pounding footsteps came to a sudden stop at the top of the stairs. Donna Gray barked, "I want him out now Erica or I'm calling the cops." There were more pounding footsteps then a door slammed shut with a loud bang!

Madison was crying. Erica picked her up and rubbed her back. "I'm sorry Joey, this is all my fault," Erica cried. "I knew better. I never should have let you come in. What was I thinking?"

"Erica, this is not your fault. I should have known better." Pacing back and forth like a wild animal, Tags said, pointing upstairs. "She's crazy. You and Madison have to come and stay with me until I can figure this out."

"Joey, right now this is the best place for us. You better go, she will call the cops."

Tags felt the sting of her words. She was right, his life was not set up for Erica, never mind a little girl. What he was doing was not good enough anymore. Even though Pastor John wanted him to provide for Erica and Madison the right way, it was too slow for Tags. Erica and Madison didn't deserve to be in this situation. It needed to change, they deserved better…so much better. Tags stood up and looked at the two of them. He had to find a way to make some quick cash and get Erica and Madison out of this insane asylum.

A multitude of conversations were happening. Joshua walked into the Gathering Room, and a red blush spread across Sarah's porcelain face. Sharise followed Sarah's gaze, her mouth practically fell open which in effect caused a chain reaction. One by one, the conversations came to a halt and a steady flow of silence filled the room. Lewis followed the direction of the distraction. Joshua entered the room, accompanied by a lovely young lady with similar features.

"This is my twin sister Brittany," Joshua blurted out.

No one moved. Odd, Lewis thought. Walking over to Brittany, Sarah extended her hand and said, "Welcome to Youth Group. I don't think we have officially met. I'm Sarah Wheaton."

Brittany took Sarah's hand, thankful for the warm reception. "No, we haven't. But from the way Josh talks about you, I feel I know you already." Brittany jabbed her elbow into Joshua's side.

Sarah brought Brittany to one of the vacant chairs. Instead of sitting down, she addressed the room knowing they were confused and not quite sure what to think about her presence.

"Look, I know you all must be shocked to see me here tonight. But I'm not the same person I used to be. I don't expect you to believe me, but things happen and that has a way of changing a person. Especially when you unmask the demons you find lurking inside of yourself."

He does not treat us as our sins deserve or repay us according to our iniquities. For as high as the heavens are above the earth, so great is his love for those who fear him; as far as the east is from the west, so far has he removed our transgressions from us. Psalm 103:10-12

"Welcome Brittany Gallo. I am Lewis Tremblay, soon to be youth pastor for Cornerstone Church. May I take your coat?" Putting Brittany's coat over his left arm, Lewis extended his right hand in welcome which Brittany accepted with delight.

Settling into their usual circle, the conversation turned to the campout.

"Speaking of the campout," Brittany began.

Hoping she wasn't about to share with the group their plot to forge their mother's signature, Joshua flashed her a look.

Ignoring Joshua's angst, she continued, "When I spoke to Erica earlier, she was upset she didn't have anyone to watch Madison for the campout."

Joshua let out his breath. Noticing, Sarah asked him if he was okay.

"Fine," he replied trying not to look into her eyes. If anyone could figure out he wasn't fine, it would be Sarah.

"I thought her mother helped out with Madison," Sharise commented. "I'm sure she'll watch her for just one night."

"Yeah, that's what I said to her. But she told me a different story. Her mother rarely has anything to do with Madison," pausing, "Erica is basically on her own when it comes to Madison."

"Wait a minute," Paul said in disbelief. "I was in class the day everything went down with you and Erica. Are you telling us you actually talk to each other?"

"Yes, we talk to each other and as a matter of fact we're friends," Brittany proudly stated.

"What? I am officially in the Twilight Zone," Titus scoffed "Brittany Gallo, what are you trying to pull here? Everyone in this room knows how you and your friends have tortured Erica Gray for the past couple of years. Now you expect us to believe that you and her are friends? Come on."

"I deserve that. But I'm telling you the truth, I apologized to Erica." Brittany defended herself, so she tried even harder. "I asked her to forgive me for all the terrible and rotten things I did to her. Yeah, I know there have been a lot. But I'm telling you, she accepted my apology." Still sensing the group's apprehension, Brittany tried again.

"Of all the people in the world, it was Erica who was there to help me when I faced something heartbreaking. She is definitely a much better person than I am and deserves good things to happen to her. Erica is an awesome mother, and her little girl is the sweetest little thing in the whole world. And that's why I have to help her go on this campout," Brittany finished.

Everyone was trying to digest what Brittany said. It was time for her big brother, by a couple of minutes, to chime in.

"It's true guys," Joshua said. "Brittany is the real deal here. Believe me, at first I was a little taken aback, too.

"I can't tell you why. But I can tell you, she's not only my sister, she's my friend. To be quite, honest it doesn't matter if you believe us or not. It just is."

"Thanks, bro," was all Brittany could choke out.

"Some of you come to church and listen to Pastor Peters preach. You sit here night after night in this Gathering Room listening and seeing what God is doing. Many of you sit in Pastor John's class and listen day after day to him teach you about God's love and still, still," Lewis repeated for emphasis "you doubt the power of God."

With man this is impossible, but with God all things are possible. Matthew 19:26

Looking around the room, he knew his point hit home. They felt ashamed of themselves for their negative attitudes.

"Oh no he didn't," Lewis sassily chided. Shaking his finger at them all. "Oh, yes, he did," he finished with a big grin.

"Checkmate," Shelby blurted out. And everyone agreed.

Dang! Lewis thought. Being a youth pastor is a lot harder than he imagined. *So much drama!*

CHAPTER 30
MOMENTS OF TRUTH

Pulling up to Lily's house, Paul decided instead of sending Lily a text, he would say hello to Mrs. Rivera. The door swung open as Paul was about to knock.

"I saw you get out of the car from the kitchen window. I hope I didn't startle you?" Theresa Rivera asked. "Come on in." She said, ushering him inside. "It's cold out this morning."

"Thank you, Mrs. Rivera." Paul answered shyly.

"It's been too long. You come by every morning to pick Lily up for school and then poof." She exaggerated with her hands.

"I know. I apologize for my bad manners. But I'm here now. How have you been? Still working a lot of hours?"

"Not as much. I try to be here for Lily as much as possible." Looking toward the stairs, Theresa whispered, "Has she said anything to you about her uncle's death or what might have happened during the summer?"

Paul knew exactly what Lily's mom was getting at. "To be perfectly honest, no. One minute everything was good the next a total 360. It's taken a while for Lily to let me drive her back and forth to school. Whatever happened she hasn't told me. I'm sorry."

Running down the stairs, Lily saw Paul standing in the middle of her kitchen. "Why didn't you text me? I told you to text me," Lily demanded.

"I haven't seen your mom in a while. It's been long overdue. Besides," he added, "if I waited for you to bring me in, I'd be waiting a very long time."

"Great. You've said your "overdue" hellos. Can we go now?"

"Sure. Do you have your permission slip?"

Annoyed she muttered. "All set. Let's go."

However, her mom was not all set. "What permission slip? I don't recall signing a permission slip."

"That's because I don't need it signed. I'm not going," sending Paul daggers, she turned to answer her mom.

Piquing her curiosity, Theresa inquired, "Tell me about this permission slip, Lily. What is it for?"

"Nothing. Can we go now?" Lily asked Paul.

Ignoring Lily, Theresa continued her questioning. "Paul, what is the permission slip for?"

Shrugging his shoulders, he answered, "It's for an overnight campout for Pastor John's classes."

"Where is it?"

"Cornerstone Church's campsite at Harbor Side Beach.

"When is it?"

"The Saturday after Thanksgiving."

"Everyone happy? Now can we go?" Lily said sarcastically.

"Not quite. Lily where is this slip?"

"I threw it away." Then with an incredulous look of defiance shrieked, "I'm not going."

Ignoring her daughter's, outburst Theresa continued. "Paul, what is the purpose of this campout?"

Hesitantly, Paul explained, "I'm not sure. The class is about God and Faith. We are studying Paul's letter to the Corinthians Chapter 13 concerning love." Thinking for a moment he recalled, "Oh yeah, Lily volunteered me and my guitar for the field trip."

Stopping for a moment to give Lily his own defiant look, "Hopefully we'll be doing smores over the campfire. You know stuff like that."

"What are the sleeping arrangements?"

"I guess there are two cabins one for the girls and one for the boys and a main lodge for eating and hanging out. There will be chaperones."

"I remember that campsite. We went years ago when Lily was young and her father was still alive. It was a beautiful place then and an even more beautiful memory now."

Looking at Lily, Theresa said in no uncertain terms, "You will go." Turning to Paul she requested. "Paul, you will get me the permission slip. Understood?"

"What are you both crazy? You can't make me go." Lily was defiant.

"If you can volunteer Paul's services, I think it's only fair you are there to lend your support."

Reaching into his pocket Paul took out a folded piece of paper. "I have an extra slip," Shifting from Lily's fierce look of objection. "I always take an extra in case I lose it." Then he handed the slip to Mrs. Rivera.

"Thank you, Paul." Taking the permission slip Theresa went into the top draw and pulled out a pen to sign her name. Handing the slip back to Paul. "You make sure Pastor John receives this?"

"Um." Confused Paul took the slip. "I, ah, will."

Lily grabbed her coat and told them. "I want you both to know I am not going. Can we go now?"

Teresa watched them walk out of the house and over to the car "Oh, I think you are going, Lily," she said to herself.

John was ecstatic at the number of returned permission slips he'd gotten back.

Even a few of the kids from detention had passed in their permission slips; Sean Sculles, aka "Scully" to his friends, Todd O'Leary and

Brian Foster, Scully's sidekick. Tags hadn't returned his permission slip. Thinking back over the week, Tags didn't seem much like himself. He was much too quiet for John's liking. Maybe Erica could give him some insight, he made a mental note to talk to her.

Tags stopped before entering the side door of one of the old brick buildings across the street from the bustling wharf. He watched the commercial vessels and fishing ships signal their way into the busy docks. One by one, they unloaded their catch and bartered for a good price before heading back out.

Opening the door, he shivered from the cold. *No!* Tags thought. *Fishing's not the life for me.* Walking all the way down the hallway to the last door on the right, he knocked three times waited and knocked two more. The door opened and Tags was ushered into a dark room.

Adjusting his eyes, he saw nothing had changed since the last time he was here. The room was littered with a few crates. A couple of guys sat on the crates with binoculars looking out the window. They could have passed for dock workers sporting flannel shirts with sleeves rolled up to the elbows, faded jeans and work boots. A single desk was situated against the left wall where a lone man, much better dressed than the other two, looked up at Tags.

"Look who is here, fellas," the man behind the desk said. "Joey Taglio. Leo, grab a chair for our friend Tags, huh?"

Tags saw a guy grabbing a chair as he was instructed.

"Thanks," Tags said and took the chair. Leo grunted and returned to the corner.

"You don't know Leo, do you Tags?" asked the man behind the desk.

"No, Mr. Robeesy. I haven't had the pleasure," Tags replied politely.

"Leo here, is my right-hand man. I'm a little surprised to see you.

Why am I seeing you now, Tags?" Mr. Robeesy asked.

"Cuz, I need to make some big money fast." Tags shrugged his shoulders. "And to be honest Mr. Robeesy, this is all I know."

"Hmm," Mr. Robeesy contemplated, sitting back in his high black leather chair. He clasped his short stubby fingers together under his drooping double chin. "The last I heard you was hanging around with some Pastor and going to church.

"Where'd you hear that?" Tags asked knowing full well it was Scully.

"Isn't God helping you out Joey?"

"Not quick enough." As soon as the words came out of his mouth, his stomach soured.

"Really? I thought God was the answer to everything, huh Tags?"

Tags shrugged his shoulders.

Mr. Robeesy considered Tags. "Okay, I guess I should be flattered I can give you something your God can't." Tags didn't find it quite as amusing as Mr. Robeesy and Leo.

"I uh, might have a job for you something that could pay big. You up for that Tags?"

"Yeah. Sounds like what I'm lookin for."

"Good." Mr. Robeesy said with a hint of a smile, adding. "You got the same number Tags?"

"I do."

"And you livin at the same place?" Mr. Robeesy asked looking down at his paperwork.

"Yeah, same place."

"I know it well." Mr. Robeesy acknowledged. "Tags, if you're in, I need you to be all in. You understand?"

"I do, Mr. Robeesy." Feeling more and more uncomfortable, Tags shifted slightly in his chair.

"Good, I'll be in touch," returning to his paperwork. "Leo, show Tags out."

Before he knew it Tags was on his feet and directed out of the room. He heard Mr. Robeesy shout from his desk, "You have a good day, Tags. I'm glad you're back."

Tags turned to reply but felt the breeze of the door slam in his face.

"Hey, Mr. R you really gonna use that loser? I mean come on, he can't even make it working for God," Leo asked him.

"Oh, Leo I'm gonna use him alright. I need a decoy for that big job we have comin up." Pausing, he decided, "As a matter of fact, I'm gonna send him with Simon."

"Simon? You know the cops are watching him."

"Exactly, let them both get pinched. Collateral damage for the greater good. Right Leo?"

"Right Mr. R, for the greater good. Our greater good you mean," Leo snorted.

Driving to pick up Erica, Tags felt uneasy. *What am I thinking?* He's supposed to trust God. Isn't that what Joseph did? Tags' inner voice rebelled. *Yeah, but Joseph didn't have two girls depending on him, did he?* "No, he did not," Tags answered out loud hitting the gas pedal.

An unlikely group of students sat around one of the lunch tables deep in conversation. They were oblivious to the looks and stares around them.

"I don't know, Shelby. Madison doesn't even know your mom or Lexy very well. I can't just drop her off for the night," Erica responded.

"I agree. That's why we'll formally introduce Madison to your mom and Lexy. It has to be this weekend. Shelby?" Brittany suggested.

"That sounds like a great idea. But my mom has to work a double on Saturday, maybe Sunday," Shelby countered.

"How many jobs does your mother have?" Brittany asked.

"Two, but sometimes another one to bring in extra money." Shelby replied, "Dad didn't leave us with much. I guess he wasn't prepared to die so soon."

"I'm so sorry Shelby. I didn't mean to bring up painful memories. I didn't know. I guess I never realized how fortunate Joshua and I are." Brittany said.

"It's okay we're used to it. I just feel bad for Mom; she works so hard.

"Well, that's it. I can't have your mother watch Madison on top of everything else she does," Erica declared.

"Erica, my mother was the one who volunteered. I never asked her. Really."

"When we told Mom about your predicament, she said to tell Erica to bring Madison to our house for the night. Lexy can't go to the campout, so she is more than happy to watch Madison. And Mom is going to be home with Stella and Ian anyway." Shelby explained.

"Think of it as Lexy babysitting and Mrs. Richardson being there for extra measure," Brittany interjected.

"Yeah, besides with Stella and Ian to entertain her, she'll be wiped out and begging to go to bed," Shelby added.

Thinking hard and weighing all her options, Erica decided. "I'll agree to Madison staying over as long as we can come over to your house after church Sunday, to get to know everyone a little better."

"Absolutely. Stella and Ian are going to be ecstatic," Shelby blurted with joy.

CHAPTER 31
ADJUSTMENTS

John wrote '*Love keeps no records of wrong*' on the white board as the students streamed into the room and settled in their seats. He turned to the class for all to see what was written.

"In Paul's passage in 1Corinthians 13:5, he writes: *Love keeps no records of wrong.* Anyone care to take a swipe at it?" he asked the class.

Erica's hand shot up in an instant, surprising even herself.

"Erica, what do you think Paul is telling us?"

"Ahem," Erica began. "I think Paul was telling us we should forgive anyone who does us wrong and then we have to let it go."

"Forgiveness, hmmm... isn't it hard to forgive people? Especially if they've done us wrong? Don't we tend to hang onto our anger?"

Brittany raised her arm.

"Please." John pointed at Brittany.

"Yeah, because sometimes the offense is so bad you can't forgive the person. It's just too hard."

"Too hard to forgive? Yet Paul tells us that love forgives. And not only does love forgive, it requires us to let go of the wrongdoing. As if it never happened."

Paul's hand went up.

John nodded in his direction. "Paul, should love forgive and forget?"

"Yeah, it's not always easy. If we hang onto to the anger, it's gonna eat away at us. I don't know about anyone else, but for me I think not forgiving someone would be worse."

"Interesting. So, both Pauls, want us to forgive. No matter what the offense." Looking around the room at the students, John hoped the class participation would continue, then the unexpected happened.

"Sometimes a person isn't able to forgive."

All eyes turned toward Lily, who continued, "Maybe the offense is too much for the person to handle so shutting down is the only way to survive."

"Good point," John agreed not wanting to make a big deal out of Lily's contribution. John looked up at the clock, only five minutes were left. "Paul says, Love keeps no records of wrongdoing. We've just heard some very different views about what Paul wants from us. They're all legit. How can Paul expect us to love and forgive someone who has hurt us? Embarrassed or humiliated us, then forget it even happened."

Students were shaking their heads in agreement.

"What was Paul thinking? Did Paul forgive? Did he love the soldiers who beat him? Whipped him? Chained him up? No…he couldn't do it either."

"What?" a student commented.

"Yeah, but Paul wants us to forgive and forget?"

"It's not our love that can forgive or forget records of wrongdoing. We are unable to erase bitterness or anger when we are hurt and offended. It is only through God's love that we can do anything. His agape love - God's love. *And so, we know and rely on the love God has for us. God is love. Whoever lives in love lives in God, and God in them. We love because he first loved us.* 1 John 4:16,19 Only God can give us the strength, the peace and yes, the love we need to forgive any and all wrongdoings."

The remaining minutes of class were left in silence letting the students ponder his final words.

"Remember your permission slips. I need you to get them in if you plan on going on the field trip. There isn't much time left," John yelled over the ringing bell as they all stood to leave.

Paul went up to John and handed him Lily's permission slip. "Here

258

you go, Pastor John."

"Paul, you already handed in your slip."

"Oh, that's not mine, it's Lily's. Her mom wanted to make sure it got to you."

After listening to Paul's explanation, Lily picked up her books, shrugged her shoulders and walked out the door.

"Paul, I don't want someone going if they really don't want to go."

"Her mom wants her to go and to be honest deep down I think Lily wants to go. I mean if she was really against it there'd be no way she'd let me hand you her permission slip. She's stubborn."

"True, she didn't say no just now," John answered and put it in the manila envelope holding the others."

"Pastor John, I'll have my permission slip tomorrow," Erica announced with a smile.

"Great, Erica. May I talk to you a moment?"

"Sure."

"I'll be out in the hall," Brittany said and went out the door.

"This is maybe nothing but...has Tags been a little distracted lately?"

"I don't know. He has been quiet; I'll talk to him." Erica sighed.

"Erica, I don't want to upset you. My concern is that he's okay. He was excited about the field trip, but he hasn't turned in his permission slip and his mind seems to be elsewhere."

"He was pretty upset that my mom wasn't able to watch Madison," Erica paused. "Maybe that has him down. He should be fine when I tell him Madison will be staying overnight at the Richardson's," Erica concluded more confident than she sounded.

"I bet you're right, that's probably what it is." John accepted.

Erica nodded in agreement, then headed out the door to where

259

Brittany was waiting.

"Everything okay?"

"Yeah. Pastor John is concerned about Joey. He hasn't turned in his permission slip," Erica said pushing the issue aside.

"Hmm. Joey Taglio?" Brittany stated elongating his name. "Someday we'll have to have a chat about him."

"What do you mean a chat?"

"Oh, I don't know. Like how? Why?"

"We'll save that tale for a day when we have nothing but time," Erica laughed.

"Pastor John, can I talk with you a minute?"

John looked up, a little startled. "Lily, I didn't see you come in, of course. What's going on?"

Lily took her army green backpack off her shoulder and placed it down on top of the closest desk with a thump.

"Wow! Sounds like you've got a lot of books in there. Are you sure that bag, or your shoulders, can handle that weight?"

"It was my dad's when he was in the Army," she explained showing the name Rivera in black lettering plastered along the front. "I guess it makes me kind of silly, right?"

John rummaged through his briefcase until he pulled out an old pocket watch. Turning it in his hand, he read aloud the scripture inscribed on the back. *"But this is the man to whom I will look and have regard: he who is humble and of a broken or wounded spirit, and who trembles at My word and reveres My commands."* Isaiah 66:2

Opening the old pocket watch, Lily could make out a picture of a woman inserted on one side. John read, *"Forever yours with all my love, Abigail.* It doesn't even work." John closed the watch and gently placed it back in the dark corner of his briefcase. "Not silly at all."

"Abigail was your wife?"

"Yes, and much, much more." John motioned to Lily to take a seat. "You're not here to discuss my Abby, so what's on your mind?"

Lily took a seat to tell John why she was there. "I want you to know I don't want to go on this campout. I'm literally being forced to go by my mother and Paul."

"I see. How about we start with why you don't want to go?"

"I have my reasons," was all Lily was willing to say.

"Okay, have you discussed your reasons with your mother?"

"No," came the firm answer.

"Lily, your mother signed the permission slip, right"?

Lily shook her head yes.

"If you really don't want to go, why are you talking to me? Shouldn't you talk to your mother and let her know how you feel?"

"I knew you wouldn't understand. No one does. I'm sorry for wasting your time," Lily spouted, grabbing her backpack.

"Wait a minute, Lily." John's appeal stopped her in her tracks. "I'm not sure I understand what you want from me. I can't help you if I don't know what's going on."

"I don't want to tell anyone. Not you, not my mother and certainly not Paul," she cried.

"Lily, maybe that's why your mother isn't backing down on this. Could she be forcing your hand, so you'll open up? Tell her what's going on. I'm sure she knows you're keeping something very powerful locked up inside you. Have you thought about talking to God about it first? Just you and him?"

Lily threw her precious backpack on the floor with force. Her fists tightly clenched at her side; she spit out through clenched teeth. "I don't have to tell God what happened. God was there and He watched it happen. I cried out to God to help me. But He deserted me!" Tears formed in the corners of her eyes.

John reached for Lily's hands, but she wrenched them away. "Lily, God didn't turn his back on you. He was right there with you going through whatever it was that happened. God cried with you then, just like He's crying with you now. Lily, there will come a time, I promise, when healing will take place."

Wiping her eyes with the back of her hand John located the tissues on his desk and handed them to her. Grabbing the tissues, Lily took out a couple, blew her nose and picked up her backpack. Flinging it over her shoulder she said with a bite of bitterness. "Well, that's really not gonna help me now, is it?"

Turning abruptly, Lily ran out of the room amidst the pastor's protests with tears blurring her eyes. How could she explain to anyone her biggest fear? If she went, she might cry or yell out in her sleep like she did every night at home. Lily always woke up in a cold sweat. The nightmare was always the same, she never gets away and the horror starts all over again.

"If I have to go to the stupid campout, I'll just have to stay up all night," she mumbled to the empty hallway.

Paul was waiting outside of his car for Lily. Time passed slowly. He wasn't even sure she'd show up for a ride home after he turned in her permission slip. Shielding his eyes from the brightness of the afternoon sun, he spotted Lily walking slowly up the sidewalk toward the black Nissan. She arrived at the car with puffy eyes and a red nose.

"Paul, I'll only get into this car if you promise not to say a word. I'm too mad and frustrated. I'm being manipulated into something I clearly do not want to participate in," Lily announced in no uncertain terms.

"Lily, I…"

"Paul no, I don't want to hear anything. I'd rather walk home than listen to anything you have to say right now." She held up her hand.

"Okay," Paul reassured her. "Not a word, complete silence. I promise."

Sarah and Shelby were talking in the backseat of Titus's car, so he used the opportunity to ask Sharise if she would like to go bowling later.

"I would love to if only to see the look on your face when I tear you up. Oh, I promised my mother I'd help her with clean-up tonight at the church," Sharise remembered. "Hey, would you like to come and help out?"

"With your mom? Sharise, you know she scares me. I'm not even sure she likes me. Why would I want to torture myself like that?" Titus asked.

"She's just keeping an eye on you, that's all. Come on, Sarah will be there and Pastor John and Lewis. You're lucky my dad has to work late. He's the one you should worry about."

"What am I doing?" Sarah asked hearing her name being thrown around.

"Helping my mother with clean-up duty at the church tonight," Sharise reminded her.

"Yes, I am. Shelby, what about you?"

"I'd love too but my mom has to work tonight, so I have to watch the kiddos," adding, "I can hardly wait until she has just one job with set hours."

"Has she been looking for other work?" Sarah asked.

263

"Yeah, she's been applying for administrative work. It's what she did part-time before Dad passed away. But there were layoffs and well, you know," Shelby sighed.

"If you can get some of the guys to come tonight, I'm in," Titus bargained.

"Okay, deal," Sharise agreed. She grabbed her phone and started texting. By the time they arrived at Sharise's house, the rain was coming down. Sarah scooted out of the back seat and thanked Titus for the ride home.

"Hey, don't think you slipped that 'whole lighting me' up remark by me. I'll take a raincheck on that challenge," Titus winked.

"I most willingly accept." Her phone went off. Looking down at the new text Sharise declared, "See you tonight."

"You know the deal, Sharise."

"I do. That was Joshua. He'll meet us at the church. Like I said, I'll see you tonight."

"See you tonight." he watched her fly up the stairs trying to outrun the rain.

"Joey, you've been quiet lately, everything okay?" Erica ventured.

"What? Yeah, everything is fine."

"Pastor John said you haven't turned in your permission slip for the campout?" Erica asked.

"I forgot it. I'll make sure he gets it tomorrow." He replied not daring to look at her.

"Great, especially now that Shelby's mom is going to watch Madison. We'll have nothing to worry about except having a good time."

"Yeah, it'll be great." He was answering her, but he wasn't involved in their conversation. A sick feeling came over Erica, reminding her of earlier days when he was off doing things he shouldn't have been.

"It's really coming down out there. You stay in the car I'll run in and get Madison," Tags said when they reached the daycare.

"Really, you don't mind?"

"Mind? Erica, she's my daughter too. It's time I stepped up. You shouldn't have to handle everything yourself."

He jumped out of the car leaving the keys in the ignition. Erica turned on the radio and found the Christian station Shelby told her about. Sitting back listening to the music Erica kept going over the conversation she just had with Joey. Something was up. "Hmm. What are you into now, Joey?"

Unbuckling her seatbelt, she turned around to look at Madison's car seat making sure it wasn't full of toys or tangled. With the rain, she wanted Joey to put her right in. Noticing something white crumbled up on the floor, Erica reached for it. Erica's worst fears were realized, in her hand was the crumbled-up permission slip.

He lied. Joey had no intention of turning the permission slip in. Was she putting too much pressure on him? Just because she was ready to trust God with her life didn't mean Joey was able to do the same. She folded the permission slip and put it in her pocket. Joey was going on this campout. If he didn't the alternative was something she didn't want to think about.

The door opened snapping her out of her thoughts and into the present. Turning in her seat, she grabbed the straps to buckle Madison into her car seat. Tags shut the door and ran to the other side and jumped in the car.

Madison was wiping her hands. "Wet mamma. Wet."

"I know baby. You'll be home soon and we'll get you nice and dry. Right, Daddy?"

"Actually, Madison will go to your house and you'll get her dry. Daddy isn't allowed." Driving away Erica said to him, "Joey, things

265

don't happen all at once. It takes baby steps. Look, God already answered our prayer for the campout. We need to trust him with everything Joey, not just some things."

"I don't have time for baby steps. Every time I've trusted someone, they've let me down. So don't talk to me about answered prayers. God doesn't have answers or time for a guy like me."

"You're wrong Joey and I'm going to prove it to you," Erica countered.

"How you gonna do that?"

"I'm going to pray for us and I'm not going to stop until God shows you, Joey Taglio, that you are worth His love and ours." Erica dared to go further. "I know something is up Joey. I don't know what, but I am begging you to look the other way. Come on the campout. I'm scared that if you don't, you'll never see me or Madison again."

"Are you threatening me when I'm trying to do right by my family?

"No, of course not," Erica shot back. "Don't you know me at all? It's because I love you." She paused clearing her throat, "This is your chance to leave all the bad things that have happened to you behind. If you don't take it, we all lose."

They drove in silence the rest of the way to the house.

"I'll get Madison out of her car seat, there's no sense in you getting drenched again." Before taking Madison out of the car, Erica reiterated what she'd told him earlier.

"We love you, Joey. I know what kind of a man you really are. You are one created for greatness. You have an amazing story to tell, but it comes with a price."

Tags didn't flinch, he kept looking straight ahead not saying a word. Seconds went by feeling more like minutes. Erica gave up. "Say bye to Daddy, Madison?"

"Bye. Bye. Daddy."

She said what she had to say. It was up to God. Sprinting up the porch steps with Madison in her arms, she was determined not to look back. Erica missed the tears trailing down Tags face as he drove away.

CHAPTER 32
A COMING TOGETHER

Paul and Joshua parked their cars and walked up the stone steps of the church together.

"Hey, Paul I wasn't sure who was going to show up tonight. What? No Lily?"

"I didn't even bother to ask her she's so mad at me."

"Hey guys," Lewis called out to them from the parking lot. "Want to give us a hand?" Turning around the boys saw Pastor John handing Lewis pizzas.

"Awesome. Pizza," Paul shouted forgetting his heartache for the moment. "I'm starving. I didn't get a chance to grab anything before coming tonight."

"I know man. I haven't had anything to eat since my sandwich after school." Joshua said.

"Seriously, Josh?" Paul shook his head. "Not the same, you ate a sandwich."

"Snack. I can't help it, my body gets into a routine from summer practice until…never mind. I always have a snack after school."

Lewis passed Paul two pizzas. He gave two more to Joshua and took the rest. "Gentlemen, we don't want the pizza getting cold. I'll go ahead and hold the doors for you." John dashed up the steps of Cornerstone. The aroma of pizzas didn't take long to waft its way through the main hallway and into the sanctuary where Louise was barking out job assignments.

Waiting for a moment to interject, Lewis yelled out "Pizza, the pizza is here."

Instantly, all heads turned toward Louise. Everyone was afraid to move until she gave them the okay.

"Go on," Louise waved her hand.

When dinner was finished, everyone broke into their assigned teams of two. Lewis and Paul were responsible for the Men's Room and two small Sunday School rooms. While John and Joshua cleaned Pastor Peters' office and the two larger Sunday School rooms. Louise paired herself up with Titus to clean the Day Care Center and Conference Room, leaving Sarah and Sharise to clean the kitchen and the Ladies' Room.

Before each group left to begin their tasks, Louise told them, "When you're finished cleaning, we'll all meet back in the sanctuary."

"The sanctuary?" Joshua dared to ask.

"Yes. The sanctuary isn't going to clean itself. Many hands make light work."

"What did you say?" Sarah asked not looking at Louise but at her father.

"What? Many hands make light work," Louise answered.

Holding her gaze, John answered for Sarah, "Abby used to say that when the congregation would get together."

"Oh, baby, I'm so sorry." Louise moved closer to Sarah. "I always use that phrase. I remember my mother saying it." Louise gathered Sarah up in a motherly hug.

"I'm happy you said it," Sarah said.

"Memories are what life is made of and we don't ever want to forget them." John smiled.

"Okay, any questions?" Louise asked. Sharise was quick to raise her hand. "Sharise?"

"Mom, can I plug in my phone to the sound system? If you want us to hustle, we need inspiration." Noticing her mom's arms moving to her hips, Sharise pressed on, "Mom, you know God loved it when David sang and danced."

"That is true," Lewis agreed.

"Sharise, do you know how to set it up?" Louise asked.

"Ah no, Lewis?" Sharise asked.

"I may know a little but not much, sorry Sharise."

"I can figure it out," Titus offered.

"Me too," Paul chimed in.

"Then get to it! And boys?"

"Yes." They both replied.

"This system costs a lot of money. I don't want to have to tell Pastor Peters that you broke it."

"Mrs. Taylor, I build sound systems in my spare time." Titus stated with confidence.

"Fine. But Titus?"

"Yes, ma'am?"

"I'll be waiting for you in the Day Care center. Don't dawdle."

"No, ma'am."

Reaching the sanctuary, he went straight to the sound system. Titus looked everything over with Paul hanging over his shoulder. "Hmm. Oh yeah."

"What's that supposed to mean? I thought you were the man?" Sharise asked.

"Give me a minute. I'm just looking this sweet system over, that's all," Titus relayed.

"Sharise, give me your phone." Paul took charge.

"Okay, okay here we go." Titus said.

Paul took Sharise's phone and attached it to the cord from one of the USB ports. Music! Titus smiled flipping switches, so the music flowed through the entire church.

Sarah was in the kitchen washing dishes as Sharise came in and grabbed a dry cloth. They belted out Merci Me's "Best News Ever".

Wiping the counters and toys down in the Day Care room, Titus chuckled hearing Sharise and Sarah singing.

"You should hear them at home. You'd think they were singing to an audience," Louise shared.

"The music isn't too bad." Titus conceded.

"Titus?"

"Yes, ma'am."

"Do you know why I'm so hard on you?" Louise asked.

"Because Sharise is your daughter, and you want the best for her."

"Yes, that's true, but there's something else. Do you know what it means to be unequally yoked?"

"When you try to put something together that isn't the same. Not equal."

"Very good. Titus when a Christian marries a non-believer the marriage is defined as unequally yoked."

Feeling a bit confused, Titus looked at Louise. "Marriage?"

"Relationships are hard enough. Don't you think, Titus?"

"Yeah."

"The difference between someone who believes in Jesus as Lord and Savior and one who does not is immense. Sharise believes in Jesus with all her heart. That's evident in the way she sings to him. She will never believe anything else." Louise held up her had to stop his reply, then continued, "I know that to be true because once saved, we will always remain his. Even if we fall away for a time." Louise watched Titus absorb everything. "I don't say this to be hurtful or mean. I am telling you this to save you from insurmountable heartache if things remain as they are."

Titus saw the compassion in Mrs. Taylor's eyes. One of the qualities he admired most about Sharise was her confidence about who she was. "Thank you, Mrs. Taylor. I understand what you're saying. I have a lot to think about."

"Yes, you do. But before you leave this room, I want you to know, you're a good man Titus. But you could be a great man if you let Jesus in."

Soon, everyone met inside the sanctuary.

"I want to know about the songs "Broken Together" and "Beautiful." Paul said. "Do you think if I learn how to play them, we could sing them at the campout?"

"Paul, I thought you were shy about playing in front of people?" John teased.

Shaking his head Paul stammered, "I… I am. I just really like these songs that's all."

"I'm teasing you," John chuckled. "Of course, you can play the songs."

Leaving the kids in the sanctuary talking about what they wanted to do for the weekend, Louise asked to talk with John in private in the pastor's office.

"What's going on?" John asked.

"I had a chat with Titus tonight."

"What kind of chat did you have?"

"I explained to him what it meant to be unequally yoked, and the affects it can have on a relationship."

"I see. How did he take it?

"Better than I thought." Louise paused to reflect. "I wish there was some way to get through to him, he's so, so, he's so…"

"Louise, he's so… what?"

"Logical," She blurted out. "You know he wants confirmation for everything."

"I do," John added. Both sat silent.

"I wish there was some way to help him see, you can be logical and scientific and still believe in God. I can see how Sharise feels about that boy. It's gonna break my heart when this comes crashing down on both of them."

"Maybe not, Louise," John exclaimed.

"What do you mean maybe not?"

"I may know a way to help Titus."

"Okay, I'll leave it to you. I just hope it helps."

"Me too."

"There isn't anything playing that my folks will let me go see," Sharise answered Joshua's question about going to the movies.

"Lewis?" Sharise asked. "Does the church have a projector set up for DVD's?"

"I don't think what the church has and what you are thinking are the same." Lewis answered.

"I have a set up." Titus announced to everyone.

"You do? Why don't we set it up in the Gathering Room for Saturday night?" Sharise said. "I have a bunch of movies. Let's watch *God's Not Dead*." She looked at Lewis for confirmation.

"Perfect," Sarah agreed.

"Lewis, what do you think?" Joshua asked.

"I like the idea, but it's not up to me," Lewis answered.

"Are we all set in here?" John walked into the sanctuary.

"Dad?" Sarah flew over to him. "Titus has a projector set up for DVD's. Do you think Pastor Peters would mind if we had a movie night in the Gathering Room Saturday night?"

"What a great idea," John affirmed then added. "Let me call Pastor Peters to be sure." He left the sanctuary with his cell phone up to his ear.

"Lewis, will you be attending movie night?" John asked, returning from his call.

"I wouldn't miss it." Lewis declared.

"What's the movie you're planning on watching?"

"*God's Not Dead*," Sharise blurted out.

"Great, then you are on for movie night," John happily announced.

CHAPTER 33
COURAGE

How Erica wished she'd been able to help at the church tonight. Except for the occasional words from Madison, there was little conversation.

"How was your day, Mom?"

"Really? We're going down this road?" Donna replied. "Erica, what do you want?"

Erica picked up her dinner plate and asked her mother if she was done with her meal. Donna answered with a simple nod. Erica kindly reached over the table and grabbed her mother's finished plate.

"There's a field trip next weekend. A campout at the Cornerstone Church's campsite."

"Do you seriously think I'm going to watch your illegitimate…her." Donna pointed at Madison through clenched teeth. "You seriously think I would help you run off on a wild weekend with that loser Joey Taglio?"

"Oh no, Mom, that's not it at all," Erica said. "There really is a field trip. My last-period class on Tuesday and Thursdays is God and Faith with Pastor John. He's running it."

"The answer is still no. Take her with you." Donna turned to walk out of the kitchen.

"Mom, wait," Erica pleaded.

Donna turned around watching her daughter run over to her backpack. Rumbling through as fast as she could Erica found the permission slip.

Handing it to her mother, she said, "I need you to sign the permission slip."

"What about her?" Donna asked.

"I've already made arrangements for Madison to stay the night at a friend's house."

"Do they know you'll be gallivanting around with that loser all weekend?"

Not taking the bait, Erica stood firm holding out a pen for her mother to use. Grabbing the pen, Donna scribbled her name and handed it back to Erica.

"Don't even think about coming back from this weekend pregnant. I don't have to tell you what that would mean."

Exhausted, Erica eased down into the kitchen chair next to Madison. "God, please help my mom. Help her to forgive." Finishing, Erica felt a tiny hand reach out and touch her arm.

"Mama. All done."

"Look at you baby girl, all covered in food. Mommy needs to clean you up and get you into the tubby."

Joshua walked into the house and hung up the keys. Taking the steps two at a time, he headed to Brittany's room.

"Joshua, is that you?" The familiar voice asked from downstairs.

"Yeah, Mom. I'm kinda tired. I'm heading into bed," Joshua answered.

"Hold on." Hearing his mother's footsteps getting closer, Joshua waited at the top of the stairs. Linda Gallo looked up at her son. "Joshua, I haven't seen you all night."

"Sorry, Mom."

"Brittany said you went out with some of your friends. Have you eaten?"

"Yeah, we got some pizza," Joshua offered up.

"Mom, I'm really beat. Between football and school…I'm gonna head into bed." Joshua headed down the hall.

"Strange," Linda said.

Quietly Joshua knocked on Brittany's door and whispered. "Brit, you in there?"

"Come in."

Opening and closing the door as quietly as possible Joshua tiptoed in.

"What's up? Why the secrecy?" Brittany asked, amused.

"I told Mom I was going to bed."

"Is Dad home?"

"Hmmm. It's Thursday night, what do you think? Brit, maybe we should tell Mom. It doesn't seem fair to keep something this important from her," Joshua said.

Sitting up from her slouched position, Brittany asked, "Do you really think she doesn't know?"

"Did you?"

"No, but he's my father. I wasn't looking for signs of cheating."

"Good point." Joshua thought.

"So why did you come in here?"

Shrugging his shoulders, Joshua said, "Advice."

"Girl advice?" Brittany teased.

"We're having movie night at Cornerstone this Saturday, so I was thinking," Joshua hesitated, "I mean I know Sarah will be going, but I thought maybe…"

"You'd ask her to go with you?"

"Yeah, what do you think? Pretty lame right?"

"Really? Are boys this dumb?" Brittany released an exaggerated sigh.

"Well…"

"No, no." Brittany waived at him. "I didn't want an answer. I already know the answer."

Feigning insult, Joshua opened then closed his mouth.

"Yes, you should ask her out. Maybe I'll go to movie night, if you don't mind?"

"Of course not. I'd like it if you came. Don't you want to know what movie we'll be watching?"

"Doesn't matter. I'll be hanging out with my friends…my real friends."

The silence in the car was deafening, except for a few exchanges between father and daughter. Tags didn't have much to say.

His mind was detached thinking about the new job. He'd been gone too long for Mr. Robeesy's liking so Tags had to prove himself once again. After dropping Madison off, the ride to school became unbearable.

"Are you upset with me about what I said to you yesterday?"

"What? No. No. I just have a lot on my mind. Can't a guy be quiet?"

"Of course. Have you thought about what I said?" Erica ventured.

"I guess. I've been thinking about a lot of things. Are we done with the fifty questions? Geez."

Something was wrong. Very wrong. How deep was he in this time? Erica couldn't even look at him when she answered. "Sure, no problem."

Reaching the school Erica wasted no time. She grabbed her book bag and said, "Thanks." Jumping out of the car, she heard Joey say,

"Hey, Erica?"

"What?"

"I'm picking you up in the library after detention, right?"

Bending down Erica managed. "Of course. Is there any reason you wouldn't?"

"Nope, see you then."

Going to the library before picking up Madison each day gave her a chance to get her homework finished. Tags was always getting detention; little did Erica know Tags made sure he got detention. He knew it was the only time she had to study.

He'd let Erica think he was in detention and meet her in the library like always.

But Erica turned in time to see Tags driving out of the school parking lot. "Where are you off to now, Joey?"

Joshua parked his car in the back school parking lot. Steve pulled up beside him, his music blaring inside his 2012 red Challenger SRT-8. Steve and his passenger Julie, jumped out of the car laughing and flirting like they were the only two people on the planet.

"You okay?" Joshua glanced at Brittany

"Yeah. It's not like it was going to work out between Steve and me anyway." Brittany didn't even glimpse their way. "Julie's only kidding herself if she thinks Steve will be content for any length of time. What's that saying, once a cheat, always a cheat?"

Brittany, Erica, Sarah, Sharise, Lily and Shelby sat together at one of the lunch tables. Looking around the cafeteria, Brittany spied

Joshua. As if he heard someone call his name, he turned to find his twin burning a hole in his back. Brittany gave Joshua a quick nod to the side in Sarah's direction. Joshua's eyes went wide. *What is she thinking?*

Brittany did it again this time a little more forceful. Knowing Brittany would embarrass him in front of the entire cafeteria, Joshua got up from the lunch table.

"Hey man, where ya going?" Steve yelled after him.

"I'll be right back."

"Sarah?"

Sarah's head shot up when she heard her name and found Joshua standing at the table. "Hi Joshua."

"Can I talk to you for a minute? Out in the hall?"

"Sure." Sarah got up from the table. Sarah looked up at Joshua with a questioning expression.

"I know it's sort of silly," Joshua initiated, "but I was wondering if I could pick you up for movie night tomorrow?"

"Like a date?"

"Yeah, like a date."

"I'd like that."

He felt like running through the cafeteria. *She said yes. She said yes.* He chose his words carefully. "Great. I'll pick you up at 7:00?"

"Joshua?"

"Is something wrong?"

"No. But?"

"But?" Josh repeated.

"You have to ask my father."

"Your father?"

"Yes, out of respect. This would be my first date and it would go a long way."

Joshua could only stare. *Was she serious?* "Your father?"

"It's okay. I understand you're not used to something like this. I can meet you at Cornerstone for the movie," Sarah smiled.

"I'll ask your father."

"Are you sure?"

"Yes, I totally understand."

"Great, he'll be in his classroom this afternoon before he heads down to detention."

"Perfect."

Sarah walked back into the cafeteria as Joshua stood in the hallway for a few extra seconds, feeling his stomach churn.

The girls stared at Brittany waiting for her to spill the beans. Instead, she gave them a slow shake of her head and a shrug of her shoulders.

"Oh my gosh girl, what was that all about?" Sharise asked as soon as Sarah reached the table.

"Can I sit down first?" Sarah teased her as she sat down with them.

"You're as bad as she is." Sharise pointed at Brittany. "She wouldn't budge an inch."

"Good to know." Sarah gave Brittany a high-five.

"Oh boy, ganging up on me already." Joshua shook his head as he passed their table. "That can't be good."

"Hey, we girls need to stick together," Brittany said.

Approaching his own table, Joshua prepared himself for the intense harassment he was sure to receive from the guys.

"Sarah?" Shelby asked with that motherly look.

"Joshua asked if he could take me to movie night." Sarah blushed.

"Tomorrow night? At Cornerstone?" Sharise asked then quickly followed with, "and you said?"

"Yes, and yes." Sarah answered.

Keeping her joy in check, Sharise covered her mouth so her screams couldn't be heard throughout the cafeteria. Everyone was genuinely excited for Sarah.

"It's about time."

"I knew he liked you."

Sarah was going to miss this group of misfits when it was time to go home. For now, she would enjoy this time and tuck away that sad thought for another day.

Joshua found Pastor John keying away on his laptop at his desk in his third-floor classroom just as Sarah said. Joshua knocked on the door.

"Come on in, Joshua."

"Why don't you take that bag off your shoulder and have a seat," John suggested, noticing how uncomfortable he looked.

"Thanks. I think I'll stand if you don't mind."

"Not at all. Is something wrong?"

"No. I mean, at least I hope not."

"Joshua?"

"Would it be okay if I took Sarah to movie night at Cornerstone tomorrow?" Joshua blurted.

"Joshua, sit down, and please breathe," John directed.

Joshua slumped down into the chair and let out his breath.

"Are you okay?"

"Yeah."

"Did Sarah put you up to this?"

"Yes."

"Do you know why Sarah asked you to ask me?"

"Because this is Sarah's first date and to show you respect."

"True to both. But it's also because we have a relationship based on trust and honesty. I could tell you it's because we're Christians and in part, that would be true. By asking my permission, you are showing both Sarah and I that you value and respect her."

"And fear me." John walked around his desk and offered Joshua his hand.

Joshua shook Pastor John's hand. "Yes, sir." At that moment everything seemed clear, by giving respect, Joshua received respect in return.

"By the way Joshua don't you have a class you should be in right now?"

"Hall pass. I have study hall last period."

Before leaving, Joshua said, "Thanks for taking the time to explain it all. I appreciate it."

"*So, in everything, do to others what you would have them do to you.*" Matthew 7:12

Making his way to the detention room, Erica met John in the first-floor hallway. Walking alongside him, she handed him Tags signed permission slip.

"Here's Joey's permission slip for the campout. He wanted me to make sure you had it. I'm heading upstairs to the library."

John stopped at the stairs that headed up to the library. Turning over the permission slip he took a closer look at it. "Mr. Joseph Taglio?" Pastor John questioned.

"Well, who else is going to sign it?" Erica chuckled with a nervous inflection.

"Erica is Tags, okay? He hasn't been to detention since Wednesday."

"Maybe he hasn't had to go," she answered shrugging her shoulders.

"Really? Since I've been doing detention Tags has been on my list. Just like he was on Wednesday. Where is he today?"

"I really don't know. Maybe he's already there," Erica uttered. "I'm sorry Pastor John, but I really have to get to the library." She turned in hopes of flying up the stairs and making a quick getaway.

"Erica?"

"Yes?"

"Don't you and Tags pick up Madison every day?"

"Yes."

"Yet, you don't know where he's been?"

"Pastor John, I'm concerned too. I don't know where he's been, he hasn't told me. But I promise I'll try and find out," offering Pastor John as much hope as she could.

John continued down the hall to detention, praying Tags would be there.

Erica wasn't in a hurry to get to the library anymore. She'd lied to Pastor John about the permission slip. What was she doing?

CHAPTER 34
WHAT IT IS

Tags was waiting for Erica. Normally, he'd go up to the library and get her when detention was over, but today was anything but normal. The task Tags was assigned had been no big deal. But it gave him some extra cash for Erica and Madison and showed Mr. Robeesy he could be trusted.

Exiting the front of the school, Erica spotted Joey's car immediately. She asked where he'd been.

"I had something to take care of is all. No big deal, Erica." At daycare, he put the car in park. "Relax. I'll go in and get Madison."

Erica needed some noise. She turned on the radio and found it was still on the Christian station. Resting her head against the seat, Erica figured Joey hadn't turned the radio on since the last time she did.

Erica smiled watching Joey carry Madison in his right arm and tickle her with his left. She turned the radio off to hear Madison's squeals of joy. As soon as Madison was in the car and buckled up the pretense of a happy family faded into the cold November air.

It was close to 4:30 when Tags pulled up in front of Erica's house. Reaching into the inside coat pocket of his brown leather jacket, he pulled out an envelope.

"Here," he handed it to Erica. "This is for you and Madison."

Erica opened it and was shocked to see one hundred dollars bills peeking out from inside. "What's this?"

"It's only the beginning," Tags stated with a sense of pride.

"Soon they'll be enough to get you and Madison out of that nut house you're living in."

"Where did you get this money, Joey?" Erica asked.

"Doesn't matter where I got it. Just be happy you have it," Tags said a little more harshly than he wanted to.

"What did you do to get this money, Joey?"

"Nothing you need to worry about, Erica. It's my butt on the line, not yours."

"Did it have anything to do with drugs?" Now it was Erica's turn to sound irritated.

"What if it was? It's not hurting you."

"It's not hurting me?" Erica repeated. "Do you even listen to yourself? You're bringing drugs into our town, Joey. How long do you think you can do this without getting caught?" Erica's voice rose. "How will you tell Madison to stay away from drugs when her father's the supplier?"

Madison's bottom lip began to tremble. "Mamma."

Realizing she was upsetting Madison, Erica reached for her book bag and jumped out of the car.

"Erica, wait a minute." Tags turned trying to soothe Madison. "It's okay Maddie. Shh, it's okay. Daddy's here."

Erica unbuckled Madison. Unable to control her anger, Erica lashed back. "But for how long?" Taking the envelope, she threw it at Joey. "Take your drug money, we don't want any part of it. I'd rather live with the devil I know, than the devil I don't." The money came flying out of the envelope and all over the front seat. Using her right foot Erica slammed the car door.

"Erica what the…?"

Running up her front stairs, Erica knew Joey wouldn't chase after her for fear of her mother. Tags collected the money and sat staring out the window. He felt like that frightened and abandoned five-year-old from his past. Well, not this time. He'd do this one job and score big. *Then what?* He thought to himself. "I don't know," he shouted.

Turning the key and pushing the door open, Erica heard the rubber of the tires screech as Joey peeled off down the street. Thankful to be inside, Erica noticed her mother was not home and breathed a sigh of relief. She took off Madison's hat and coat and hung them up. With Madison in her arms, she walked over to the brown velvet sectional. It was too small for this living room but a perfect fit in their old one. Sitting down, Erica recalled how adamant her mother had been about keeping the couch no matter how ridiculous it looked.

"That was another life," she said, placing her daughter on the couch beside her. Erica retrieved her book bag and returned to the couch and Madison. She pulled out her Bible. "Now let's see." Erica thumbed through the pages until she got to the book of Psalms. "*Sing joyfully to the Lord, you righteous; it is fitting for the upright to praise him.*" Psalm 33:1

"Brittany?" Linda called, waited, then trudged up the stairs and knocked on her daughter's bedroom door. Not getting a reply, Linda opened her daughter's door. Brittany was on her bed, books opened, pen in hand and earplugs from her phone stuffed into her ears.

"Brittany?" Linda yelled.

"What's the matter?" Brittany jumped, pulling the earplugs from her ears.

"The matter! I've been calling you for about five minutes now," Linda exaggerated.

"Sorry. I was getting my homework done."

"Joshua has football practice, and your father has plans tonight. How about you and I go to the club for dinner?"

The last thing Brittany needed was to run into Julie or one of the other girls. Since befriending Erica, it was clear they were tolerating her presence as captain of the cheerleading squad until the end of the football season. Running into any of those girls would cause her mother to ask questions.

Thinking fast she suggested, "I have a better idea, Mom. How about we watch a movie and get a pizza for tonight? You know have a girl's night. Just you and me?"

"Hmm. I was really looking forward to going to the club, but..." Linda said mulling the idea over. "You know that does sound like fun! What movie?"

"Your choice Mom," Brittany replied.

"Okay, there are so many good ones out right now. I hope I can decide," Linda answered.

"Pizza." Linda stopped abruptly at the door.

"Luigi's, large pepperoni." Brittany answered before her mom could turn around.

"Of course. What else?" Giggling like a little girl, Linda agreed.

Brittany pondered the idea of a night with her mom. *Maybe it won't be that bad.*

While Mrs. Gallo was busy with her preparations downstairs, Brittany thought it was a good time to call Sarah.

"Hi Brittany."

"Hey Sarah. I hope I'm not catching you in the middle of anything?" Brittany asked.

"Nope. Shelby and I are trying to help Sharise put together her playlist for the campout. What's up?"

"I was wondering who's going tomorrow night?" Brittany asked feeling a bit insecure.

"Hold on, let me put you on speaker so we all can weigh in," Sarah volunteered.

Brittany was about to protest when she heard the other girls chime in.

"Hey girl," and "What's up, Brittany."

"Hi Sharise, Shelby. I was just asking Sarah about tomorrow night."

"Are you coming?" Sharise asked.

"I was thinking about it. Who's going?"

"I'm going," Shelby called out.

Sarah spoke next. "You know your brother and I are going. Titus, Sharise, and you just heard from Shelby."

"It's not a couples night, is it?" Brittany asked suspiciously.

"No. Lexy and Jamie are coming as well. Mom doesn't have to work," Shelby broke in.

"Shelby, do you think your mom would watch Madison for a couple of hours so Erica could go? It would give Madison some time to get familiar with your family before the campout. What do you think?" Brittany suggested.

"I'll ask and let you know."

"Okay. I won't say anything to Erica until I hear back from you, Shelby."

"Good idea. Just in case," Sarah agreed.

"Is anyone going to tell me what movie we'll be watching?"

Sharise proudly announced, "*God's Not Dead.* What else?"

"Talk to you guys later." As soon as Brittany hung up the phone and tossed it on her bed, she heard her mother's footsteps.

Linda poked her head into Brittany's bedroom. "The pizza will be arriving in about forty-five minutes. Then we can start the movie."

"Sounds good, Mom."

Brittany quickly turned her sights to finishing up her task at hand. Homework.

Dressed in their pajamas Brittany and her mother lay sprawled out on each end of the teal blue, leather couch, filled with the pizza they had just devoured. Brittany was enjoying herself until her mother announced her movie choice.

"I know it's an oldy, but I just love Fatal Attraction."

Of all the movies. *Really, about a cheating husband?*

About halfway through the movie, Linda jumped up from the couch. Clicker in hand, she pressed the pause button and announced. "Time to make the popcorn. I'll be right back."

"Do you need any help?"

"No relax, I'll be right back. Isn't this movie great?" Linda asked walking out to the kitchen.

"Yeah. Great." Brittany answered trying to hide her true feelings.

Linda returned with the large bowl of salted popcorn smothered in melted butter and placed it on the coffee table. Pulling the brown cashmere throw from the back of the couch, Linda covered them.

"Mom, before we start the movie can I talk to you for a minute?"

"Of course." Linda placed the remote back on the table.

Brittany wasn't sure how to broach the subject, but she had to know. "I was wondering."

"Yes?"

"What do you think about men, or boys for that matter, who cheat?"

"Are you just asking because of the movie we're watching or has something happened?" Linda inquired.

"I don't know. I mean take Steve for example. He's such a stud and girls are always falling all over him. If I caught him cheating, should I forgive him or break up with him? I mean once a cheat always a

290

cheat, right?"

"I can understand your apprehension. But Brittany, boys will be boys and men will be men. Look, since the beginning of time men have always had this need, to live life on the edge. It plays to their ego. They have their little flings. Who does it really hurt? I say let them have their night of fun because at the end of the day it's us they come home to."

"But Mom what if one night they don't come home?"

"Don't be ridiculous Brittany if they don't want to lose everything they've worked for, they'll come home. Trust me, Brittany. Your father knows I'd take him for everything he has including his reputation."

She knows and it doesn't bother her. Astonished at the realization, Brittany sat dumbfounded while her mother rattled on.

"Steve reminds me of a younger version of your father. He had a roving eye. But I knew even as a young girl what it took to keep his eye coming back to me. Steve's going places Brittany, and you want to be the one he takes with him. The best advice I can give you is not to get hung up on the small stuff."

Joshua was right. Even if their mother knew what was going on she didn't care if it didn't upset what she had.

"Are we all set now? Can we get back to the movie?"

"Sure Mom, all set." Brittany got her answer. The old Brittany would have relished their conversation. *But now… everything was different.*

Being early in the evening, Sharise asked if she could drive Shelby home. When they arrived at Shelby's house, she asked them if they wanted to come in for a few minutes.

"Sure, but only for a few minutes or my mom will have the police looking for us," Sharise warned.

Mary emerged from the living room at the same time the girls entered the kitchen escaping from the frigid night.

"Hey, Mom."

"Hello, Mrs. Richardson."

"Girls you must be freezing, anyone for hot chocolate?" Mary offered.

"Normally, I wouldn't hesitate, but we can only stay for a few minutes. New driver laws and all," Sharise pointed at the clock that read 10:05 p.m.

"I'll have a cup with you, Mom." Shelby took off her coat.

"Sounds like a plan, Shelby," Mary walked over to the stove. "That was very sweet of you girls to stop in. Are you going to movie night at the church tomorrow?"

Big smiles spread across the girls' faces.

"Indeed, we are. Hopefully, this will be just the first of many at Cornerstone," Sarah answered.

"Which reminds me," Shelby interjected.

"Would you mind watching Madison tomorrow night so Erica can see the movie? It would only be a couple of hours? Before you answer," Shelby rushed on, "Erica doesn't know we are asking. We didn't want to get her hopes up in case you can't."

Before Mary could get an answer out Sharise interrupted. "Please don't feel pressured. We realize it's last minute and you could already have plans with Ian and Stella."

Mary found the girls amusing and considerate. "I appreciate your thoughtfulness and to be honest I haven't planned a thing for tomorrow night. The idea of just being home with my children was enough for me."

Thinking out loud Mary confessed, "You know this might be a great way for Madison to get to know us before she spends the night. Yes, we would love to watch Madison for her."

"Really Mom?"

"Really," Mary affirmed.

On the ride home Sarah sent Brittany a text. "Mrs. R said yes."

Brittany had made an excuse of not feeling well after the movie and went up to bed.

"Too much popcorn," Linda teased.

She was sick to her stomach from listening to her mother. Brittany's phone went off and she read the text. She responded by sending a red heart.

CHAPTER 35
MOVIE NIGHT

Brittany ate her freshly poured cereal at the breakfast nook early Saturday morning. She was texting Erica when Joshua strolled into the kitchen, rubbing his eyes from the night's sleep. Walking over to the refrigerator, he opened the door and reached in for the milk then grabbed a bowl and a spoon. He sat down next to his sister.

"Pass the cereal, please?"

Brittany picked up the box of Fruity Pebbles and passed it to her twin brother. "Here ya go."

"Thanks," Joshua replied taking the box.

The siblings sat quietly, watching the ocean waves spraying foam against the rocks. The luminous light of the morning sun created a rainbow above the waves. The only noise they heard was the crunch each mouthful of cereal made.

"How did it go last night?" Joshua asked.

Glancing around the room Brittany answered in a whisper. "I can't really get into it right now. Later, at Cornerstone."

"You're going?"

"Yeah, don't act so surprised. I told you I might."

"I know but…" Joshua left it at that.

"How did practice go?"

"Awesome. I think we might have a chance to win it all this year."

"Good. I, for one, can't wait for the season to be over."

The moment was cut short when Linda entered the kitchen.

"Okay, I'm off to run a few errands," she announced.

"Where to?" Brittany asked.

"To start," Linda began, "tonight, is the Silent Auction at the club. I have to pick up my new dress at the tailors and your father's tux at the dry cleaners." Linda grabbed her car keys. "Which reminds me," directing her attention to the two of them, "What are your plans for tonight?"

"Just hanging out," Brittany responded.

"Yeah, I think everyone is meeting down at Murphy's," Joshua interjected.

"Oh, fun. How was practice? I heard Coach has been working you boys pretty hard."

"You have to put in the time if you want the reward. Besides, Coach fed us, so no one complained."

"I'll leave you both some money before we go out tonight." Without another word, Linda disappeared.

"Murphy's?" Brittany asked.

"Yeah, why?"

"What if Mom bumps into some of the parents at the auction? I'm sure they're all going."

"She can bump into all the parents she wants. The plan for tonight is to meet at Murphy's, at least that's what Steve said."

"Oh, I guess I didn't get the invite," Brittany moved the last of her soggy Fruity Pebbles around in her pink milk.

"Sorry Brit, that was pretty inconsiderate of me."

"It's not your fault. Even though I know they're a bunch of selfish, egotistical jerks that don't care about anyone but themselves, it still kinda hurts."

"I know, but hey, the good news is you're not staying in. You're going out with friends who have your back and a fantastic brother who'll let you hang out with him."

"Hah, it's you that should feel honored with my presence, Bro."

Brittany teased.

"Can you drop me off at Sharise's house when you pick up Sarah?" Brittany asked Joshua.

"Why don't you just come with us to Cornerstone?" Joshua offered.

"As much as I would love to be the third wheel on your much-anticipated date, Sharise is driving tonight. We're picking up Erica and Madison then onto Shelby's house. Madison is staying with Mrs. Richardson so Erica can go. This way Mrs. Richardson can get to know Madison and vice versa before the campout."

"Sounds like you guys have it all figured out. Just be ready by six-thirty."

"Six-thirty? It only takes 15 minutes to get to Sharise's house."

"I know you Brit, 6:30."

"But I've changed."

"Not that much." Both knew Joshua was right.

Sarah and Sharise were busy getting ready for the much-anticipated movie night. The adults were completing their agenda for the evening.

"John, you are the only logical choice. Dwayne and I are not very tactful. This youth group is in its infancy. The kids need to understand how it's going to be, in a more compassionate tone."

"Dwayne and I will be chaperones a little later down the line." She was good, but John wasn't ready to give up.

"Why me? I have a million things to do before the campout. Isn't Lewis going to be there? He is the youth pastor after all."

"Lewis is the acting youth pastor until he finishes school. And, I might add, he's a student who has eyes for Shelby Richardson." Dwayne chimed in.

"What? Shelby?" John questioned.

Dwayne and Louise looked at each other in utter disbelief. "John, no offense but did you really write that book, *Children of the King*?" Dwayne teased him.

John started to open his mouth.

"Lewis is doing a great job leading the youth group. But he could use some direction, think of it as a learning curve," Louise explained. Adding with a calculated smile, "Isn't Joshua picking Sarah up to take her to movie night?"

Around 6:30, the girls came downstairs to find John with his coat on and keys in hand.

"Dad, where are you off to?" Sarah asked her father.

"To Cornerstone."

"No offense Pastor John, but why?" Sharise inquired.

The apple doesn't fall far from the tree, John recognized. "Well someone has to chaperone this evening. We could ask your mom and dad if you prefer Sharise?"

"Maybe next time," Sharise volunteered.

"Dad?" Sarah questioned. "Isn't Lewis going to be there tonight? Or are you chaperoning because Joshua is picking me up?"

Always honest with Sarah, he wasn't about to change that now.

"Yes. Lewis is going to be there. But it was pointed out to me earlier today, he's still a student. I'll be the adult overseeing the night's activities. As far as Joshua, we had a very nice chat. So no, it's not personal, it's a necessity that I will be there tonight."

Both girls looked at each other and shrugged their shoulders. "Okay."

"Okay?" *Well, that was easier than I thought.* "I'll see you there."

"Are you going somewhere?" Donna pried, noticing Erica's coat thrown across the couch and Madison's backpack next to it.

"Yeah, it's movie night at Cornerstone. Shelby's mom said she'd watch Madison for a couple of hours so I can go."

"Are you really going to see a movie or meeting up with that baby daddy loser of yours? Mrs. Richardson is a fool."

"No Mom, Joey isn't going. Mrs. Richardson is not a fool. She's a very nice person." *Unlike you.*

Erica finished getting Madison into her pajamas and put on their jackets to head outside. They could wait for Sharise out on the porch, opting to face the cold outside rather than inside.

Gathering Madison and her backpack in her arms Erica said, "We'll be home no later than eleven, Mom." Dashing for the front door, she hoped to get out of the house.

"Erica?"

"Yeah Mom?"

"What movie will you be watching?" Donna asked.

"*God is Not Dead*, because Mom, God is NOT dead." Erica walked out the door.

Donna stood in the middle of the living room. "Well, he is to me."

Titus and Lewis were meeting to set up the projector and screen. Arriving at Cornerstone, Titus found Pastor John with Lewis. "Hi Pastor John. I didn't know you were coming tonight."

"That seems to be the consensus. I'll be in the Pastor's office if anyone needs me," and he was gone.

Titus and Lewis were finishing up when the others arrived. Joshua and Sarah walked into the Gathering room and immediately noticed the seating arrangement left a lot to be desired.

"Do you think the screen might be better against the wall on the far end of the room?" Sarah asked.

"We're getting there, we're getting there. Perfection takes time, little lady," Titus explained.

"Funny, Titus. While you work on perfection," Joshua needled, "maybe Lewis and I can rearrange these chairs."

"I'm going to go into the kitchen and get the snacks together," Sarah informed them.

"I hope somebody brought popcorn," Titus called from behind the screen. "I'm just saying. You can't watch a movie without popcorn."

"Really?" Lewis asked, tossing a crumpled piece of paper hitting Titus on the top of his head.

"Really," Titus shot back, tossing the ball of paper back from where it came.

"And furthermore, every kernel should be saturated with butter and seasoned with just enough salt to keep the palate wanting more."

"Titus, you're making me hungry." Sarah made her way to the kitchen.

Suddenly the church was alive with the sound of music.

Shaking her head, Sarah knew it could only mean one thing, Sharise had arrived. Flinging open the office door, John greeted the merry group parading through the entry way. Sharise and Shelby led the group singing with unabashed passion, fists pumping high in the air.

Brittany politely tapped Sharise on the shoulder who was oblivious to everything around her except the song in her heart. Turning her head toward where Brittany was pointing, Sharise found herself staring into Pastor John's startled, amused face.

Immediately, Sharise turned off the music and squeaked out a polite, "Sorry!"

Giggling, the girls scurried down the hall towards the Gathering room.

"Anyone want to help me get snacks together?" Sarah cornered the girls at the doorway to the kitchen hoping to get some help with the snacks. A couple of them had bags of their own.

"Sure. Erica and I can help out," Brittany volunteered.

"Sarah, I'll be back to help out, but I have to see how the room is set up first," Sharise proclaimed.

"Me too," Shelby announced, right behind Sharise.

Lexy and Jamie were standing at the doorway with bags in their hands.

"Come on you two," Sarah said coming to their rescue. "We need to get the popcorn popping."

Bringing the snacks to the Gathering Room, they bumped into Joshua.

"I thought I'd ask your father if he would like to join us."

Sarah rewarded Joshua with brilliant smile and mouthed the words, "Thank you."

Joshua knocked on the office door.

"Come in." John immediately asked. "Is everything okay? Why aren't you watching the movie?"

"We're about ready to begin. I just thought. I mean." he stammered. "Would you like to watch it with us?"

"Oh. Thank you. But I'm finishing up some last-minute details for the campout. But maybe I'll pop in a little later."

"Okay, the door's open," Joshua replied.

"Joshua?"

"Yeah?"

"Did Sarah ask you to ask me?"

"No, I just didn't want you to feel left out." Joshua turned for the door.

"Do you know the story of Joshua from the Old Testament?"

"No, can't say that I do," Joshua replied.

"Ask Sarah to tell you about him. I think you'll like the story and the man."

"I'll do that."

Back in the Gathering room, Joshua spotted Sarah sitting at the far end corner of the couch. She'd saved the seat next to her for him.

"He said maybe in a little while."

Sarah responded with a nod and a smile.

"You weren't going to start the movie without us, were you?" Paul asked walking in the room with Lily.

"Glad you could make it, Bro," Joshua shouted genuinely happy to see Paul.

Shelby yelled out, "We have snacks laid out on the back table and a bowl of perfectly-popped popcorn."

After a quick jaunt to the back table, Lily and Paul sat down next to Lexy and Jamie.

"Is everyone ready now?" Titus asked. "No more trips to the kitchen or the bathroom. Because once I push this start button that's it, people." Titus looked so serious the room fell momentarily silent, except for Sharise's giggles.

Everyone let him know he could start the movie. "Good." He pushed his glasses up the bridge of his nose. "Now. Let the movie begin…" Finishing with a childish grin, he hit the start button and triumphantly sat down, smiling from ear to ear. Then from every direction, Titus was bombarded with handfuls of popcorn accompanied with squeals of laughter. "Okay, okay. I guess I deserved that."

The music started and the movie began…

Standing in the doorway, John noted the movie was at its climatic point - the final debate.

"If God does not exist then everything is permissible. God gives us the choice to believe or not believe," declared the young college freshman as the professor mocks him.

"Why do you hate God?" The student repeatedly asks the professor. He screeches at the students sitting in the Lecture Hall. "Yes, I hate God with every fiber of my being."

The freshman calmy asks the professor in a quiet voice. "How can you hate someone that doesn't exist?"

"Wow!" Titus voiced out loud, "I did not see that coming."

One by one the students in the Lecture Hall rise from their seats declaring, "God is not dead."

The room erupted with everyone clapping and cheering. However, Titus, Lily and Brittany although smiling, showed hints of confusion.

Noticing her father for the first time, Sarah gave her dad a shout out.

Everyone turned to see Pastor John standing in the doorway. "What? This is my favorite part."

The movie concluded a short time later. Sharise and the girls sang along with the Newsboy's, "God is Not Dead, (He is surely alive)."

CHAPTER 36
FOUNDATIONS

It was a little after 10:30 when Joshua parked his car out front of the Taylor's home. Turning to Sarah he said. "When I went to ask your dad to join us for the movie, he asked me a question. He asked if I knew the story of Joshua from the Old Testament. I told him I didn't, I mean I know Joshua is a character in the Bible, but I don't know his story."

"I see," Sarah replied with a bit of hesitancy.

Hoping not to sound too ignorant, Joshua had wandered off topic and onto a minor bunny trail. "Sorry. I'm not doing a very good job of explaining. Your dad told me to ask you to explain the story to me." Joshua finished feeling a little foolish.

"He did, did he?"

"Yeah, really he did."

"Do you want me to tell you the story? Be honest," Sarah asked earnestly.

"I do. I really do." Joshua exclaimed.

"Okay, I'll give it my best." Sarah faced Joshua. "Israel is made up of twelve tribes and Joshua is from the tribe of Ephraim. He was born in Egypt and was part of the Exodus that Moses led out of Egypt. One day, when the Israelites were in the wilderness, the Lord came to Moses and spoke, "Send out 12 spies, one from each of the tribes of Israel to scout the land of Canaan. This was the land the Lord was giving to the Israelites, the land of milk and honey..."

Peeking out the window in the front room, John had a great vantage point.

"John, what you are doing?" Dwayne cautiously asked.

"I'm spying on my daughter," John explained.

"Oh. Well, what's happening?" Dwayne wanted to know.

"Sarah's telling Joshua a story."

"Interesting and you know this because…" Dwayne drifted off.

"Because I told Joshua to ask her to explain the story of Joshua from the Old Testament. If you could see Sarah's hands right now, moving every which way."

"Let me see," Dwayne pushed John aside. "Yes, siree. I agree that's one heck of a story she's telling him. Hm, hm." Then Dwayne asked, "Why?"

"Simple. I think they really like each other. I thought with Sarah and I moving back to Nebraska, I wouldn't have to deal with it."

"And now, what's changed your mind?"

"Tonight, he came in on his own to ask if I wanted to join them for the movie."

"Hmph, you mean he was kissing up to you?"

"That's what I thought at first, but I think he's genuine. More important, I think Sarah does too." John moved away from the window. "Sarah loves telling stories from the Bible. You should see her on Sundays, teaching the younger ones back home. Either Joshua will appreciate her, or he will know they are not alike and move on. Hmm. Sarah's already suffered tremendous heartache for one so young. I won't stand by and let it happen again," John concluded.

Dwayne shook his head in agreement.

"So, you see. Joshua is not just a character from the Bible. He's real. God chose him and made him a leader. A hero in the eyes of his people because he led them to the land of milk and honey." Sarah wrapped up her story.

"I've noticed names are very important in the Bible," Joshua said after a moment of silence.

"Yes, they are. A name describes one's character," Sarah agreed.

"The name Sarah means "Princess", right? She was the wife of Abraham and from what I've read very beautiful."

"Yes," Sarah said. Soaking up the moment uniquely their own.

Knock! Knock! The noise on the passenger window startled the pair. Sharise opened the passenger door.

"What are you two doing out here? I dropped your sister off about twenty minutes ago," Sharise informed Joshua.

"I better get in. My father is probably pacing the living room floor," Sarah heeded.

"Thanks, I really appreciate you taking the time to explain things to me."

Sarah shook her head knowing he was being sincere.

"I'll see you at service tomorrow?" Joshua asked.

"Of course. My father's a pastor you know," Sarah joked getting out of the car.

Joshua watched as Sarah and Sharise ran up the stairs and into the house.

Watching again from the living room window, John noticed Joshua didn't drive off until the girls were safely inside. "Abby, I could really use your help right now."

Paul took Lily for a ride by the beach before he dropped her off at home.

"What did you think of the movie?" Lily asked.

"I thought it was great, very powerful. I mean I know it's just a movie, but it has a powerful message. I do think God does send us multiple chances throughout our lives. Hoping that one of those times we'll accept him into our hearts and make Jesus our Lord and Savior," Paul said thoughtfully.

"Yeah, but the question is how many chances do we get?" Lily thought. "I mean, that girl's brother sees a miracle happen right in front of him and disregards it as a fluke. But the professor who spent most of his life hating and blaming God gets a last chance."

"God is the God of second chances, Lily. It doesn't matter how many chances you get, it's the one you don't take that could sentence you."

"Paul, do you really believe that?" Lily asked.

"I do Lily, with all my heart." Finding a great spot across from the beach, Paul pulled over.

"I know without question or doubt God loves us so much he sent his one and only son Jesus Christ to save us. Greater love has no one than this: to lay down one's life for one's friends." John 15:13 Paul swallowed. He was about to share with Lily something he had not shared with anyone, not even Pastor John.

"I've accepted Jesus Christ as my Lord and Savior," Paul stated with strength.

From the flickering lights of the passing cars Paul watched Lily's facial features lay bare her uncertainty. Giving her the space, she needed, Paul sat silent in his seat.

"You sound so sure. I wish I was that confident." Lily looked away from Paul. The ocean glistening behind him. Lily stared out into the darkness.

"Not too long ago, I was spiraling out of control like I was falling down a rabbit hole. Then Pastor John came to Gilford. He helped me to trust God. When I did, God reached down and pulled me out of that hole."

"Right now, I feel more like the professor did in the movie. Mad and... and..." Lily stuttered. "Never mind, it doesn't matter. We should get going." Lily was done sharing with him tonight. At least they were beginning to talk.

"Lily. I will be here for you as your friend...nothing more and nothing less."

Lily nodded acknowledging Paul's devoted friendship above all else. He nodded and put the car in drive, heading to Lily's house. Before dropping her off, Paul told her if she wanted to go to service the next morning to text him and he'd come and get her. Remembering the passage Pastor John once shared with him. Paul at last understood.

"Be still and wait upon the Lord." Psalm 37:7

Joshua arrived home breathing a sigh of relief. His mother and father hadn't returned from the Club's Silent Auction. Famished, he headed for the kitchen, not even pausing long enough to turn on the kitchen light. Seeing Joshua pull up from her bedroom window, Brittany closed the book she was reading. Making her way downstairs she turned the light on to find her twin poking around in the freezer.

"What are you looking for?"

Jumping back, he hit the top of his head on the freezer door. He yelped, "Ice cream." Rubbing his head, Joshua gave it another try. "Aha, found it." He grabbed the pint of Vanilla Chocolate Almond Haagen-Dazs. "Dad loves to stash the Haagen-Dazs in the back. He thinks no one knows it there."

"Well, I didn't know," Brittany confessed.

"Are you kidding me?" He headed to the cabinet for a bowl. "You want some?"

"No thanks." Brittany scooted herself up on one of the stools at the kitchen island. Placing his bowl of ice cream down, Joshua joined her.

"What's up with you?" He questioned, noticing her subdued mood.

"I don't know," she replied releasing a deep sigh resting her chin on both elbows.

"You know if Mom was home, she'd tell you to get those elbows off the table," Joshua teased.

Ignoring his comment Brittany pried, "Didn't that movie affect you?"

"What do you mean, affect me. In what way?"

"Hmm… I've never thought to question whether God exists or not. I mean all through our lives, Mom and Dad only made us do the essentials. We went to Sunday school when we had to. We made our First Holy Communion and Confirmation, that was enough. Even now, we only go to church on special occasions."

"We 'make an appearance' so Mom and Dad can show everyone how perfect we are."

"Joshua." Tears pooled in her eyes. "I never really thought about God. He's been this fictional character. There, but not there. I don't even know if I'm making any sense."

Joshua broke a silence between them. "Like an old uncle. There in the background. Talked about occasionally, but never comes to visit."

"Yes. Exactly!" Brittany jumped down from her stool wrapping her arms around Joshua's neck. "You understand. So do you feel the same way?"

"I do. I have," Joshua shrugged, "for a while now."

"Joshua, what do we do about it?"

"I don't know about you Brittany, but the more I learn the more I want to know. I want God to show me who He is."

308

"But how?"

"Sarah said if you want to know God, if you want a relationship with Him, if you want to see Him do good works in your life, then read His book."

"That's it? Read the Bible?"

"That's where we start, Brit.

"Do you want to go to church with me tomorrow?" Joshua gambled.

"I would love to, Brother. But if I do, we may not make it to the campout. I don't know about you, but I have a feeling the campout is going to be something special."

"Yeah, I know you're right but it's not fair to you," Joshua acknowledged.

"Mom already thinks you're being brainwashed into a cult. If she thinks we're both being brainwashed she'd have the police at the Taylor's house Monday morning. We need to get to that campout. After that, we come clean to Mom and Dad. And Pastor John." Brittany laid out her plan.

"I'm not looking forward to that."

"Me neither."

Joshua took his bowl and spoon to the sink, rinsed them off and opened the dishwasher to put them inside.

"Are you kidding me?" Brittany asked

"What? Mom's going to be mad at me in the morning as it is. I don't want to add to her anger." Joshua said.

Brittany giggled. "Smart." The twins headed upstairs.

Brittany got back into bed and picked up the book she was reading before she went down to Joshua. Opening to the page where she placed her bookmark, Brittany resumed reading.

"This is how the birth of Jesus the Messiah came about." Matthew 1:18.

CHAPTER 37
BATTLES

Sitting on the beat-up mattress and box spring Tags got for cheap money some years back, his brain was wrestling with right and wrong. Trying to alleviate the stress of his predicament, he focused on the only other furnishings in the room. There was the old lamp Erica had given him back when they were tight and the framed 5x7 picture of Madison.

Mr. Robeesy had just informed Tags that he had to work on Thanksgiving. And the job he was counting on to score big was the same night as the campout.

What am I supposed to do?

"Trust God? I've been on my own since I was a kid. Where've you been God?" he asked.

When he was reading his Bible, which was now stored on the top shelf in his closet, something stirred inside. Flickers of hope?

"Hope for what? A future? A life with Erica and Madison?" He focused on the present.

"You're a loser Tags, always was, always will be. Humph! Tags. Isn't even your real name." Erica's mom was right.

"Why did you abandon me? Why are you abandoning me now?" What are you looking for Tags? That little boy you once were? Tags laid down, rolled his face into his pillow to muffle the screams. "Help me. Please?"

His fists began throwing punch after punch into his mattress while his pillow soaked up his tears until Tags fell asleep.

In his dream he was running as fast as he could in every direction.

He tried to escape, but from what? Every street had a dead end. He saw a fence and started to climb, but when he reached the top, the fence grew higher and higher. He climbed back down and found himself in an alley. Ahead was a wooden door with a black iron latch for a handle. It was like the buildings he visited on the wharf. He ran to it and pulled on the latch until the door finally sprang open to a brick wall. Cornered, sirens were blaring, and flashing blue lights were getting closer and closer. There was a little boy with his back to him, he heard his cries. Walking to the little boy, he tapped him on the shoulder and asked. "Are you okay? Do you need help?"

The little boy turned around. Stumbling backward he stared into the face of the five-year-old boy. It was him. The little boy screamed at him, "Nobody loves me. Why doesn't anyone love me?" He reached for the little boy, but he ran away down the alley toward the blue lights. Screaming, "You don't love me either. You're hurting me. Stop hurting me!"

Tags awoke with a jolt, sweat gleaming off his face. Choking back tears, he cried out to the little boy, "I won't hurt you. I won't hurt you."

Lily finally fell asleep, only to be assaulted by the horrors that frequented her nights. Tonight's terror found her crouched in the corner of her uncle's living room. Her hands covering her ears trying to block out the voices of the people passing her by. Her mom, Paul, even Pastor John. Each one calling out her name with their hands extended. She refused them all.

A dark image with no real form floated above her coming closer and closer each time it passed by. She was tired of fighting. It would be easier to give up and let the darkness consume her. Sensing her submission, the dark image descended toward her. Suddenly a flash of bright, blinding light appeared. The darkness exploded and was no more.

Gazing into the light, she witnessed a prism of colors so spectacular a warmth permeated her body. Two arms appeared, reaching out to her. She was unable to look away as the image began to take form. Emerging from the light, her father's face appeared, smiling at her just like he did when she was little and afraid. She reached for his hand, but he faded away.

"Daddy! Don't go! Please Daddy. Don't go. I need you, I'm so scared!" Lily awoke to find her mother consoling her.

"Shh, Lily, it's okay. It's okay."

Wrapped in her mother's comforting arms, Lily relaxed.

"Why don't you come into my bed tonight like old times?"

"I'm good Mom, really," Lily replied.

"Okay. But if you need me for anything. I mean it, anything Lily, you call me."

Before Theresa left the room, Lily dared to ask, "Mom?"

"Yes."

"Did Dad believe in God? I mean I know he believed in God. But did he believe that Jesus was the Messiah?"

Returning to the side of Lily's bed, Theresa sat down. Tenderly brushing back the hair from Lily's face, Theresa smiled when she replied, "Do you remember when your father was still alive, and we went to church?"

"Yeah, I do."

"Well, that was a non-negotiable requisite from your father before we got married. After he passed away, I was so hurt and mad at God for taking him from us that I stopped going to church. When I finally came to terms with your father's death, I was working so much church was never an option. The truth is Lily, because your father took me to church every Sunday, my faith in God helped me through the grief and pain. I've always been thankful to Paul for taking you to church. It made me feel like part of your father was still around to help you where I couldn't. So, to answer your question. Yes, your father believed Jesus was and is the living Messiah." Choking back tears Theresa recalled, "Do you remember him saying to you. "Feel the Spirit, Lily. Feel the Spirit?"

Lily nodded in response.

"It was the Holy Spirit he was referring to."

"Thanks, Mom."

Back in her own bed, Theresa made a mental note. Tomorrow morning, she was going to tell her supervisor she needed Sundays off. Even if it meant losing her job. She could always get another job, but she could never get back the time with her daughter they both so desperately needed.

Titus was unable to fall asleep. "Torn between two worlds." He released to the universe as he tossed and turned.

The one he's been living in. *Quite contently.* He thought and the turbulent one. "Sharise!"

Sharise Taylor was enough to make a young man's head spin. Lovely, passionate. *And don't forget beautiful. But, what about...*

"The Plan." Titus knew the Plan; to graduate high school with top honors, have his pick of Stanford, MIT, or Harvard, receive his Doctorate in Physics with a minor in Astronomy. Tossing it over, he wavered. "Or space science. Either way. Get my dream job, Space Scientist for NASA. Maybe even win a Nobel Peace Prize." Titus' smile turned into a frown. "How am I supposed to become a scientist and believe in God at the same time? That's an oxymoron."

The movie really shook him up. "How can I have both? 'The Plan' and Sharise." Who was he kidding, there's no way he could have both. Wasn't that what Mrs. Taylor was trying to tell him the other night? "But...what if?" Titus thought. "What if?

What if? Drifting off to sleep, Titus held onto to that one thought.

Standing all by himself in the middle of a stage there was an audience silently waiting. What's he supposed to do? Why was he there? To his right was a group of scientists from all over the world, some laughed while others shouted at him.

"You can't be a scientist. You believe in God."

"You're crazy," while a few even called him 'A Mad Scientist.'"

"No. No. You've got it all wrong," Titus explained.

A movement to his left caught his eye. "Sharise?"

Running through a field of wildflowers in shades of yellow and pink, blue, and purple. She looked beautiful with a daisy caught up in her long dark hair. Laughing, she ran in a flowing white dress. "Titus, come on. This way Titus," she called to him.

Reaching for her hand he could feel the warmth in her fingertips. Before he could grasp her hand, she started slipping away.

Slowly…slowly…and she was gone.

TORN ROBES:
RECKONING

Pride goes before destruction, a haughty spirit before a fall.   Proverbs 16:18

TORN ROBES: RECKONING PROLOGUE

Getting together at Breakers, the local food and game hangout, Julie, Lisa, and Andrea snagged a corner table to plan what Julie considered 'a necessary retribution'.

"I want tears, lots of them. Nothing will give me more satisfaction than to watch Brittany Gallo running off the stage with nothing but laughter and total embarrassment hot on her heels. This will be her last rally."

"That's harsh Julie. I mean I get it she chose Erica Gray over us. But you have her boyfriend and the top spot in school. So why bother?" Lisa was hurt by Brittany's decision, but she didn't like playing these mind games anymore.

"There's one thing I don't have. I'm not captain of the cheer squad, but I will be. I want Brittany and everyone to know who owns Gilford High. Are you in or not? Lisa, it's just as easy for me to plan for two rather than one."

"Of course, I'm in. I was curious, that's all," Lisa replied.

"Foods here," Andrea announced placing the tray of food down on the table. What did I miss?" She asked with malicious glee, before shoving a handful of French fries into her mouth.

"Nothing, we're just getting started." Julie watched her in disgust. "You just sit there filing your face with French fries and let me worry about the details."

"That was uncalled for," Lisa said.

"I'm sorry. Did I hurt your feelings, Andrea?" Julie asked in a condescending childish tone.

"No…not at all," Andrea's voice cracked.

"See, all good." Julie glared at Lisa. "Now can we get down to why we're here?"

"Sure."

After a successful movie night, John looked forward to the campout. He picked up his phone and took a deep breath, then hit the number.

"It's good to hear your voice too, Mom. Yes, Sarah's doing great, but you already knew that. Don't play coy with me. I know you speak to her on a regular basis," John teased.

"Mom," he'd delayed the inevitable long enough, "Sarah and I won't be coming home for Thanksgiving. I know. Yes, I know. This will be the first time we've been apart for the holiday since…" John's voice trailed off. He listened patiently as she related her disappointment. Catching a break in the conversation, John jumped in.

"Mom, let me explain. If you don't agree, Sarah and I will be on the next flight home."

With a full heart, Mrs. Wheaton listened as John told her about the upcoming events. She noticed his voice held the same excitement he'd had when he was a little boy.

"The Cornerstone Church has this great campground, and you won't believe it, but it sits right on the beach…"

Life is a storm, my young friend. You will bask in the sunlight one moment, be shattered on the rocks the next. What makes you a man is what you do when that storm comes. -- Alexandre Dumas

TORN ROBES: RECKONING
CHAPTER 1
CROSSROADS

"Let's go Lexy, we're going to be late," Mary shouted upstairs to her daughter.

Shelby, Ian, and Stella were waiting patiently at the door with their coats on ready to leave for Sunday service.

"Coming," Lexy called out.

"Mom, I'll get Ian and Stella in the car. We're getting overheated standing here waiting," Shelby offered.

"Good idea," Mary answered, then shouted, "Lexy, we are leaving right now with or without you."

"I'm ready. Sorry, so sorry guys." Lexy flew down the stairs and into the kitchen.

"Better button up it's cold out there." Shelby threw Lexy her coat.

"Yes, Mom." Lexy replied smartly.

Tags waited outside Erica's house; he was thankful she agreed to go to church with him. Especially after their fight.

When Erica and Madison came down the porch stairs, Tags got out of the car and opened the back door to help get Madison in her car seat. Then opened the passenger door for Erica.

"Joey, this doesn't mean I've changed my mind." Erica placed her hand on his arm.

"Yeah, I figured Erica. Let's just agree to disagree."

Erica shrugged in response.

The clouds billowed in the sky, threatening to bring down a cold freezing rain. Snow was not in the forecast, but the fierce gale winds of the Northeast were showing their bluster. The blazing colors of autumn a mere memory, all the trees were bare now.

"Halleluiah, praise Jesus!" The congregation rocked in song, voices praising in worship.

Stepping up to the pulpit Pastor Peters shouted again, "Halleluiah, praise Jesus!"

The glorious replies came, "Praise Jesus!"

"Welcome! We certainly have the Spirit working here at Cornerstone this morning," Applauding the choir, Pastor Peters began his message on choices.

"Satan is always at work with his demons looking for ways to derail our salvation. You see, he knows he's lost but that won't stop him from taking as many souls as he can with him. Now most of us imagine Satan or Lucifer red in color with horns sticking out from his head." Pastor Peters indulged his audience placing his two index fingers at the top of his head. "But nothing could be further from the truth. Who is the Satan? Ezekiel 28:14 and 17 says.

You were anointed as a guardian cherub, for so I ordained you. You were on the holy mount of God; you walked among the fiery stones. Your heart became proud on account of your beauty, and you corrupted your wisdom because of your splendor. So I threw you to the earth; I made a spectacle of you before kings.

"Satan is a fallen angel. Don't kid yourself into thinking Satan roams the Earth coming at you with great horns, red and nasty, disfigured by hate and evil. SATAN..." Pastor Peters bellowed, "is the great deceiver. He knows every one of our failings and uses them to tempt us. *And no wonder, for Satan himself masquerades as an angel of light.*" 2 Corinthians 11:14

"Satan deceives us into thinking our choices are righteous and good. When in fact they can bring us nothing but destruction and hurt. In order to have victory over the evil one and his minions, we must put on the full armor of God. The belt of truth, the breastplate of righteousness, the gospel of peace, the shield of faith, the helmet of salvation and the sword of the spirit." Pastor Peters continued for another fifteen minutes.

"In conclusion, I ask you to take heart and remember the following passage from Philippians 4:6-7 as you face difficult choices. *Do not be anxious about anything, but in every situation, by prayer and petition, with thanksgiving, present your requests to God. And the peace of God, which transcends all understanding, will guard your hearts and your minds in Christ Jesus.*

Singing the final song led by the church choir, "The Reckless Love of God", Sarah stopped singing and asked Sharise, "Who are you looking for?"

"Titus," Sharise whispered. "I was hoping after the movie last night he'd, you know, come to church."

"Sharise. Titus is a stubborn boy. I think it's going to take more than a movie to open his eyes. Besides, he's already been to one service, and he still came to help clean the church. He probably got tied up with family stuff."

Knowing Sarah was right, Sharise couldn't help but be a little disappointed.

Mary stopped at the church bulletin board, a habit of hers since coming to Cornerstone. Parishioners posted everything from yard sales to babysitters needed. However, this Sunday, Mary noticed something very special was posted.

"Oh my," she said out loud.

"What Mom?" Lexy inquired standing next to her.

"The church secretary is retiring and Pastor Peters is looking for an executive administrator to replace her."

"Really? You're going to apply, right?" Lexy urged.

"I'd like to. Do you think I should?"

"Shelby, come here," Lexy demanded.

She was speaking with Lewis and was a bit annoyed about being pulled away. Marching over to Lexy and her mom Shelby fumed. "What Lexy?'"

"Look," Lexy said pointing at the notice. "Pastor Peters is looking for a secretary. Don't you think Mom should apply?"

"What…let me see. Oh my gosh, Mom. Of course, you should apply."

"Have you done administrative work before Mrs. Richardson?" Lewis had followed Shelby over to see what was going on.

"Yes. I worked part-time as an executive admin for the VP of one of the produce markets downtown. After my husband passed away, I had to look for something full-time. Unfortunately, there weren't any admin jobs available." Mary sighed. "This job would be a dream come true. It's full-time days which means I would be home at night with the kids."

"Mrs. Richardson, please follow me." He guided Mary toward

Pastor Peters' office.

Spotting Jamie with her mom and dad, Lexy announced to Shelby. "This is the first time Jamie's parents have attended Cornerstone. I'm gonna go over and say hi."

"Okay," Shelby took Stella and Ian over to the refreshment table where her friends were conversing.

The munchkins were much too tempting for Stella and Ian. Reaching for them, Shelby advised, "Remember only two apiece, choose wisely little ones."

"You're not the mom, Shelby," Stella pouted.

"No, but until she gets back, I'm in charge Stella Richardson." Stella made a face at Shelby and reached for a chocolate munchkin.

"Where's your mom?" Sarah asked.

"Lewis took her to Pastor Peters' office. There's a job posted on the bulletin board for a new church secretary. I guess the one they have now is retiring."

"That would be incredible for your family Shelby!" Sharise exclaimed.

"I know. Mom has been praying nonstop about finding a new job. I walked by her room the other night and she had just gotten home. I wanted to let her know how the night went. Her door was cracked and I peeked in. She was down on her knees praying to God to help us. But before she ended her prayer, she thanked him for the new job he was sending her way that would allow her to be home with us." Befuddled, Shelby asked her friends, "Why would she thank him for something she hadn't received?"

"Because Shelby, by thanking God beforehand, she is telling God she believes without a shadow of a doubt that He will deliver her." Sarah paused for a moment. *"Therefore I tell you, whatever you ask for in prayer, believe that you have received it, and it will be yours.* It's from the book of Mark 11:24."

"Hmmmm. Prayer is a powerful tool. Sounds like your mother is a prayer warrior," Sharise said.

"Maybe you should take a page from Mrs. Richardson, Sharise," Sarah teased.

"What's she talking about Sharise?" Joshua asked.

"Please Sarah," Sharise shot back. "I'm way ahead of you on that one."

"Hey Paul, how are the songs going for the campout?" Joshua asked, not wanting to get involved in any girl stuff.

"Wow, you're really into this," Lily said.

"Yeah, well someone volunteered me," Paul smiled at her.

"Madison. Madison, you little cutie," Stella and Ian yelled, running toward the Kid's Room. All eyes turned to see Madison running as fast as her two little legs would carry her, screeching with the same enthusiasm.

Mary was leaving Pastor Peters office and intercepted Madison scooping her up. "I've got you. You little rascal." Erica and Tags joined Mary who held their squealing little girl.

"Can we play with Madison, please?" Stella begged. Mary looked to Erica and Tags for their permission before setting Madison down.

"Sure," Erica smiled.

"What about me?" Ian asked not wanting to be left out.

"I think Madison would love to play with both of you," Erica told Ian. Bending down to Madison, "Wouldn't you Madison?" The three of them ran off chasing one another.

"They just love her," Mary said.

"Believe me the feeling is mutual," Erica laughed.

"You must be Madison's father?" Mary inquired.

"Forgive me and my lack of manners," Erica said.

"Nonsense," Mary waived off. "You were enjoying your little girl."

"I was," Erica admitted. "Mrs. Richardson this is Joey Taglio. Joey this is Shelby's mom, Mrs. Richardson."

"Nice to meet you Mrs. Richardson. Thank you for watching Madison," Tags said, reaching to shake her hand.

"It's very nice to finally meet you, Joseph," Mary replied, taking his hand into her own.

"You can call me Joey or Tags, that's what my friends call me."

"If you don't mind," Mary asked. "I like the name Joseph, it's a strong and loving name. It was my husband's name and it's what I called him."

"Sure. But it might take some getting used to," Tags forewarned.

On their way to search out Stella, Ian, and Madison, Mary had a wonderful idea.

"Why don't you, Joseph and Madison come to our house for dinner?"

"Dinner?" Erica repeated.

"Yes, I have chili cooking in the slow cooker and corn muffins I pulled out of the oven just this morning," Mary revealed.

"Joey, what do you think?"

"What, I'm...I don't know. I guess," he answered taken completely off guard.

"Great, then it's settled. I'll see you at the house." Mary smiled heading off to gather her crew.

"I'll have to stop at home first if you don't mind?" Erica asked. "I need to pack a bag for Madison."

"Sure. Madison and I can wait in the car while you run in the house," Tags suggested and off they went.

On the road Mary announced. "Joseph, Erica and Madison are coming over for Sunday dinner.

"Joseph?" Shelby repeated.

"Yes, I prefer to call him his given name. Does anyone have a problem with that?"

"I like it, Mom. That was Daddy's name."

"Me too, baby. That's just what I thought."

"Okay, now that we have the important things settled," Shelby declared sarcastically, "could you please tell us what happened when you met with Pastor Peters. Please?" Shelby begged.

"Yeah, Mom what happened? Did you get the job?" Lexy grilled her.

"I have to go online tonight and fill out the application. Then I have an interview set up tomorrow in between my shifts. I hope you don't mind, Shelby. I won't be able to stop at home like I usually do."

"Mom, I think I talk for all of us when I say, whatever it takes," Shelby said.

"Yeah Mommy," Ian said.

"That's right Mom, we'll help out anyway we can," Lexy reiterated.

Mary chocked out a grateful, "Thank you."

ABOUT THE AUTHOR

K.M. Quinn lives on the east coast where she was born and raised. She is a devoted wife, mother, and grandmother. In 2004, K.M. began writing her first novel *TORN ROBES: CHOICES*, fitting her writing time between work and raising a family.

The second novel in this series *TORN ROBES: RECKONING*. It will be released midyear 2023. *TORN ROBES: THE KING'S HIGHWAY* the third book to be released in the series. Follow K.M. Quinn's website for details.

Along with writing her next project, K.M. enjoys spending time with her family, horseback riding, kayaking, walking, snowshoeing and being at the beach. Having grown up along the coast, the ocean has been her constant companion and still to this day is her, "happy place." An avid researcher, she loves history, learning, and exploring new things.

K.M. firmly believes that with God everything is possible she has witnessed it firsthand in her own life. As K.M. has changed roles and made career moves, God has been preparing her for her time as an author.

"This is, the most rewarding season of my life! It is an absolute joy, pleasure and honor to share God's undying love with you, my readers. Thank you!"

AUTHOR'S NOTE

I am deeply grateful for all the people in my life who've made this dream a reality. I've benefited from a determined work ethic passed down through the mighty women in my family. My loving and supportive husband, my children, and grandchildren sustain me.

I am thankful for the many friends and acquaintances who have accompanied me along this weathered path. I'm thankful for my editors and publisher who are wise, compassionate and supportive. They enabled me to deliver beyond my own expectations. A shout-out to the Christian Writer's Sanctuary. Their support and encouragement helped me believe – and know that my stories would be published. TORN ROBES: CHOICES is now a reality, and there are more stories to come!

For many years, TORN ROBES: CHOICES has been my constant companion. It became a labor of love driven by an undeniable passion that God sealed into my soul long ago. What began as a need, slowly developed into an intense commitment to share God's unconditional love, constant forgiveness, and the many promises I've experienced throughout my life.

Whether it be a school board member, a parent, or one of the students in the story, these characters are ordinary people with many imperfections. Through their imperfections, they display uniqueness and courage. I have journeyed with each one of them for quite some time and developed a fervent attachment to them!

My hope is with each page you will laugh at their humor, scoff at their sarcasm, feel the depth of their sorrow and embrace their hope. Please remain steadfast during their moments of confusion, and indulge yourself in the miracle of God's love.

Thank you for choosing TORN ROBES: CHOICES.

K.M. Quinn
January 2023

Made in United States
North Haven, CT
27 May 2023